'You are a v...

'Like England h...
fact, I shall call y...

'Do not be so fo...
dress is Indian. T... ...and the
style Roman. My mask is Venetian. My pearls
are Oriental. I think my shoes are from Spain.
There is nothing of England here.'

His finger traced the edge of the demure bodice
of her dress, where the fullness of her breasts
was only hinted at. He hooked his finger under
the material and pulled it away from her skin,
allowing a soft touch of what was below.

'I suspect,' he murmured, stroking her skin and
gazing into her eyes, 'underneath you are pure
England.'

'Not pure, my lord,' she whispered as his
fingers did lovely things to her soft skin. 'Not
pure at all.'

As a psychiatric social worker, **Diane Gaston** spent years helping others create real-life happy endings. Now Diane crafts fictional ones, writing the kind of historical romance she's always loved to read. The youngest of three daughters of a US Army Colonel, Diane moved frequently during her childhood, even living for a year in Japan. It continues to amaze her that her own son and daughter grew up in one house in Northern Virginia. Diane still lives in that house, with her husband and three very ordinary house cats. Visit Diane's website at www.dianegaston.com

**Mills & Boon® Historical Romance™
are proud to publish this Golden Heart
award-winning novel from new author Diane Gaston**

THE MYSTERIOUS MISS M

Diane Gaston

MILLS & BOON®

All the characters in this book have no existence outside the imagination of the author, and have no relation whatsoever to anyone bearing the same name or names. They are not even distantly inspired by any individual known or unknown to the author, and all the incidents are pure invention.

MILLS & BOON and MILLS & BOON with the Rose Device are registered trademarks of the publisher.

*First published in Great Britain 2004
Harlequin Mills & Boon Limited,
Eton House, 18-24 Paradise Road, Richmond, Surrey TW9 1SR*

© Diane Perkins 2004

ISBN 0 263 83968 0

*Set in Times Roman 10¼ on 11¼ pt.
04-0704-88278*

*Printed and bound in Spain
by Litografia Rosés S.A., Barcelona*

For Helen and Julie,
who have been with me in this writing venture
from the very beginning, and Virginia,
who made our circle complete.

Chapter One

London, September 1812

Madeleine positioned herself on the couch, adjusting the fine white muslin of her gown and placing her gloved hands demurely in her lap. The light from the branch of candles, arranged to cast a soft glow upon her skin, enhanced the image she was bid to make. Her throat tightened, and her skin crawled from the last man's attentions.

This wicked life. How she detested it.

She checked the blue-feathered mask, artfully fashioned to disguise her identity without obscuring her youthful complexion or the untouched pink of her full lips. 'The Mysterious Miss M' could be any girl in the first blush of womanhood. It was Farley's contrivance that she appear so, and the men who frequented his elite London gaming hell bet deep to win the fantasy of seducing her. Escape might be out of the question, but at least the mask hid her face and her shame.

Unable to remain still, Madeleine stepped over to the bed, discreetly tucked into the corner and covered in lace-trimmed white-and-lavender linens like some virginal shrine. She perched on the edge of it and swung her legs back and forth, wondering how much time was left before the next gentleman had his turn. Not long, she surmised. She had taken more care in the necessary toilette than usual, thoroughly washing away the memory of that odious creature who had not departed too soon for her taste.

Male laughter, deep and raucous, sounded in the next room. Stupid creatures, seated around tables, as deep in their cards as in their cups, just waiting for Lord Farley to make away with their fortunes. The girls who ran the tables, tonight dressed as she was, like ingenues at Almack's, were meant to tantalise, but, for a select few, the Mysterious Miss M was the real prize.

Farley would not allow his prize to flee. She had learned that lesson swiftly enough. No matter. There was nowhere for her to go.

Voices sounded outside the room, and she blinked away the memory of how Farley had doomed her to her fate, or, more precisely, how she had doomed herself.

The next man, thankfully the last, would appear soon, and she had best be ready. She checked her hair, fingering the dark curls fashioned in the latest style to frame her face, a pale pink silk ribbon threaded through them.

Something thudded against the door. Madeleine hopped off the bed and hurried to her place on the couch. In staggered a tall figure, silhouetted against the brighter light of the gaming room. He stood a moment with his hand to his brow.

A soldier. He wore the red coat of a British uniform, festooned with blue facings and looped gold lace, unbuttoned to reveal the white linen of his shirt. If only she were a soldier. She would battle her way out of this place. She would be in the cavalry and gallop away at breakneck speed. How lovely that would be.

The soldier, who looked not more than five years older than she, swayed as he swung shut the door. Lord Farley's generous supply of brandy, no doubt.

Madeleine sighed. He might be foxed, but at least he was not fat. With any luck, his mouth would not be foul. She hated a putrid-smelling mouth. With all his lean muscle, he looked as a soldier should, strong and powerful.

'Good God!' he exclaimed, almost tripping mid-stride as he caught sight of her.

'I am afraid I am not He, my lord,' she retorted. The candles illuminated a handsome face, grinning with such good humour she could scarcely keep from grinning back.

'Yes, of course not.' His green eyes twinkled. 'And fortuitous for me that you are not, Miss...?'

'Miss M.' A charmer. She had met charmers before. The charm wore thin after they took what they wished from her.

'"The Mysterious Miss M", I recall now.' He flopped down on the couch next to her. 'I beg your forgiveness. You quite startled me. I had not expected you to actually look like a young lady.'

'I am a young lady,' she said, playing her part.

'Indeed,' he agreed, masculine approval shining in his sea-green eyes and a dimple creasing his left cheek. 'I swear you are the vision of one. England does offer the finest ladies. I find I must apologise for this humble uniform.'

He presented her with his boot-covered foot and winked at her while she tugged on it. Though properly polished, her fingers felt the leather's scratches and scrapes. From the battlefield? she wondered. When his foot finally gave up the boot, he nearly fell off the couch. She rolled her eyes.

He laughed. 'Have I impressed you with my finesse, Miss M?'

'Indeed, my lord. I cannot recall when I have been so entertained.'

He chuckled softly and swung around, bringing his face close to hers, his expression more full of mischief than lust. 'And I thought you were here to entertain me.'

She felt a smile tickling the corner of her mouth. He placed his finger on her lip and traced the edge. His eyes filled with a wistful expression that surprised her. A heat she was not quite prepared to feel made her wish to fan herself. As she wiped the disturbing touch from her mouth with her tongue, he took a swift intake of breath and gazed into her eyes so intensely that she lowered them.

He was like the fantasy she conjured up in her loneliest hours. A knight on a huge white stallion, who faced the evil lord in the joust, winning her away. Or the pirate who fought the blackguard and sailed her away in a ship with a dozen sails. He was the soldier, riding in with sabre flashing, to rid her of Farley and keep her safe forever.

Such nonsense. He was none of these, for all the splendour of his uniform, dark, curling hair and sun-darkened skin. He certainly looked the part, though, with his eyes wondrously expressive and a face lean, as if honed by battle.

Once Farley had been a fantasy, when she'd dreamed he was taking her to a marriage bed instead of the one in this room.

The soldier shrugged off his coat, and his loose linen shirt revealed a peek of black chest hair. Madeleine's eyes fixed on the wiry patch and her fingers itched to discover how it would feel.

As if it would feel any different than the other lust-filled men who forced themselves so hard against her that she pushed on their chests to give herself room for breath. She placed a hand on her breast. What fancy had captured her to give way to such thoughts?

He grinned impishly at her again, the dimple deepening in his cheek. 'You are a vision, Miss M. Like England herself, beautiful to behold. Nothing mysterious about it. In fact, I shall call you Miss England.'

'Do not be so foolish, sir. The fabric of my dress is Indian. The design is French and the style Roman. My mask is Venetian. My pearls are Oriental. I think my shoes are from Spain. There is nothing of England here.'

His finger traced the edge of the demure bodice of her dress where the fullness of her breasts was only hinted. He hooked his finger under the material and pulled it away from her skin, allowing a soft touch of what was underneath.

'I suspect,' he murmured, stroking her skin and gazing into her eyes, 'underneath you are pure England.'

'Not pure, my lord,' she whispered as his fingers did lovely things to her soft skin. 'Not pure at all.'

He slowly leaned closer so that she could feel his breath on her lips. With a gentleness she did not know existed, he placed his lips on hers and lingered there, moving so softly, she was only half-aware of him urging her mouth open and tickling the moist inside with his tongue.

She moaned and positioned herself closer to him. Her arms twined around his neck and her fingers played with the curls on his head. He tasted of brandy, but she decided she might like brandy the next time she was compelled to drink it.

He urged her down on the couch, covering his body with hers. The hard bulge of his arousal pressed against her. To her surprise, it pleased her.

Only once before had a man's arousal not filled her with revulsion. That day in the country when her father's house-guest, the Lord Farley her older sisters prosed on about, met her out riding and showed her what happens between a man and a reckless, unchaperoned fifteen-year-old girl. She had thought it a splendid joke to be the first of her sisters kissed by a man, but, all too easily, that kiss had led to delights she had not imagined.

The soldier's muscles were firm beneath his grey wool trousers. His mouth played lightly on her cheek, and Madeleine's long-suppressed desire tugged at her again. She must not allow herself the weakness. She must control her sensibilities.

His kisses trailed down the sensitive skin of her neck, and she said her rehearsed lines: 'Shall we go to the bed, my lord?'

Immediately he rose, grinning his dimpled grin. 'Whatever you command, my lady.'

He gallantly extended his hand to assist her up. His grasp

was firm and warm, even through her lavender-kid glove. As she led him to the bed, he kept hold of her hand, the gesture unexpectedly setting off a storm of yearning inside her.

Vowing to get her feelings under control, Madeleine continued her duties, turning back the covers on the bed and facing the soldier. She slowly pulled off her gloves, one finger at a time. Her fingers free, she unlaced his shirt, caressing his warm bare skin as she pushed it off his shoulders. When she unfastened his trousers, the bulge therein attested to the success of her endeavours. She tried not to watch his green eyes darken with passion.

A guttural sound emerged from his throat. Madeleine collected herself and proceeded with the task she was bid to perform. This was the moment for him to pounce on her. She must temper his lusting, so that her dress not become ripped from his impatience.

Even completely free of his clothes, he did not pounce. Instead, he simply gazed at her. All the unwanted cravings of her body rushed back as she gazed at him in return. Usually she avoided a view of the men who bared themselves before her. When Farley first seduced her, she had been too shy to look, but her gaze freely drank in this soldier's body. He was more beautiful than the drawings of Greek statues in her father's books. Her eyes widened with surprise at the pleasure of seeing him.

'Good God, Miss England,' he exclaimed. He moved toward her. With gentle hands on her shoulders, he turned her around and fumbled with the laces of her dress, his progress painfully slow.

He chuckled. 'I am woefully out of practice.'

With a resolute purse of her lips, Madeleine spun back to face him and made quick work of the laces. The dress fell to the floor. She tackled the corset next. When she let her shift drop from her body, his gaze was as rapt as hers had been, and her resolve to simply perform her task fled.

His eyes met hers. 'I feel home at last.'

He ran his hand over her breasts, his fingers barely skimming the soft flesh. Her breasts ached. How could they ache? He'd barely touched them.

'Wh—where have you been?' She would distract herself. These feelings were too disturbing. 'In the Peninsula?'

'Last at Maguilla.' His manner turned solemn and his sparkling eyes lost lustre.

Maguilla. So exotic a name, like a magic kingdom far away. But what had happened there to cause his change in mood?

Sadness lingered in his eyes, but he smiled. 'I have been too long at battle and not long enough at home to have seen what I most have missed.'

'I do not understand you, my lord.' She chewed on her lip. 'What have you most missed?'

His gaze travelled up and down the length of her. 'England,' he said in a reverent voice. 'Every hill, curve, and thicket. All lush beauty and honest comfort.'

Madeleine felt herself blush. She stilled the impulse to cover her most female parts. 'Well,' she said, 'shall we proceed, my lord?'

Quickly she climbed on the bed, her mouth set in a determined line. He followed her, more slowly than she would have guessed. That he was not so eager to slake his desire unsettled her, but not so much as her own yearning. When he climbed in the bed and positioned himself over her, she nearly burst with excitement. It felt too much like what had brought her to ruin, but she wanted this soldier. Wanted him very much.

She stiffened and panic raced through her.

He halted immediately, searching her face. 'What is wrong?'

Her heart pounded. 'Nothing. Nothing is wrong.'

He cocked his head sceptically. 'You are frightened. I do not understand. What frightened you? Did I hurt you?' He shifted to lie beside her.

She avoided the puzzled look in his eye. 'No, you did not hurt me, my lord. I am not frightened. You may proceed.'

His hand grasped her chin and brought her face closer. 'I'll not *proceed*, as you say, until you explain.'

She could not explain what she did not understand. Even when Farley had seduced her and her body responded so wantonly, she had not felt like this. So…so excited and breathless.

Was this what young women felt when they loved the man they bedded? Was this a feeling she could never have or deserve?

A tear trickled down her cheek. As it appeared from beneath her mask, he wiped it away with his finger. 'There now,' he murmured, stroking her cheek. 'No need to cry.'

'It is of no consequence,' she said, stifling a sob, furious at her tears. Farley would be even angrier, if he knew. Weeping was not in the carefully fashioned script. 'Please don't tell Lord Farley about this.'

'Now, now.' He sat up and settled her in front of him, wrapping his arms around her. 'Why would I ever do that? Come. Tell Devlin what troubles you.'

'Devlin?' His arms felt like a warm blanket around her. She wished she could remain cosseted within them and never, ever leave.

'That's my name. Lieutenant Devlin Steele of the First Royal Dragoons. Youngest brother of the very honourable Marquess of Heronvale. At your service, Miss England.' He cuddled her closer to him. 'Tell me what is wrong.'

She released a deep, shuddering breath. 'Sometimes…sometimes I wish to be what I appear, not what I am.' The tears came in earnest now, soaking the feathers of her mask.

If only she had not gone riding that fateful day. If only Farley had not seen her scandalous attire, her brother's old clothes already too small for her. If only she had known that kissing a man could lead to so much more.

She fingered the damp feathers of her mask, hoping they would dry without losing shape or she would be punished.

'Shh, now, it will be all right,' he whispered.

No, nothing would ever be all right again.

The lieutenant held her and rocked her and murmured comforting words into her ear. It was a long cry, longer than any she had allowed herself since the night she'd learned Farley had other plans for her besides marriage.

Soon enough, though, she recovered. She pulled away from him and turned so he could not see her face as she removed the mask to wipe her eyes with the linen sheet. When she turned back her mask was in place.

'Now have you finished, little watering pot?' he asked, his lovely green eyes the kindest she had ever seen.

She nodded.

'Silly goose.' He tapped her on the nose and slid off the bed to grope on the floor for his clothes. Still unsteady, he stumbled and bumped against the bedpost.

'What are you doing?' she asked.

He laughed softly. 'Getting dressed. Do not worry, miss, I will forgo your favours tonight.' He cast her a long glance, a woeful expression on his face. 'Though it may be more difficult than piquet duty in freezing rain.'

'No, you mustn't.' She pulled him back, trying to urge him back on top of her. 'It would not suit. I am expected to perform.'

'No, sweet Miss England. You have performed enough tonight.' He stood again.

Madeleine stared at him, trying not to be transfixed by the flexing of his well-defined muscles as he groped for his trousers. She could not bear it if he should leave so soon.

He turned that mischievous grin upon her, his dimple emerging. 'We must, of course, give a show for the others in the next room. Create proper noise. Make the poor buggers envious.'

She giggled.

'Not laughter. Passion. Like this.' He let out a loud moan. 'More! More! More!'

'Yes! Yes! Yes!' she returned. They both burst out laughing, holding their mouths to keep it silent.

He collapsed on the bed. 'Stop. It hurts to laugh.' He grabbed his side. 'Ow.'

She pulled his hand away. To the side of his abdomen there was a scar, jagged and still pink from recent healing.

'You were injured at…at…?' She traced the scar with her finger.

'At Maguilla? As you would say, it is of no consequence.' He smiled, but without joy. 'We chased a regiment of French cavalry until the tide was turned and their reserves chased us. I made a foolish attempt to rally the men. A Frenchman met me with a lance instead. The wound is healed now. In two days' time I return to my regiment.'

'Back to the war?'

'Of course. It is a soldier's duty.'

Two days and he would return to war. He could be injured again. He could lose his life. Never again see his precious England. And, if she knew Farley, Devlin Steele would also return to war penniless.

'Lieutenant?'

'You must call me Devlin.'

She waved her hand dismissively. 'Devlin, then. Have you won at cards tonight? I mean, in addition to winning me?'

He laughed. 'Will you be in search of my money next?'

This offended. She had principles, after all. 'I want none of your money, but you must refuse to play further. Make some excuse.'

'Whatever for?'

'The game is not honest.'

The silly men who lost fortunes to Farley while trying to win a second chance with her never comprehended. No one won her twice in a night.

'The devil,' he mumbled. 'I never thought to inquire of

Farley's reputation. I should have known better. I shall make my excuses to him. I am indebted to you. You are quite a lady.'

'Don't elevate me, sir. I am just as I seem.'

He laughed. 'You seem quite like the misses in the marriage mart. A young lady of quality.' He smiled. His eyes turned kind and his voice tender. 'Indeed, that is what you are. A young lady of quality.'

Her face grew hot with shame. 'No.'

He struggled to get into his trousers, hopping on one foot and making no progress.

She did not wish him to leave. 'Lieutenant?'

'Devlin, remember?'

'Devlin. Will England win the war?'

He momentarily ceased his struggle. 'Without a doubt. It is nearly done, I think.'

'Wellington will see to it, will he not? And you soldiers who fight the battles with him?'

'Worry not, little miss.' He ran his finger over her brow. 'England will endure.'

Madeleine reached out and placed her hand over his scar. 'Lieutenant?'

'Yes?' He had become still, too, looking directly into her eyes.

'I wish to make love to you.' She slid her fingers up his chest.

'Miss England, it is not necessary.'

She reached behind her head and untied her mask. With trembling fingers, she removed it. His eyes darkened.

She moved closer. 'I will make love to you. It will be my gift, because you must return to battle.' With one hand stroking his hair, the other moved downward. Farley had taught her where to touch to arouse. This time, with Lieutenant Devlin Steele of the First Royal Dragoons, it gave her pleasure.

He moaned, softer this time. She clasped her hand behind his head and brought him uncomplaining to her lips. Urging him atop her, she gasped as the firmness of his body bore down on her. Her heart beat faster. She would truly make love to this soldier, this kind man who had been willing to comfort her.

He eased himself inside her with exquisite gentleness, and what typically caused her to deaden all emotion gave unexpected delight. She thrilled to the feel of him filling her, revelling in each stroke, each scrape of his chest against hers, each breath on her face. The only sound she heard was the clap of their bodies coming together and their panting breath. She matched his rhythm, stroke for stroke, press for press, and the sensations he created in her became urgent, spurring her on with each thrust. His pace quickened and her need grew. She would burst with pleasure, she was sure. She would shatter into a thousand sparkling shards. She would escape herself, this life she was forced to lead, the dismal future, in this brief space of time with Lieutenant Devlin Steele.

He collapsed on top of her, his need satisfied with hers. Sliding off, he lay facing her, his eyes half-closed, his skin aglow with a sheen of sweat. Madeleine let her gaze wander languidly over his face, memorising each feature, committing each curve and line to memory. She needed to remember him. She needed to dream of her Dragoon returning victorious from the war, coming to whisk her away. She would need for him to come to her tomorrow and the next day and the next.

The fantasy would comfort, though it would never come true.

'Sweet England,' he murmured. 'Thank you.'

She kissed him again, boldly giving him her tongue, tasting him. Brandy would never again taste so vile. It would be how *he* tasted. She inhaled his masculine scent, filling her lungs and memory with it, as his seed had filled her. She entwined her legs with his. He moved away from her kiss and grinned at her as she arched her pelvis to his.

'Ah, England, you shall be most difficult to leave.' As she placed her finger in the dimple on his cheek, he pressed his fingers into the soft flesh of her buttocks. She felt his passion flare back to life and she made a primitive sound deep in her throat.

As he entered her for the second time, Madeleine whispered. 'Lieutenant Devlin Steele. I shall remember you.'

Chapter Two

London, April 1816

Devlin Steele glanced up from the cards in his hand. The acrid smoke and dim light muted the gaudy red velvet of the gaming room. He reached for his glass and set it down again. The prodigious amount of brandy he had already consumed threatened to fog his brain.

His months back on English soil were as hazy as his present thinking. Snatches of memory. His brother, the imperious Marquess, rescuing him from the dirty makeshift hospital in Brussels. Days drifting in and out of consciousness at Heronvale, his sisters hovering around him, dispatched there to return him to health. Eventual recovery and a flight to London for a frenzy of dissipation meant to banish images of blood and horror and pain. Thus far, Devlin had managed to gamble and debauch away his quarter's entitlement. What capital he'd possessed had gone to money-lenders, but at present his pockets were flush, an unexpected surprise at Lord Farley's table.

'Your bet, Steele?' Farley's smooth voice now had an edge. His foot tapped the carpet.

Devlin stared at his cards, blinking to focus on the hearts and spades and diamonds. He had avoided Farley's gaming hell until this night, preferring an honest game, but damned if the man had not sought him out at White's. Predictable, Devlin figured, after he'd been tossing blunt all over town. Ripe for fleecing, by all accounts. A perfect pigeon for Farley.

He smiled inwardly. Farley had not yet heard the River Tick was already seeping into Devlin's boots. All the fleece had been long shorn.

'I'll pass.' Devlin barely glanced at the man seated across from him, concentrating instead on keeping his wits about him. Knowing Farley dealt a dishonest hand gave Devlin a slight advantage, if he could but hold on to it.

The cards were too good, though. Farley must be seducing him with a run of luck. He bet cautiously, against the cards, and avoided losing the successive hands. Farley's brow furrowed.

Rumour had it that Farley had lost a fortune in bad investments. Moreover, Napoleon's exile to St Helena had brought an end to the lucrative smuggling business everyone knew he ran. Farley was mortgaged to the hilt, a situation to make a man desperate—and desperate men made mistakes. War had taught Devlin that.

Farley indeed became more reckless, and Devlin stacked his chips higher.

Farley dealt the next hand, and Devlin carefully watched his expression. The man could still be considered handsome, though hard living had etched lines at the corner of his mouth and eyes. With his thin elegant nose, hair once fair, now peppered with grey, he had the look of the aristocrat he was, though his family fortunes had been squandered by an ancestry of fools. Typical of society, Lord Farley might not be a welcome suitor to the daughters of the *ton,* but, in the world of gentlemen who enjoyed his brandy, his card tables, and the young woman whose favours he doled out to the select few, Farley was top o' the trees.

Farley's fingers tapped a nervous tattoo on the table. 'Steele, I believe I could allow you some time with our Miss

M. She is delightful tonight. A Spanish maiden. Perhaps she
will remind you of your service in Spain.'

Devlin peered over the fan of cards in his hand. 'I have no
wish to be reminded of Spain.'

He placed his cards on the table, and Farley blanched, pushing another stack of chips to Devlin's side.

The man plastered on a smile, but a nervous twitch had
commenced under his right eye. 'I think you might recollect
you won a time with Miss M once before. I assure you, she
remains in good figure and has added to the delights she may
offer.'

Devlin remembered her. Indeed, memory of her lovely face,
so pale against her dark hair, had often warmed lonely nights
as the British waited for Napoleon's army to attack. Her spirit
and sensibility had intrigued him more than young ladies in
drawing rooms could do. Not that he had mixed in society to
any great degree. Good God, he'd never even set foot in Almack's.

Devlin smiled at his host. 'I'm sure I'd be delighted to
renew my acquaintance, sir. Perhaps after a hand or two.'

How long ago had he shared that memorable space of time
with her? Three years and more? Just after Maguilla. What
had her life been like under the thumb of this man?

Farley's brow broke out in beads of sweat. Devlin suppressed his smile. The man was in trouble. Throwing caution
to the wind, Devlin made a hearty bet. The tic in Farley's eye
quickened.

The cards were called, and the man on Devlin's right let
out a whoop. So intent on besting Farley, Devlin had forgotten
the other player. As Devlin gave up half his stack of chips,
he vowed not to continue such carelessness.

'Enough for me, gentlemen. I think I shall stop before
Barnes here takes my whole stack.'

Barnes bellowed with laughter. 'I'd be pleased to do that,
Steele.' He gathered his winnings, leaving Farley with a scattering of chips too small to stack.

'Another time,' Devlin said, standing.

'One more hand.' Farley's voice was thick and tense. 'Don't deny me the chance to recoup, Steele. One more hand is all I ask.'

It would hardly be civil to refuse. Devlin bowed slightly and sat back down. One more hand couldn't break him, though that last loss had hurt a bit. Farley would have been wiser to quit. The man had lost all card sense. Devlin doubted he could even cheat effectively at this point. Barnes, too, was flush with his winning streak and eager to extend it.

Play was fierce. Devlin bet moderately, intent only on preserving his present winnings, but the cards came like magic. Was Farley setting him up, or had true luck shone upon him?

Caution be damned, he thought. Life's the real gamble. Devlin bet deep.

And won.

Barnes good-naturedly laughed off his losses, still ahead with his one spectacular hand. Farley slumped back in his chair, his face drained of all colour.

'You will accept my vowel, sir?' Farley's question did not demand an answer.

'But of course,' Devlin replied amiably.

As Farley wrote out his vowel, Devlin gazed around the room, into the dark recesses where Farley's girls, looking like Spanish tarts, ran the tables.

'Shall I make Miss M available to you?' Farley asked, his voice flat.

Devlin considered, sweeping his gaze over the too-opulent room. Had this place truly impressed him three years ago with its wainscoting and brocades? Now it appeared as false as glory.

Perhaps it would be preferable to seek the relative silence of the street and preserve The Mysterious Miss M as a memory.

A shout came from outside the parlour. The door opened and a burly man dragged in a girl who was beating at his chest and kicking his legs in protest. She wore a mask.

'Lord Farley,' the huge man said, 'she's brawling again.' He dropped the girl at Farley's feet. Her pale delicate fingers grabbed the edge of the table to pull herself up. She lifted her head regally and smoothed the skirt of her red silk dress. Black sensuous curls tumbled to her shoulders in a tangled mass. The lace mantilla had slipped off and hung on one of her shoulders.

'I have no patience for this,' Farley growled. 'What now?'

'She refused a patron.' The man tossed her a scathing look. 'She bit him in…a most unfortunate place.'

The girl faced Farley with her chin held high, her face half-covered by a red leather mask. 'I warned you I would do so.'

Farley shot out of his chair and with a loud clap struck his open hand against her cheek.

'The devil!' Devlin sprang from his seat to catch her before she hit the floor. Both her hands clutched her head, and Devlin supported her with an arm around her waist.

'Farley, I must protest. That was most poorly done.'

'I'll thank you to stay out of my business, Steele,' Farley snarled. 'You have no say in the matter.'

'If you strike her in front of me, I claim the right.' Devlin spoke through clenched teeth. 'You might hear her out.'

Farley rubbed his face. 'I have treated her with more consideration than she deserves, and she still defies me. I'm done with her. You found her pleasing once. Take her in lieu of my debt.'

Devlin combed her hair away from her mask with his fingers. He would leave no woman to suffer such treatment. He leaned close to her ear. 'What say you, Miss England?'

She blinked uncomprehendingly, her eyes unfocused. Suddenly her vision seemed to clear and she stared at him, the bright red imprint of Farley's hand remaining on her cheek. She smiled faintly and flung her arms around his neck.

He gazed over the top of her head to Farley. 'Your debt is settled, sir.'

A half-hour later Devlin paced the pavement in front of Farley's establishment, cursing himself. In the space of a moment, he'd tossed his winnings away and incurred further expense. All for a lightskirt with whom he'd once spent a pleasant interval. He could almost hear the Marquess ring a peal over his head. 'Brother, how many times must I caution you? Think before you act.'

Ah well, he could not very well leave his Miss England with Farley, could he? Perhaps she had some family. His winnings ought to be sufficient to send her wherever she wished to go.

At least the money bought him a little more time. Only two months left before his brother released his quarterly portion.

Two cloaked and hooded figures hurried from the alley. Devlin instinctively kept a watchful eye on them. In this neighbourhood one could easily be set upon and relieved of one's winnings. Indeed, Farley might attempt to recoup his losses. The two shadowy figures came to a stop in front of him, one carrying a large portmanteau.

'We are ready, my lord,' the other one said, breathing hard.

Devlin peered at her. In the lamplight, her face was all but obscured by the hood, and she was wrapped entirely in her cloak, clutching some bundle beneath its folds. Still, he could not mistake his Miss England.

'We?' he asked, one eyebrow arching.

'Sophie accompanies me. I will not leave her.' The resolute tilt of the young miss's head was the same defiant gesture she'd made to Farley. 'Please, we must hurry.'

'She is your maid?' Mentally, Devlin doubled the expense facing him.

'Yes, but more so she is my friend.' She glanced about nervously. 'Truly, haste is in order.'

'Haste?'

'We did not secure Lord Farley's permission for Sophie to accompany me, but I'll not leave her.'

The other woman was a wisp of a thing almost overwhelmed by the portmanteau. Devlin massaged his brow.

What the deuce. In for a penny, in for a pound. 'Very well, Miss England.' Devlin glanced around the street for a hack. 'Shall I relieve you of your bundle?'

She shrank from him. 'If you could take the portmanteau from Sophie, sir, I would be most grateful.'

'Indeed. Sophie, allow me to carry that for you.'

The maid hesitated, backing away as if it were a precious burden unsafe to hand over. He nearly had to wrestle it from her grasp. The portmanteau weighed a ton. Surprising she had strength to lift it off the ground.

'Where is your carriage, sir?' Miss England asked.

Devlin laughed. 'You mistake me for my brother, the Marquess. Perhaps we can find a hack hereabouts.'

'Please, let us remove ourselves.'

He led the way, and the women fell in step behind him, like sari-clad females of India, keeping a respectful distance.

Perhaps he should have cast his lot with the East India Company. There were fortunes to be made, to be sure, but he had no wish for foreign shores. Not after Spain and Belgium—truth was, he had no idea what to do with his life.

Devlin glanced behind him, checking on his two shadows. The memory of his Miss England's soft lips and bold tongue drifted into his mind.

A hack ambled to a stop at the end of the street, and Devlin quickened his step to arrange its hire. He assisted the women into the conveyance, and the driver stowed the portmanteau.

Devlin sat opposite his cloaked companions. 'Where shall I instruct the driver to deliver you?'

The little maid huddled against Miss England's shoulder. Miss England faced him, but he could barely make out her features. 'We have nowhere to go,' she murmured.

He rubbed his hands. 'Is there no relation who might be

persuaded to take you in?' The coil he'd gotten himself into had just developed more tangles.

'There is no one.' She turned her head, but held it erect. 'Leave us where you wish.'

Indeed, drop them into the street? They would be gobbled up in a trice. How long could he afford to put them up at some inn?

At that moment, the bundle in Miss England's arms emitted a squeak. Two small arms poked out of the wrapping and wound themselves around her neck.

'Deuce,' Devlin said.

The cloak opened to reveal an equally small head with a mop of hair as dark as her own. The child cuddled against her chest, fast asleep.

'This is my daughter, Lieutenant.' Miss England faced him again and spoke in a trembling voice, both wary and defiant. 'Linette…England.'

'Good God.'

Miss England spoke again. 'I do wish you would order the hackney somewhere away from this place. I care not where.' She grasped the child more firmly. 'Lord Farley might have a change of mind.'

Devlin instructed the driver to take them to his address. Where else could he take two women and a child when his brain was foggy with brandy and fatigue?

The passengers lapsed into silence. Miss England pointedly avoided conversation, and Devlin, angry at himself for his rash behaviour, clamped his mouth shut.

The thin light of dawn seeped through the London mist as the hack pulled up to a plain, unadorned building near St James's Street. His rooms were at the edge of the unfashionable district where the rent was cheaper. It was an area best known for housing Cyprians of the *ton* and, therefore, acceptable for a gentleman.

His entourage spilled out into the street, the little maid

grabbing the portmanteau before Devlin could reach it. He began to chuckle. To anyone passing by at this hour, the women would appear as two more fancy pieces under protection. As long as the bundle in Miss England's arms remained covered, that is.

Devlin walked to his entrance halfway round to the back.

Wait until Bart saw what he had won at cards. The sergeant's face when they came in the door would make this whole escapade worthwhile.

Devlin had once saved Bart's life on the battlefield. Ever since, the older man made it his mission to take care of him. Primary among Bart's self-imposed duties was tempering Devlin's rash, impulsive nature—a task at which he was doomed to fail.

Live for the moment. As a creed, it was as good as any.

Hmmph, more like a curse, Devlin thought. That particular creed had gotten him sent down from a school or two, but, from the time his late father had purchased his colours, it had meant survival. Now, however, it meant he had the charge of two women and a child.

He glanced over his shoulder. The women were not following. They stood on the spot where the hackney had left them, looking as lost as waifs.

Devlin cursed himself. They presumed he would abandon them. When had he ever passed by a creature in need? In his youth, one of his impulsive habits had been collecting stray animals which he'd then had to conceal from his father.

He walked back to the women. Three more strays to add to his collection.

'This way, if you please.' He wrested the portmanteau from the maid again. 'My abode is humble, to be sure, but will have to do.'

Miss England stood her ground. 'You need not trouble yourself, Lieutenant.'

'Nonsense,' he replied. 'We shall contrive something. The streets are too dangerous for you.'

With halting steps she followed him through the narrow alley. Her maid crept close behind. The sky had brightened, showing signs of becoming a magnificent day.

Devlin knocked on the door and only a moment passed before it opened. 'Good morning, Bart,' he said in a cheerful manner. 'I trust you have not been up all night waiting for me.'

'Half the night is all, then I consigned you to Jericho and took to—' Pale brown eyes in a weathered face widened.

'I've brought guests.' Devlin smiled as he dragged in the portmanteau. Bart's astonished expression was as rewarding as he could have wished. 'Not guests, really. Charges, you might say.' He stepped aside to let the women enter. 'Bart, may I present my charges.' He swept his arm in a graceful gesture. 'Miss England and Sophie.'

The little maid stepped forward cautiously and curtsied.

Devlin tossed Bart an amused glance as he shrugged off his coat. 'Where are your manners, Bart? Take the lady's cloak.'

Bart, mouth open, did as he was bid.

Devlin turned to Miss England. 'Allow me to assist you.' He stepped behind her and unclasped the fastening under her chin, removing the garment.

As the cloak fell away, the child in Miss England's arms whimpered in her sleep.

'My God,' exclaimed Bart.

Devlin laughed. 'This is Miss England's daughter…um…'

'Linette.' Miss England turned to face Devlin, and he had his first good look at her.

His memory had not failed him. Her face was almost regal in its loveliness. Her skin shone like fine porcelain, except for finger-shaped splotches of blue. Her lips were the identical colour to a rose that had grown in his mother's garden. Her lush mahogany-coloured hair cascaded down her shoulders, the perfect frame for a perfect face. She met his appreciation with a bold gaze, her intelligent blue eyes reflecting both youthful innocence and knowledge far beyond her years.

Devlin's breath left his lungs.

'I...I do not know your true name...' he managed, feeling his throat tighten at the vision of so much beauty.

She paused, her eyes searching his face. 'My name is Madeleine.' She added a faint smile. 'Madeleine England.'

He remembered the feel of her bare skin next to his, the lushness of her full breasts, and the ecstasy of her passion. His eyes swept over her as his body came alive to her again.

The child sleeping against her shoulder brought him back to his senses, a tiny girl, a miniature of the mother, very much resembling the wax dolls on his sisters' old toy shelf. The child's feathery long lashes cast shadows on the rosy cheek that lay against Madeleine's shoulder.

What the deuce was he to do with the lot of them?

Bart broke out into guffaws of laughter. 'Cast yourself into the briars again, have you, Dev?'

Madeleine lifted her chin, refusing to let it tremble in disappointment as she regarded the two men. At Farley's, her vision blurred by Farley's blow, she'd thought she dreamed Lieutenant Devlin Steele. Lord, she'd dreamed of him often enough. But when she'd blinked her eyes, it truly had been he.

She understood too well the look he'd given her a moment ago. It spoke of wanting to bed her. Foolish of her to forget this would be his motive for rescuing her. He could not be the brave and gallant dragoon of her fantasy. It had always been a silly fancy, after all, even if visions of him riding up on a tall stallion had comforted many a night.

Especially the nights Lord Farley came to share her bed.

The lieutenant ran his hand through his hair and replied to the other man's remark. 'I've not quite worked out what to do.'

She knew what he would do. He would cast them off as soon as he could. He must dislike her bringing Sophie and

Linette. Perhaps if she'd come to him alone he'd have been content to keep her.

No matter. She would go nowhere without her daughter and her friend. They depended upon her.

She avoided looking at him. 'We shall not trouble you, sir. It is light outside. I am sure we may be safely on our way.' She reached for her cloak. 'Come, Sophie.'

The slight figure was in mid-yawn, her lank yellow hair falling across her face. The other man reached out an arm for her as she staggered.

'The lass is dead on her feet,' he protested.

The lieutenant rubbed his brow, as Madeleine struggled with her cloak. The child squirmed and started to whimper. The cloak slipped to the floor. She tried to comfort Linette, swaying to and fro with her as she had done since her infancy.

'Do not be foolish, Miss England.' He picked up the cloak and tossed it out of her reach. 'You confided you have nowhere to go.'

'It is none of your concern.' She attempted to pass by him to reach her cloak.

He stepped in her path and put his hand on her arm. 'You will stay here.'

She wrenched her arm away. The child started to whimper.

'You have made her cry,' Madeleine said. Much easier to be angry at him than to worry about where she would go if they did walk out the door. What would happen to Linette out there in the streets?

'I have made her cry?' His eyebrows lifted. 'Do you believe she will fare better if I allow you to leave? Do you have money enough to take care of her?'

She could not meet his eye.

He gently took her chin in his hand and made her look at him. 'You do not have money enough even for a hackney coach, do you?'

Her little girl stopped crying and stared with wide eyes at the man. 'Coach?' the child said.

Madeleine clucked at Linette, taking advantage of the opportunity to turn her back on Devlin. Inside panic reigned. Where would they go? Not back to Farley. Never back to Farley, but where? 'I do not need your concern.'

He marched around to face her again, and his voice became quieter. 'I beg to differ with you. If you will recall, it was I who intervened when Farley struck you.' He reached toward her cheek.

She shrugged him away, refusing to let him touch her. 'What does that signify? It is not the first time he has hit me.'

His hand remained poised in the air, his expression conveying acute sympathy. She should not allow herself to believe he truly cared, no matter how much the fantasy of that very thing had sustained her these few years.

The child squirmed in her arms and pulled away to grasp his fingers. The child giggled. Devlin stepped closer, and the tiny girl tugged on his neckcloth. This time when he touched Madeleine's bruised cheek, she did not draw away. Could not draw away. Speech became impossible.

'He will not hurt you again,' he murmured.

He became the hero of her daydreams again. How could she believe in him? Other young men had vowed to place her under their protection. They never returned, or, if they did return, never spoke such a promise again. Farley had seen to it. Why had Farley allowed this man to take her? Was it some sort of trick?

She glanced at her lieutenant. His eyes were warm and full of a resolve she would at least pretend was real. His face again became the one in her weary daydreams, conjured up after her toils were done and she was free to seek her bed alone. He always smiled at her in her dreams, his dimple winking at her.

Now his manly face filled her with excitement. The memory of his gentle kiss and peace-shattering lovemaking returned and agitated her. It was acceptable to dream and remember, but to let herself feel again? To hope? No, her only hope was to contrive to support Linette and Sophie, two people she could depend upon because they needed her so.

Linette tore out the folds of Devlin's neckcloth as he leaned down. His lips came closer. Madeleine's heart thudded against her chest.

'I settled the lass in my cot.' The voice of Devlin's servant, Bart, broke in, full of indignation.

Devlin smiled at the man. 'In your cot, Bart? Quick work.'

'I'll harbour no insults, if you please.' This man did not speak as servant to master. 'If you've managed to get us any funds, I'll see about some food. Some milk for the wee one.'

Devlin marched over to the table and emptied his pockets. 'Good news. We shall eat well.'

Bart picked up a few coins and shoved the rest back to Devlin. 'See you try to hold on to these for a bit.' He reached for a coat on a hook and went out the door, closing it silently.

'He is your servant?' Madeleine asked, conscious of being alone with him once more.

As if reading her thoughts, Devlin regarded her with smouldering eyes. 'More than that, I suppose. We managed through Spain and Belgium together.'

'Belgium,' she murmured. After news of Waterloo, for days she had pored over the names of the dead, weeping in relief when she finally found him listed among the wounded.

No matter. Now that his servant had absented himself, her lieutenant would soon wish payment for her rescue.

Her heart pounded. She must not feel this excitement at being near him. She must expect him to be as selfish and capricious as other men. Madeleine adjusted her hold on Linette, who rubbed her eyes and flopped her head on Madeleine's shoulder again.

Devlin came near to her again. 'The child must be getting heavy for you. Come. It is time for bed.'

Devlin led her into his bedchamber, acutely aware of blood thundering through his veins. By God, she was more desirable than that first, magic time with her.

As she regarded the room with dismay, he saw it through her eyes. A smallish room, furnished with a tall double chest of drawers in a style long out of fashion and a large four-poster bed with faded curtains. His old trunk was tucked in the corner, clothing spilling out.

Her gaze rested on the bed. What might it be like to share that bed with her? To tangle with her in its sheets?

This would not do. She appeared as if she would collapse at any moment. The child was no infant, nearly three years old, he'd guess. A sturdy bundle, and Madeleine had not let go of her for nearly an hour.

'Where shall Linette sleep?' she asked nervously.

'In the bed, where else?'

She straightened, her defiant chin lifting. 'My lord, I am prepared to repay you for your generosity, but I must insist on privacy for Linette. She must not be in the same room, let alone the same bed.'

He raised his eyebrows. Did she think him unmindful of the child? Did she think him so base as to take advantage of her?

'And I'm loath to leave her alone in a strange place,' she continued, her mouth set in firm determination.

He stared into her blue eyes and the breath left his lungs. He let his gaze travel down the length of her. Her red silk dress clung to her form and the weight of her daughter pulled its low neckline down lower. The attire was pure tart, but her bearing regal. The combination set his senses aflame, though he had no intention of acting upon them, ill timed as they were.

A smile not absent of regret spread across his face. 'I meant for you and the child to share the bed. Did you think I meant otherwise?'

She blushed, bringing a most innocent pink to her cheeks, her eyes downcast. 'You know very well what I thought.'

He stepped behind her and put his hands on her shoulders. The little girl's curls tickled his fingers. For a moment he let his fingers caress Madeleine's soft flesh. He held her against him, inhaling the scent of lavender in her hair. From behind her, he planted a chaste kiss on her cheek and gave her a push toward the bed.

'Sleep well, Madeleine.'

Chapter Three

The damp chill seeped through Devlin's clothing. His twisted limbs would not move. Pain had settled into a constant ache, made worse with each breath, worse still by the rancid stench of blood. Of death. Moans of the dying filled the night. The sounds grew louder and louder, until they merged into one piercing wail. An agonised sound. The sound of fear and horror and pain.

Coming from his mouth.

He woke, his heart pounding, breath panting. His vision cleared, revealing faded red-brocade curtains made moderately brighter by sunlight. What were brocade curtains doing at Waterloo?

He sat up, his mind absorbing the round mahogany table in the corner with its decanter of port, the mantel holding one chipped porcelain vase. His back ached from contorting himself on the settee. It had been the dream. He hung his head between his knees until the disturbing images receded. Had he cried out in his sleep?

The wail again sounded in his ears, coming from the bedchamber this time, not from his own soul.

He leapt from the settee and flung open the door. Madeleine paced the room, clutching her little girl. The child cried and struggled in her arms. Madeleine's red dress was creased with wrinkles. That she'd not bothered to undress before sleeping moved him to compassion. How exhausted she must have been.

The child gave a loud, anguished cry, and Madeleine quickened her pace.

'What the devil is going on?'

She spun toward him, her youthful face pinched in worry. 'She is feverish.'

'She is ill?' Devlin's head throbbed from the previous night's excess of brandy.

'Yes. She coughs, too.' Her voice caught. 'I have never seen her so ill.'

'Good God,' Devlin said. 'We must do something.'

'I don't know what to do!'

Tears glistened in her eyes. The child's wailing continued unchecked. He had not bargained for a sick child.

'Bart!' he yelled, rushing back into the parlour. 'Bart! Where are you?'

Bart emerged from his room, Madeleine's small companion like a shadow behind him. The sergeant, his craggy eyebrows knitting together, protectively held her back. The gesture irritated Devlin. Did Bart think him dangerous to young females?

'What in thunder?' A scold was written on Bart's face.

'The child is sick. We must do something.' He stood in the middle of the room, doing nothing.

'The wee one is sick?' parroted Bart, standing just as paralysed.

'Linette!' Sophie rushed past Bart and ran to Madeleine, who had followed Devlin into the room. She frantically felt the child's forehead.

'She is burning up!' she exclaimed. 'Maddy, sit down. Let's loosen her clothes. Mr Bart, if you please, some cool water and some clean rags.

'Clean rags?' Bart said, still immobile.

'Make haste!'

At Sophie's words, Bart sprang into action, drawing water from the pump and bringing it to the women, both fussing over the child. Finding clean rags was more of a challenge. He finally brought a stack of towels and bade them to cut them up, if necessary. Sophie dipped one towel in the water, wrung it out and placed it on the child's chest. Madeleine mopped the little girl's brow with another.

The child seemed to settle for a moment, but, before Devlin could relax, broke out in a spasm of coughing.

'Deuce,' said Devlin, barely audible and still rooted to the floor.

Madeleine flashed him an anxious look. 'I am attempting to quiet her, my lord.'

'I did not complain,' he protested.

Her eyes filled with tears. 'I am at a loss to do more.'

'I would be honoured to assist, if someone would instruct me.' No one heeded him.

Madeleine sniffed and patted Linette's head with the damp cloth.

Her friend regarded him with a wary expression. 'We could try to give her a drink of water.'

Before Devlin could move to the small alcove that served as the kitchen, Bart delivered Sophie a cup of water.

'Let me try to give her a sip,' Madeleine said.

Linette flailed her arms, jostling Madeleine, who spilled the water on her daughter and herself. Devlin walked to the cupboard, removed another cup, and placed in it a tiny bit of water. He handed this to Madeleine.

'Try a bit at a time,' he suggested.

She did not look up to acknowledge his act, but she was able to pour a small amount into the child's mouth. He took the empty cup and poured a bit more from the fuller one. Again the child accepted the drink.

Devlin was feeling rather proud of himself at having been so useful, when the child began another spell of coughing.

Madeleine sat the little girl on her knees and leaned her over to pat her gently on the back.

The child promptly vomited the water all over Devlin's stockinged feet.

'Damn.'

Madeleine gasped. Sophie grabbed the wet towel and wiped his feet, kneeling like a slave girl. Bart glared at him as if he were somehow solely responsible for the child's ill health.

'Enough. Enough.' He stepped away from Sophie's ministrations. She burst into tears and ran from the room.

Bart glared at him. 'Now look what you've done. You've frightened the lass.' He rushed after her.

Devlin reached for his head. Bart, he supposed, would not be inclined to brew the remedy for his excess of brandy. The child wailed again.

The sound triggered memories. Voices of dying men. His knees trembled, and he feared them buckling underneath him. The dream of Waterloo assailed his waking moments. With it came the terror that had only been too real.

Clamping down on his panic, he rushed into his bedchamber and pulled fresh stockings from the chest. He shrugged into his coat, and retrieved his boots from the parlour where he'd left them. Without a word, for he could not guarantee his words would be coherent, he rushed out of the apartment, slamming the door behind him.

Madeleine flinched at the sound and held her coughing daughter against her shoulder, still patting gently. Well, good riddance to Lieutenant Devlin Steele, she told herself, battling the disillusion of his abandoning her at such a time.

'Was that the door?' Bart asked, coming back into the room.

'He left,' she said, shrugging her shoulders.

'Hmmph.' The man pursed his lips.

Linette settled into a fitful sleep. Though her skin burned like a furnace, Madeleine could not let go of her.

The stocky man surveyed her. Not as tall as the lieutenant and a good ten years older, he seemed solid as a rock.

His gaze softened when lighting on Linette. 'Ma'am, would you and the lass be all right if I went out for a bit? I've a mind there are some things we may be needing.'

A rock that easily rolled away. She sighed inwardly. It was foolishness to hope for assistance from any man.

But Devlin had assisted her in the most consequential way. He had rescued her from Farley, when he need not have done. He was under no obligation to assist her further, however. After Linette's distress he would surely wish them speedily gone. Madeleine's lips set together in firm resolve. He would have to put up with all of them until Linette became well.

If Linette became well.

Her throat tightened. Her child meant everything to her. She'd risked Farley's wrath to give birth to Linette and to keep her. Her daughter was the only worthwhile part of her life.

Sophie appeared at her side. 'Mr Bart went out. Do you think the master will return soon?'

'Lieutenant Steele?' Madeleine would not call him master. 'I very much doubt it. I fear Linette's illness displeases him.'

'Is Linette better? She's quiet.' Sophie leaned over and brushed the child's dark curls with her fingers.

'She sleeps fitfully and is so very hot.' She dabbed at the child's face with the cool cloth.

Sophie wandered about the room aimlessly, and Madeleine watched her, needing some distraction. The room was comfortably fitted to double as parlour and dining area, but its once-fashionable furnishings showed signs of wear. The carpet had lost its nap in places, and the cushioned seats looked faded and worn. Had not Devlin said his brother was a marquess? Perhaps the family had more title than blunt. Not that it at all signified. It was far superior to Farley's richly done-up rooms.

Unbidden thoughts of home came, mahogany tables polished to mirror finish, sofas and armchairs covered in rich velvet. No threadbare furnishings there. She could see herself bounding through the rooms, her scolding governess in hot pursuit.

Linette stirred and Madeleine's attention immediately shifted to her. It never did any good to recall those days, in any event.

'Should I unpack our clothes, do you think?' Sophie asked.

Perhaps if they appeared settled in, they might delay an eventual departure. 'That would be good. I fear I cannot help you, though.'

'Oh, Maddy, do not trouble yourself. You have your hands full.' Her waiflike friend smiled at Linette. 'You ought to lie down with the babe.'

Her arms ached from holding Linette, and she had slept only a couple of hours before the child's cries woke her. 'I suppose you are right. I will bring her into the lieutenant's bed.'

She carried Linette to the bedchamber, placed her in the centre of the bed, and climbed in next to her. The sheets and pillow held Devlin's scent as they had the night before. She had dreamed of him walking toward her to a bed like this. He would gently brush the hair from her face and lean to kiss her. She had dreamed of this Devlin many times.

It took no more than a moment to fall exhausted into sleep.

The banging of the door woke her. She immediately felt for Linette's forehead, still too hot.

'Where the devil is she? I've brought a doctor.' Devlin's voice came from the other room. 'Where's the child? Has the fever broke? Deuce, I've been to Mayfair and back. Found the doctor three houses down.'

As the door of the bedchamber opened, Madeleine had a glimpse of Sophie skittering away. Devlin charged in, a short, spry figure behind him. He had mentioned a doctor. For Linette.

The doctor wore a kindly smile in a round countenance. His coat was shabby and the leather satchel he carried was battered and worn. He came directly to Linette. 'Is this our little patient? Here, let me have a look at her.'

Madeleine rose quickly and handed Linette over to him. He sat in a wooden chair and spoke softly to the child as he peeked into her mouth and examined her all over. Madeleine watched the doctor's expression for a clue as to his thoughts. She chewed on her lip. Devlin came to her side and put his arm around her. Needing his strength, she leaned against him.

Finally the doctor handed Linette back to her. 'She has a putrid throat. Nothing to signify under ordinary circumstances, but I cannot like her fever. How long has she suffered thus?'

'This…this morning,' Madeleine stammered. Devlin squeezed her closer.

The doctor smiled, kind crinkles at the corners of his eyes. 'Well, she seems a sturdy child. A little bleeding may suffice to throw off the fever.' He rummaged in his bag.

'Bleeding?' Madeleine said warily.

'Yes, just a little. Come hold her.'

Madeleine sat on the bed and placed Linette in her lap. The doctor opened a small container and, with long pointed tweezers, removed the ringed worm.

'Hold her arm, if you please.'

Devlin stood his ground, though every impulse shouted at him to flee. He recalled the doctors placing such creatures on his arm. The memory belonged to the time of delirium and pain, when he fancied the leeches would consume him alive. Madeleine sat so composed, so resolute in assisting the doctor.

His arms prickled with the sensation now being experienced by the little girl. She was too weak to struggle, as limp as his sister's dolls when they carried them about, as he had been those months ago in Brussels.

The child will feel better after the bleeding, he reminded himself. It had been so for him.

Finally the leech fell away, satiated, and the doctor placed the creature back in its container. He packed up his bag while Madeleine tucked Linette into the bed.

The doctor took Madeleine's hand. 'You have taken good care of her thus far. Try not to lose heart. I have some powders that may assist, as well.'

Madeleine nodded, looking unconsoled. The doctor frowned worriedly at Devlin and gestured for him to follow out of the room. Devlin escorted the doctor out.

When outside, the doctor paused, glancing worriedly back into the apartment. 'The child's fever is very high. Only time will tell if she will recover.' He handed Devlin a packet of powders and gave instruction how to use them. 'I shall return tomorrow to see how she fares.' He patted Devlin's shoulder.

Devlin pushed some coins into the man's palm. The doctor placed them in his pocket, not glancing at the amount. Smiling reassuringly, he took his leave.

Devlin returned to the bedchamber. Madeleine stood beside the bed where the child slept.

'He told you it is hopeless, did he not?' she said, rubbing her arms.

Devlin attempted a smile. 'Indeed, he said no such thing. He gave me the powders and told me how to mix them. He will return tomorrow to see how she fares.'

'She will not die?' Her voice trembled.

He walked over to her and gently brushed the hair off her face. 'She will recover. You are overwrought. Come, sit. I will wager you have not eaten.' He found a chair and brought it next to the bed. 'Where did your friend and Bart go?'

'Her name is Sophie, Lieutenant.' Her voice still shook.

'And mine is Devlin.' He tapped her nose with his finger. He gazed at the little girl. 'The child will sleep, I think.'

'*Her* name is Linette.'

Devlin touched a lock of the child's hair. 'I know.'

He heard the door open and went into the other room. Bart entered, carrying pieces of wood.

'What's all this?' Devlin asked.

Bart cleared his throat. 'I took the liberty of procuring a bed for the wee one. A rocking chair, as well. The poor babe needs a place to sleep.'

Devlin smiled at him. Bart was a practical man. 'Well done, my friend.' He had not thought of such a necessity.

Madeleine stood in the doorway. 'A bed for Linette?'

'Aye, miss. And a chair to rock her in.'

The look she gave Bart was almost worshipful. Devlin's skin grew hot. By God, he was jealous. Of Bart. He wanted Madeleine's gratitude all to himself.

'Set the bed up in our room for now, Bart,' he said and received not a glance from her.

Sophie peered out from the closet where Bart slept. 'Can I help you, Maddy? What would you have me do?'

'Prepare some food for Madeleine,' Devlin said. Sophie shrank from his voice, but scurried to do what she was told.

Devlin sat Madeleine at the small table and took a seat across from her. He poured a small glass of port. 'This will fortify you a bit.'

He sat so near to her, Madeleine again became aware of the scent that had surrounded her in his bed. The lines in his face were clearly visible and told of years spent on battle-fields. Her heart gave a lurch. He was too much like her dreams.

'Drink,' he commanded, handing her the glass.

Madeleine obeyed. The sweet liquid warmed her throat, but Devlin's solicitude frightened her. The doctor must have given ominous news indeed.

He continued to speak to her in a kind voice. 'We will put the child into her bed as soon as Bart has put it together. Sophie can see to the linens. You must try to eat something, Madeleine.'

Sophie scurried from the scullery. Madeleine sipped her port, keenly aware of Devlin's eyes upon her.

Bart announced the bed to be ready, and Devlin accompanied her to the room. She placed Linette gently into the small wooden bed and carefully tucked the linens about her. The child settled, and Devlin took Madeleine's arm and urged her away.

When she returned to the table, Sophie put a plate in front of her with a fat slice of bread and cheese. Madeleine ate, because she did not know what else to do.

When darkness fell, Devlin lit the candles in the bedchamber to dispel the gloomy shadows that had crept into the room. The soft glow of the candlelight illuminated Madeleine, who looked vulnerable as she sat by Linette's bedside. She had barely moved from the little girl's side all day, though he could not fault her. Little Linette was an appealing child and it pained him to see her suffering.

Madeleine glanced at him. 'Do you go out this evening, my lord?'

He put his hands on the arms of her chair and leaned over her. 'My name is Devlin.'

'Very well. Devlin.' Her eyes drifted back to the child.

He pulled up a chair next to her. 'Now, how could I go out when our babe is ill?'

She gave him a sharp glance. 'You are not obligated to stay. I would not hold you.'

'Fustian,' he said.

She rocked gently. He wished he could convince her all would be well. He'd been trying to do so all day, but she did not believe in reassurances.

Devlin heard Bart's deep voice coming from the next room. He smiled to himself. The old sergeant was taken with that mouse of a female. It was amusing. Devlin always imagined Bart would shackle himself to some sturdy country girl to match the farm he used to dream of owning. To make a fool of himself over a wisp of a city chit amused Devlin no end.

'Devlin?' Madeleine's voice was barely more than a whisper.

'Yes?'

'I have never thanked you for…for the doctor and for… allowing us to stay.'

'Deuce, Madeleine. What do you take me for?' Tossing her out, indeed. 'Did you think I'd send you back to Farley?'

She twisted around to face him, alarm lighting her face. 'You would not!'

He stroked her cheek. 'Of course I would not.'

She turned back to Linette, but her hand went to the place he had touched. Devlin leaned back in his chair, balancing it on its back two legs. 'How the devil did you come to be at Farley's? You are too young, surely.'

She rocked at a faster pace. 'I am old enough.'

'Nonsense, you are hardly out of the classroom.'

She tossed him an insulted look. 'I am eighteen.'

'Eighteen!' he cried, unbalancing the chair and nearly pitching over. Linette stirred, whimpering.

'Shh.' Madeleine reached for the child, rubbing her back.

'Good God.' He lowered his voice. 'How old were you when you came to him?' He'd made the computation in his head, but could barely believe it. She'd been so young, and he'd made love to her. How could he have done so?

'I was fifteen.'

'Damnation!' So painfully young. He had left her there when she was younger than the silly chits making their come-out, the ones he thus far had successfully avoided. 'The man's a damned reprobate.' Devlin had bedded her, as well. What did that make him?

She gave him a sideways glance. 'You assume me the hapless victim, Devlin. Don't make me so good.'

'You did not join him willingly.' He would not believe it.

She continued her rhythmic rocking. 'Is this any of your concern, my lord?'

'Not a whit.' But that would not stop him. 'Why did you join that cheating lout, then?'

She sighed. 'This is a sordid story. Hardly of interest.'

'Of interest to me,' he persisted.

'Very well.' She paused to stroke Linette's hair. 'He seduced me. I was ruined. What else could I do?'

She made being ruined sound like getting a soiled spot on her gown. This was a rum story if ever he heard one. Farley was forty, if he was a day. Seducing a girl of her tender years—abominable. Devlin ought to have rescued her from him back then. Saved her from that abominable life.

She adjusted the blankets around the child, the candle behind her placing her profile in silhouette. His breath caught. She was a beauty. As fair as a cameo. As exotic, with her thick black curls, as a goddess from foreign shores. As skilled in the sheets as would fuel any man's dreams.

Her fingers gently touched the child's forehead. When she drew them away, they covered her face. Shame on him. Her child's life hung by a fragile thread, and he thought of bedding her.

'She will recover, Madeleine. Do not fear.'

She leaned back in the rocking chair and closed her eyes. Her silence stretched into the night, and Devlin felt guilty and useless. He watched her rock slowly back and forth in the chair. Back and forth. Back and forth.

'Devlin?' Her voice came as if from a great distance.

'Yes?'

'Do you believe God punishes sinners?'

Chapter Four

Devlin woke sharply, still sitting in the chair. The candles had burned down to stubs and the peek of dawn came through the windows. Madeleine cradled the child in her arms. The child was still.

'My God, is she…?' No, it was unthinkable.

'She's sleeping.'

Devlin's heart started beating again.

Madeleine shuddered. 'Her fever broke and she fell asleep. I thought I would lose her, Devlin. It is what I deserved.'

'Nonsense.' Weak with relief, he stretched his stiff limbs. 'She is through the illness, then?'

She nodded, her cheeks wet with tears.

While she had kept her anxious vigil, he had fallen asleep. Damned if he was not a useless sot. He stood up and, with a tentative hand, stroked the child's hair.

He kissed the mother on the forehead. 'Now you can get some sleep, as well. To bed, Madeleine, the babe can lie with us.'

He urged her up by her elbow and put an arm around her waist as he escorted her to the bed.

She looked about to protest.

He grinned. 'Now don't get in a twist. I'm too tired to

remove my clothes and so are you. We will be as proper as peas.'

She removed her slippers and laid Linette on the bed. Devlin's boots had long been tossed into a corner, as had his coat and waistcoat. He turned down the covers, and she crawled in. When he took his place next to her, he tucked her against him and promptly fell back to sleep.

When Madeleine woke, she was alone in the bed.

Linette. Where was Linette? She scrambled out of the covers and ran to the door.

Opening it, she saw Devlin seated at the table, Linette on his lap. The child giggled as she pulled on Devlin's nose. Two dark curly heads so close together.

Devlin turned his head to escape the assault on his nose. He spied Madeleine. 'Good morning, sleepyhead.'

'Deddy's nose,' cried Linette, pushing Devlin's head back with two chubby hands on his cheeks. Devlin pretended to resist.

'Would you like some nourishment, miss?' asked Bart, pulling out a chair for her.

She glimpsed Sophie perched on a stool near the kitchen alcove, looking smaller and more childlike than ever. Sophie jumped down and disappeared into the scullery.

'Our girl has made a remarkable recovery, wouldn't you say, Maddy?'

Hearing Devlin say 'our girl' gave her heart a lurch. Nor did the familiarity of him calling her Maddy escape her notice.

'She seems fit,' she agreed.

'Mama!' Linette scrambled off Devlin's lap and flung herself into Madeleine's. 'I got Deddy's nose!'

'I saw, sweetling.' She kissed the top of Linette's head and felt her forehead with her hand. It felt blessedly cool.

Bart brought a tray of tea things, followed by Sophie carrying a plate of biscuits. He set the tea service beside her and poured her a steaming cup. 'Do you want some tea, Dev?'

Devlin nodded.

Linette pointed to the biscuits, 'I want one.'

Madeleine placed a biscuit on a plate and lifted Linette on to the other chair to eat it.

'Maddy, you're a sight.' Devlin blinked at her over his cup. 'That awful dress.'

She glanced down at the crumpled red silk.

'Would you like Bart to fill you a bath? We have a tub hereabouts, don't we, Bart?'

'I believe so,' Bart responded.

Before Madeleine could think of what she wished to reply, Bart fetched the large tub, carrying it into the bedchamber while Sophie put on more water to boil. When they began to carry buckets to fill the tub, Madeleine offered to assist, but Devlin would not let her. Even Linette helped, carrying small pitchers of water, spilling more than made it into the tub. It felt all wrong to be so pampered.

When the bath was filled, Devlin brought her into the bedchamber. Bart and Sophie took charge of Linette, but Devlin remained. Madeleine began to understand.

Devlin closed the door and leaned against it. 'Shall I play lady's maid for you?' His voice was velvet.

It was time for her to pay for his kindness. Farley had taught her how.

She cast Devlin a demure look under her lashes and strolled over to the bath. 'As you wish, sir.'

He moved closer, as smooth a motion as a stalking cat. Presenting her back to him, she lifted the long tangled curls off her shoulders. His hands slid up the length of her back. Slowly he undid her laces, his fingers light and dextrous. She remembered him fumbling with her laces all those years before. Her body lapsed into a languid state. His hands slipped under her dress and ran over her skin like warm liquid.

The wrinkled red silk dress fluttered to the floor. Next came her shift. When she was fully naked, she knew he would wish to see. She turned to face him.

As she expected, his eyes feasted on her, darkening with arousal. She had learned to stand still for a man's visual pleasure.

He took time to regard her, longer than she thought she could bear. His gaze disturbed her. Not precisely as the ogling from Farley's clientele had done, but in an indefinable, unsettling way. His eyes finally reached her face.

'You are lovely.' The corner of his mouth turned up, and his dimple deepened.

The next move belonged to her. She stepped toward him and reached out her hand to caress his neck. She had not intended to kiss him, but he leaned down, and she had only to rise on tiptoe to reach his lips. He crushed her against him, standing wide-legged so she could feel his arousal pressing into her. For a moment she forgot her role and simply revelled in the strength of his muscles, the sweetness of his mouth, the feel of his hands pressing into her back, sliding down to hold her tightly against his groin. She did not realise how quickly she removed his shirt, how efficiently she freed him from his trousers, how she clung to him as he carried her to the bed.

'Madeleine.' His voice was a groan as he placed her on the bed and climbed atop her. His lips feathered her cheek and neck, soft, warm, and hungry. Her heart raced in excitement. His tongue circled the pink of her nipple, and all her senses sprang to life. She ached with wanting him.

She was spiralling out of control at the precise moment she ought to check herself. She had succumbed to the ecstasy of Devlin's lovemaking once, but that interlude belonged to daydreams. She must shield herself, protect herself from feeling, just as she'd done when required to endure the attentions of other men. The Mysterious Miss M could not be hurt, or humiliated, or betrayed, because The Mysterious Miss M felt nothing at all.

The Devlin of her daydreams was not the same Devlin whose hand now stroked the flesh of her belly, whose mouth rained kisses over her breasts. She would not be fooled, no matter what kindnesses he chose to make. Ultimately, all men served their own needs, and demanded payment for any small favour they bestowed. If they were refused, they could be very cruel.

It had been that way after the enchanted night with Devlin so many years ago. Farley had come afterwards to claim his pleasure, but Madeleine refused him. He went into a rage that left her bruised and in pain. The next day, Farley departed on one of his mysterious long trips. By the time he returned, Madeleine knew herself to be with child.

Now Devlin's hands and lips threatened to engulf her in sensation. She remained still, resolving to repay him for rescuing her, for taking in Sophie, for snatching her child from the clutches of death, but she would not allow herself to feel anything.

She pushed on his shoulders, and he lifted his head.

'Shall I pleasure you now, my lord?' She modulated her voice to a velvet smoothness, as she'd rehearsed many times.

He leaned on his elbow, his expression puzzled. 'Pleasure me?'

She deliberately slithered out from beneath him, facing him instead. She ran her finger in circles on his chest. 'I wish to please you. Tell me what I must do to pleasure you.'

He grabbed her hand and searched her face. 'What the devil…?'

She laughed, making a throaty sound Farley insisted she learn. 'Oh? Would you like me to be wicked? I can be wicked, my lord, if that is what you wish.'

He dropped her hand and sat up, rubbing his face.

She pretended to look wounded. 'What is amiss, my lord? I shall do whatever you desire.'

'Stubble it, Maddy.' He swung his legs over the side of the bed and grabbed his clothes.

'Do not be vexed.' Retaining her velvety voice, she pressed herself against his back. 'I would not wish you unhappy.'

His muscles stiffened. 'And I do not wish to play this game of yours. We are not at Lord Farley's establishment, Miss M.'

'Game?' She sat back, blinking in confusion.

He shoved his arms into the sleeves of his shirt and groped around for the rest of his clothes, donning each piece as he came to it. 'You are acting like cheap Haymarket-ware.'

She blinked at him, covering herself with the bed linens. 'I do not know what that means.'

He glared at her. 'It means lightskirt, Cyprian, dolly-mop. Shall I continue?'

Her eyebrows knitted together. 'But that is what I am.'

He grabbed at the linens covering her and yanked them away. Before Madeleine could protest, he picked her up and dumped her into the now-tepid bath water.

'How dare you!' she shouted before she remembered that men did not like it if you showed them anger.

He lunged down at her face, and she drew back, fearful of the price he'd exact from her show of temper. Only an inch lay between their lips.

His voice became disturbingly low. 'You cannot fool me, Maddy. You wanted me as much as I wanted you.' As quickly, he strode out the room, slamming the door behind him.

Dripping with water, Madeleine burst into tears, but she did not know if it was because she had angered him or because what he'd said had been only too true.

'Can you make it fit, Sophie?'

Madeleine stood in the centre of the bedchamber while her friend pulled on the strings of her dress. Though her hair, now in a braid down her back, remained damp, all other signs of the bath had been removed. Not from Madeleine's mind, however, where Devlin's angry eyes continued to haunt. She rubbed her temples.

Sophie tugged on the material of the dress. 'It is too small, Maddy, and the seams cannot be let out.'

'Oh, bother,' she mumbled.

The door slammed. Footsteps sounded in the outer room. 'Bart! Bart!'

Madeleine felt the blood drain from her face. Devlin had returned.

'Where is everybody?' He entered the bedchamber.

Sophie shrank back to a corner. Madeleine braced herself.

Surprisingly, he wore a grin on his face. He walked briskly over to her, lifted her off the ground, and swung her around. 'I have a surprise for us. Where is Bart?'

'Here I am, Dev.' Bart appeared in the doorway, holding Linette's hand. Linette had her thumb in her mouth.

Devlin released Madeleine. 'We're moving. Right now. We have to pack.'

'Did you get us tossed out of here?' Bart asked, his eyes narrowing.

Devlin clapped Bart on the shoulder, smiling broadly. 'No, I've merely secured lodging spacious enough for the lot of us.'

Madeleine's hands flew to her face. For all of them? What of sending them away?

'Explain yourself, lad.' Bart said.

'I have procured the lease to Madame LaBelmonde's apartments,' Devlin responded, grinning.

'Madame LaBelmonde?' Madeleine raised an eyebrow.

'Two bedchambers above stairs and two below. A parlour, dining room, and a proper kitchen.' He placed his hands on his hips in satisfaction. 'It should do very well.'

'A sizeable rent, I suppose?' Bart pursed his lips.

Devlin shook his head. 'Not beyond our touch, once my quarterly portion is in hand.'

Bart clucked his tongue. 'How do we pay until then?'

Devlin tossed Madeleine a broad wink before answering Bart. 'I wagered the first month's rent on a roll of the dice and won. My recent winnings should pay the second.'

'You wagered the rent?' Madeleine gasped. Visions of foolish, ruined men, their faces bleak and despairing, leaving Farley's gaming rooms flashed through her mind. She remembered the sounds of angry words, overheard years ago outside her parents' bedchambers.

'Lord Devlin is a sad gamester, ma'am,' Bart told her.

'What else was I to do with my time but play cards?' Devlin countered. 'We shall go on very well, I promise.'

Madeleine wondered about more than the rent. 'Who is Madame LaBelmonde?'

Devlin smiled at her. 'A close neighbour.'

'Close?'

'Indeed. She has found a new protector. Lord Tavenish, I believe. He purchased a town house for her. She leaves her furnishings.'

'Lord Tavenish,' Madeleine repeated. A frequent visitor at Farley's, Lord Tavenish had been well over fifty with sagging skin, and a sour smell. Would a town house be worth such a man?

Bart blew out a breath. 'Well, what is done is done.'

'Indeed.' Devlin grinned. 'We have not a moment to lose. There is a tenant interested in these rooms.'

'These rooms? Already?' Bart asked.

'The matter is completely settled. I called upon our landlord and made an arrangement with him. If we move out today, our debt to him is forgiven.'

Little Linette let go of Bart's hand and tottered over to Madeleine. 'Up, Mama.' She reached her hands up. Bart turned on his heel, muttering about setting to the task and hotheadedness. Sophie quietly crept along the wall until she, too, reached the door.

Devlin turned to Madeleine, his smile taking her breath away. She spun to face the wardrobe, gathering Devlin's clothing to pack in the trunk.

'You rented these accommodations to include us?' She could not believe it. There must be some mistake.

He put his hands on her shoulders and turned her to face

him again. 'Yes, to include you. We could not get on here, all of us, in this small space.'

She dipped her head, hiding her face from him. 'You are not obliged to house us.'

He tilted her face to him, his fingers under the soft skin of her chin. 'I am obliged.'

Not that he understood it, but Devlin felt keenly responsible for them. What would happen to them otherwise?

She shook her head.

He held her gaze. 'As you have said, you have nowhere else to go.'

She cast down her eyes.

'Madeleine, you are no prisoner here, if you wish to go.'

Her glance flew back to him. 'I do not wish to leave. You are correct. There is no place for me.' Her voice cracked.

His finger drew a line down her cheek. 'Let us not speak of this now. We have much to do.'

He watched her turn away, stooping down to hand Linette some clothing. 'Put them in the trunk, Linette.'

The laces on the back of her dress were undone. 'Let me lace you,' he said, reaching for them as she stood up again.

She twisted away from his hand. 'It is no use. The dress no longer fits.'

'Change to another then. I will leave the room if you desire privacy.'

She kept her eyes on her daughter, a doll-like miniature of herself. 'I have no other dress.'

'No other dress?'

'Well, there is the horrid red one, but Sophie washed it and it is quite wet still. I must have grown out of this one since last wearing it.'

He studied the frock, and it did indeed look unfashionably old and slightly girlish. 'A long time ago, I collect.'

'The day Farley brought me to London.'

Devlin heard the edge in her voice. How had she come to be in Farley's clutches? 'You brought only one extra dress?'

'I did not want Farley's clothes.'

Devlin raked his fingers through his hair. He had not cal-culated on having to purchase a wardrobe. Did the little maid and the child need to be clothed as well?

Madeleine regarded him, her eyes serious. 'Do not worry. Sophie will know how to alter it. She is clever at such things. In the meantime, if I go out, I shall wear my cloak. It covers everything.'

'We will get you clothes, Maddy.'

She lifted her eyes to him before walking over to Linette.

Later that afternoon, Madeleine held Linette's hand as she walked through their new rooms. Linette chattered, and she answered automatically, trying to stay out of the way of Dev-lin and Bart, busily carrying in trunks and boxes.

She had feared Madame LaBelmonde would have furnish-ings as gaudy and garish as in Farley's establishment, but these rooms were genteel, the golds, reds, and greens muted and beautiful. She might have chosen them herself. Would it not be lovely if this really were her house? She the mistress, and Devlin...

No, she must not pretend. But as she strolled through the rooms, she could not help herself.

She entered the parlour and ran her finger across the pol-ished mahogany and silk upholstery. She pictured herself seated on the couch, and Devlin, on the nearby chair, reading the latest newspaper. Linette sat at her feet, playing with a doll. She ought to be doing something in this fantasy, but what? Her attempts at embroidery used to wind up in tangles, and she had never paid enough attention to sewing to know how to mend.

Sophie walked in the room in such high spirits her usually pale face was flushed with pink.

'Oh, Maddy, it is the loveliest set of rooms I have ever seen. Do you think we may really stay? Look at the furniture.

I should like to keep such nice tables polished. Do you think lemon oil or beeswax would do?'

Madeleine stared at her, not having any notion of what best polished wood, nor whether they might stay.

Sophie did not seem to notice she had not responded. 'I shall ask Mr Bart.' Sophie swept out of the room as quickly as she had come in.

'Mama, I want Mr Bart!' Linette pulled at her hand to follow Sophie.

'No, Linette. Mr Bart has much to do right now. He's moving boxes.'

'I want boxes, too.'

'Let's explore the kitchen, shall we?'

She led Linette to the kitchen where the little girl opened cabinet doors, momentarily distracted by new discoveries within. Madeleine ran her hand over the cupboard, imagining life inside this kitchen. She saw herself kneading bread, and Devlin entering, kissing her cheek, and asking for his meal.

Folly! She knew not the first thing about making bread, nor how to cook a meal.

Devlin entered the kitchen, carrying a big wooden box. 'Maddy, is the kitchen well supplied?'

She opened a cupboard. 'There are things in here. Do you suppose it is adequate?'

Devlin stood next to her and peered in the open cupboard. 'Hmm. Well, Bart will know.' He set the box down on the table and walked out.

Much later, the five of them sat around that rough wooden table, having finished a hastily prepared meal of bread from the nearby bakery and hard cheese. Devlin poured each of them another glass of wine, giving Linette, seated on his lap, a small sip from his own glass. The little girl puckered her lips at the taste, and he laughed.

Madeleine gazed at all of them. She pretended they were a

family, without a care, sharing a simple meal and pleasant conversation. The thought made her smile.

Devlin caught her eye and winked at her. 'I propose a toast.' He raised his glass.

'I want toast,' Linette said.

'To our new abode,' Devlin said.

'New 'bode,' Linette parroted.

'Hear, hear,' Bart responded.

'It is a lovely place.' Madeleine sipped her wine and swept her gaze from corner to corner.

Devlin gave her a smile. He'd had no idea that pleasing her would make him feel mellow and strangely content. He raised his glass again while Bart sliced a piece of cheese and handed it to Sophie. Little Linette banged on the table with both hands.

The mellow feeling returned. 'Tomorrow, ladies, we shall visit the mantua maker. Outfit you properly.'

Panic came over the shy Sophie's face. 'Oh, no, my lord.'

Devlin at last saw an opportunity to befriend the skittish young woman. 'Would you not like a pretty dress or two?'

Sophie shook her head and dared to glance up at him for a moment. 'No pretty dress. Nothing pretty. A bit of fabric will do, if it is not too dear. I do not presume to ask, my lord.'

'Sophie, you are part of our household. You deserve decent clothing.'

'Yes, my lord.' She slid off her stool and cleared the dishes.

Devlin rolled his eyes and caught Bart's disapproving look before the man followed Sophie out of the room.

'Do not mind her, Devlin,' Madeleine said. 'She does not want presents, I think.'

He took a gulp of his wine. Linette relaxed against his chest, still at last.

'She is afraid of you.'

He gave a dry laugh. 'Indeed.'

'It is because you are a man.'

He ran a finger through Linette's hair, brushing it off the child's forehead. 'Bart is a man, I've noticed.'

'True.' She looked quizzical.

'Well, Maddy, shall you and I visit the modiste or do you choose to be your own dressmaker, too?'

He meant to be good-tempered, but she responded with a wounded look.

'I cannot sew.'

Lord, women were difficult.

'It is of no consequence,' he said, hoping to return to her good graces. 'I'm sure we can find a skilful mantua maker. I would be pleased to see you in a pretty new dress.'

Her countenance changed, as if he had said something of great importance that had never occurred to her before. 'Of course. I understand perfectly.'

He wished he understood. Devlin poured himself more wine and drained the entire contents of his glass. It was easier to evade the musket balls of an entire French battalion than to navigate a simple conversation with a female.

'Linette is falling asleep. I need to make her ready for bed.' Madeleine rose from her chair.

'I'll carry her.' Devlin lifted Linette, and the little girl relaxed against him, a warm bundle more than comfortable against his shoulder.

He followed Madeleine into the bedchamber where they had set up Linette's bed. A connecting door joined the two upstairs bedchambers. He wanted to think of Madeleine knocking softly on that door and coming to him in the night, but, after the morning's débâcle, he was sure she would not do so.

Madeleine pulled out a tiny nightdress from the bureau. Linette's meagre supply of clothing barely filled half a drawer, and Devlin vowed to ensure the child, as well as the mother, had a pretty new wardrobe.

'Place her on the bed, please.'

He did so as gently as he could. 'Toast,' Linette murmured, opening her eyes momentarily.

Madeleine glanced at Devlin and smiled. How pleasant it felt. He had no idea domesticity could be so comfortable.

After she settled the child into bed and kissed the soft pink forehead, Devlin wrapped his arm around her and squeezed. 'She's a fine child, Maddy.'

'She is everything to me.' Her voice shook with emotion.

Madeleine leaned her head against Devlin's shoulder. His strong arm felt so comfortable, she could almost imagine he belonged to her and they were gazing upon their own—

No, she must not lapse into that particular fantasy. She must remember that Devlin wished to see her in pretty dresses, just as Farley had. She must remember that she owed him for his kindness.

'Shall I ready myself for bed as well, sir?' She modulated her voice as she had been used to doing for these last years.

He placed her away from him and looked into her face. Madeleine knew how to control her expression. She smiled, half-demurely, half-seductively. She gently caressed his neck, leaning forward so when he glanced down, a peek of the rounded shape of her breasts was clearly visible. She led him to the connecting door, pulled him into the other room, closing the door behind her.

'Shall I kiss you?' she purred, wrapping her arms around his neck. Not waiting for his answer, she stood on tiptoe and touched her lips to his.

Yes, she could do this, she thought, keeping her body in firm control. She could indeed pleasure Devlin and repay his kindness without ever pleasuring herself.

Devlin wound his arms around her and pressed her against him. Desire flared inside him, and he deepened the kiss. She reached her hands around to loosen the already loose strings of her dress. It fell to the floor, leaving only her corset and shift. He ran his hands across her bare shoulders.

So lovely. So soft. Like honey. He wanted her. Wanted to plunge into her, join himself to her and not feel so alone.

'Shall we go to the bed, my lord?'

The words echoed in his mind, from long ago.

He released her, watching as she moved toward the bed. She tossed a seductive glance over her shoulder.

She climbed onto the bed and turned to face him. 'Come, let me remove your clothing.'

He rubbed the back of his neck. And stood his ground.

'Come,' she purred, reaching her arms above her head, arching her back. 'Come, my lord.'

Devlin spoke quietly. 'You must call me Devlin. Did you forget that, Maddy?'

She rolled to her side and stared at him.

'This is not Farley's establishment.' He stared back.

She twisted the sheet in her hand.

'Go to your room, Maddy. Your daughter might need you this night.'

She sat up. 'No.'

'I do not want your favours.' Something else from her, perhaps, but not what Farley required of her.

'But you must.' A desperate look came over her.

'No.'

She scampered off the bed and gathered her dress, holding it in front of her, covering herself with it. 'Please, Devlin, you must let me make love to you. You must.' Her words came out between laboured gasps.

'No, Maddy.'

He walked to the door and opened it.

'Devlin, I am used to this. It is not difficult. I will pleasure you. It will be pleasant, I promise you.' Tears sprang to her eyes.

With every sensation in his male body, Devlin wanted to accept her offer, but he could not bear the emptiness in her seductive words. He well remembered what had passed between them that first time and this was not it.

She rubbed her eyes, now red and swollen. Her nose had turned bright pink. 'I…I wish to show you my gratitude.'

'Gratitude? Do you think I desire your lovemaking out of gratitude?'

Confusion wrinkled her brow. Devlin suspected that was not part of her practised repertoire. She clutched her dress in her hands. 'You want me, I know you do. Men like to…to… You liked it, too.'

He had indeed, but not when her eyes stared vacantly and her words were rehearsed.

'Go to bed, Maddy. Your own bed, not mine.'

She dropped her dress to the floor and wound her arms around his neck, kissing wherever her lips could reach. At least her rehearsed seduction had fled, but her desperation was no better. None the less, his body flared to life. He picked her up and she sighed in relief, nuzzling his neck. He carried her through the doorway and dropped her on to the large bed in the other room.

'No, Devlin.' She grabbed the front of his shirt, trying to pull him back. 'You do not understand. I must do this.'

He moved her hands away, trying to be gentle, but not succeeding. The demands of his body were making him harsh. 'You do not need to bed me. It is not something I demand of you.'

'But it is the only thing I can do.'

Madeleine watched him turn away from her and walk toward the door. 'You do not understand,' she whispered. 'It is the only thing I can do.'

He did not look back, but closed the door behind him, leaving her alone.

Devlin fled down the staircase and out into the damp night air. He strode through lamp-lit streets until reaching the nearest gaming house. Instead of sounding the knocker, he stood staring at the entrance. What would he find inside? Cigar smoke? Bad brandy? The luck of the draw? It was not ennui he sought to dispel this night, but the turbulence left in Madeleine's wake.

Why not accept her gratitude and bed her? He'd rescued her from Farley's, hadn't he? Taken in her child and her mouse of a maid. Provided them proper lodgings.

Devlin turned from the door of the gaming establishment and walked back to the street. When he had first met her, she had come to him, not with gratitude, but desire. Almost like loving him. He had never forgotten.

He wandered slowly through the streets, until he found himself back at the door of his expensive new rooms. The place was quiet as he entered, a single candle providing light. He glanced toward the back of the place where the two other bedchambers were located and wondered what might be occurring behind those closed doors. Was Bart holding the frail Sophie protectively, lest the 'lord' attack her in the night? Had Sophie offered her body to Bart, as well? Had he accepted?

Devlin would bet a month's blunt Bart had not made a mull of things as he had, and that, on the morrow, the little maid would gaze upon Bart's craggy features with adoration.

Devlin entered Madeleine's room quietly. The dim illumination of the street lamp shone on Linette's sleeping figure, her thumb in her mouth. Devlin smiled and gently pulled out her thumb. The little girl stirred, her long dark eyelashes fluttering. She popped the thumb back in.

Madeleine's bed was empty, and he felt a moment's anxiety, until he spied her curled up on the windowseat, sound asleep, as innocent and vulnerable as her daughter.

They were both beautiful, these charges of his, and totally dependent upon him. It frightened him, worse than leading men into battle. Soldiers knew the stakes were death, but they had the tools to fight. If he failed Madeleine and Linette, they would be at the mercy of creatures like Farley and would have no weapons with which to protect themselves.

He would not fail them, he vowed. He would see to their needs no matter what the cost.

Devlin gathered Madeleine in his arms, her weight surprisingly like a feather. He carried her to the bed.

'Only thing I can do,' she murmured, resting her head on his shoulder, much like her little girl had done earlier.

'Hush, Maddy,' he whispered. 'You'll wake Linette.'

'Linette,' she murmured. 'All I have.'

'Not any more, Miss England.' Devlin laid her carefully on the bed and tucked the covers around her. 'Now you have me, as well.'

Chapter Five

Madeleine held tightly on to Devlin's arm as they strolled the pavements of London in the bright morning sun. She pulled the hood of her cape to obscure as much of her face as possible. Still, she felt exposed.

'You will not take me to a fashionable modiste, will you, Devlin?' The thought of walking down Bond Street filled her with dread.

Devlin regarded her with an amused expression. 'No, indeed, Maddy. Would I subject you to such a terrible thing?'

That made her laugh. 'Do not tease me. It is merely that I would not want to be seen.'

'Do not worry, goose. You were always masked, were you not? No one will recognise you.' He patted her hand comfortingly.

'Of course. So silly of me.'

She took a deep breath. He did not understand. Farley's patrons did not concern her, but perhaps those she did fear encountering would not recognise her either. Surely the years had altered her?

'Where are we bound, then?' She gazed up at Devlin, so tall and handsome. His green eyes sparkled in the sunlight, like emeralds on a necklace a young man had once bestowed upon her before Farley snatched it away. If necessity bade her to walk in daylight, it pleased her to be beside him.

'Bart found a dressmaker only four streets from here,' Devlin said. 'How he should know about dressmakers foxes me.'

She laughed. 'Bart is very clever, isn't he? He and Sophie. I do believe they can do everything.'

'Unlike me, I suppose.' He smiled, but the humour did not reach his voice.

'You are the hub around which all revolves.' She spoke absently, transfixed by a coach rumbling down the street. 'Oh, look at the matched greys. How finely they step together. They are magnificent, are they not?'

'Indeed,' he answered.

She watched the coach-and-four until it drove out of sight. 'Oh, my.' She cast one last glance in the direction it had disappeared. 'What were you saying, Devlin?'

'I was remarking about how utterly useless you find me.'

She glanced at him. 'You are funning me again. What would have happened to me and Linette without you, Devlin?'

Madeleine felt her face flush. She should not have spoken so. To suggest he had any obligation to her was very bad of her. She had awoken in her own bed this morning. The only service she could render him, he'd refused.

'It is I who am useless, not you, Devlin.' She sighed. 'I am skilled at nothing…well, nothing of consequence.'

A curricle drawn by two fine roans raced by. Madeleine stopped to watch it.

'Do you like horses, Maddy?'

'What?' She glanced at him. 'Oh, horses. I used to like horses.'

'Not now?' His mouth turned up at one corner.

'I have not been on a horse since…for many years.'

'You ride, then?'

She had careened over the hills, giving her mare her head, clearing hedges, sailing over streams. Nothing unseated her. She outrode every boy in the county and most of the men.

When she could remain undiscovered, she spent whole days on horseback.

Had she not been out in the country on her mare, unchaperoned as usual, she might not have met Farley, might not have succumbed to his charm. Never riding again was fitting punishment for her fatal indiscretion.

She blinked away the regret. 'You might say I used to ride horses as well as I now ride men.'

'Maddy!' Devlin stopped in the centre of the pavement and grabbed her by the shoulders. 'Do not speak like that. I ought to throttle you.'

She tilted her chin defiantly. 'As you wish, sir.'

He let go of her and rubbed his brow. 'Deuce, you know I will not hit you, but why say such a thing?'

'Because it is true. I know what I am, Devlin. There is no use trying to make me otherwise. It is my only skill. Bart and Sophie can do all sorts of useful things. You, too. You can win at cards and go about in society. You have fought in the war. What could be more useful than that? But me, there is nothing else I know how to do.'

He extended his hand to her, wanting to crush her against him and kiss her until she took back her words. Though the kissing part might not prove the point, exactly, he admitted. He dropped his hand and, putting her arm through his, resumed walking.

After a short distance in silence, he said, 'That's what you meant last night. Saying it was the only thing you could do.'

She did not reply.

Devlin held his tongue. This was no place for such a conversation in any event. Besides, each time some handsome equipage passed by in the street, she slowed her pace a little.

He chuckled. 'Horse mad, are you?'

She pointedly turned her head away from him.

'Now do not deny it, Maddy. You are horse mad. I recognise the signs. I was myself, as a boy. Why, I liked being with the grooms better than anyone else. My brother, the heir, could not keep up with me when I rode, though he's a good ten years my senior. Nothing he could do but report to Father that I was about to break my neck.'

He threw a penny to the boy who had swept the street in front of where they crossed.

'Oh, look at all the shops!' Madeleine exclaimed. 'I had not reckoned there to be so many.'

Like a child at a fair she turned her head every which way, remarking on all the delicious smells and sights.

'You have not been to these shops?'

She laughed. 'Indeed not. I always wondered what the London shops would be like.'

'You've been in London three years and have never seen the shops?' This was not to be believed.

'Lord Farley did not take me to shops.'

This time Devlin stopped. 'Do you mean that devil did not let you out of that house?'

'Not as bad as all that, I assure you.' She patted his hand and resumed walking. 'When Linette was big enough, I was allowed to take her to the park across the street. But only in the morning, not when other people might be about. And there was a small garden in the back of the house. Sophie and I were allowed to tend it, though I mostly had the task of digging the dirt, because I did not have the least notion how to make the flowers grow. I enjoyed feeling the soil in my hands, though.'

Such a small space of geography in which to spend more than three years. 'I wish Farley to the devil.'

She gave him a look. It struck him as almost the same expression Sophie bestowed on Bart.

As they stood at the entrance to a shop with an elegant brass nameplate saying 'Madame Emeraude', Madeleine shrank back. Devlin had to practically pull her into the establishment. She held her fingers to the hood of her cloak, covering her face.

A modishly dressed woman emerged from the back. 'May I be of assistance?'

Since Madeleine had turned away, Devlin spoke. 'Good morning. Madame Emeraude, I collect?'

The woman nodded.

Devlin gestured to Madeleine. 'The young lady is in need of some new dresses.'

'Certainly, sir. Shall I show you some fashion plates, or do you have certain styles in mind?'

It irritated Devlin that the dressmaker addressed him directly instead of Madeleine, as if Madeleine were his fancy piece to dress as he wished, but, he supposed, in this neighbourhood, her clientele were almost exclusively from the demimonde.

'Shall we step into the other room?' She gestured elegantly.

He pulled Madeleine along to the private dressing room in the back. 'The young lady is in somewhat of a fix. You see, she has only the dress she wears and we were hopeful to purchase something already made up.'

Understanding lit the woman's eyes. 'Let me see her.'

Since Madeleine was acting like a stick, Devlin had no choice but to treat her that way. He turned her toward the dressmaker and removed the cloak that obscured her.

'Oh,' said the woman in surprise. 'Miss M, is it not? How delightful to see you again.'

'How do you do, ma'am,' Madeleine murmured politely, though Devlin did not miss the splotches of red on her cheeks.

'Deuce,' said Devlin.

'Why, I believe I have a dress ready for you,' said Madame Emeraude helpfully. 'Do you recall we fitted it not a fortnight ago? Wait a moment and I shall see—'

'No!' Madeleine cried.

Devlin interceded, putting his arm around Madeleine. 'We do not wish that dress.'

Madame Emeraude looked from the one of them to the other. 'I see. It is a new day, is it not? Well, I am pleased for you, miss. That other one was charming, but I shall have no business with him, I tell you, until he pays—' She caught herself. 'I beg pardon. I only meant I wish you well, Miss M.'

'Thank you,' Madeleine said, continuing to look miserable.

Madame Emeraude smiled and began to consider her, stepping around her. 'Oh, my,' she said as she saw the open laces of Madeleine's dress. 'This dress does not fit. No, no, no. This will never, never do.'

'You see our predicament.' Devlin smiled. Madeleine fixed her interest on the floor.

'Let me show you a few things I have on hand.'

Madame Emeraude signalled an assistant, who carried in one dress after another. Madeleine seemed to regard each garment with horror. They were, Devlin thought, merely dresses. A little fancy, perhaps.

As Madame conferred with her assistant, Madeleine whispered to him, 'Devlin, please do not make me wear those dresses. This one I have will do, or Sophie can make me a plain one.'

'What is wrong with them?'

'They are not…respectable.'

He regarded her, rubbing his chin. 'I see.'

When Madame Emeraude came back to them, Devlin took the woman aside and spoke to her. Madeleine watched them, the modiste nodding and looking her way. She dearly wished to leave this place where the proprietress knew her as Miss M.

Devlin came back to her. 'Madame Emeraude is ordering a hack. She has given me the direction of another dressmaker where we will go next.' He held her cloak open for her.

'I do not wish to. Let us go home, please.' This short excursion had already been mortifying.

'We will try this other place first. You need clothes, Maddy.'

In the hack she continued trying to persuade him. 'I believe

Sophie could teach me to sew, Devlin. A piece of cloth would be enough.'

He would not listen. He did not understand. Though it was exciting to be out among the carriages and shops, it was frightening, as well. She would always be face to face with what she was.

Madeleine peeked out at the passing scenery, the bustle of London with the pedestrians so intent on their destinations and the tradesmen so occupied with peddling wares. She could not hide forever. How could she rear Linette if she hid? Her daughter would have to go out into that world, too. She was determined that Linette's life be respectable, though nothing could ever change what Madeleine was inside.

If Devlin Steele was determined she should have clothes, she was determined they be respectable ones.

'Are you taking me to Bond Street?' she asked, meaning to sound merely curious, but her voice shook.

He smiled at her. 'Not to Bond Street. We are directed to a modiste who dresses the worthy daughters of our bankers and merchants.'

'Very well.' Not the fashionable part of town. No chance of encountering members of the *ton*.

They discovered a goldmine. The wealthy daughter of an East India merchant had abandoned her trousseau for one made at a fashionable address. The young woman was of Madeleine's size, and the dresses were exquisitely tasteful attempts by the modiste to expand her clientele.

Madeleine quarrelled with Devlin over the number of dresses he would purchase, wanting no more than two or three. She adamantly refused to let him include even one evening dress and would not even discuss the riding habit. His easy acquiescence in these last two matters made her momentarily suspicious, but he whisked her off to the milliner next door and a new set of arguments became necessary.

As he made arrangements for the delivery of his final purchase of several bonnets for Madeleine and one very plain one for Sophie, Madeleine gazed in the mirror.

She wore a pale lilac muslin walking dress adorned only by vertical tucks in the bodice edged by a plain purple ribbon. A blue spencer, lilac gloves, and a modest straw bonnet, simply adorned with a blue bow, completed the ensemble. She even carried a reticule.

Studying herself in the glass was like gazing into the distant past.

Devlin's image appeared behind her. 'You look very well, Maddy.'

She swallowed the surge of emotion that had risen in her throat. 'It seems like too much...'

He held up his hand. 'No more of that. We still need to stop by the shoemaker.'

She opened her mouth to protest, but as he took her hand and tucked it in his arm, he quickly added, 'Do you suppose we could convince Sophie to be measured for new shoes?'

For all his generosity to herself, his thinking of Sophie most touched her heart. She cast him a smile. 'Perhaps we should charge Bart with such a task.'

He laughed as he escorted her out the door to the street. 'Very wise idea.'

Madeleine had an illusion of being transported to the town of her childhood. The pavement was more crowded, indeed, and the shops more varied and numerous, but it was a most respectable street, and her dress indistinguishable from other young ladies shopping. Or so she thought. She still received many curious looks.

'Devlin, are you sure my appearance is acceptable?'

Devlin had noticed the admiring glances of the men and appraising looks of the women. He could not help but be proud to be Madeleine's escort. Beautiful even in her own ill-fitting frock, she quite took his breath away in her new walking dress.

'You look lovely,' he whispered back.

This news did not appear to cheer her. She furrowed her brow. Too bad some choice piece of horseflesh did not come into view to distract her.

Devlin caught sight of a shop window. 'We must go in here.' He pulled her into the shop. 'Must not forget our girl.'

They entered a toy store with shelf after shelf of dolls, toy soldiers, and miniature coaches and wagons. An exquisite wax doll with real hair as dark and curly as Linette's caught Devlin's eye. He vowed he must purchase it for Linette. Madeleine adamantly refused, saying the child was too young to care for such a treasure. He settled instead for a porcelain-faced baby doll, a ball and blocks. As he finished giving the direction for the toys to be delivered that afternoon, he spied a carved wooden horse and, thinking perhaps the little girl might be horse-mad like her mother, added it to his purchases.

Back on the street, a handsome carriage drawn by a set of matching bays approached in their direction. Devlin frowned as he spied the crest. The carriage stopped next to them. As Madeleine shrank back, Devlin stepped forward to greet its passenger.

'Devlin, it has been too long,' the fair-haired lady at the carriage window exclaimed.

'How are you, Serena?' His sister-in-law was a good creature, well intentioned, eminently correct, with classical looks and very little in common with Devlin except a connection to his brother.

'I am well, as usual,' she responded in her soft voice. 'And you, brother? We do worry when you do not call.'

'I have been shockingly remiss, but I'm fit, I assure you.'

His sister-in-law gazed curiously at Madeleine. It had never entered his mind that he'd be required to introduce Madeleine to anyone, least of all his sister-in-law, the Marchioness.

He pulled Madeleine forward, needing to exert a little physical effort to do so. 'Serena, may I present Miss England. Miss England, the Marchioness of Heronvale, my sister-in-law.'

Madeleine executed a very correct curtsy.

'Have we met before, Miss England? I do not recall.'

Madeleine, with her eyes downcast replied, 'No, madam.'

'Well, perhaps I may convey you both to your destination? I would be pleased to do so.'

Devlin suspected Serena would be very pleased for an opportunity to find out who her brother-in-law escorted unchaperoned through this shopping district. He felt Madeleine painfully squeeze his arm.

'I believe Miss England has one or two more shops to visit, but that was kind of you, Serena.'

'Are the shops worthwhile, Miss England? I confess I have never visited the ones on this street.'

'They suit me very well, madam,' responded Madeleine in a quiet voice.

'Perhaps you could recommend one to me,' the Marchioness persisted. Devlin knew her inquiry to be meant in a friendly way, but he also knew his brother's wife was nearly as fixed on him securing his future as was his brother. She wanted nothing more than to see him happily married; the Marquess wanted merely to keep his brother's fortune secure.

'I would not presume to.' Madeleine looked miserable. Only his firm hold on her arm kept her from bolting, he suspected.

A hackney coach came from behind, its driver shouting for the carriage to move on.

'Oh, dear,' said Serena. 'We had better go.'

'Indeed,' replied Devlin.

'Please call soon, Devlin. My pleasure, Miss England.' The carriage moved forward and these last words faded with distance.

'Devlin, may we please go home now?' Madeleine raised a shaking hand to her bonnet.

'No,' he said mildly, determined for her not to be made uncomfortable by her encounter with Serena. 'We need to have you measured for shoes and I must not return without cloth for Sophie.'

'Oh, yes, I quite forgot Sophie's cloth,' she murmured. A racing phaeton whizzed by. She did not even notice.

'Maddy, were you made uncomfortable by my sister-in-law?'

They walked a few steps before she answered. 'It was very improper to introduce me to her.'

'I disagree. It would have been ill-mannered not to introduce you. An insult to you.'

He glanced at her, seeing her brows knitted together and her bottom lip trembling slightly. 'A fine lady like the Marchioness should not be made to converse with one such as me.'

'Maddy, I refuse to allow you to speak so. You have studied your appearance. You could not be more presentable.' He did not yet know the story, but he would wager she'd not chosen her life with Farley. But who would choose such a life? Only a woman with no other choice.

'My appearance does not alter the fact that you should not have introduced a marchioness to…to Haymarket-ware.'

'I refuse for you to speak so,' he said.

She did not look at him. 'I will endeavour to obey you, my lord.'

He yanked open the door to the shoemaker.

After he'd ordered various pairs of shoes for her, he seemed relaxed again. By the time they'd selected several pieces of material at the cloth merchant's shop, they were back in temper with each other.

Devlin hailed a hack. As he negotiated with the driver, Madeleine noticed a gentleman across the street looking at her.

Farley.

He saw her look in his direction and tipped his hat to her. Her heart pounded wildly, and she feared she might vomit. She felt Farley's eyes on her the entire time it took for Devlin to lift her into the hack.

As they pulled away, he saluted her once more.

* * *

Lord Edwin Farley watched the hack start off down the street. He had taken to frequenting a tobacconist on this row, one of the deplorable economies he was forced to make in his constrained financial circumstances. At first he'd noticed the young lady in the lilac and blue with a connoisseur's appreciation, but when he saw it was Madeleine, he froze. All that beauty, and he'd let her fall into the hands of Devlin Steele. It irritated him beyond belief.

He'd hoped to recoup from his recent bad luck by playing until Steele owed him a bundle. The Marquess of Heronvale would have redeemed his little brother's vowels, even if the sum had been large. Everyone knew the older brother doted on the younger one. But Farley had lost instead. If that were not bad enough, he'd impulsively used Madeleine to settle his debt. Damned Steele.

The hack turned the corner and disappeared from his sight. He resumed his stroll down the pavement. Madeleine had looked quite fetching in that lavender confection. His body stirred merely thinking about her.

He'd have her back, he vowed. He'd unpeel those layers of clothing from her and bed her like she'd never been bedded before. He'd make her beg for him, make her pant with wanting him. She'd been easy to seduce as a girl. He'd only had to say a few pretty words to her, and she'd been his. He laughed, remembering how easy it had been to entice her to his room that night, her father bursting in at the perfect moment—when she'd been naked on top of him.

Yes, he'd get her back, he vowed. This time without the child she was stupid enough not to prevent. Perhaps he could make some money on the child. He knew men whose tastes went to ones as young as that. A little beauty like her mother, she would likely sell at a good price.

What revenge ought he to exact upon Steele? It would give him added pleasure to give that matter some thought.

Humming and jauntily swinging his walking stick, Farley continued on his way.

Chapter Six

The packages from their shopping expedition arrived that afternoon amid much excitement. The wide eyes of little Linette as she opened hers made all the extravagance worthwhile. Sophie, whom Devlin did not expect to break out in raptures, reverently fingered the cloth they had purchased.

'Thank you, my lord,' Sophie whispered, though she did not meet his eye while saying it.

'You did tolerably well, Dev,' Bart said, watching Sophie's every movement.

'Indeed?' He laughed. 'I am unused to such high praise from you.'

'The lass is happy. Mind you do not tease her, now.' Bart shook his finger in warning.

Devlin tried to stifle his grin. 'I shall endeavour not to.'

Madeleine was unusually quiet. She excused herself, saying she wished to unpack her dresses. Thinking of it, Devlin realised she had been just as solemn on the ride back home.

Linette held the horse up to Devlin, pulling on his trousers as she did so. 'Horse! Horse!' she said excitedly. It was inevitable. The horse captured the little girl's attention and the expensive doll was ignored. Devlin sat down on the floor.

'Shall we build a stable for your horse, Lady Lin?' He gathered the blocks together and started building.

'Wady Win,' Linette parroted.

'How much did all this cost, might I ask?' Bart's voice was deceptively casual.

'I think you had better not ask,' Devlin said ruefully. 'I thought I might pay a visit to my brother tomorrow.'

Madeleine walked back into the room. 'You will visit your brother?'

She did not need to know he intended to ask his brother for a small advance. 'I promised my sister-in-law, as you recall.'

'Oh.' She sat on the settee and watched Devlin and Linette build the promised stable with the blocks.

'Would you like me to make tea, Maddy?' Sophie asked, dropping her fabric back into its box.

Madeleine popped up. 'I will do it.'

'You, Maddy?' Sophie said. 'It is not necessary.'

'I want to. It is not so difficult, is it?'

'Neigh! Neigh!' Linette galloped her wooden horse, trying to make it jump over the blocks. The blocks tumbled.

'Now, I was building that.' Devlin ruffled the girl's hair, making her giggle. He kept an eye on the mother.

'I will do it, Maddy. Do not trouble yourself.' Sophie started for the kitchen.

Madeleine insisted. 'No, *I* will do it.'

'It is my job,' Sophie said, visibly upset.

Madeleine put her hands on her hips. 'I would like to make it. I am tired of being waited upon as if I am no use at all.'

'But, but…' Sophie burst into tears and ran out.

'That was badly done, miss.' Bart gave her a stern expression. 'The lass wishes to serve you. She credits you with sparing her much hardship.' He marched after Sophie.

Madeleine glanced at Devlin, her hand rubbing her throat. 'I did not mean to make her cry.'

Devlin understood. She wanted to feel she had some use beyond the bedchamber. He had even less to offer, except the money his brother controlled, if he could get it. If Madeleine wished to make tea, what was the harm?

He turned back to the blocks. 'Maddy, if it would not be too much trouble, would you make me some tea?'

The next morning Devlin walked up to an impressive town house on Grosvenor Square and rapped with the shiny brass knocker. The heavy door opened and a solemn-faced butler almost broke into a smile.

'Master Devlin.'

'Barclay, you never change.' Devlin did smile. 'I trust you are well?'

The man took his hat and gloves. 'Indeed, I am, Master Devlin.'

'Is my brother here?'

'He is expected directly, my lord. Shall I announce you to her ladyship?'

'If you please.'

He followed Barclay to the parlour, decorated with Serena's usual perfection, couches and chairs arranged to put visitors at ease. A moment later, the Marchioness came through the door.

'Devlin, you kept your promise. How good to see you.' She reached out her hands to him.

He clasped them warmly and kissed her cheek. 'Serena, you are in excellent looks, as usual.' His brother's wife had the cool beauty of the fine china figurines gracing the mantelpiece, disguising her warm-hearted nature. Her reserve and unceasing correctness could so easily be mistaken for coldness.

She coloured slightly. 'Do sit with me and tell me how you go on. I've already rung for tea.'

He joined her on the couch. 'I am well, Serena.'

She peered at him worriedly. 'Are you sure? You look a little pale. Do your wounds still pain you?'

He laughed. 'I am quite well. Thoroughly recovered and there is no need to fuss over me. Where is Ned?'

'Attending to some business.' Her brows knit together. 'Are you in trouble, Devlin?'

'Good God, no, Serena.' Her solicitude rivalled his brother's. 'I have something to discuss. Nothing to signify.'

The tea arrived and she poured with precision. He sipped the liquid, brewed to perfection, and thought how different this cup was from the strong, leaf-filled concoction Madeleine had made the day before.

Serena spoke. 'It was pleasant seeing you yesterday.'

'Indeed.'

'That young lady—Miss England, I believe—was lovely. Who is she, Devlin?'

He should have expected this question. He gave Serena a direct look. 'An acquaintance.'

Her eyebrows raised.

He held her gaze.

Serena glanced down demurely. 'Does she interest you?'

Did Madeleine *interest* him? Keeping her safe interested him. Making love to her interested him, but he would not explain that to Serena. At least Serena must not suspect Madeleine to be anything but a well-bred young lady, unchaperoned though she had been. She would not have mentioned Madeleine at all if she had thought her to be Haymarket-ware, as Madeleine called herself.

'She is an acquaintance, Serena,' he repeated in a mild voice.

She tilted her head sceptically, but was much too well bred to press any further.

They sat in awkward silence.

'I should tell you I have moved, Serena.'

She peered at him. 'Moved? For what reason?'

Devlin paused. 'No reason.'

'Some difficulty with the rent?'

'No.' Devlin hid his impatience with a small laugh. 'Why

do you suppose I should have difficulty with the rent? You and Ned. I cannot say who is the worse. I am not in difficulty. I am well able to take care of myself. At six and twenty I should know how to go on. I survived Napoleon's army, if you recall.'

Serena looked stricken. 'But you were so badly injured. We feared you would not live. You do not realise how close a thing it was.' She fished a lace-edged handkerchief from her sleeve and dabbed her eyes. 'And you have been gambling so. Ned was concerned because no one has seen you for days.'

'Ned can go to the dev—' This was too much. 'Good God, what does he do, scour the town for news of me?'

Serena's eyes glittered with tears. 'I believe he hears word of you at White's,' she replied in all seriousness.

Devlin burst into laughter. He sat down next to her and put his arm around her, squeezing affectionately. 'Dear sister, I beg your pardon. I do not mean to upset you. I know you and my brother mean well, but you forget I'm out of leading strings.'

She blushed and straightened her posture. 'I am sure we do not.'

'Tell me how you and Ned go on? Is my brother still managing the family affairs to perfection?'

Serena lifted her chin protectively. 'Ned has much on his shoulders.'

Devlin gave her a kind smile. 'Indeed he does. He is a man to admire, Serena. I mean that.'

'I have heard from your sisters and brother. They are excellent correspondents.'

Unlike himself who wrote little and visited less.

'Indeed? What is the family news?'

Serena, with a wistfulness in her voice, chattered on about the trifling activities of his nephews and nieces. Percy's son, Jeffrey, the eldest, at Eton. Rebecca, Helen's daughter, learning the pianoforte. All the little ones merging into a blur. He listened with as interested an expression as he could muster.

Serena doted on all the children. By far she was their favourite aunt. And he, the Waterloo Dragoon, was their hero uncle, even though he had difficulty keeping their names straight.

What a pity Serena had not had a child. Fate had no notion of fair play. She would make a perfect mother, and a loving one, as well. He suspected her disappointment in that quarter was immense.

'And you, Serena? How do you go on?'

'I am well.' A sad look came over her face.

Devlin gave her another hug. She would not wish to speak of her disappointment at not presenting the Marquess with an heir.

'Dear sister,' he murmured.

She recovered herself. 'Ned will be here directly. Will you wait for him?'

He had little choice. 'Serena,' he said, surmising a change of conversation was in order, 'do you suppose Ned would mind if I borrowed a pair of horses some morning? I've a notion to ride.'

'You will ride again?' she said brightly. He had not been on a horse since charging the French, east of the Brussels road. 'Indeed he will not mind. He will be glad of it, and I will personally ask Barclay to instruct the stable to provide any horse you wish.'

'Any two horses. I…I wish to have Bart join me.'

'Two horses it is.' She smiled.

The parlour door opened and the Marquess strode in at a quicker pace than was his custom. Devlin stood to greet him.

'Devlin, how good to see you.' Equally uncharacteristic of him, he embraced Devlin heartily.

This idol of his childhood, his oldest brother Ned, usually did not betray emotion. Ned always could be counted on to remain unflappable when his youngest brother came begging for his help out of the latest scrape. Because of those days, Devlin always felt in awe of that tall, ramrod-straight figure. He always expected to crane his neck to look at Ned. It never failed to be a shock when he found himself half a head taller and his brother going grey at the temples.

'What brings you to call?' Ned asked with such surprise, it suggested he had given up altogether on a visit from Devlin.

'I wished to see you and Serena, of course, but I also have a matter of business to discuss with you, if it is convenient.'

Ned regained that strict composure. 'Indeed. We shall go into the library. You will excuse us, Serena?'

With a nod to his wife, he preceded Devlin out the door. Devlin followed dutifully, feeling much like that little boy, in a scrape once more.

Inside that book-lined room, Ned poured two glasses of port. Devlin glanced at the shelves and had the incongruous thought that Madeleine might enjoy a good book. Not the sort of book to be found in this room, he supposed, but perhaps a Miniver Press novel such as his sisters had read when they sat by his sick bed.

Ned handed him his glass. 'What did you wish to discuss?'

Devlin sipped and paced the room, trying to figure out the best way to present this.

'Are you in trouble?' Ned's voice was low and steady.

Devlin flashed him an irritated glance and muttered, 'You and Serena.' Speaking more firmly, he said, 'I am not in trouble.'

His brother's face remained impassive.

Devlin took a gulp of port. 'I have moved.'

'Yes?'

'To a larger place.'

'You required a larger place?' A disapproving tone crept into his brother's speech.

'It was too good an opportunity to pass up. On the same street, but a much better situation.'

'And?' One of Ned's eyebrows rose.

Devlin took a deep breath. 'I am short of money as a result. I would ask if you would advance me some additional funds until next quarter.'

His brother did not drop his gaze, nor did his expression change, even a muscle. Devlin knew he was considering, weighing the matter silently in his head.

As a child, this silence had been a comfort. It meant Ned was reckoning a way out of his difficulties. As a man, he was less certain.

His brother stared implacably into his port. 'How wise was this move?'

'Devil it, Ned, the move is made. Whether it was wise or not is moot.'

'You engaged in this impulsively.' This was not a question but a statement of fact, a disapproved-of fact.

Devlin put his glass down on a table and faced his immovable brother. 'It is done, Ned, and I need some money to get through to next quarter. Will you give it or not?'

Ned sat in a nearby chair and casually crossed his legs. 'You have been gambling heavily, little brother.'

Devlin knew that was coming. 'As your spies have reported? I do not suppose they were present when I won back my losses?'

Ned's cronies would never have been present at such an unsavoury place as Farley's. If they had, his brother would be discussing what else Devlin won that night.

'I have heard your losses to be steep. This gambling must stop, Devlin.'

If his brother had not ordered him to stop gambling, he might have informed Ned that he'd come to the same conclusion. Now he would not give his brother that satisfaction.

'And what else might I do, Ned? What is there for me to do? The war is over, and I'm damned if I'll go anywhere else in this world to fight. India? Africa? The West Indies? I'm no longer keen on dying on foreign soil.'

Ned swirled his port and tasted the rich, imported liquid. 'It is time you took your rightful place in the family.'

'Rightful place?' Devlin prowled the room. 'What the deuce is my rightful place?'

Calmly his brother spoke, 'You need to assume the control of your estate. It should not fall to our brother Percy, who has enough of his own to oversee.'

'You know I cannot.' Devlin glared at him. 'You and my father saw to that. I cannot take control until I marry. I must subsist on what you obligingly provide me until I marry a suitable woman of whom you approve. Good God! What possessed you and my father to contrive that addle-brained plan?'

'You know why.' Ned spoke in the most reasonable voice possible. 'You lack control. You have always been devil-may-care. Father had the wisdom to know you would cease your wild ways when you had another person dependent upon you. A wife.'

'Damn it, Ned, would you have me marry merely to get my fortune? Would you have married under that fancy bit of blackmail?'

At least Devlin had the satisfaction of seeing his brother betray emotion. Ned's cheek twitched. 'Leave Serena out of this.'

Devlin felt a pang of guilt for speaking of his brother's marriage. He never knew for certain if his brother loved Serena, though he suspected she loved Ned. When he saw Ned and Serena together, there was such a reserve between them, who could tell? Had Ned married her out of duty? Pity Serena, if he had. Their father was behind the match, of course, and Ned would never have gone against their father's wishes. Two peas in a pod, his brother and father.

'I am not speaking of Serena,' he said more mildly. 'I am speaking of myself. I have no desire to marry at the moment, but I am more than ready to assume control of my property. Indeed, I long to run it. Let me take the task from Percy and work the farm. I do not give a damn if the rest of the money is under your thumb.'

It would be an ideal solution. Bart and Sophie would fit in neatly on the estate. Madeleine and Linette would be a bit more difficult to situate, but he was sure he could contrive something.

Ned regained his damned composure. 'Doing so would deprive you of an opportunity to make an advantageous match. The Season has begun and there are all manner of eligible young ladies from whom you may choose.'

Devlin clenched his fist. 'I have no desire to marry.'

Ned rose and walked to the desk by the window. He fussed with papers stacked there, glancing through them, and restacking them. Devlin would have liked to think his brother was considering his proposal, but he suspected Ned was simply showing him who was head of the family.

Ned did not look up from the papers when he spoke. 'Our father's wishes will continue to be honoured. You will receive your allotted portion on the quarter, not before. When you marry an acceptable young lady, your estate and your fortune will pass to you, and I will have no more to say of it.'

Devlin leaned down, putting both hands on the desk, forcing his brother to meet his eyes. 'Both you and Father were mistaken, Ned. You could at least let me work. As it is, you and our dear departed father have deprived me of any responsibility at all and have kept me as dependent as if I were still a schoolboy. Had I something of value to do, I might have reason to be steady. As it is, I have nothing.'

'You will have everything you desire if you marry.' Ned spoke through clenched teeth.

'But I do not wish to marry.'

The two men glared at each other.

Devlin swung away from his brother. 'You and Father never trusted me to find my own way. You knew, did you not, that he almost refused to purchase my colours?' He fingered one of the volumes on the shelf. 'I would have enlisted as a common foot soldier had he done so. Father could not force me to do anything and neither can you, Ned.'

'You are being foolish, Devlin. This is for your own good.

You have always been too wild by half and too wilful to behave with any sense.'

'You dare to say such a thing to me? Do you forget what I have been doing these past years? Do you think I have been on a lark?'

The Marquess stood. 'I know it killed our father to have you traipsing all over the continent risking your neck.'

Devlin shook with rage. 'Unfair, Ned.'

'You should have been seeing to your duty to the family.' Ned raised his voice.

'I *was* seeing to my duty to the family. How well do you think the family would have fared under Napoleon?' Devlin matched his brother's volume. 'Go to the devil, Ned.'

Ned stepped from behind the desk and faced his brother. 'Our father worried every day that you would meet your death. Not only during the war, but every day of your sad youth. You have been a rash care-for-nobody and it is past time you became a grown man.'

Devlin clenched his fists, standing nose to nose with his older brother. 'I fought for my life before I ever went to war. To be a man means more than following the dictates of a father who thought he could pull a string and have all his bidding done. When will *you* assume manhood, Ned? Have you ever had a thought of your own?'

'You are addressing the head of the family, little brother.'

'I am addressing my father. You may as well be him, Ned. You always did whatever he said. You and Percy and our sisters. You all blindly did his bidding. If he said jump, you jumped. If he said marry this young lady, you made the offer.'

'Leave Serena out of this!' Ned's eyes blazed. He shoved hard against Devlin's chest.

Devlin automatically shoved back, his soldier's reflexes operating. With his greater height, youth, and war-honed strength, he knocked his brother to the floor. 'Leave me to live my own life! I will choose when and who I marry.'

'Indeed you shall, you insufferable ingrate.' Ned picked

himself off the floor and, to Devlin's surprise, came at him with a swinging fist that connected smartly to Devlin's jaw.

'Deuce,' yelled Devlin, lunging back at him, toppling them both to the floor. They rolled, grunting and punching, knocking down a small table and sending the wine decanter crashing to the floor, red wine splashing.

'Stop this! Stop at once!' Serena cried from the doorway.

The two men paid her no heed. On their feet now, they smashed into a bookcase and books rained down from the shelves. Blood dripped from Ned's nose and Devlin's coat ripped.

'Barclay! Barclay!' Serena screamed for the butler as she ran over to her husband and brother-in-law. She pulled on Devlin's back to get him off Ned.

'Master Devlin. Master Ned.' A voice of authority seemed to boom directly from their childhood. White-haired Barclay entered the room. 'You ought to be ashamed.'

They stopped fighting at once.

Ned recovered first, dabbing his nose with the lace-edged handkerchief Serena offered him. 'Thank you, Barclay. We are quite in control again. Your help is no longer necessary.'

Devlin felt a pain in his stomach that was not the result of a punching fist. How had he wound up brawling with his older brother? He'd seen Percy and Ned in a scrap or two, always carefully kept from their father, but it was unthinkable that he should actually strike this man who'd searched all through the wounded and dying in Brussels until he found his younger brother.

'Ned, I—'

'Enough, Devlin.' The Marquess folded the handkerchief.

Serena looked as if she might swoon at any moment, filling Devlin with more guilt. Her face was pale as she righted the toppled table and tried to pick up the glass fragments. How could he have distressed her like this?

Ned straightened his clothes and brushed himself off. He glanced at his wife. 'Serena, would you leave us, please?'

'I would not wish—' she began.

'Leave us. We shall not come to further blows.' Devlin had not thought his brother could speak so softly.

With a worried look at them both, she left the room, one hand covering her mouth.

Ned composed himself and returned to his desk, showing no signs that they had been rolling on the floor moments before. 'Serena tells me you were in the company of an unchaperoned young woman.'

Devlin rolled his eyes. He might be standing before his father again. Too many times his father ignored what Devlin tried to say and went directly to whatever would hurt him most.

'Your point, Ned?'

'Did you introduce my wife to your fancy piece?'

Amazing. Ned managed to provoke his anger again. 'Ned, I assure you, I would not do anything to embarrass my sister-in-law. I have the highest respect and sympathy for her.'

'What do you mean "sympathy"?' Ned sounded ready to punch him again.

'I meant nothing.' He meant he was sorry she had not conceived a child, but this was not the time to address Ned on that subject. He had no notion how the wind blew for his brother on that score.

'Who was the woman you were with? Do you have a light-skirt who costs you?'

Good God. Did Ned wish another jab in the nob? 'She is an acquaintance who does not deserve your insults.' Devlin would say no more. He merely wished to get away from his brother. 'Ned, we have said more than is prudent. I will beg your leave.'

'Indeed? We have resolved nothing.' Ned looked like a stranger. No, he looked like their father, not at all like his adored older brother.

'It doesn't matter. I will wait for my money to come due.' He walked to the door.

Ned's mouth set into a thin, grim line. 'When your money comes due, it will be half the amount.'

'What?'

'Half the amount.' The Marquess studied his papers before glancing up at Devlin. 'You need to search for a wife. Perhaps penury will serve as an incentive.'

Devlin fought the rage that erupted inside him. How would he care for Madeleine? How would he feed little Linette? 'Damn you, Ned. You have no idea what this means.'

'Remember who is the head of the family, little brother.'

'I'll not forget.' He spoke through his teeth.

Devlin hurried out of the library and almost ran into his sister-in-law, who was walking back and forth in the hall.

'Devlin, what happened? Why were you fighting?' she whispered, her voice filled with anxiety.

He stroked her arm. 'A brothers' quarrel, nothing more. Do not worry, sister.'

She looked unconvinced. He gave her a long reassuring hug and let her weep against his shoulder a little. 'It was entirely my fault, Serena. You know how I can provoke Ned. Do not cry.'

The library door opened. An icy voice such as Devlin had never heard said, 'Unhand my wife and take your leave.'

Chapter Seven

Misery assailed Devlin as he walked through the doorway of Ned's town house. He'd made a mess of things. What a colossal fool, provoking his brother, though he could not precisely remember what he had said to set Ned off. They had disagreed reasonably for a short time. How had he ended up punching Ned in the nose, for deuce's sake?

Worse than bloodying the nose of the Marquess of Heronvale was jeopardising Madeleine's future and that of her child. How would he care for them now?

What a damned coil. What a fool and idiot.

He set a slow pace in the direction of St James's Street.

He ought to have conserved his money, not rented the bigger apartment, not purchased as many lengths of fabric for Sophie, as many toys for Linette. He should not have purchased an entire wardrobe for Madeleine when she argued for only two or three dresses. Most of all, he should not have lost his temper with his brother. He should have remained calm. He should have rehearsed several cogent arguments why his brother should advance him the money. Instead, he'd allowed Ned to goad him until they came to blows.

He might laugh at rousing emotion in his brother, if only the result had not been the halving of his funds. Ned's calm, dispassionate control, so comforting to him as a child, irritated him as a man. To think he used to shake with fear when Ned and Percy pummelled each other with their fists, Ned as out of control as Devlin so often was. It had been like watching the foundations at Heronvale crack and crumble.

This time it was his own would-be estate that crumbled—Edgeworth, twenty miles from Heronvale and ten from Percy's estate. His father had aimed to keep them close, tied to the land that he'd purchased from neighbours who let their property slip through their fingers.

'Land, my boy.' Devlin could hear his father's firm voice, his fist pounding the dinner table. 'If a man has land, he has a future.' His father would gesture to Devlin's plate. 'Land gives you good food and drink to fill your belly. Mind, you have never been hungry in my house.'

True, but Devlin had known hunger on the Peninsula where supplies were often low, and he had known thirst when wounded at Waterloo, waiting twelve hours in the mud to be found.

Devlin was ready for the land his father bequeathed him. Ready for work. He longed for hard physical labour. He yearned to work next to the men in the fields, as he had fought beside their brothers. Wouldn't that give Ned apoplexy!

Devlin stopped in the middle of the pavement and rubbed his brow. What good did it do to think of Edgeworth? He needed to think of Madeleine.

It would not be at all difficult to find positions for Bart and Sophie somewhere in the family. Percy, especially, had a kind heart for a person in need. Indeed, anyone would be fortunate to hire Bart. And, if he knew Bart, the man would care well for Sophie. As for himself, he could plague Ned by visiting one sister after another, never complying with the Heronvale dictates. What prime sport that would be.

But what about Madeleine and Linette? He would go to the devil and drag Ned with him before he'd allow Madeleine to return to the only profession she knew and her daughter with her. Damn, he needed money to save her from that fate. Enough money for her to live comfortably and to rear Linette.

Devlin's mind spun round and round. The only thing he knew with a certainty was that he was a damned fool and had failed the people who depended upon him.

Failed Madeleine.

Too soon he neared the lodgings. With a heavy heart, he turned the knob of the front door.

Madeleine stole a surreptitious glance at Devlin during dinner later that evening. He was unduly quiet. Something troubled him, and she did not know what. Did she even have the right to inquire?

If he were like other men, she would not care what problems he had. But he was not like other men. Would another man be so kind to her daughter? When it had been time for Linette to go to bed, it had to be Devlin to carry her up and tuck her in. For a moment she worried about leaving Linette to a man's care, but that was foolish. Devlin would not harm her.

Indeed, he should not be so kind. It made her feel she could depend on him. It was dangerous to depend upon anyone. They fooled you, then tricked you into doing what they willed.

She cast her gaze on Devlin again, and made an attempt at conversation. 'Did you have a pleasant visit with your brother?'

He glanced up and paused so long she thought he would not answer. 'I spent an agreeable interval with my sister-in-law.'

What did that mean?

'Scrapped with your brother, did you?' Bart snorted. 'That explains your black looks.'

Devlin did not banter back at Bart as was usual. Instead, he rubbed his forehead and stared down at his plate. Madeleine frowned. Bart should leave off scolding this time. Something was indeed wrong.

Sophie, her usual wary expression on her face, popped up to gather the dirty dishes. She had a cat's sense for danger.

Little had been eaten from Devlin's plate. 'Leave the dishes a bit, Sophie. I wish to speak to all of you.'

Madeleine's pulse accelerated. No good news could be forthcoming.

'Let us clear the dishes first,' Madeleine suggested. 'It will be more comfortable.' And it would delay the inevitable.

Devlin released a breath. 'Very well, remove the dishes, but return promptly, if you please.'

'I will help.' Madeleine picked up her own plate and Devlin's.

'I can do it, Maddy,' Sophie said.

'I want to help,' Madeleine countered. She was able to clear dishes, at least. No special skill needed for that. Besides, it helped quiet her nerves to be busy.

Madeleine returned to her seat next to Devlin. He had poured small glasses of port for all of them and his eyes held such a pained expression, the fear rose in her once more.

What other kind of bad news could there be, except she, Linette and Sophie would have to leave? She clenched her hands together in her lap.

Devlin toyed with his glass of port. He cleared his throat. 'I visited my brother to request an advance of the money due me in two months' time. We have wound up a little short—'

'Because of my dresses.' Madeleine moaned, misery and guilt swirling inside her.

He held the glass still. 'Not only your dresses, Maddy. My mismanagement is primarily the blame.'

'Now, lad…' Bart began, an uncharacteristic soothing tone in his voice.

Devlin cleared his throat. 'You see, I had decided the way out of our difficulties was to make the request of my brother. Unfortunately, I had not counted on the Marquess refusing.'

'The man refused?' Bart's thick eyebrows shot up.

'I fear so.'

'No worry, Dev. We shall manage.' Bart nodded his head as if convincing himself as well as the others. 'We can practise some economy. We shall do nicely.'

Devlin gave a dry laugh. 'You have not yet heard the worst of it, my friend. Not only did my brother refuse an advance, he cut my allowance in half. I do not see how we can go on at all.'

Bart's mouth opened. 'Half?'

'What does it mean, Maddy?' Sophie leaned over the table to whisper to her.

'It means you and Linette and I must leave.' Madeleine's hand went to her throat. She thought her words would strangle there.

'No,' Devlin protested. 'It does not mean that.'

'Oh, perhaps not today,' she went on. 'We should have a little time to make other arrangements. Nothing hard-hearted about it.' Her voice trembled now.

'Maddy.' Devlin grabbed her hand. 'It does not mean you must leave.'

She met his gaze. Along with pain, she saw a tenderness that took her breath away.

'I do not know how, Maddy, but I will take care of you.'

She blinked.

He turned back to Bart and Sophie. 'I think I should be able to find you both positions with some member of my family.'

'I will not leave Maddy,' Sophie cried.

'And I will stay with you, lad. We have endured worse than this.' Bart lifted his glass in a salute.

Devlin looked from one to another. 'We did not have women and a child to care for in those days.'

'We will take care of ourselves.' Madeleine lifted her chin in a show of bravado she could not feel.

'How, Maddy?' Devlin said. 'You have no means of income.'

Bart stood and held his glass high. 'We are in this together, do we agree? We solve it together.' He stared at them until they all lifted their glasses in return.

'I could take in laundry,' Sophie said in a quiet voice.

Devlin laughed. 'I hope it does not come to that, little one. I thought I might speak to some people I know tomorrow. Perhaps someone can find a use for me.'

'If there's labour to be done I can do it,' Bart said.

Madeleine toyed with her glass. 'There are three or four men who would pay much for time with me.'

They all stared at her.

'It should not be difficult, I think. I can give you the names and you can find out how to communicate with them.'

'Good God, Maddy.' Devlin's face drained of colour.

Madeleine gave him a surprised look. 'It would pay handsomely, I am sure.'

He spoke through clenched teeth. 'I do not give a deuce how well it would pay, you will not bed other men on my behalf.'

'Not on your behalf, but for us all.' He could not prevent her from doing her part, not when she was the cause of the problem.

He slapped his hand on the table. 'I will hear no more of this.'

Sophie's eyes grew wider. With a nervous glance, she slipped off the chair and skittered into the kitchen. His arms crossed against his chest, Bart regarded Madeleine and Devlin with a disapproving expression.

Madeleine continued. 'I believe it would bring in a good sum of money.'

He stood up and leaned over her. 'No.' He strode out of the room.

She followed him. 'Why not?'

He wheeled around to face her. 'You have to ask?'

'Devlin, it would not be difficult for me to do this. It is not as if I have not done it before.'

His eyes flashed.

'What objection can you have? It is the perfect solution.'

'You will allow me to solve our problems, Maddy. You will not do it by lying on your back.'

He did not need to speak to her in such a crude manner. 'It is what I do best, if you recall.'

'Deuce,' he said. 'And where shall you perform this lucrative act? In this house? With Linette in the room?'

'Of course not!' How dare he suggest such a thing. 'I have always kept Linette out of the way. Sophie would take her.'

'Much more proper,' he said, the corner of his mouth turning down in contempt.

'I have told you, I am not proper.'

'And where would Bart and I be? Collecting the money at the door?'

'Do not be absurd. I cannot talk to you. You do not see reason.' She stalked off.

How could he not see she must resolve the difficulties she had placed him in? She owed him that much. It was not that she wished to bed anyone, except…except… No, he must recognise how much she was indebted to him. He had rescued her from Farley. For that she would do anything for him. Anything.

She ran up the stairs, but he came right behind. At the top of the stairs, he caught her by the shoulders and spun her around.

'We will finish this, Madeleine. We will not solve our financial woes in this way, do you hear? You will not speak of this again.' He dug his fingers into her shoulders.

'How is it that you could object, Devlin? You know what I am.' She lowered her voice.

He made a strangled sound. 'Do you think I wish to think of another man's hands all over you?'

She stared at him. The hands of many men had touched her.

His fingers slid down her arms. 'Do you think I could accept money for another man to bed you?'

She swallowed. 'Farley did.'

'I am not Farley, Madeleine. I thought you understood that.'

He stood so close, all she needed was to stand on tiptoe and touch her lips to his. She could smell the port on his breath and the taste of it resonated in her mouth. The wish to taste it on him was almost too difficult to bear. He made no move to close the gap between them. It was clearly her choice.

His hands rested gently on her arms. Those hands had once caressed her bare skin. She craved the joy and terror of his body joined to hers. Her feet arched and raised her higher. He uttered a guttural sound and closed the gap between them, his mouth plundering as if he were a man starved. Her own hunger surged as she pressed herself against him and wound her arms around his neck. His lips travelled to her neck, sending sensations straight to her soul.

She wanted him again with all the wantonness of her wretched body. The body that had betrayed her and led to her deserved ruin. She had learned to erase all thought and all feeling in order to play the role Farley bid her play, but Devlin made her tremble with longing. He tore away the safety of her detachment.

She struggled to speak. 'Do you want me, Devlin?' Her voice sounded more controlled than she felt. 'Do you wish to bed me?'

He stilled. Straightening, his eyes narrowed. Her knees began to shake as his silence grew longer.

Finally, he spoke, his tone cold. 'Am I able to afford you, Miss M?'

He turned and hurried down the stairs and out the front door.

*   *   *

At the town house in Grosvenor Square, the Marquess of Heronvale pushed food around his plate. The cavernous dining room echoed with the clink of his silver fork against the china.

He glanced at his wife. She looked absorbed in her own thoughts, the corners of her eyes pinched with unhappiness. A ball of misery sat in his stomach where food should have been.

He had disappointed her once again, more inventively this time. Indeed, rolling on the floor, trading punches with his youngest brother could hardly have lowered him further in her estimation. Especially since he had lost the fight.

Humiliating.

She had probably championed Devlin, in any event. He could not blame her. She was at ease with his brother in a way she was not with him. There was so little emotion between Serena and himself he would have been surprised if she had taken his side. Serena undoubtedly would think him too severe with Devlin, that a marquess should wield his power with more compassion.

But Devlin had infuriated him with those comments about his wife. Success with women came as easy to Devlin as riding, shooting, gaming. His youngest brother did everything without effort, as well as without thought, while he, the bearer of the title, had laboured for every accomplishment.

How well he remembered Devlin's birth. He had been home on school holiday, old enough at ten years to take charge of Percy, Helen, Julia, and Lavinia during his mother's confinement. He smiled inwardly at his less-than-learned explanation to his sisters and brother of exactly what would transpire during the birth. From the moment he'd held the newborn baby in his arms, Ned had been full of pride in this littlest brother. He made a solemn oath, that day, to always protect and defend him.

Devlin had made keeping that vow a challenge. A more reckless individual had never been born. It had been no surprise to Ned that Devlin joined the cavalry. Had Ned not been heir, he might have served his country as well, fighting at his brother's side, but all he could do was bring a near-dying Devlin back home.

'Ned? Is something troubling you?' Serena's sweet voice broke through his reverie.

'What?'

'I thought you might be troubled.' She averted her eyes.

'No, I am not.' She would think him weak, for certain, if she knew his thoughts.

'I beg your pardon,' she murmured.

He wished more to beg pardon of her, for his abominable behaviour, but did not know quite how. It seemed to him the silence between them was a condemnation.

'You disapprove of my dealings with my brother,' he blurted out.

Her eyebrows flew up in surprise. 'I would not question your judgement.'

'You think me too harsh.'

'I would not presume...'

He dismissed her words with a shake of his head. With trembling fingers, she picked daintily at her food.

After eight years of marriage, his wife remained a stunningly beautiful woman, her restraint the epitome of what became a lady. He could not complain. She was biddable, even when he pressed his carnal urges upon her, something he did as rarely as he could tolerate. The marital act was too painful for her sensibilities, but she craved children and he wished to give them to her.

Another failure on his part.

Ned drained the wine from his glass for the third time. 'Do you go out tonight, Serena?'

She jumped at the sound of his voice and barely glanced at him. 'No.'

It was his turn to be surprised. She had lately developed the habit of accompanying friends to the evening entertainments, the ones from which he begged off with increasing frequency.

She pressed her fingertips against her temple. 'I shall retire early. I…I have the headache.'

He had made her ill. He poured another glass of wine, wanting to express his concern, to offer to get her headache powders, to escort her up to her room and help her into bed.

He did none of those things.

'If you will excuse me…' She rose and, without waiting for a reply and probably not expecting one, left him alone in the room.

A footman entered and moved quickly to clear the table. Ned gestured for him to take away the plate from which he had barely eaten. When the man set the brandy in front of him, Ned began to see how much of that bottle he could finish.

Chapter Eight

Devlin picked a secluded chair at White's far from the bow window. He intended to sip his brandy in peace, away from the curious passers-by in the street. He wished to steel himself before circulating among the gentlemen of the *ton* in another attempt to procure employment. But what reason was there to expect this afternoon to differ from the last two weeks? He had made inquiries with the few of his senior officers still alive and exploited every imaginable family connection.

He might as well have bivouacked in a field. In fact, he would have preferred it, sharing cold, damp nights and bawdy soldier's tales with men who knew life could end with a musket ball the next day.

'May I join you?'

Devlin glanced up. The elegant figure of the Marquess stood before him. He shrugged his assent.

His brother signalled for a drink and settled in the comfortable chair across from him. 'How do you go on, Devlin?'

How did Ned think he went on? He and Bart had counted every coin that morning. They had a few days' escape from the River Tick, no more.

'Tolerably well,' he said.

Ned regarded him with a bland expression. What lay beyond that inscrutable countenance was a mystery. Devlin could wait out the silence, even if his brother never spoke.

Ned did not betray a thought, let alone a feeling. 'I understand you have inquired about employment around town.'

Devlin cocked his head, ever so slightly.

The waiter placed a glass before Ned. 'Without success, I recollect.'

Devlin favoured him with an ironic grin. 'I am pleased you are so well informed. Unfortunately, there seems to be a surplus of men such as myself. Soldiers needing work.'

'A pity.' Ned raised his glass to his lips.

'It does not help that the men from whom I seek employment instead contrive to introduce me to their daughters.'

'Indeed?'

Damn his brother's implacability. 'It was not you who spread the tale of our father's peculiar arrangement for me?'

Ned's eyes flickered with surprise, not guilt.

Devlin laughed. 'Not you, I collect. A sister, perhaps?'

Ned's control returned. 'Helen is a likely suspect.'

'Likely,' Devlin agreed. 'She has a crony in town, I believe.'

'And meddling proclivities.'

For a moment the ease between them returned and Devlin could almost forget that his revered brother had unwittingly placed a young woman and her innocent daughter in jeopardy. Ned would disapprove if he knew of Madeleine, but would he be less tight-fisted? Pride prevented Devlin from revisiting his monetary request on his brother. He was less sure why he did not confide about Madeleine.

'How is Serena?' he asked instead, seeking neutral ground.

The Marquess's eyes narrowed. 'Well.'

Serena was not neutral ground, then. Had Ned's anger something to do with Serena? Devlin studied him. The Marquess's bland expression had a hard edge.

'Good God, Ned. Is there some trouble between you and Serena?' The sudden thought burst into words.

Ned's face turned to chiselled granite. 'Mind your loose tongue. Your voice will carry.'

'I am sorry,' Devlin mumbled. Deuce, he had managed to blunder into more disfavour. If others had heard his ill-conceived words, the rumour-mill would carry the tale throughout the *ton*. He glanced around the room, but no one seemed to have given them the least heed. He hoped.

Ned had not looked around, but maintained his damnable composure. What a soldier he would have made, thought Devlin. He would bet Ned could face down a battalion single-handed without flinching. But would he be able to muster enough emotion to strike? A soldier eventually had to tap into rage. Until their fisticuffs of a fortnight ago, Devlin would not have believed Ned capable of rage.

Devlin felt light-headed. He ought not to have imagined battle. Images, sounds, and smells enveloped him. The thud of horses' hooves, the cry of battle, the smoke and smell of musket fire. Men screamed. Horses squealed. Metal clanged against metal before thrusting into flesh. Blood sprayed and the stench of death grew stronger.

Devlin pressed his fingers to his temple.

'Are you unwell?' Ned's voice held genuine concern.

Beads of perspiration dampened his forehead, as if the day had not been cool. The incessant thunder of French cannon echoed through his brain and his vision blurred into smoke-filled chaos. He could see the men, the shapes of their noses, the yellowed colour of their teeth, the stunned expressions as his own sabre sliced their throats.

'Dev, you are white as death. Let me summon a doctor.'

At his brother's voice, the images dissolved as suddenly as they had come, leaving his emotions in tattered pieces. Devlin suppressed an urge to laugh. As in childhood, his brother had rescued him, this time from his own personal demons.

'No doctor.' Devlin's voice was not quite steady. 'I was woolgathering for a moment.' He stood. All notions of grovelling for employment fled. 'Would you excuse me, Ned? I must leave.'

The brow of the Marquess wrinkled slightly. 'Are you sure you are not ill?'

Devlin's mouth lifted at the corner. 'Poor, perhaps, but not ill. You needn't worry.'

'I have my barouche. I will take you home.'

'Not necessary, brother. The walk will do me good.' His heart still pounded and his hands trembled. All Devlin wished to do was flee. He touched Ned on the shoulder and hurried away.

A light rainfall greeted him on the street and he closed his eyes for a moment, savouring the cool droplets pattering on his upturned face.

'Good day, Steele. Been at White's, I see.'

Devlin opened his eyes and met the affable grin of Lord Farley. He merely nodded and made to continue on his way.

Farley put a hand on his arm. 'Pray, what is your hurry? Come with me to my establishment. I shall buy you a drink.'

'I think not.' Again Devlin tried to leave.

'Come. You may give me news of Madeleine,' he persisted.

Devlin shrugged off the man's hand. 'I think not.'

Anger flashed through Farley's eyes for a moment before the amiable expression reappeared. 'How does she go on? I hope she still pleases you, but perhaps you have tired of her.'

Devlin's emotions were ragged enough to plant his fist squarely in the centre of Farley's face. He pushed past.

The man fell in step with him. 'I say, Steele, I hear you are seeking employment. Consider working for me. I could use a skilled gamester, and, I promise you, I would compensate you generously. I am again flush in the pockets, you see.'

Devlin stopped, his fingers still curled into fists. He'd heard the tale of Farley's change in fortune. 'Tell me, would my employment include fleecing green boys—like young Boscomb? He put a pistol to his head after a visit to your tables, did he not?'

Farley's eyes narrowed but his grin remained. 'An unfortunate incident.'

Devlin attempted to walk on, but Farley kept pace. 'Perhaps, if you are in need of funds, you would return Madeleine to me. In return for the money you won from me, of course.'

Devlin's fists tightened. If he'd had his sword in his hand, he would relish the sound of its steel plunging into Farley's gut. Devlin gritted his teeth. 'Do not speak of her.'

'Oh?' Farley remarked casually. 'She has become troublesome to you, perhaps? She has a habit of doing so. I assure you, I know precisely how to deal with her.'

Devlin spun toward Farley and, with the strength of both arms, shoved him away. Better that than attacking and killing him. Farley fell, splashing into a puddle on the pavement.

Farley struggled to rise. 'You have ruined my coat.'

Devlin leaned over him. 'I'll ruin more than your coat if you dare speak to me again, Farley.'

He turned his back and crossed the street, not heeding the stares of others walking by.

Madeleine stood in the hall, pushing the broom here and there, wondering how one contrived to get all the dust into one spot so that one could use the dustpan. She decided to experiment on a little pile of dust, but couldn't work out how to hold the broom and the dustpan at the same time. Linette sat in the corner galloping her wooden horse back and forth, while her doll sat abandoned on a parlour chair.

Bart had accompanied Sophie to the dress shop. How could any of them have guessed that little Sophie would be the only one to find paying work? Bart searched each day for labour, coming home talking of scores of veterans like himself lining up for one job. And Devlin. More lines of worry etched his face each day.

When Madeleine and Sophie took some of her new dresses to the dressmaker in the hope that they might return them,

Sophie came home with a large package of piecework, Madeleine with the dresses she had sought to sell.

She struggled with the sweeping. She was determined to do her part. While Sophie sewed and Bart and Devlin searched for work, she would care for the house.

Madeleine tried a different way to hold the broom, sticking it under her arm and levering it against her hip. She pretended to be a simple country housewife. She cleaned the house and tended the child while her husband—Devlin, of course—tilled the earth. Their lives were a quiet routine of hard work, peaceful evenings in front of the fireplace, and nights filled with loving. Madeleine leaned on the broom and sighed. How wonderful it would be.

She should not waste time in fancy. This silly habit of hers did not do her credit. She needed to solve her problems such as they really were. She needed work. Employment as a housemaid would not be the means, she supposed, although housework had never seemed difficult for the housemaids she once knew. They sped through chores with no apparent effort.

She jabbed at her pitiful pile of dust with the broom, scattering it everywhere except into the dustpan. 'Deuce.'

As she uttered this unladylike but Devlin-like epithet, the door opened and Devlin walked in, his head bent and his shoulders stooped. When he saw her, he smiled, but his eyes remained sad. 'What the devil are you doing?'

'Sweeping.' She looked down at the floor. 'Or trying to do so.'

'Deddy!' Linette popped up from her corner and propelled herself into Devlin's arms.

'How's my little lady?'

Linette wrapped her little arms around Devlin's neck. 'Deddy play?' She batted long lashes and smiled sweetly.

'Not now, Lady Lin.' He put Linette down and the child ran back to her toy horse. Devlin rubbed his forehead. He turned toward Madeleine and again smiled.

She stepped over to him to take his hat. 'You are wet.'

'It is nothing. A little rain.'

'Let me help you remove your coat.' She reached for the lapels. He held her arms and stared at her a moment before clutching her to him.

She could hardly breathe, he held her so tight.

'Do not worry so, Devlin. We shall come about.' She wound her own arms around his neck.

Linette ran to them, arms raised. 'Me! Me!'

Devlin scooped her up and enveloped them both in a hug, the kind of coming-home greeting she had imagined a moment ago, but infused with pain instead of pleasure.

'Come into the kitchen, Devlin. I'll make you a cup of tea.' She liked the sound of that, the housewife giving comfort to the labourer.

'I want biskis!' Linette cried.

Devlin, holding them both more loosely now, gave her a perplexed look. 'Biskis?'

'She means biscuit. I believe we still have a good number that Sophie made.'

He smiled. 'Tea and biskis it is, then.' Still carrying Linette, he followed her into the kitchen.

Bart and Sophie entered from the rear door as Madeleine poured Devlin's tea. Devlin merely raised his eyebrows to Bart, who shook his head.

'These are hard times.' The sergeant frowned.

Madeleine bade Bart and Sophie sit for tea and 'biskis', and, amid Sophie's protests, she served them all. Linette had climbed upon Devlin's lap. While the others traded news of their efforts of the day, she surveyed the scene. Their situation was dire, but the moment filled her with peace.

Her family, she thought. She put a hand to her brow. She must not think of family.

'Perhaps I have something of value to sell,' Devlin mused. 'I must have a stick pin or something with a jewel in it. Or perhaps my sword would fetch a good price.'

'You must keep the sword.' Bart nodded his head firmly. 'To honour the others.'

'You are right.' Devlin's voice was barely audible.

'I could try another shop to sell the dresses,' Madeleine offered.

He winced. 'Yes, you could.'

Sophie rose and dropped a few coins into Devlin's hands. 'My earnings, sir.'

Madeleine watched the look of pain flash over his face, replaced by a gentle smile for Sophie.

'Thank you, indeed, little one. This is a welcome contribution.'

Sophie flushed with pride.

He stood, having drained the contents of his cup and set Linette upon a chair. 'If you all will pardon me.'

Madeleine watched him walk out of the room, his tall figure ramrod straight. A moment later the front door closed.

Later that evening when she was putting Linette to bed, she heard Devlin's footsteps on the stairs. He entered his bed-chamber. Half-listening for sounds from his room, she sang softly to her sleepy daughter. Within a few minutes, the child's eyelids fluttered closed. She kissed Linette's soft, pink brow, tucked the covers around her, and tiptoed over to the chest. Quietly opening the top drawer, she removed a small package wrapped in cloth.

Madeleine tapped lightly at the connecting door between her room and Devlin's. Without waiting for an answer, she entered.

He sat on the edge of his bed, bare-chested, his elbows resting on his knees, his hands clasped together. He glanced up.

'May I speak with you, Devlin?'

He nodded.

She walked over to the bed, handed him her parcel.

'What is this?' He took it in his hand.

'Something for you to sell.'

He unwrapped the cloth and lifted a delicate gold chain with a teardrop pearl. In the cloth were matching pearl ear-rings.

'These are lovely. Where did you get them? From Farley?'

'No,' she said, indignant that he should think so. 'They were mine before I met Farley. You may sell them.'

He stared at the jewellery and at her. 'Not quite yet, Maddy. Keep them for now.'

She carefully rewrapped the package.

'I have been thinking.' He rubbed his hands together. 'I have depended upon all of you too long. Poor Sophie, her fingers sore from sewing. You, ready to sell your treasures. Bart, searching for labour I'd not ask an enemy to perform.'

She stroked his cheek. 'I have caused you this trouble.'

He clasped her hand and held it.

Suddenly shy under his gaze, she glanced down. Her eyes rested on his chest and widened. 'Devlin, you have scars.'

His torso was riddled with them. Now, thinking about it, she realised she'd felt rough areas on his chest, that day she had touched him and almost made love with him. She had not looked, however. Now, so close to him in the candlelight, she recognised the long scar from the injury in Spain, but there were so many others, short and jagged.

'It is repulsing, is it not?' he said.

She touched one of the scars with her finger. 'Oh, Devlin, how could you think such a thing?' With gentleness, she traced it, still pink from healing. 'What happened to you? How did it come about that you have so many?'

'Waterloo.'

She placed her palm against his firm chest. 'I know it was at Waterloo. I should like to hear what happened to you.'

He rose, walking over to his window. 'The tale is not fit for fair ears.'

'Fustian. Nothing about me is fair.' She followed him. Standing behind him, she marked the scars on his back with her fingers. 'You had to endure this. It cannot be worse for me to hear of it.'

He turned to face her. She placed her hands on his shoulders as he gazed at her. The green of his eyes turned soft as moss. 'I have a proposition for you, Miss England.'

She stiffened, pulled away, but he held her firm.

'Not that kind of proposition.' He took her chin between his thumb and fingers. His expression turned serious again. 'I will tell you about Waterloo on one condition.'

'What condition?' She could imagine no other condition but bedding him. He meant a proposition, after all, no matter how he coloured it. When he touched her like this, she dared hope for it.

He gave her a light kiss on the lips, which merely gave her an urge to kiss him harder in return. 'I will tell you about Waterloo, if you tell me about how you came to be with Farley.'

She pulled away and rubbed her arms. 'Nonsense. I told you already that he seduced me. What else is there to tell?'

He crossed the room and picked up the cloth wrapping her necklace and earrings. 'I want to know how a girl who owned these came to be in Farley's gaming hell.'

She turned away. She had never spoken of her past to anyone, not even Sophie. In fact, she chastised herself if even a thought of the past invaded her mind.

She faced him. 'Very well, I will tell you, but not this night. I do not wish to speak of it this night.'

'You have a bargain, Maddy.' He returned to her, kissing her on the cheek. 'I do not wish to speak of any of it tonight.'

The chaste kiss disappointed her. She wished something else from him. She wished to pretend she was the farmer's housewife readying for bed with her husband. There was no Farley, no Waterloo, no shortage of money. Just days full of useful toil and nights filled with love.

He walked back to the window and stared out at the street for countless minutes. She knew not whether to stay or leave, but she did not want to leave him, especially with the weight of all their problems on his shoulders.

'Sophie is teaching me to sew.' Her voice sounded foolish in the face of his troubled silence.

But he turned to regard her with a kind look in his eye. 'That is very well. Had you not learned before?'

'Oh, I was taught, but I did not heed the lessons.'

He chuckled. 'Your head too full of horses?'

She smiled. 'Sadly, you are right. I never could keep my mind on much else.'

He sat on the window seat, his long legs stretched out before him. 'I know precisely what you mean.'

She sat next to him, tucking her legs beneath her and leaning against him. His arm circled around her shoulders. 'It is a pity that I could not procure employment in a stable. I could do all manner of things there.' She sighed.

He became silent again, and she struggled to think of some other topic to converse upon. She rested her hand on his knee and in a moment, he covered it with his own warm, strong hand.

'No, I shall find the way,' he murmured.

She snuggled against him, the moment acutely precious.

Devlin lifted his hand to her hair, stroking gently. Her locks felt like spun silk beneath his fingers. He inhaled the faint scent of lavender in her hair, and recalled that fragrance from his first meeting of her. After Waterloo, when fever made him delirious and his sisters bathed his forehead with lavender water, his Miss England swam through his dreams.

He had never expected to see her again, and here she was, more wonderful than he could have believed.

He snuggled her closer. She tilted her face to him, the pupils of her eyes wide, her pink lips moist and irresistible.

He kissed her, tasting the sweetness of her, wanting to remove every pain and care from her life and resolving once again to do so. No matter what he must bear.

As his lips gently rested against hers, she whispered, 'Devlin, I...'

He moved to the tender skin beneath her ear.

'I will make love to you, Devlin.'

He stopped and searched her face. 'Only if you truly wish it.'

She cast her gaze down. 'I do wish it. I know it is wicked of me.'

Lifting her chin with his finger, he forced her to meet his eye. 'It is not wicked.'

'But it is,' she insisted. 'I know it is.'

'Well, then, I must be damned indeed.' He ran his lips over her brow. 'I wish that much to make love with you.'

Her face flushed pink. 'It is different for a man.'

'And how is it different, sweet goose?' He pulled the pins from her hair, freeing it to tumble over her shoulders.

'It is no shame for a man to take his pleasure.' Her countenance was solemn. 'Men even boast of it.'

The truth of her words shamed him.

He drew his fingers through her hair. 'Women are made to feel the pleasure, too, Maddy. They are merely expected not to speak of it.'

'Do you truly believe so?' Her wide eyes made her appear as innocent as a young virgin. As she must have been, before Farley.

He smiled. 'I do indeed.'

She gazed at him, a dreamy look on her face.

'Come.' He led her to the bed.

She followed almost shyly, like a bride on her first night. He was determined that she should feel every pleasure he could provide for her. He wanted to show her that lovemaking could be beautiful. Enlightening. Forgiving.

He undid the laces of her dress and gently peeled the cloth from her skin. She released a long breath. Next came her corset. As he pulled her shift over her head, she raised her arms, bringing them down again around his neck. Clinging tightly to him, she kissed him.

Though he throbbed to mate with her that instant, he kept his kiss light. He sensed she also could succumb to the passion of the moment, but he held her back. All she'd known was frenzied, impersonal coupling. He wished to show her more. He wished to show her love.

And he wished to savour each moment of it.

She unfastened his trousers and slid her hands under the cloth until she'd pushed them down to his ankles. As she stood again, she slid her hands up his legs, torso, and shoulders, nearly causing him to abandon his resolve to proceed slowly. He captured her hands in his own and tasted her lips at leisure.

Lifting her on to the bed, he settled beside her, letting his eyes drift down the naked length of her.

Miss England, he had called her that first time, half in jest. She was still so very much like the homeland he loved. Peaceful and pleasing. Exciting and teasing.

He slid his tongue down her neck and covered the rose of her nipple with his mouth. She moaned and arched toward him.

Not yet, Miss England, he thought. This must be a journey with so languid a pace every part would be savoured and committed to memory.

As dawn tried to poke its fingers through the thick morning mist, Devlin sat in shirt and trousers, staring out the window. Madeleine rolled over in the bed, making endearingly incoherent sounds as she did so. His attention shifted to her.

Her beauty took his breath away, as it had that first moment he'd seen her in Farley's gaming hell. Her dark hair such a contrast to her fair skin; her long eyelashes, so like Linette's, full against the pink of her cheeks. He memorised her image, just as he had done before returning to Spain.

The eyelashes fluttered and she opened her eyes. The smile she gave him, so peaceful and satisfied, tugged at his heart.

He would see that peace stay with her forever, no matter what the cost to him.

'Good morning,' she said, sleep making her voice raspy.

'Did you sleep well?' He already knew her reply. While he had hardly captured two winks all night long, she had slept as sound as a kitten.

'Indeed.' She stretched, arching her back and extending her arms above her head. 'And I have the feeling that this will be a lucky day. Today you will find the solution to our problems.'

'I have done so already.'

She brightened, sitting up straight. 'You thought of it in your sleep?'

Sleep, indeed. 'I thought of it last night, but I only decided this morning.'

She sprang from the bed and rushed over to climb into his lap. With her arms around him, she rested her head against his chest. 'What is the solution, Devlin?'

He closed his eyes. As if lances were piercing his skin again, he steeled himself against the pain.

'I must marry.'

Chapter Nine

Madeleine's heart pounded. Marriage had figured too prominently in her fantasies of late.

'It was my father's plan.' Devlin's voice vibrated through her body, but it did not soothe. 'And it is the only means I have of solving our problems.'

He held her more tightly. 'You see, Maddy, I am a wealthy man. My father bequeathed me a fortune, as he did my sisters and second brother. Ned, of course, has the title and all the entailed property and is as rich as Croesus, but my father saw that each of us would prosper.'

'I do not understand. You are wealthy, but your brother refuses you money?' He made no sense.

He laughed drily. 'There is the rub. My father thought me unfit for my property and wealth. Ned controls the lot until I marry a lady of whom he approves.'

She buried her face into his chest so he would not see. Her fantasies had indeed been foolish. He must marry someone of whom his brother approved. A lady such as the beautiful Marchioness. Not one who came as the prize in a game of cards.

She took a deep breath. 'So you must marry.'

'Marriage shall steady me…or so Father believed. I have resisted, Maddy. It seems an abominable reason to marry.' He squeezed her, his strength conveying his frustration. 'It is too soon for me, in any event. I have just done being a soldier. I do not wish—' He broke off.

Madeleine pulled away and retrieved her clothes from the floor. Suddenly conscious of her nakedness and ashamed of even more that that, she donned her shift, aware of his eyes upon her. She glanced at him and he averted his gaze. Tossing her hair over one shoulder, she slipped into her dress and fumbled with the laces. Devlin came and tied them for her, the light touch of his fingers sending shimmers of pleasure down her back.

'It is because of me…' She felt sick inside, unsure if it was because Devlin would once again pay the price for her freedom, or because he might think of bedding her, but never, never would he think of marrying her. 'I will not allow it.'

'You have no choice.' His voice was bleak.

'I could leave here.' She set her chin firmly. 'You would not need to marry, then.'

He turned her around and held her arms firmly, forcing her to look at him. 'You would be driven back to Farley. Or worse. Believe it, there can be worse.'

'I will never go back to him.' She shuddered at the thought. 'I will find employment. I am already learning to sew.'

He regarded her with tenderness. 'Yes. I am proud of your efforts, but, even if you attain Sophie's skill, it is but a pittance to earn. I counted her money, you recall.'

'I will contrive something.'

'No, you will not. I have been around this in my mind in all manner of ways.' He released a ragged breath. 'I must marry.'

Someone else. Some other woman. A lady.

'You are not responsible for me,' she continued, struggling to keep the misery at bay.

He brushed a lock of hair off her forehead. 'But I am, Maddy. I am responsible for the lot of you.'

'I could walk out. You could not stop me.' She glared.

He shook his head. 'Do not be foolish. You must think of Linette.'

She closed her eyes. He was correct. She would sell her soul to spare Linette a future like hers.

Pulling away, she went to Devlin's bed and smoothed the covers they had disordered, trying not to recall the wanton pleasure of loving him. Her carnal pleasure had come at great cost.

He spoke from behind her. 'I will see to both of you, Maddy. A snug little house for you. Whatever you want. School for Linette. I will make her future secure, and you will not want for anything.' He turned her around to face him. 'It is the only way. I will not permit you and Linette to suffer.'

His countenance, so sincere, with a look so loving, caused tears to prick her eyelids. 'I cannot like being a burden to you,' she said lamely.

He gathered her in his arms, holding her tightly against his chest. 'You will never be a burden. My wealth is such that I may easily afford to provide you and Linette a life of ease.' He took a deep breath and his chest rose tighter against her. 'But I must have a wife to do so.'

He would be that rich? But he had been satisfied to count pennies and seek common employment. Why had he done so?

Her mind seized on an anxious thought. 'Is there a woman for whom you have already spoken?'

He petted her hair. 'No, my sweet, there is no one else.'

She glanced up at him. His green eyes were soft, though tiny lines of worry etched their corners. She lifted her fingers to feel the rough stubble of his beard. Her childish fantasy of a pirate whisking her away flashed through her mind. Would that it could be true, that this unshaven, half-dressed, hot-blooded man would whisk her away. Not send her away, as fate decreed.

His eyes darkened with passion. Adjusting his hold on her, he captured her lips. The kiss, rough and as yearning as her heart, sent fire through her. She uttered a deep, needful sound and grasped at his shirt, wanting to tear it away from where her hands longed to touch.

His hands untied the laces of her dress as he backed the two of them against the bed. She let her dress slip to the floor, not caring if she stepped on it. He lifted her on to the bed and moved back to rid himself of the shirt and unfasten his trousers. She lifted her shift. He climbed atop her and she relished the weight and nearness of him. His male scent filled her nostrils along with the more primitive smell of desire.

He kissed her again and she arched to him, wanting to join with him, the need more urgent now that she knew this golden time with him would end. She whispered for him to proceed with haste, and he made ready to comply.

'Mama!' Linette's plaintive cry sounded through the door.

'Deuce,' Devlin muttered.

'I have to see to her.' Madeleine said, fighting her body's craving to do otherwise.

'I know.' Devlin sighed and moved off her, grabbing her dress, which she hurriedly donned. He worked the laces as she headed for the door.

He stopped her at the door with a quick, regretful kiss. 'See to the child. I'll come below stairs soon.'

With one glance back, Madeleine opened the door to her room and headed for the outstretched chubby arms of her daughter.

Devlin dragged his hand through his hair and stared at mother and child, desire still churning through him. He closed his eyes and took deep breaths. Arousal faded little, but calm did not return.

He watched Madeleine tend to her child with confidence, efficiency, and calm good humour. How could she manage that when his body still throbbed with wanting her?

Lord, he did not want to leave her when their passion flamed like this. Marrying would not have to cause this to end, would it? He could continue to visit her, still warm her bed.

He quietly shut the door.

No, he would not see her again after the damned marriage. It would be too cruel to this hapless future wife for their marriage to include a mistress.

The wretched course he had decided upon was the correct one. The only one. But it sickened him all the same. To damn another lady to a future without love merely to secure his fortune was detestable, but not to do so meant damning Madeleine and her child to a living hell.

He prowled the room, unable to quiet the storm of emotion inside. He must give up Madeleine. It was the only way to ensure her a good life. Marriage was his only choice.

The walls of the room closed in on him, and his breathing quickened. He shut his eyes and yearned for escape, for freedom.

Until Waterloo, soldiering had been his freedom. Living by his own wits with men who understood what was essential in life. Making the most of each day. Grateful for food, shelter, the occasional warmth of a willing woman. Laughing and drinking and sleeping under the stars. Surging with excitement, raging against the enemy. Testing skill, courage and luck. He would trade everything to go back to those days in Spain.

What blithering nonsense. Those days had vanished with Waterloo.

A heavy fatigue overtook him, but he proceeded to shave and dress. He would put the best face he could on this day, for Madeleine's sake.

Below stairs, he walked past the dining room and smiled. Their little household rarely supped at the table there, except for the last meal of the day. He liked the informality of the kitchen where they gathered as equals in this venture to survive.

That would vanish, too, with his decision. When his money flowed again, he would be master.

As he neared the kitchen door he heard Madeleine's voice.

'Sit, Sophie. Please do. I will tend to the meal.'

Sophie's inevitable protest dissolved into a fit of coughing.

Madeleine looked up as he entered. Linette clambered over the chairs to get to him.

'Deddy!' The little girl jumped into Devlin's arms.

'Devlin,' Madeleine said, 'please tell Sophie to sit and allow me to do the work. She is ill.'

'I am not ill.' The little maid, sallow-faced with dark circles under her eyes, choked on her words and turned her head to cough some more.

Devlin opened his mouth, but had no chance to speak.

'I cannot see how she fooled Bart. He never would have gone out had he known.' Madeleine fussed at putting bowls on the table.

'Deddy play?' Linette batted her long lashes at Devlin.

Madeleine whirled to the child. 'No, Linette, sit here and eat.' She swept over and took the child from Devlin's arms.

She put Linette back in her chair, raised high by a wooden box upon which Linette now stood, not sat. Madeleine continued, 'Dev, please do something. Sophie will not listen to me.'

As if to prove Madeleine's words, Sophie pushed her hands on the table to raise herself. Devlin pressed his fingers to his brow.

'All of you, sit!' he commanded.

The three sat, like obedient soldiers.

He glared from one to the other. 'Linette, do as your mother says. Eat. Maddy, stop fussing. If you wish to ready the meal then bloody do it.' He softened his voice for Sophie. 'Little one, do not exert yourself. It is foolishness when Maddy is capable of a simple breakfast.'

Sophie did as she was told, coughing softly, eyes downcast.

Madeleine rose to pour a cup of tea for Sophie and Devlin. 'You need not have snapped at me.'

He glanced at her, regretting his burst of temper, but her

eyes held the hint of a smile and a softer expression that spoke
of what had passed between them the previous night.

'I apologise.' His eyes held hers for that moment. He hoped
she knew he was sorry for more than a fit of temper.

Between coughs, Sophie said, 'I need to tend to my sewing.'

Madeleine started to protest, but Devlin shot her a glance
to keep quiet. She spooned him a bowl of porridge.

'You need sew no longer, little one. We have had a change
in fortune. In fact, I intend to return your earnings to you.'

Sophie's eyes grew wide. 'We have money?'

'We will by this afternoon, I expect. I will call on my
brother again. He will give me the money this time.' He cautiously took a spoonful of the lumpy porridge. Perhaps by the
morrow they would be feasting on boiled eggs and ham.

'You see, I will do as my brother wishes and he will advance me the money.' Devlin would leave further explanation
of their change in fortune to Madeleine, not knowing how to
tell Sophie about his need to marry.

'May…may I continue with the sewing?' Sophie asked, her
eyes darting warily.

He leaned to her and placed his hand on her arm. 'You
may do whatever you wish. I do shout and bluster, but you
are a free woman, Sophie. Not mine to command.'

Madeleine stood behind him with the pot of tea. She
brushed against him as she poured.

'Where the devil is Bart?'

'Gone to find work,' Madeleine said.

'Deuce, you did not stop him?'

'He left before I came down.'

Bart would be out searching for some sort of back-breaking
labour, or something so dangerous, only a few of the out-of-
work war veterans would compete for the job.

'He went to a lead factory in Islington,' Sophie said, before
a cough stopped her.

'When?'

She held her throat, as if that would hold back another coughing spell. 'An hour or more, I think.'

He could hire a hack and catch up to him. Devlin took a quick sip of his tea and rushed off to warn his sergeant not to risk his neck another time for Devlin's sake.

He found Bart at the factory door where he and others hung about, hoping to be chosen for a job. The factory billowed black smoke and flecks of black ash covered the pavement and buildings. How could anyone abide such dismal surroundings?

'Come on, Bart. Let us get you out of this damned place.' He gestured his friend over to the hack.

Bart did not leave his place in the ragged line that had formed. 'It is honest work, Dev, and pays well.'

'You no longer need to break your back. Our fortunes have changed.'

Bart stared at him, hands on his waist. After a moment he abandoned the line and walked over to the hack.

Devlin explained the whole business as they rode back. Bart responded with a grim expression. 'It is right enough, Dev, but I do not like it all the same.' He shot Devlin a suspicious glance. 'Are you certain you have thought this through?'

Devlin nodded, frowning. 'This is not one of my impulsive acts. I have sat up half the night figuring this. We are mere days from having no blunt at all. What else can we do?'

The two men stared at the buildings passing by, the only sounds the horses' hooves on the cobblestones and the shouts of vendors selling their wares.

'When the time comes,' Devlin said at last, 'I want you to stay with Madeleine.' He did not have to explain what he meant.

'We have not been apart since Spain. I'll not desert you now.' Bart's thick brows knitted together in one straight line.

Devlin regarded his friend with a wan smile. 'Sophie will

not wish to leave Madeleine, I expect, and I doubt you will wish to leave Sophie. Am I correct?'

Bart did not answer, but neither did his craggy brows move from their stern expression.

'I can only do this if I know they remain safe.' Devlin's voice became low and insistent. 'I must depend on you to look out for them. I will not be able to see to it myself.'

Bart stared at him as the hack neared St James's Street. 'I will do as you say.'

That afternoon, Madeleine was alone in the house. Linette napped. Sophie, who had insisted herself fully recovered, went to return her sewing to Madame Emeraude and get another batch. Bart accompanied her, so she need not carry the basket.

Devlin left to see the Marquess, to announce his decision to seek a wife so as to release his allowance.

Madeleine hated this solitude. Busy all morning, she had given herself no time to think of Devlin searching for a wife. And leaving her.

Now there were no distractions.

The only fantasy she could muster was of Devlin in a church with a beautiful lady like the Marchioness at his side, saying his vows. If she shook off that unwanted reverie, she saw him facing the same lady in his bed.

She grabbed her sewing and settled herself in the parlour's window seat. The day was clear, the kind of day she once might have spent on horseback, galloping over the hills near her home. Those days felt as unreal to her as her fantasies about Devlin. She frowned over her stitches. Sophie had helped her design an apron to protect her dresses during the day. They had found an old bedsheet to make it with. Stitching was laborious, but she was determined to finish the garment when she was not needed helping Sophie with the dresses.

Sewing simply did not occupy enough of her mind, and

this morning of all mornings she did not wish to think. Devlin would marry and she would be sent away.

She supposed she should be grateful that he intended to take care of her and Linette. It was a good fortune, a perfect solution to all their problems. Perhaps Devlin would visit after he wed. Lots of men kept mistresses, she knew. Several had offered her a *carte blanche*, but Farley inevitably found out and they never offered again.

She refused to rank Devlin the same as those odious creatures who used to drool over her. He was not like them. Being with him was so different than being with other men. So wonderful. Devlin was a man like no other.

She turned back to her stitches. Perhaps if she became truly skilled at sewing, she and Sophie could earn enough for a little place to stay, enough to feed and clothe themselves and Linette.

Devlin would be free.

Madeleine concentrated on speeding up her sewing, necessary for a seamstress. She tried very hard to keep the stitches the same size and close together. Sometimes she would forget to use the thimble and push on the needle with her bare finger. More often, she poked herself with the needle's point instead of moving her fingers away.

For a few moments, the effort consumed her mind, but a noise in the street distracted her. A shiny barouche with a splendid pair of matched bays pulled up in front of the house. The horses were as fine as any she had ever seen. What stable had bred them? she wondered. They were identical in size, their markings so similar one would suppose they had been twins. She wished she had seen them in motion.

The knocker of the door sounded, and she jumped. She peeked out the glass to see who knocked. An unknown man stood there. The driver of the elegant equipage?

She opened the door.

The man who stood before her was more refined than any she had ever seen. His buckskins and driving coat were so finely tailored they looked moulded to his well-formed frame. His eyes, regarding her with a startled expression, seemed familiar, as did the set of his chin.

'I was given this as Lord Devlin Steele's direction.' He eyed her as men usually did, but without the typical prurient gleam.

'Lord Devlin is not presently at home,' she said.

He stepped past her, across the threshold, though she had not given him leave to do so. Her heart beat in alarm and she was acutely aware of being alone in the house.

She straightened her posture. 'Perhaps you would wish to leave your card.'

He removed his hat. 'I wish to wait.'

She bit her lip. She dare not betray being alone. His eyes still carefully assessed her.

'Who are you?' His question was more like a command.

She bristled. Smiling with bravado through her nervousness, she said, 'Forgive me for not introducing myself. I had thought it proper for visitors to announce themselves first.'

His eyes flashed at her insolence. She supposed he was not one accustomed to having his behaviour questioned. She smiled again and cocked her head as if waiting.

'The Marquess of Heronvale,' he said impatiently.

Her smile vanished. Devlin's brother.

'You are?' he commanded again.

She waved her hand as if his question was foolish, but curtsied politely. 'Miss England at your service, my lord. I am the...the housekeeper.'

'Indeed?' His eyebrows lifted in a top-lofty expression and his eyes flicked up and down her person once more.

She took a breath. 'Lord Devlin intended to visit you this afternoon, my lord. Perhaps you might find him at your residence.'

He made no move to leave. 'I will wait for him.'

She took his hat and showed him into the parlour, where he stood continuing to watch her. She scooped up her sewing from the window seat and twisted the material in her hand, wishing she had finished the garment so it could cover her pale yellow muslin dress.

'I shall bring tea.' It sounded like what a housekeeper might do. He still stood, watching her.

As she moved to leave, his voice stopped her, sounding less imperious. 'Tell me, Miss England. My brother…is he well?'

An odd question. 'Yes, he is. Very well, my lord.' She curtsied again and hurried out the door.

The Marquess watched the retreating figure, wondering what to make of this surprise in his brother's household. Housekeeper, indeed. The young woman—lord, she looked more like a girl—was a breathtaking beauty with startlingly blue eyes and dark unruly hair. Where had Devlin found her? He had heard no rumours of his brother forming a liaison.

He strolled around the room, intrigued, as well, with the genteel furnishings. The place must have commanded a respectable rent. With this 'housekeeper', it was easy to see why Devlin wished to move. And he could see why his little brother had overspent his due. A woman of Miss England's face and figure would not come cheap, as her tasteful new attire could attest.

He'd not reckoned on his brother living with a mistress, had not conceived the notion even when Serena reported seeing Devlin with a woman. Devlin had introduced Serena to her as if she were respectable. Devlin should have told him about her.

He should not be surprised Devlin had not. Ned wandered over to the window. He would have disapproved. He would have given Devlin a list of cogent reasons why keeping a mistress was irresponsible and he would have reminded Devlin of his duty.

Ned had often thought about keeping a mistress himself. There were times when his masculine urges raged in a manner he could not inflict upon his delicate wife, and a willing woman would have easily slaked his desires.

But he had not.

In any event, Devlin had no business keeping a woman. He had no fortune of his own to command. Ned stood again and peered out the window. He had planned merely to assure himself Devlin was not ill and be on his way. He pulled on the bell cord.

Miss England appeared at the door. 'Yes, my lord?'

At least she played her role of housekeeper well. Puzzling, she spoke like an educated miss. Still, her youth did not make sense. She could be no more than nineteen.

'Please have someone instruct my tiger to walk the horses.'

'Yes, my lord,' she replied.

He watched from the window to see it done and was surprised when Miss England went from the house to speak to his tiger.

A few minutes later, she entered with a tea tray. She poured the tea prettily and offered some lemon cakes, as well. He noticed tea leaves swimming in his cup.

He could not resist baiting her. 'Tell me, Miss England, how long have you been in my brother's…employ?'

'Not long, sir,' she replied, an edge to her voice.

'He had not spoken to me of having a housekeeper.'

She did not lower her gaze at this question. She smiled instead. 'Indeed? Do gentlemen discuss such matters?'

He narrowed his eyes, 'Was it you whom my wife met with Devlin—Lord Devlin?'

Her cheeks flushed. 'Yes, my lord. She kindly spoke to me.'

He ought to wring Devlin's bloody neck. How dare he put Serena in such a position, to speak to one such as this Miss England? He glared at her.

But at the moment she looked more like a timid young girl, nervous and uncertain. It was difficult to maintain his anger.

'May I be excused, my lord?' Her cheekiness had fled, at

least. He wished to ask more questions, but could think of none.

'Deddy?' A small voice sounded from the doorway, and Miss England turned pale.

Ned turned to come face to face with a tiny child, no more than a baby, rubbing her eyes and yawning.

The very image of his brother.

Chapter Ten

Ned stared at the child, a doll-like little girl who clutched a wooden horse in her hand. Even the toy was like one Devlin had carried with him at that age. She had blue eyes instead of green. Even so, this little girl was a female version of Devlin twenty-five years ago. The child stole a wary glance at him and ran to Miss England, who scooped her up in her arms.

'I want Deddy,' the child said.

Miss England flushed.

'Daddy?' Ned asked, raising an eyebrow.

The young woman blinked rapidly.

'The child's word for papa?' Perhaps the child had picked up the Scottish term from the faithful Bart.

Her eyes darted. 'No, indeed, for a…a…toy.' She looked at the girl. 'Go above stairs now, sweetling. Mama will be up directly.'

The child flung her little arms around Miss England's neck. 'No!'

Ned remembered that feeling. Chubby arms clasping his neck, the awesome knowledge that such devotion could be directed at him. His littlest brother, following him everywhere when he was home on school holiday. Worshipping him. Needing him.

'She is Devlin's child.' He did not ask.

A panicked look flashed across Miss England's face. She recovered quickly, meeting his eye. 'She is *my* child.'

Her child? She looked barely old enough.

The little girl studied him with wide lash-fringed eyes. 'Who zat, Mama?'

'He is the Marquess,' she responded.

His title would mean nothing to the child. But it would warm his heart if he again heard a childish voice call him Ned.

The little girl squirmed and her mother set her down.

Ned squatted to the child. 'And what is your name?'

'Winette,' the shy little voice said, a thumb popping into her mouth.

'Winette?' He looked to Miss England.

'Linette,' she said.

Ned smiled at the child. 'That is a splendid horse you have, Linette. May I see it?'

Linette thrust the hand holding the horse in Ned's face.

'A splendid horse, indeed. Does your horse have a name?'

She released her thumb. 'Deddy's horse.'

Ned glanced at Miss England. Her hand had flown to her mouth. With a halting gesture, he touched Linette's dark curly hair. His brother used to run to him for comfort, he recalled. Ned would mop up his tears and stroke his hair just like this.

'Markiss play?' the little girl asked, cocking her head and batting her eyelashes.

Ned laughed and ruffled the child's hair, a smile lingering on his lips. Yes, he would like to play again, to sit on the floor and gallop a wooden horse.

He stood instead. 'I shall take my leave, *Miss* England. Please tell my brother he shall hear from me.'

'Yes, my lord.' She hurried to fetch his hat and gloves and to open the door for him. The child hovered behind her, and he gave the little girl a final smile as he walked out of the door, his barouche pulling up in front of the house.

Linette ran out the door, pointing. 'Horse! Horse, Mama!'

Miss England rushed out to grab her. Ned caught the child first and held her until Miss England took her hand. Regretting he had to leave the child, Ned continued towards the barouche. He stopped, a thought interrupting the plan half-formed in his head.

He turned back. 'Miss England?'

She hesitated. 'Yes, my lord?'

'Are you married to my brother?'

Surprise flashed across her face and she blushed deep red. 'No, my lord.'

He continued on his way, climbing onto the barouche and snapping at the rungs while his tiger leapt on to the back.

From an alleyway across the street, black eyes watched the retreating vehicle and glanced back at the mother and child re-entering the house.

What was meant by that tender scene? Lord Farley wondered. The Marquess of Heronvale going all mawkish over Madeleine's child? Perhaps the man's fancy ran toward young ones. Rumour said he had no fancy for his ice-maiden wife.

Farley tried to calculate what small fortune a marquess might spend for the rare chance to dally with such a child. He rubbed his hands at the thought.

Perhaps he should have sold the child to settle his debts instead of giving up Madeleine. Madeleine had become so much more difficult since the child was born. He should have got rid of it straight away.

Cursed chit—Madeleine had vowed to slit her own throat if he so much as touched the child, and he'd decided to keep her happy. He'd counted upon her being grateful enough to come willingly to him, like the first time when she'd been flushed with delight. That was what he desired again.

Farley leaned against the lamppost. He removed a pinch of snuff from its box and inhaled it. After a spasm of sneezing, he glanced back at the door she'd walked through, recalling the sway of her hips. She was made for seduction. If ever there was a woman created for passion, it was Madeleine.

So why did she withhold that passion from him? It enraged him. He thought he'd taught her a lesson when he forced her to become the bribe in his crooked games. He'd intended to offer her only a few times, but she'd made him a tidy profit. Men would come to his establishment every night, hoping to win time with her, especially if he offered her only every now and then. Then they returned often, losing more blunt each time.

While she was fat with child she'd earned him nothing. If he'd been in London he'd have dealt with her before it had grown too big to get rid of, but one did not refuse an emperor's summons or, to be more accurate, one from an emperor's emissary. Not when the emperor paid well for information gleaned from brandy-loosened tongues and gentlemen desperate to settle gambling debts.

He should have taken her to France with him, but that night before he left she'd angered him, and it had suited him well enough not to set eyes on her for a while. Besides, she'd become something of a patriot. More than once he discovered her poring over newspapers filled with stories about the war. If she had discovered his business dealings with Napoleon, she might have been stupid enough to pass the word to some fool willing to put country above fortune.

Stepping out of the alley onto the pavement, Farley gazed once more at the apartments where Madeleine lived with Devlin Steele. He thought of her naked beneath Steele, and his own loins ached.

He'd have her again, even if he had to kill to get her.

Madeleine paced the floor, wishing Devlin would hurry home and dreading when he would.

What could be worse for Devlin than the Marquess of Heronvale learning of her existence and that of her child? She knew what could be worse—his suspecting the child to be Devlin's.

Oh, she should never have opened the door. He would have gone away none the wiser had she not.

Linette walked up to her. 'Mama? Where's Markiss's horse?'

'Gone, Linette,' she said for what seemed like the hundredth time. Linette had not stopped speaking of those cursed horses. They were beautiful animals, she had to admit.

After what seemed like hours but could barely have been more than one, Devlin walked in. Linette reached him first and was lifted into his arms.

'Markiss's horse! Markiss's horse!' Linette chattered.

Madeleine tapped her foot in impatience.

Devlin frowned at her. 'My brother was not at home, so we remain penniless.'

'He was here.'

Her words were drowned out. Linette grabbed Devlin's cheeks and yelled, 'Markiss's horse!' as if getting louder would help.

'What the deuce is she talking about?' Devlin asked.

'I told you. Your brother was here. He came here, Devlin. He saw Linette. Markiss. It is her way of saying the Marquess.'

'Good God,' Devlin said. 'What did he want?'

'To see you.'

'For what purpose?'

She lifted her arms in frustration. 'I do not know. He did not confide in me.'

'Good God. He met you?'

'Of course he met me.' Her voice went up an octave. 'I have told you.'

She knew it was a terrible thing for Devlin's brother to learn of her existence. Still, it stung to realise Devlin thought so, as well.

Devlin set Linette down, putting his hand to his brow.

'You need not worry.' She lifted her chin. 'I told him I was the housekeeper.'

He threw his head back and laughed, the sound bouncing off the walls of the hallway.

Madeleine glared at him. 'It is not a jest, Devlin.'

Grinning, he drew her into his arms, even though she tried to pull away. 'You are nothing like a housekeeper.'

She pushed at his chest. 'Be serious. What are we to do?'

Linette ran up with her toy horse. 'Deddy play!'

'Not now, Lady Lin.' Devlin continued to hold Madeleine. Linette pulled at his trousers.

'We do nothing, Maddy,' he said. 'Ned would know of us sooner or later. My brother always discovers my secrets.'

Madeleine settled against him. As long as her presence remained a secret, she had an easier time pretending. In the full light of day, however, her existence was a shameful one.

Madeleine rested her head against the comforting beat of Devlin's heart.

'Are Sophie and Bart here?' His deep voice resonated in his chest. It was like feeling the sound, as well as hearing it.

Madeleine did not move from his warm, strong arms. 'They went to Madame Emeraude's, but that was a while ago. I believe they may be dallying.'

He chuckled, producing more interesting vibrations. 'They are the unlikeliest pair.'

No, she thought. *We* are. A man of Bart's class may marry a girl, no matter what her reputation. A lord may not.

The next morning Devlin woke, tangled in Madeleine's embrace. He stared at her face, inches from his and, in sleep, looking innocent as a lamb, so very young and vulnerable. His heart ached with tenderness for her.

She had not come to him in the night. He'd been restless and eager, desire heating his loins until he could wait no longer. He crossed the room, opened the door, and lifted her into his arms. She'd not protested when he carried her to his bed.

He intended to make love to her this morning. More than once, if the child slept long enough. Knowing he must give her up made him hungry for her, as if he needed to get his fill of her while he could. Enough to sustain him for the rest of his life.

Her eyes fluttered open, immediately filling with tenderness. A heartbeat later those eyes registered alarm and then, slowly, carefully, turned blank.

'Shall I make love to you, Devlin?' She spoke in that sweet voice that sounded as if it came from someone else. Her hand slid across his scarred chest and descended, nearing to where he was already hard for her.

He caught her wrist. 'Do not trouble yourself, Miss M.'

He had not expected to see this side of Madeleine again. He'd resigned himself to a limited time with her, but he expected her passion. Had not that much passed between them?

It angered him, made him want to teach her a lesson. He could show her how a man takes what he wants. He could climb atop her and force her to love him, before their time ran out.

Devlin sat up and ran a hand raggedly through his hair. His heart pounded and his throat tightened so that he could not take a breath. The walls of the room closed in on him and he heard the beat of the French drums, the pounding of horses' hooves charging. Retreat! he thought. Run. Ride. Gallop until your lungs feel like bursting and you are safe behind the line.

He swung his legs over the side of the bed and searched for his clothes.

'What are you doing?' Madeleine's modulated voice trembled a bit.

He could show her his anger, but he would be damned if he would let her see this panic that so frequently beset him.

'I am going out.' He left the room, still buttoning his trousers.

Madeleine, her breath coming rapidly, waited a few moments before donning her nightdress.

The previous night had been more than her daydreams could have imagined. He created sensations in her that she'd not known possible. Her body had responded to him, and she had performed all the tricks she had been taught to perform. But this time she had *meant* them. She had wanted to share her pleasure with him, wanted to feel him under her hand and her lips, wanted to bind him to her forever.

She must not allow herself to love him. She must give up foolish dreaming and prepare for leaving him. She must hope that the lady he wed would be worthy of him, and that he would eventually fall in love with her and be happy.

Such a thought was too miserable by half.

Madeleine opened the door connecting her room and Devlin's. Linette still slept, but in a short space of time the sun would send its fingers through the window to poke her awake. Madeleine hurried to dress herself and to drag a comb through her unruly curls. In the scratched mirror, her lips looked swollen from Devlin's kisses. She lightly touched her breast, remembering how his hand had felt there the night before, remembering the ferocity of their lovemaking.

Her body sprang to life. The light from the rising sun increased its brilliance. The sounds of Linette's breathing grew louder. From the open window, she could smell dampness in the cool morning air. She could not afford to feel so alive again. She vowed to tame the desire he aroused in her and to become dead again. As she had been at Farley's.

After all, leaving Devlin would be a little like dying.

Devlin strode through the streets with only one thought in his mind. To run. To ride. To be on horseback again with the sensation that nothing could catch him. No man, no musket ball, no blue eyes that stared blankly through him.

He quickened his pace as he neared his brother's stable. Entering, he called a 'halloo' and walked past the gleaming berlin carriage, a well-sprung curricle, and what appeared to be a brand new barouche. The smell of hay, so long missed, came back to comfort him.

A squat, wiry figure emerged from the most distant stall, wiping his hands on a rag. 'Yes, sir. What is it, sir?'

Devlin peered at him as he walked closer. The man was about his age and familiar. 'Jem, is that you?'

The man broke into a wide smile. 'Lord Devlin, well I'll be. Good to see you again, sir.'

They had grown up together at Heronvale, separated by their stations in life. Jem had been born to the stable, while Devlin belonged in the great house with its portrait hall of ancestors, its armour and family silver. When he and Jem met in the horses' stalls, however, they were of one mind. Horses. They could spend hours talking of horseflesh. On horseback, they rode for miles.

Devlin reached out his hand, which Jem accepted with hesitation. 'What are you doing here, Jem? By God, I have not seen you in years.'

'Yes, sir, since you went off to fight the Frogs.' Jem glanced around proudly. 'His lordship gave me the running of the stable here.'

'Indeed?' Devlin surveyed his surroundings again. 'Well done, Jem. He could not have chosen a better man. How goes it with you? You are well, it seems. What of your mother?'

'Passed away two years ago, I'm sad to say.' Jem's mother had worked in Heronvale's kitchens. She had been a jolly, generous soul.

'I am sorry. I had not heard.' Devlin felt guilty for not having known, not having even thought of her in that many years.

'I'm married now, sir,' Jem said, a proud expression on his face. 'I have a son and another babe on the way.'

'That is excellent news.' It was on the tip of Devlin's tongue to tell all about Madeleine, Linette, Bart and Sophie, but it could not be right to do so. Jem had a real family. His was not.

They stood awkwardly for a moment before Jem asked, 'And how can I be serving you today?'

Devlin had almost forgotten his purpose, though it now seemed less necessary to thunder away on horseback at break-neck speed. 'I had a fancy to ride this morning. Did the Marchioness send word of me using the stable?'

'She did, m'lord.'

Devlin clapped the man on the back. 'Show me your animals, Jem, and help me select the best bit of blood.'

As they toured the stable, Devlin selected Ned's black gelding, the only horse to truly tempt him. He spied another spirited animal, a mare.

'Jem, I have another request…'

From the kitchen where she washed the morning dishes, Madeleine heard the front door open. Devlin's voice roared, 'Bart!'

She ignored it and returned to her chores. Sophie had become more accustomed to Madeleine's insistence on helping with the work. The little maid's success as a seamstress helped her relinquish her hold on every menial task that needed to be done. That and the fact that her cough had become no better.

Linette came barrelling into the kitchen.

'Mama! Mama! Horses. *Horses*.' The little girl pulled her by the hand and there was no refusing. Madeleine followed, though she preferred to avoid Devlin.

Linette led her out the front door to where Bart was holding the reins of two of the most beautiful horses she had ever seen. The gelding was so black the sun on its coat reflected blue. The mare was a rich chestnut. The steeds' eyes shone with intelligence and good breeding. Their superior long legs impatiently pounded the cobblestones of the street.

She noticed the mare was saddled for a lady to ride.

Linette squealed something incoherent, and it was all Madeleine could do to keep hold of the child's hand.

'What are you about, Bart?' she asked.

'Dev asked me to hold them.' Bart scooped Linette up in his free arm, cooing to the child, 'Now, lass, pet the nose gently.'

Linette was in raptures, hardly able to be contained in Bart's arm.

Madeleine smiled at her daughter's enthusiasm. 'What is this?'

Devlin appeared at her side, responding to her question in a low voice. 'Have you forgotten what riding horses look like, Maddy?' He reached for Linette.

He was dressed in riding gear: buckskins clinging to his muscular thighs, top boots gleaming with polish, a riding coat of deepest blue. Her heart caught in her throat and she turned away from him.

'Horses, Deddy!' the child cried.

'Indeed, Lady Lin.' He grinned at Linette and placed her on the back of the black horse, holding on to her as he did.

Linette looked tiny atop the huge steed. 'Devlin, please take her off. She is too little—'

He spoke stiffly. 'I'll not let any harm come to her.' Without turning toward her, he continued, 'Madeleine, you will accompany me for this morning ride?'

The lady's horse was for her? A thrill rushed through her, replaced by trepidation. She should not spend time with him.

'I have no clothes.'

'Yes, you do. On your bed is the riding dress.'

She had refused the riding dress at the modiste. He had ignored her. 'I told you I'd have no need of riding clothes.'

'You were wrong. You need them now.'

More useless money spent on her. Perhaps if he had simply given her the money he spent on clothes, she could have found her own place to live and he would be free not to marry for her.

She crossed her arms in front of her chest. 'What else did you buy that I asked you not to?'

'The evening dress.'

'The evening dress!' Her voice became shrill.

'And shoes to match.'

She gritted her teeth. 'Useless waste of money.'

Devlin spoke firmly. 'Madeleine, change into the riding dress and return here forthwith. We will ride.' It was a command straight from a battlefield.

'Yes, my lord.' She turned and made sure she did not rush up the steps and into the house.

Once out of his sight, her anger blazed. She stomped into her room, and saw the riding dress laid out on her bed. It was an elegant outfit, a deep crimson, the colour rich and luxurious. She fingered the fine weave of the cloth and could not help but admire the garment's excellent cut.

She picked up the matching hat. A single feather adorned it, curled into a crescent to accent her chin. The hat had netting she could pull down over her face.

She had never expected to ride again. Indeed, she had settled in her mind that giving up horses was fitting punishment for fate to bestow upon her. When Lord Farley had first seen her on horseback, she had worn her brother's outgrown breeches and shirt instead of a proper riding dress. His old clothing was tight on her newly emerging curves. Now she knew how such garments must have inflamed Farley's senses, and she'd had no sense to restrain herself.

Yes, it was a fitting punishment to never ride again.

She walked over to the window and peered out. Devlin was now astride the black horse with Linette seated in front of him. He urged the horse into a sedate walk and she could hear through the closed window Linette's squeals of delight.

Devlin looked as if he were born to the saddle, and, as he held Linette protectively in his arm, Madeleine felt her heart yearn for him.

No. She must refrain from such feelings. She would ride,

as he commanded her to do, but she would not allow herself to feel a thing. Not for him. Not for anything, except her daughter. She would not allow herself to care about how the horse felt beneath her, how the hooves pounded in her ears, how the wind beat against her face.

She turned back to the bed and began undressing.

A quarter-hour later, she allowed Bart to toss her into the saddle. She remained silent while Devlin handed Linette down to Bart and they cantered through the London streets.

They made a solemn pair as they rode next to each other through neatly kept streets, still quiet at this early hour. The shops made way for rows of houses, each larger and more elegant as they progressed. She did not ask where they were headed.

Devlin finally spoke, though more to himself than to her. 'I have not been on horseback since…since Belgium.' His voice was flat, expressionless.

Her mouth dropped open in surprise. She must have tugged on the reins because the horse broke its gait. She hurriedly righted it again, but remembered the battle's evidence on his chest and back. In spite of her resolve to be angry with him, her throat tightened with emotion.

'We are here,' he said. They had stopped in front of a large stone gate.

Hyde Park.

Beyond the gate was a landscape of green, a fantasy of countryside in the midst of a city. 'Oh, my,' she gasped.

'It is early. No one will heed us at this unfashionable hour.' His horse led the way.

So many years ago, it had been her girlish wish to gallop down Rotten Row in Hyde Park, while her sisters had merely aspired to sedate afternoon drives.

As she and Devlin rode, Madeleine tried to imagine row after row of fashionable equipages with beautiful ladies and finely dressed gentlemen perched on the seats. The less prosperous would stroll along the pavement. She admitted to curiosity about such a sight, even though she had disdained the role of passenger. In those innocent days, however, she had never expected to feel like a trespasser in a world to which she no longer belonged.

Devlin led her to a dirt path where it was clear they could let the horses have their heads. Rotten Row. There were a few other riders, and Devlin ignored them. Madeleine pulled the netting of her hat over her face.

'We will race.'

He was back to giving commands, was he? Well, she would do as he commanded. She would race.

She did not wait for his command to begin. She pressed her knee into the horse's side. The mare leaped into motion. Madeleine leaned forward almost flat against the horse's neck. She inhaled the mare's scent, heard the panting of the mare's breath and the pounding of her hooves. Madeleine's heart ignored her bidding to play dead and leapt with delight. For the first time in years, she felt exhilaratingly free.

Other hooves sounded and Devlin's horse, neck pumping, pulled alongside. She glanced at him. His beaver hat was gone, and his hair blew wildly around his head. His eyes, too, blazed with excitement.

She urged her horse faster. Joy overwhelmed her and she laughed out loud. She glanced at Devlin, his horse neck to neck with hers. He grinned. They ended the course together.

They slowed their horses to a walk. Devlin, breathing as hard as his horse, circled around Madeleine. He gazed at her. To Madeleine, the green of the park faded and was replaced by the green of his eyes. She held his gaze, memorising it. No matter what her resolve, she vowed to remember the passion she saw in his eyes, the passion that mirrored her own.

A slow grin came over his face. 'Shall we do it again?'

Before she could figure out what the *it* could be that they would do again, he launched into a gallop. She recovered quickly and urged her horse on his heels. He smiled proudly at her when she caught up. Again they finished the course together.

'I won,' he said, a smug look on his face.

'You did not,' she countered. 'I would have been a length ahead if not for this infernal saddle.'

His brow wrinkled. 'Is something amiss with the saddle?'

She felt herself redden. 'No, I…I am accustomed to riding astride. Or I used to be.'

His expression turned solemn and she suspected he could imagine the scandalous picture she made in those days.

A bird fluttered noisily out of a nearby bush, startling Devlin's horse. He quieted the animal and glanced at Madeleine. Her face was flushed and her blue eyes sparkled. No matter what happened to him from this day forward, he would never regret this moment with her. Nor would he forget.

They remained that way, staring into each other's eyes, their mounts restless underneath them. Neither looked away.

More riders arrived in the park. Some greeted Devlin and tossed curious glances toward Madeleine. She held her head down.

'Perhaps we had best head home,' he said.

'Perhaps.'

He rode to retrieve his hat and led them to the gate. She followed closely.

They returned through the most fashionable streets, to streets full of shops, to their own nearly respectable address.

Madeleine spoke, 'Why did you hire horses today?'

He glanced at her. 'They belong to my brother.'

'The Marquess?' Her voice was anxious.

'Yes, but do not worry, Maddy. I have my brother's permission.' It was not entirely accurate, but he had Serena's permission, and Ned would never counter her wishes.

They lapsed back into silence.

Soon they neared their street. Madeleine asked, 'Why did you do this?'

'Fetch the horses?'

'Make me ride with you.'

He frowned. How could he explain what he did not truly understand? He had not meant to invite her. At first he had meant to escape her. 'I did not wish to ride alone.'

'You could have taken Bart with you.'

To Bart horses were like tools, a means to get a job done. His wish to ride was more ephemeral. A last chance for freedom? Bart would never have understood.

He had not even thought of Bart, though. He had wanted Madeleine. Who else would understand the need? The pleasure?

'I wished it to be you.' His voice had turned low and he was not sure if she heard him.

As they rode up to their apartments, Linette's face disappeared from the window. A moment later she was out the door, tugging away from Bart's firm grip.

'Horse! Horse! Mama. Deddy.'

'Hello, my darling,' Madeleine called to her.

'Me, too, Mama. Me, too.' Linette cried, squirming to get free. Even a strong man like Bart could barely hold her.

'Bring her here, Bart.' Devlin reached down and scooped the child into his arms, holding her securely in front of him. 'Maddy, come with us.'

Devlin, Madeleine, and Linette rode sedately to the end of the block, quiet at this hour, and back again. The little girl's delighted laughter filled the street.

'More. More.' Linette shouted.

'Enough for today, Lady Lin.'

Bart reached for the child. Devlin slid easily off the horse and turned for Madeleine, holding her firmly by the waist to assist her to dismount.

She looked him directly in his eyes and whispered, 'Thank you, Devlin.'

He held her there, suspending the moment.

When he finally slid her down his body to touch the pavement, Madeleine blinked, turned and took Linette from Bart.

She allowed Linette to pat the horses and say goodbye to them.

'Would you return the horses, Bart?' Devlin asked.

Bart nodded, taking hold of the reins. 'Dev, a note was delivered for you. It is on the table inside the door.'

Devlin, his emotions in a tangle, ran up the steps and into the house. He had not wanted that time with Madeleine to end. He removed his coat, gloves and hat, and picked up the envelope.

Madeleine and Linette came inside, and Linette ran to the window for her last glimpse of the horses. 'Bye bye, horses!'

'What is the note?' Madeleine asked as she pulled off her hat. Her hair tumbled down to her shoulders.

He handed her a piece of paper.

Her eyes grew wide. 'It is a voucher for Almack's!'

'Serena certainly lost no time procuring it for me.' He wrinkled his brow. 'The other paper is an invitation,' he said, though she was paying little attention. 'No, a command, really.'

'A command?' She gingerly fingered the voucher.

'We are commanded to dine with my brother and his wife this evening, at their town house.' He tapped the card against his palm.

'You are?' She said absently.

'*We* are,' he corrected. 'You and I.'

Her face turned pale. 'No.'

Chapter Eleven

'Oh, yes,' Devlin said. 'The invitation is very specific. It is for us both.'

'I will not attend.' Her voice sounded as if she were being strangled. 'I will not expose myself to…to a society dinner where I do not belong.'

Devlin saw the rising panic in her eyes. 'It is a private dinner. You and I are to dine with Ned and Serena, *en famille.*'

'No.'

Devlin rubbed his brow. What the deuce could Ned be thinking of? It was not like his brother to play games. Impossible to believe he would invite Madeleine to his home to dine with his wife. Ned might not love Serena, but he certainly would never deliberately cause her any discomfort. And, then, there was the matter of the voucher to Almack's. An invitation to bring his mistress to dine, and a blatant entry into the marriage mart in the same package. It made no sense.

Madeleine stared at him, her chin now tilted in defiance, anxiety lingering in her eyes. He looked back at the card, not so much to read it again as to collect his thoughts.

He wrinkled his brow. 'I think the voucher must mean Ned intends to give me the money, but…' he glanced up at her '…I cannot understand why he wishes us to dine.'

'I will not go.'

'I do not think there would be any harm in it.'

She crossed her arms over her chest. 'I will not go.'

Devlin attempted a cajoling smile. 'You would find use for the evening dress.'

She threw the voucher at him and fled up the stairs.

As he bent to retrieve it, Linette toddled in from the parlour where she had been on sentry duty at the window. She pulled on Devlin's sleeve, her little mouth turned down and her big blue eyes mournful. 'Horses gone.'

Devlin almost smiled, even amidst his confused thoughts. He picked her up. 'That's right, Lady Lin. Horses gone.'

Linette flung her chubby arms around Devlin's neck. He clung tightly to Linette. The freedom and joy of the ride with Madeleine receded. Walls blocked his escape and the air seemed in short supply.

Run, he heard himself shout. *Run*. He was on horseback again, this time screaming for his cavalry to withdraw. They had gone too far, drunk with the carnage they'd wrought on the French, still swinging their sabres into retreating backs, until the pounding of fresh French cavalry sounded in his ears.

He opened his eyes and caught a glimpse of himself in the hallway mirror, Linette's curly dark head leaning trustingly on his shoulder.

He took a deep breath. 'Come on, Lady Lin. Let us see if Sophie left us some lemon cakes in the kitchen.'

Madeleine flung herself dramatically on the bed. As a child, she might have indulged in a fit of angry tears, but now she knew tears achieved nothing.

She rose and unbuttoned the riding dress, choosing her yellow muslin to wear. After fastening the laces, she picked up the riding dress again and held it to her nose. It smelled of horse. She closed her eyes. The ride had been glorious. The exhilaration, the freedom of speed, Devlin, hatless and grinning beside her.

Another memory to store. She pored over every detail, fixing each in her mind. With another whiff of the lingering scent, she laid the garment carefully on top of the trunk at the foot of her bed. Later she would brush it off as she had seen Sophie do, and she would hang it up to air out.

The door opened. 'May I come in?'

She stiffened at his voice. 'You might have knocked first.'

Devlin closed the door and leaned against it, his legs crossed at the ankles. 'You might have refused me entry.'

She picked up the riding dress and brushed it off with her hand. It was something to do, to look busy.

'May we talk, Maddy?'

He looked appealingly long limbed, taut with strength, but infused with gentleness. She did not wish to see him thus. She closed her eyes, but that only brought the memory of him wild-eyed on a galloping horse. She shrugged.

'First, let me assure you that the decision is yours. I will not mention this matter again, do you understand?'

She nodded, but did not look at him.

'I do not know why my brother made this invitation, but I cannot believe he would mean any harm. He is a good man.'

'I am not so certain of that.' The Marquess represented danger to her, even though he had been gentle with Linette.

Devlin continued, choosing not to argue the point, 'The invitation must have something to do with Ned advancing my money, or else why would he include the voucher? I think that in order to get the money, we must do as he says.'

She stiffened. 'I do not have to do as he says.'

He softened. 'Of course you do not. But I wish that you would. Nothing is more important to me than securing your future. And Linette's and Sophie's and Bart's.'

'Why?'

He looked surprised.

Her vision blurred with useless tears. 'Do you wish to go to Almack's and search for a wife?'

She watched one of his hands clench into a fist, then relax again. 'I do not *wish* to do so, but I must.'

'I cannot like it,' she said lamely.

One corner of his mouth turned up in an ironic smile. 'I cannot like it either, but we must do it for Linette's future.'

Did he mean this, or was he saying it because he knew she would do anything for Linette's sake? Her child was more important than all the rest of it. Even more important than Devlin's happiness, though it killed her to have to make that choice. She truly wanted to believe that Devlin cared so much for Linette, but men had said many things to her over the past years and she'd learned not to believe any of it.

'Linette is my concern, not yours.' She strode to the window and looked out.

He came behind her and put his hands on her shoulders. 'I have told you before. You all are my responsibility. You. Linette. Sophie. Even Bart. What kind of man would I be if I did not see to your well-being? But I need the means to do so.' He gently rubbed the tender skin of her neck with his thumbs. 'My brother controls the money, so I must do as he says for the time being. It is the price of my independence and your survival.'

'He is making you marry and you do not want to do so!' she blurted out. 'And the fault is all mine.'

He put his fingers to her lips to silence her. 'I choose to do this. Ned does not make me. Just as I will not make you go to this dinner, though I want you to do so.'

With all her heart, she did not want to go. She did not belong in polite society, and she did not trust the top-lofty Marquess, even if he did show a soft spot for her daughter.

It was unfair of Devlin to ask her to do such an unsuitable thing. How would she endure it? Madeleine pursed her lips. She had managed more unendurable things. She could manage this.

'Very well, I will attend your brother's dinner. For Linette's sake.'

'That is also why I attend,' he murmured, gazing into her eyes with a softened expression. 'Madeleine,' he whispered, his lips inches from hers. His fingers gently stroked her cheek.

The passion flared inside her, making her ache for him here in the middle of the day with the whole household up and busy. She had lost all claim to respectability with her wantonness. Worse, she had tied herself to him with her body.

He leaned closer. She felt his breath on her own mouth. She wanted him again, felt urgent for his kiss. She considered how to loosen his buckskin breeches.

Small steps pounded on the stairs. 'Mama, Mama!'

Devlin took a step back, a rueful smile on his lips. 'In here, Lady Lin.'

The Marchioness of Heronvale felt uncommonly nervous as she waited with her husband for the arrival of their dinner guests. She was anxious that her new guest approve of her, a silly worry. Since when did one concern oneself with the approval of a…such a woman?

Her husband's plan filled her with excitement, but she was afraid to even think of that, so huge were the hopes that could be dashed. So she thought instead about how scandalous it was to invite to their respectable home a woman whose attachment to a man involved carnal matters. Serena put her fingers to her cheeks to conceal her blush. What would Devlin's woman be like? What would be different about this woman that she could hold a man by bedding him? Serena felt almost unbearably wicked for pondering such things. What would Ned think of her if he knew?

Rarely did Ned require her to face the carnality of the marriage bed. When he did, all she managed to feel was anxiety that she would displease him. Displease him she always did, though he was too much of a gentleman to tell her so.

She wondered if Ned would look upon this mistress of Devlin's in that sensual way she had often glimpsed at the opera, where young dandies eyed gaudily dressed women in the pits.

It frightened her unbearably that Ned might do so, just as it frightened her to think he might have a mistress of his own. He gave her no signs of doing so, but how would she know?

As usual when she let herself dwell on such matters, she felt her eyes sting and her throat tighten. Ned would not approve if she looked as if she might cry. She steeled herself to assume a placid expression.

'My brother is late.' Ned stood at the mantel where the clock had chimed the half-hour.

Ned was always prompt, sometimes embarrassing Serena when they arrived first at a social gathering. She could never convince her husband that the time on the invitation was not the time one was expected to arrive.

She opened her mouth to make an excuse for Devlin, but shut it again. For some unknown reason, Ned lately became angry whenever Serena spoke on Devlin's behalf.

She was glad, though, that Ned had decided to advance Devlin his allowance, but it puzzled her why Devlin had now decided to pursue a wife when he was obviously involved with this mysterious woman, Miss England. It was hard to reconcile the idea that the pretty girl she'd met with Devlin was a wanton demimonde sharing his bed.

Barclay appeared at the door. 'Lord Devlin and Miss England,' he announced.

Serena rose, her heart pounding with excitement.

Devlin entered, looking handsome in his evening attire. It had been a long time since she'd seen him dressed so. His plain coat of black superfine complemented his dark hair and superbly fit his soldier's broad shoulders. Still, he managed to wear the formal clothes in that careless manner so typical of him. Serena fixed her gaze upon the young woman who stood a step behind him.

She was dazzling. Her hair, as dark as Devlin's, was piled high on her head. Natural curls framed her face and caressed the nape of her neck. She wore a delicate pearl necklace and matching teardrop pearl earrings. Not at all the jewellery one would expect of a mistress, more like a set Serena had received on her twelfth birthday.

The gold silk evening dress Miss England wore was cut in classical lines and free of adornment except for matching gold beading around the neckline and hem. Serena had seen more revealing necklines on the *ingénues* at Almack's, but this young woman's figure was such that a man's eye would certainly be drawn to that part of her. Serena glanced hurriedly at Ned, to see his reaction. He merely lifted an eyebrow.

'Ned. Serena. How good to see you!' Devlin spoke with cheerfulness. 'Let me formally present to you Miss Madeleine England. Miss England, the Marquess and Marchioness of Heronvale.'

The young woman curtsied perfectly to each of them and then stood regally, directly meeting their gazes. 'I am pleased to renew your acquaintance.' Her voice was cultured and correct, indistinguishable from one who'd had a respectable upbringing.

'Good of you to come,' Ned said stiffly. He turned to Devlin, just of hint of worry in his eyes. 'Are you well, brother?'

Devlin rolled his eyes. 'Good God, Ned, I am no longer at death's door, you know.'

Serena watched Miss England glance in surprise at Devlin's comment, concern flashing across her face. Devlin caught the look and disarmed it with the hint of a smile.

Serena was fascinated.

Barclay entered with a tray of aperitifs. They were still standing. Serena was embarrassed at her lapse of manners.

'Barclay, Miss England and I will sit on the sofa. Come, Miss England, let us sit and become better acquainted.' Serena led her guest to the sofa. The two women sat and accepted the small crystal glasses from the butler.

Serena had no idea how to converse with this beautiful young woman. 'I hope our coach brought you here satisfactorily.'

Miss England smiled cordially. 'It was kind of you to send it.'

'Well, we could not have you walk, and Devlin could not hire—' Serena stopped. It was poor manners to refer to Devlin's lack of finances, especially since Ned was the cause.

Miss England seemed to ignore her embarrassment. 'Indeed. It was most generous.'

Serena listened carefully to the expression in Miss England's voice. She was not sure what she expected—for the girl to be nervous? She did not seem so. For her to be insolent and mocking? There was none of that. Miss England seemed perfectly composed.

'I must also compliment you on your appearance,' Serena said, searching for conversation. 'Your dress is lovely.'

Miss England blushed at this and seemed for the first time to look ill at ease. What woman was not pleased with a compliment to her clothes?

'Thank you,' the girl murmured.

Serena's distress increased. She was not handling this well at all. She glanced to see if Ned noticed, but he was deep in conversation with Devlin. It pleased her to see the two brothers not slamming fists into each other. Ned loved Devlin more than he did anyone else in the world, Serena knew.

'They had a disagreement, I believe,' Miss England said, turning her head toward the two men.

The directness of this statement surprised Serena. She would never have mentioned the topic to anyone. 'Yes, they did.'

Miss England gave a faint smile. 'Perhaps Lord Devlin lost his temper with his brother.'

'I believe my husband provoked the trouble,' Serena said.

'It seems forgotten now.'

Barclay announced dinner.

'I will escort Miss England,' Ned said, bowing to her and holding out his arm. Serena felt a pang of jealousy. The young woman took the offered arm and waited until Serena, escorted by Devlin, walked ahead of her.

Devlin gave Serena a brotherly squeeze. 'Tell me, Serena, what is this about?'

She blinked. 'What is what about?'

He frowned at her. 'You know very well. This invitation.'

She bit her lip. 'We…that is, Ned… We wished to see you.'

He tossed her a sceptical glance. 'Fustian,' he whispered. 'Why did you invite Maddy?'

'So you would come?' Her answer came out like a question.

They entered the formal dining room with its crystal chandelier glittering from the candle flames. Serena wished they had set up a small table in one of the more cosy parlours, but Ned had wanted Miss England to see the opulence of the house. It was odd, though, that the young woman seemed to accept the frescoed ceiling, long mahogany table, and multipiece silver service as a matter of course. Serena had instructed the servants to set the table so that they sat at one end. Ned at the head, of course, and she to his right. To his left sat Devlin and Miss England.

Serena watched the young woman throughout dinner. Miss England never hesitated over her choice of cutlery, and she seemed completely at ease with having servants present the food. The conversation was confined to topics of general interest, upon which Miss England conversed easily, but Serena noticed that she never spoke unless she was addressed first.

Serena also watched Devlin. He checked Miss England often, concern or pride alternating in his face. She looked at Ned, whose expression never changed. Serena was struck with a pang of envy so strong she feared she might burst into tears right over the chocolate truffle.

When the port appeared, Serena was relieved to leave the dining room to the men and return to the parlour with Miss England.

Miss England selected a single chair, waiting politely for Serena to sit first. A small fire had been lit in the fireplace to ward off the chill of the damp spring night, its hiss and sputter loud in the silence between the two women.

'Would you like tea?' Serena asked finally.

'No, thank you, ma'am.' The young woman remained composed, her hands folded in her lap.

'I do wish you would call me Serena.'

Miss England glanced at her in surprise. 'I would not presume.'

'But you are Devlin's friend, and he is so dear to us.' Serena fingered the lace trim on her dress.

Madeleine's nerves were beginning to fray. She had managed the role of guest long enough. 'I am not Devlin's friend.'

This pretence seemed even more dishonest than those she was forced to enact for Farley. It was shameful for her to even set foot in this house, more flush with money than Farley could have wrested out of her in one hundred years. She wished she could excuse herself and run.

Instead she regarded the Marchioness. What could have induced this high-born, titled lady to entertain her? To ask for the intimacy of first names? There was no sense in it.

The beautiful blonde woman in her pale blue dress edged in delicate lace looked even more uncomfortable than Madeleine. Madeleine suspected the Marquess was behind this visit, and his wife compelled to go along. But why?

It certainly did not help matters that the Marchioness looked as if she might cry at any moment. 'I apologise, ma'am. I did not mean for my words to distress you.'

The Marchioness smiled faintly, blinking. 'Do not concern yourself about me. I fear I am proving a poor hostess.'

Madeleine blinked in surprise. 'Why should you be a good hostess? You ought not be compelled to entertain me at all.'

Her hostess looked up. 'Compelled? I assure you I was not compelled. It was my idea to invite you to dinner.'

'Why?' It was presumptuous of her to ask, but the word simply burst out of her.

Distress again pinched her ladyship's brow, and she gave Madeleine a pleading look. Madeleine felt a different kind of shame for distressing such a lady. Lady Heronvale had truly laboured to be kind. There had not been a moment when she had shown even a hint of the disapproval Madeleine deserved.

Madeleine glanced around the room, her eyes lighting on the figurines on the mantelpiece. 'They are Meissen, are they not?' she said, trying to find something comfortable to talk about.

'What?' The Marchioness still looked distressed.

'The figures on the mantel. They are Meissen.'

'Why, yes they, are.' Her ladyship's eyes widened with surprise.

Madeleine smiled. 'They are lovely.'

After nearly half an hour of more awkward conversation, Ned and Devlin entered the parlour. The brothers looked congenial. Madeleine did not know if this boded good or ill. In any event, what more pain could the Marquess inflict than making Devlin leave her? Devlin would leave her no matter what. The Marquess could not, after all, know her identity.

Ned surveyed the parlour and elected to stand near the mantel, upon which he leaned casually. The leg nearest the fire felt too much heat, but he ignored the discomfort. He had a good view, a position of power.

He had been pleased to be able to converse with his brother in an amicable way, though he sensed Devlin's wariness. He glanced at his wife and perceived her discomfort, as well. Miss England was more of a puzzle. She seemed serene, poised, untouched by the tensions crackling throughout the room.

Ned rubbed the elegant carving of the mantel with his thumb. The time had come. He met his wife's eye. She inhaled sharply. He would bring Serena her heart's desire.

He looked down on the young woman who should never have been invited to his wife's home. 'Miss England,' he began in a mild voice, hoping it sounded friendly.

She lifted her gaze to him, the impassive expression still in her eyes.

'What think you of our house here in town?'

A flicker of surprise showed in her face, but she quickly changed her expression to one he could not read. Mocking? Melancholic? 'It is a magnificent home, my lord. Very fine.'

He smiled. 'I am pleased that you think so.'

She returned his smile. 'I did not realise you sought my good opinion.'

That statement must be sarcasm, but he could not tell for certain. He ignored it, clearing his throat. 'This house pales in comparison to Heronvale. Heronvale is a piece of heaven.' Ned glanced at Devlin. 'It was a marvellous place to be reared, was it not, Devlin?'

Devlin's eyes narrowed suspiciously. He lounged in a chair, but one leg crossed over the other swung with nervous energy. 'It had fine stables.'

Ned laughed, hoping to dispel his brother's tension. 'My brother saw little of Heronvale except on the back of a horse. Did you know that, Miss England?'

The smile was fixed on her face. 'Indeed.'

This woman gave up little of her feelings, Ned thought.

'Miss England is an accomplished horsewoman,' Devlin said.

'Is that so?' Ned remembered the child's excitement seeing the horses of his curricle. He had assumed her passion for horses had come from her father. 'You and my brother have that in common, then.'

Miss England shrugged her reply.

This was like fencing with an opponent reluctant to reveal his skill. Perhaps he should begin the attack.

He strolled over to a decanter of claret, lifting it to offer its contents to the others. Devlin shook his head and Serena mumbled 'No, thank you.'

'I should like some,' Miss England said, and Ned had the foolish impression that they had each chosen their weapons. He handed her a glass and poured one for himself. He took a sip.

First lunge. 'Did you know my brother is a wealthy man, Miss England?'

Her glass pressed against her lips and her taste of the wine was long and delicate. 'Is one wealthy who has no money to spend?' Parry.

Riposte. 'You know, then, that Devlin must marry?'

Her brows lifted. 'For his wealth, he must marry, unless you declare otherwise.' Well parried. Too well parried.

'He must marry. His heritage demands it. Do you understand?'

She stared at him, bringing her glass to her lips again.

Ned abandoned the fencing and indulged in a rare display of anger. 'His behaviour with you has been irresponsible. Unbecoming in a gentleman—'

Devlin rose from his chair. 'Enough, Ned. These are words to be spoken to me in private. I will not have you do so in front of Madeleine.'

Ned took a step toward his brother. 'You took a mistress when you knew full well you could not keep her in clothes or jewels—'

'She does not want—'

Ned closed the distance on his brother. 'You involved a child, Devlin. A child. How irresponsible is that?'

Serena gasped.

'You know nothing of this matter, Ned. I have said I will find a wife, what more do you want? I'll accept my bloody heritage and be damned, but you owe Madeleine an apology.' Devlin's eyes blazed with anger. 'She has done nothing to deserve these words of yours.'

'She has borne a child, has she not?' Ned paced back to

the mantel. Devlin stood his ground. Turning to face them again, Ned saw the alarm in Serena's face. Miss England looked on, alert.

'The home you have contrived is no place for a child,' he said. 'The little girl needs comfort and education and a solid moral foundation. You cannot give that to her, Devlin.'

'I can and will take care of the child. Why do you think I agreed to marry? You've left me no other way to take care of them, have you? Well, brother, you may bet on it that Madeleine and Linette will be well cared for.' Devlin's fists were clenched and his body poised for a fight. 'By me.'

Ned paced the floor. 'You cannot provide her a good home. What will the child learn of life in a household like that, with you arriving at odd hours to warm her mother's bed?'

'Damn you, Ned. You have stepped too far over the line.' Devlin's face became a rigid, angry mask. Ned thought this might be how he appeared galloping toward a company of bayonet-wielding Frenchmen.

'Ned?' Serena's fingers crushed the fabric of her dress.

He glanced from Serena to Miss England, her hands folded demurely and her gazed fixed on them. Damn his brother for compromising that young woman.

And damn himself for being glad of it.

He would not back away now, not when he had come so far. He slowed his breaths and moderated his voice. 'I do apologise. I did not intend to ring a peal over your head.'

Devlin's hands curved into fists.

'Serena and I wish to help. It is why we invited you here.'

Miss England raised her head.

'We believe it would be advantageous to everyone, if you agree with our proposition.'

Devlin still glowered, but showed a hint of curiosity, as well.

Ned went on. 'We wish to adopt the child and raise her as our own…'

Chapter Twelve

'**G**ood God, Ned.' Devlin turned away from his brother and
drew a tense hand through his hair. Ned wanted the child?
'What right have you to propose such a thing?'

He heard the Marquess take a deep breath. 'I am head of
the family, you might recall.'

'What the deuce has that to do with it?' Devlin swung back
to him.

Ned made no effort to respond, simply staring back.

Devlin's mind reeled with his brother's words. Ned thought
he had seduced Madeleine. Thought she pined for dresses and
jewels. Thought he could take Linette from her.

'Serena and I realise—' Ned's voice was steady and reasonable '—that there may be talk about our raising your child,
but we are prepared—'

'*My* child?'

'Linette.' Ned went on. 'Such talk would disappear as soon
as something more interesting came along. So I would not—'

'My child?' Devlin repeated, raising his voice.

'Of course,' Ned glanced at him and continued talking. 'It
would be no time…'

Devlin stared at his brother, impeccably dressed in white
breeches and superbly cut black coat. His hair, flecked with
grey, remained neat and orderly. Did his ever-perfect brother

think he'd seduced Madeleine, got her with child, then abandoned her to go off to war? Only a cad would do such a thing.

Devlin longed to explain to Ned he was not that sort of man. Explain that Madeleine had been Farley's prize. That the child might be anybody's. Serena might blush, but how scandalised could she be? An occasional tumble with such a woman was expected of young men. His brother might lift a disapproving eyebrow, but he could not damn Devlin's character. Yes, all that was needed to clear his name was to expose Madeleine's life under Farley and shame her in front of Ned and Serena.

Devlin tried to keep his voice steady. 'What causes you to think the child mine?'

Ned gave him a look of exasperation. 'She looks like you.'

'She looks like Maddy.' A vision of Linette flashed through Devlin's mind. Her curly dark hair always falling from its ribbon. The clear blue innocence of her eyes. The pouty mouth when she did not get her way. So much like Madeleine. From his first glimpse of the child, his heart had reached out to the little girl. She was Madeleine as a child.

'She is the image of you at that age,' Ned countered. 'If you do not believe me, come to Heronvale and check the family portrait in the music room. She is even named for you. She was obviously conceived during your leave from Spain. The timing is correct. How you supported them in your absence is a mystery, but there is no mystery about the fact that she is your child.'

'My child.' Stunned, Devlin made his own calculation. His one brief encounter with Madaleine. The child's age. He'd never considered.

Madeleine stared down at her lap, her knuckles turning white as she gripped her hands. The Marquess's words echoed as if emerging from a distant cave. Saying he wanted to take Linette. Saying Linette was Devlin's child.

She stood and spoke with cold rage. '*My* child.'

These men were no different than Farley and the ones he had sent to her bed. They all wielded power over her. The power to control her life, to violate her body…and to steal from her all that was dear. This rich Marquess controlled with his title and money. What chance had she against such weapons? Even Devlin, for all his pretty words, held her life and her daughter's in his hands. He could crush them both in an eye blink. He could cast them into the street. Abandon them to his brother.

Send them back to Farley.

Madeleine's body trembled. Panic mixed with rage. Three sets of eyes stared at her. The Marquess's with a look of impatience. His wife's with tears rolling down her cheeks. And Devlin's with confusion and surprise.

Madeleine held herself erect, lifting her chin high. These people would not see she feared their power. Indeed, she would not fear it. She would defy it. No one would take Linette from her. No one.

She let a faint smile cross her face and spoke again, her voice mild. 'Linette is my child.'

And, as they stood poised to hear more, she bolted. She ran out the mahogany parlour door, down the white marble stairs and through the hall, glittering with gilt. She heard Devlin shout her name. Heard the Marchioness wail, and the Marquess call for someone to stop her.

No one did. She flung open the front door and ran out into the street. She cared not that she held her skirts high away from her ankles, nor that the silk slippers scuffed roughly against the pavement. She would get to Linette first. She would grab Linette and Sophie and run.

She had only a vague notion of which direction to take, but trusted that her need to protect Linette would lead her home. Shouts sounded from behind her. She dared not look back. She'd always been fleet-footed. None of the lads she'd grown up around could best her in a race and no one would best her now.

'Maddy!' It was Devlin's voice.

She ran faster, past the elegant houses and neatly swept streets, ghostly in the lamplight. Ahead was a jumble of carriages, polished and shining, clogging the street. Elegantly liveried footmen milled about. Candlelight blazed from a house and, as she neared it, Madeleine heard sounds of music and revelry coming from the windows. She also heard Devlin's shoes pounding behind her. Coachmen and postilions glanced curiously in her direction. There was nothing to do but head straight for them. She plunged into the crowd.

Devlin's lungs strained and his legs ached as he pushed himself into greater speed. His months of recovery had robbed him of more strength than he had known. Madeleine was in sight. He gained on her slightly when she disappeared into the throng of vehicles and men lounging in front of the elegant town house. A satisfactory crush by the looks of it, but he had been out of society so long he could not even remember whose house it was. He only knew Madeleine would draw attention to herself in her flight. He must catch her before danger befell her. What could she be thinking of running into the night alone and unprotected?

He slowed, trying to get a glimpse of her in the confusion.

'Lord Devlin?' A man panted as he came up behind him.

Devlin greeted him with relief. 'Jem. Help me find her.'

Bless Jem. He asked no questions, but immediately ran to search from the edge of the line of carriages. Devlin headed through the jam where he'd seen Madeleine disappear. The commotion ahead of him told him he was close.

'Hey, missy, what is your hurry?' Men's voices laughed. 'Stop now, missy.'

Would she appear to be a lady to them? The coachmen and postilions would be whiling away the hours of waiting with a bit of drink. Boredom and drink were dangerous companions. He glimpsed her, seeing only a bit of her gold silk before men closed behind her, calling after her. Were they grabbing at her? Please no. They would not molest her here in Mayfair. St James's Street was the danger. Not Mayfair.

She turned, giving Devlin an anguished look. Jem had circled behind her. He caught her in flight.

'It's all right, Maddy. Jem is a friend,' Devlin said to her, as she struggled to get free. 'You are safe with us.'

'Let me go,' she cried. 'Let me go.'

Jem did let her go, but not until Devlin had her firmly in hand, one arm encircling her waist.

Devlin saw one of the footmen look curiously in their direction. He thought it prudent to avoid further trouble. 'Come, let us get away.'

Jem led them to the entrance of an alleyway. Madeleine thrashed and kicked as Devlin half-dragged her into the alley. 'I want to go.'

Devlin kept his arm tight around her waist. 'Jem, can you send the carriage? I assume you made it ready for us.'

'Yes, sir.' He ran off.

Madeleine squirmed and struggled in Devlin's arms. 'Let me go,' she cried feebly. 'Let me go.'

He leaned her against the cold stone wall and secured her with his body, his arms embracing her. Her struggles quieted, but she trembled against him, her breath ragged.

'You are safe now, Maddy,' he whispered in her ear. 'I will not hurt you.'

'You will let him take Linette,' she cried.

'No, I will not,' he spoke soothingly in her ear.

'He will make you do it,' she insisted. 'Just as he makes you get married.'

The truth in that statement stung. Ned held the power over his fortune, and he needed that fortune to safeguard Madeleine and Linette. Devlin had no means to combat him.

A few weeks ago Devlin would have bet his entire fortune that his brother would never to do anything so dastardly. Now Ned was like a stranger, capable of anything.

Trying to sound confident, he assured her, 'Ned will not take Linette from you, I promise.'

'I am sick to death of gentlemen's promises.' She spat out the words. 'Promises mean nothing.'

'Mine do,' Devlin insisted, offended and hurt that she would think him like other men, after all they had been through.

She met his eyes, her own a challenge. 'Do they?'

What was the use? She would not believe him. He cursed Farley and every man who had failed her. He cursed himself. It had not occurred to him to take her away from that life when he first met her. Had he done so, she'd have been spared years of suffering, of rearing her child in such a scandalous place.

Her child. His child, perhaps? Had he left his own flesh and blood to Farley's evil whims? Perhaps Ned's ill opinion of him was well deserved.

Her struggles ceased, but though his body was pressed against hers, he felt her distance.

The carriage pulled up with Jem on the box beside the driver. Devlin walked her to it.

She looked up. 'I will not ride in *his* carriage.'

'Do not be foolish, Maddy. Let us get out of here.' Curious bystanders started to gather, doubtless trying to see the crest on the side of the vehicle.

'No.' She tried to pull away.

'Enough of this,' Devlin said, more to himself than to Madeleine. He picked her up and tossed her into the carriage, jumping in behind. 'Go!' he shouted to Jem.

The carriage lurched, and Devlin fell against her. She pushed him away. Crossing her arms over her chest, she huddled against the side of the carriage, as far away from him as possible. A tear trickled down her cheek.

Feeling miserable, Devlin rubbed the back of his neck. Her dress was wrinkled and dirty, her shoes near tatters, her hair half-tumbled from its pins.

She glanced at him briefly before turning back to the curtain.

'Maddy?'

She did not respond.

Devlin took a breath. 'Linette…is she…is she my child?'

Madeleine shut her eyes and focused on the rhythmic sounds of the horses' hooves against the cobbles. She had intended for this moment never to come.

She turned to him. 'I do not know.'

There was little light in the carriage, and she could only dimly see his face. She could not read his expression.

She continued, 'She could be your child.'

He made a sound, an aching one. 'How? From that first night, I suppose, but how could you know?'

He meant how could a woman who had been with countless men say that one of them fathered a child? She winced.

'I do not pretend to know.' She had promised herself never to believe Devlin fathered her child. She'd always told herself naming her Linette was in memory of a man who had been kind to her, nothing more. But sometimes, when she gazed upon her daughter, she believed otherwise.

'It is possible, nothing more.' She felt her throat tighten. The memory of that night, both with him and afterward, was etched in her mind.

'I was a foolish girl. You undoubtedly will think me so.' She attempted a light tone to her voice. 'When you left that night, I did not do as I was supposed to do. I did not wash myself. I fancied it would keep you with me a little longer.'

She heard his breath quicken.

'And when Farley came to me, I refused him.' She winced at this part. 'I had never refused him before, and he beat me soundly, but he did not bed me. The next day, he left. He was gone a long time, more than a month.'

Those rare times when Farley left had been the best her life had to offer in those days. She was guarded against running away, but none of his lackeys dared touch her and the gaming hell ran without her as the prize.

'Maddy.'

He reached for her, but she twisted away. 'By the time Farley returned, I knew I was with child. I hid the fact from him as long as possible. He wanted to get rid of the baby, but I threatened to kill myself if he did.'

'Maddy, I'm sorry.' Devlin reached out to her, but she pushed his hand away.

'Linette has been reward enough. I ask for nothing more.'

'I should have been there to help you.' He sounded anguished.

How like a man to be sorry for what he had not done, though he probably gave not a thought to it until this moment. Did Devlin think his regret made any difference to her? He had not believed Linette to be his child and looked for excuses not to believe so now. His words were empty.

'I will not let the Marquess take Linette,' she said. 'Sophie and I will take her away this night. You need not trouble yourself further with us.'

'You will not leave, do you understand?' He spoke sharply. 'It is not safe for you.'

'You cannot make me stay.' She twisted toward him. 'Unless you plan to hold me prisoner like Farley did. Under guard every moment.'

'He kept you under guard?'

'At first. After Linette was born, he guarded her.'

'Damn.' The word barely reached her ears.

They rode in silence, the creaks of the carriage and the sounds of the horses' hooves filling their ears until the carriage came to a stop. Jem hopped down from the box and opened the carriage door. Devlin lifted Madeleine out.

'Wait for me, Jem,' Devlin said.

'You are going back?' Madeleine said, fear creeping back.

'I need to speak to my brother.'

They would plot the stealing of her child. Devlin would

give Linette to the high-minded Marquess and flawless Marchioness.

'Do you keep me here? Do you alert Bart to guard the door?'

He attempted to take her by the elbow, but she pushed him away and ran hurriedly to the door. He caught up with her there, pulling the key from his pocket. He gripped her arm with his other hand as they entered the house. The hallway was lit with two candles, the rest of the house, quiet.

Devlin took her by the shoulders and forced her to look at him. 'Nothing is changed, Maddy. I promised you that I would take care of you and Linette, and I will fulfil that promise. I will not take Linette from you, nor let my brother do so. I promise you on my honour.'

She glared at him and tried to back out of his grasp. 'More talk of promises.'

He kept his grip on her shoulders and kept in step with her. 'You must stay here, Maddy.'

'You do not command me, my lord.' She backed into the wall.

He moved towards her still. 'I must command you in this. There are dangers out there for you and Sophie and Linette. Men like Farley and far worse. You would not be safe if you left, and I would not be able to protect you.'

'I am not safe here.' He was too close now, his hands on the wall and his legs spread apart like a cage entrapping her. 'You would give my child away.'

He gave an exasperated bark. 'Damn it, Maddy. I will not.'

She stared at him as he loomed over her. His features blurred in the dim light. More vivid was the scent of him, the warmth of him.

He rubbed his cheek, rough with stubble, against hers and brought his lips near her ear. 'You may not believe my promises, but I will believe yours. Promise me you will not run away. You will stay here until I have the means to set you up in your own house, wherever you wish.'

Her breath quickened, swelling her chest so that it touched his with each breath. She wanted to believe him. Wanted to believe he was the soldier returned from the war to rescue her, to whisk her and her daughter to a pretty little cottage where they would live happily forever.

His lips touched the sensitive skin of her ear. 'Promise.'

She squirmed under the sensations his lips created, making her press against his pelvis. She forced herself to place her back flat against the wall.

She also forced herself to think realistically. It was more likely he would barter her child to his brother. Linette would be wrenched from her arms and sent to live in the Marquess's house, and Devlin would be free to pursue whatever pleasure he wished. Linette would have sugared treats and pretty clothes and a pony of her own. There would always be a fire warming her room and food filling her belly. She would learn to call the kind-hearted Marchioness 'Mama' and the Marquess, who had looked upon her with such tenderness, 'Papa'.

A sob escaped her lips. Devlin gathered her into his arms and she soaked his jacket with her tears.

'Promise you will not run away,' he murmured. 'Let me keep you safe.' He lifted her chin and placed his lips on hers.

For a moment she melted into him and allowed him to pet her and taste the tender interior of her mouth. For a moment she believed him. Catching herself, she struggled in his arms, wrenching her face away from him. He released her, pain written on his face.

She ran up the stairs without a backward glance.

Devlin returned more than two hours later. The candles in the hallway were burned to nubs. He pinched them out before ascending the stairs. His heart pounded in his chest.

Had she stayed?

When he had arrived back in Grosvenor Square, his brother and Serena still sat in the parlour. Serena's eyes were red with crying. She twisted a damp handkerchief with her fingers. His brother poured from an almost-empty decanter of brandy.

Serena had gasped when he reappeared.

'She is safe at home,' he announced.

He then endured his brother's lecture, watching the clock on the mantel pass midnight, wondering all the while if Madeleine waited for him, or if she had run. He declared to Ned that he, not the Marquess, would care for Madeleine and the child, had explained that their care was his whole motivation for marrying. He accepted Serena's shocked protests regarding such a marriage plan and allowed his brother to exact from him a promise to disengage from Madeleine and her child after his marriage. Ned rang another peal over his head about the destructiveness of debauchery and the necessity of relieving Madeleine of the disreputable status of mistress. Devlin had resisted the temptation to tell Ned the promise was unnecessary. Ned renewed his offer to adopt the child. Serena even proposed the unlikely option for Madeleine to become the governess.

Before Devlin bid Ned and Serena goodnight, Ned had discussed with him the financial obligations of engaging in courtship. They had come to agreeable terms.

Now, as Devlin mounted the stairs to where his two charges should be sleeping, his pockets were weighted with gold coin and a promise had been extracted from him to accompany Serena to Almack's the coming evening. All of which seemed of no consequence at all.

Devlin paused upon the top step, trying to sense if he would find Linette's little bed unoccupied, drawers void of contents, trunks bare.

Madeleine gone.

He knocked gently on Madeleine's door and opened it. The lamplight from the street provided dim illumination to the room. The light rested on Linette's bed.

The little girl slept peacefully. Her long lashes brushed the tops of her chubby cheeks and her little pink lips moved around the thumb tucked securely in her mouth.

He leaned over to watch her. My child? he asked himself.

He still could not see it. The little girl looked like a tiny, innocent Madeleine, before she'd encountered life's ugliness. Devlin reached out his hand and brushed his fingers through the child's dark curls.

Did it matter to him if she were his child or not? Would he feel the same ache in his heart at the prospect of losing her if he knew her to be from the seed of some other man?

He would never know.

Devlin glanced toward the larger bed, expecting to see Madeleine looking similarly peaceful in sleep, but the bed was empty. His heart accelerated and panic rushed back. Had she gone? He pressed his fingers against his temple.

And felt the point of a sword sharp in the small of his back.

Chapter Thirteen

'You will not take my child, Devlin.'

Madeleine pressed the point of the sabre into Devlin's back.

She had waited in the shadows of the room for over an hour. Each moment he had been away convinced her he was plotting with his brother to take Linette. She was furious with herself for being too cowardly to grab her child, wake Sophie, and flee.

She had finally decided that if Devlin returned home and went directly to his room, he was worthy of her trust. But if he entered her room, thinking her asleep, it would be to take her daughter. And she would be ready for him.

She had taken the sword from where it rested against the wall in his room, unsheathed its curved blade, and waited in the darkness. When he entered, she moved like a cat, silent and predatory, until the sword's point rested against his back.

'Maddy.' He started to turn.

'No!' She pushed on the sword. Its sharp point pierced the cloth.

He became still. 'I was not attempting to take her.'

'I do not believe you.' She kept pressure on the sword.

'I kept my word to you. Remove the sword.'

Her hand trembled. His coat ripped.

'You are piercing my skin, Maddy.' His voice was mild. Deceptively so, she thought.

'Why did you come in this room, if not to take her?' Madeleine's voice quavered. She had not truly intended to draw his blood.

He did not answer. He remained very still for what seemed to be an eternity. 'I merely wished to look at her.'

Something wistful sounded in his voice, and Madeleine faltered. Perhaps it mattered a trifle to him that Linette might be his child. Her grasp on the sabre relaxed slightly.

Devlin whirled around, his movement so swift she was not sure how he achieved it. He grabbed her wrist and wrenched the sabre from her grasp, catching the hilt of the falling sword in his other hand.

She cried out.

He whipped the sword to point at her. Madeleine shrank back. His face held no expression at all.

'If you must use the sabre, Maddy,' he said in a rumbling tone, 'it is not for stabbing, but for cutting and slicing.'

The sword whirred as he cut and sliced the air, fluttering the lace of her nightdress. He pointed the sword inches from her nose. Her heart hammered painfully against her chest.

Ever so slowly, his eyes not leaving hers, he lowered his arm so that the blade pointed to the floor.

'Now, heed me, Maddy.' His eyes narrowed. 'I offer you my protection. That includes Linette and Sophie, as well. You may accept or leave. You know the world you face if you spurn my offer, but perhaps you would prefer the dangers of the street...' he paused and blinked '...to me.'

Madeleine's heart slowed and she allowed herself to breathe, her thoughts a hopeless muddle.

She dreaded the idea of leaving him. Dreaded the thought that he would marry. She had persuaded herself he would steal Linette from her. How could she have thought that? He had rescued her. He planned to marry to support her and Linette. But how could he not have accepted the offer his brother had made? Linette would receive everything as the child of the Marquess.

'What is your wish?' he snapped.

Her wish? What she could not have. Her throat constricted, with frustration and despair. 'I will stay with you.'

He whipped the sword blade up into a salute, then turned and left the room.

Madeleine collapsed on to her bed and squeezed her eyes tight. She had cut him and made him bleed. She had torn his clothes.

She heard him slamming and banging things in his room, as well as the muffled sounds of swearing. She lay in the darkness and listened. What would happen in the morning? The one time she had totally defied Farley he had beaten her senseless. She had done so much more to Devlin. His forgiveness was impossible.

The cuirassier rode his midnight-black steed over a mass of writhing blue-coated bodies. Sunlight glinted off his metal breastplate and the sharply honed blade of his sword. The wind whipped the horsehair plume on his helmet while his black moustache quivered. The Frenchman laughed, and the sound echoed, merging with the moans of the wounded. The stench of war's carnage filled Devlin's nostrils, and he struggled to run, to retreat, but bloody hands clasped his ankles, holding him fast. Escape was impossible.

The huge Frenchman, a grin showing his yellow teeth, slowly raised the sword over his head and brought it down, closer and closer—

'No!' Devlin cried.

Hands grabbed him and shook him.

'Devlin, wake up! You are dreaming. Wake up!'

He fought, bucking and rearing and pushing the hands away. The voice became more urgent. 'Wake up!'

He opened his eyes, expecting to see each face of each man he had ever killed.

He saw Madeleine. She was straddling him, her nightdress hiked above her knees. Her hands were clasped around his wrists and he pushed against them, trying to free himself.

'It was only a dream, Devlin,' she said, her tone soothing.

He stared at her. *Madeleine.* Was she real? Perhaps she was the dream and if he closed his eyes again, the faces of the dead would return. He widened his gaze. His sheets were damp with sweat and his heart pounded like the drums of the French.

'There is no danger now.'

Madeleine. He ought to be furious at her, he dimly recalled, but he was so damned glad she was here. He relaxed his arms and, by so doing, caused her body to lie flush against his nakedness. As the last wisps of the nightmare evaporated, he turned his face from her, ashamed of his terror.

Madeleine stroked his hair. 'There, there.' She spoke as to a child awoken by dreams of goblins. 'It is all gone now. Nothing to signify.' Her lips touched the sensitive skin of his neck. Her body was warm, like a blanket.

'It will never go away,' he mumbled.

The first light of dawn shone through the window and the clatter of workmen's wagons testified that ordinary life proceeded, in spite of his private horror. His eyes moistened. Madeleine took his chin in her hand, turning his head to face her and kissing each eyelid.

Relief and gratitude washed through him, leaving him drained. He lifted his head to kiss her and tasted the salt of his tears on her lips. If only his world could consist solely of this. Why could life not be as simple as a man and woman making love?

She moaned softly and opened her mouth, giving, yet demanding more. Devlin pulled her nightdress over her head, his hands sliding against her smooth skin and full breasts. He was hard and urgent beneath her and desperate to feel the comfort she offered. He lifted her slightly and, as if she anticipated his desire, she gave him access.

Devlin's world became simple. Madeleine was here and his body pulsed with the sensation of her. Her hair tumbled forward, her curls tickling his face. Her pink lips parted with passion and her eyes half closed. She felt warm and smooth beneath his hands, her breasts soft on his chest. He grasped at her, feeling greedy and fearing she, like all that was beautiful, would disappear and he would fall into the cauldron of destruction and death from which he would never escape.

'Madeleine,' he growled, his need for her primal.

She gasped, and he felt her convulse around him. He exploded inside her, pleasure and peace filling him.

She relaxed, lying next to him and gazing at him. Devlin wanted nothing to break this moment.

Her blue eyes searched his, concern filling them.

He attempted a smile. 'I am quite all right now.'

Her concern did not disappear. 'I have heard you restless in your sleep before this.'

The nightmare came often enough. 'And you did not offer this comfort?' he joked.

The familiar masked look came over her and her body tensed. 'You had only to ask, my lord.'

'Shh, Maddy,' he whispered. 'I meant only a poor jest. Do not spoil this moment.'

She slipped away and reached for her nightdress. The moment had been spoiled. 'Your dream,' she said, thrusting her arms through her sleeves. 'Was it of Waterloo?' Her tone was almost conversational, but she had brought back the horror with the word.

Waterloo.

'I do not wish to say.' He spoke through clenched teeth.

'You promised you would tell me of Waterloo,' she reminded him. It sounded a scold.

'You promised me you would tell me of Farley,' he countered, mimicking her tone.

'I will,' she said. 'But first you must tell me of Waterloo.'

He turned his back on her. He felt her move toward him on the bed. Her fingers touched the sabre cut she had inflicted.

He wished to run from the memories, as he tried to run from the visions that plagued him at odd moments during the day and the dreams that tortured him at night, the ones drinking and debauchery had never quite erased.

'And if I do not, do you impale me with my sword again?'

She inhaled sharply, then kissed the wound she had made. 'I am sorry, Devlin.'

His words made him feel small.

'You carried the sabre that day, did you not?'

Damn her. She would not leave it alone. Well, she would hear it, then. All the horror. She would see what kind of man had lain with her.

'It is not a story for delicate ears.' Let it not be said he did not warn her.

'My ears have heard much that is not delicate.'

He had forgotten for a moment that her world had contained its own version of hell.

He took a deep breath. 'First there were the guns…'

French cannon had thundered and pounded destruction through the allied ranks before the relentless rhythm of the drums signalled the first French infantry assault. Devlin again heard the screams, and saw bodies being torn apart.

Wellington's motley mix of untried Allied troops was far outnumbered by the thousands and thousands of French, resplendent in new glittering uniforms, eager to bring glory to the emperor who had miraculously returned to them.

By the time the order came for the cavalry to charge, Devlin and his men lusted for French blood. They became drunk with vengeance, wreaking destruction on French infantry who broke and ran. He remembered the exhilaration of slashing his sword at men who were merely trying to run to safety. The air reeked of blood and sweat, gunpowder and grass. He told Madeleine how he rode over bodies and their severed parts, over men still moving and men who would move no more.

She listened. He sat facing her, his legs crossed in front of him on the bed. She kept her eyes on his, but he saw nothing but the memories.

'The killing did not last,' he said.

She reached over to him, placing her hand on his arm.

'The cuirassiers came.' He closed his eyes, again seeing them, hundreds of them mounted on fresh horses, shiny in their gold-tasselled uniforms. 'They rode slowly at first, then picked up the pace, like rocks tumbling from a cliff, faster and faster, until, raining down so fiercely, they bury you. I called out for the men to retreat, but they did not hear me.'

She squeezed his arm.

He met her gaze. 'Our horses were blown. We were no match for them. The cuirassiers had their revenge. My men screamed and died as the French infantry had done at our hands.'

'You watched this?' she asked, her voice hushed.

If he shut his eyes again, he would see it still. 'I was alone for the moment, the dead on the ground around me. Only for a moment…'

'Oh, Devlin.' Her hand stroked his arm, sending shivers.

'I was not alone for long. A French officer mounted on a huge black horse headed toward me. There was no escaping him. I was hampered by the dead and dying, you see. My horse could not manoeuvre.'

Devlin could still recall the man's chipped and yellowing teeth, each pockmark on his face, the glee of victory in his near-black eyes.

'Did he attack you?'

Devlin gave a dry laugh. 'He attacked my horse.'

Poor Courage. Courage had been a clod-footed, stout-hearted animal with an instinct for battle. The horse had saved his life more than once.

'That is the best means of crippling cavalry.' He gave a half-smile. 'We are nothing without our horses.'

Madeleine did not smile back.

He rubbed his hands. 'The Frenchman slashed at my horse with his sword. Skilful job, it was. Threw me off. Almost lost my sword. I managed to recover it, but he'd already had a go at me.' He fingered one of his scars. 'I cannot fathom why he did not finish me off. He jabbed at me. I rolled in the mud to escape him, while my horse screamed and stumbled nearby. Not exactly a heroic end.'

'But it was not the end,' she said.

'He meant it to be. I can still hear him laugh at my feeble attempts to fend him off. I kept rolling, until I rolled into an irrigation ditch. He slipped at the edge and tumbled down on top of me, impaling himself on my sword.'

She gasped.

'I heard the Frenchman draw his last breath, and my horse fell dead across the ditch, entombing me with my dead enemy.'

'Oh, my.' Her hand went to her mouth.

Devlin, suddenly chilled, wrapped the bed's blanket around him. Again he felt the cold mud seep into his back and the still-warm blood of the Frenchman soak his chest.

A tear trickled down Madeleine's cheek. Devlin was surprised at the tear's effect on him. Something near pain, near pleasure.

He would spare her the real horror. The sounds of the battle raging above him. The cries of the dying and wounded. The cold bleakness of the endless night, looters rustling above him. The stark terror that he would be discovered and killed for his silver buttons and leather boots.

'Bart found me the next day.'

'How did he find you among so many?' she asked, her voice raspy.

He gave her an ironic smile. 'I was quite hidden from view. He found my horse.'

'Your horse?' Her eyes widened again, this time with surprise.

'I had remained in the ditch, under the horse, under the Frenchman.'

'Devlin…' she whispered, reaching to stroke his cheek.

He moved away, not from her sympathy but from the memory that provoked it. 'I do not remember much of the rest. Bart carried me to Brussels. Then Ned came. Days had passed, I've been told. Ned brought me home on the yacht, to die at Heronvale.'

'But you did not die,' she said, as if that had been of some significance.

'That is it,' he whispered. 'Why did I not? Why great numbers of other men and not me? I killed many. Why did that damned Frenchman not kill me?'

Madeleine watched his face break. He squeezed his eyes shut and grimaced. She wrapped her arms around him and pressed his head against her breast. Sobs racked his body and his breath came in heaves.

'So you could save me,' she told him. 'That is why the Frenchman did not kill you. So you could save *me*.'

He drew away from her and stared, stunned.

Madeleine looked upon him and filled with tenderness. She memorised each line on his face. She repeated his words in her head so she would never forget what he had endured. The incident at his brother's faded. She pushed it from her mind. There was no stabbing him with his sword, no conspiring to steal her child. There was only the need to ease his suffering, his pain and guilt. And to think of how close she had come to losing him.

He leaned back against the bedboard and took a deep breath.

'Do you feel better?' she asked.

He nodded.

'Nothing helps more than a good cry.' She smiled. A good

cry had never helped her, but it seemed the proper thing to say.

He smiled back, this time wide enough for the dimple to crease his cheek. His eyes were still red and puffy, and his nose bright pink. She thought, perhaps, he had never looked so appealing. She smoothed his hair, her heart tender for him.

There was a jiggle at the connecting door and it opened. 'Mama?'

Linette stood in the doorway rubbing her eyes. Devlin hurriedly wrapped the blanket around him. 'Mama?' she said again, finally finding Madeleine.

She trotted to the bed and climbed atop it. Madeleine gathered her in her arms. 'Good morning, my darling.'

'I heard you and Deddy.' The little girl peered at Devlin who clutched the blanket around him. Linette touched his damp cheek and looked puzzled. 'Deddy cry?'

'A little,' explained Madeleine. 'He had a bad dream.'

Linette scrambled out of her mother's arms and into Devlin's, giving him a big hug. 'There, there,' she said, patting his back. 'All gone now.'

Devlin's gaze caught Madeleine's, his eyes moist again.

'Thank you, Lady Lin,' he said. 'I think I am better now.'

Linette grinned in triumph. Devlin fingered the dimple in her cheek.

'Young lady, shall we get dressed for breakfast?' Madeleine asked, her throat tight with emotion. 'Bart and Sophie will be expecting us.'

The child jumped off the bed. 'Deddy come, too,' she said imperiously as Madeleine took her hand.

'I'll be down directly.'

Madeleine glanced over her shoulder before walking back to her room. He remained on the bed, staring back at them.

A half-hour later, Devlin entered the kitchen. He overheard Bart asking, 'Did his brother advance him the money?'

He sat at the table. 'Indeed he did, my friend.'

Madeleine spooned some porridge into a bowl and poured him some tea.

Devlin glanced at the bowl with dismay. 'Today you must replenish our larder, Bart. Bacon and boiled eggs for breakfast tomorrow.'

'Bacon, bacon, bacon…' sang Linette, a white moustache of milk on her lip.

'And wages for you both,' Devlin continued.

Sophie, whose eyes had remained downcast when he entered the room, looked up with awe.

Bart turned red. 'Now, I was not asking about my wages, but there is a matter I wish to discuss.'

'What is it?'

Sophie slipped out of her chair and retreated to a stool in the corner.

Bart fidgeted with his spoon and for once avoided glancing toward Sophie. 'I…er…um…'

'Out with it, man,' Devlin insisted.

'I wish to arrange for the banns to be read.' He gripped the spoon. 'For Miss Sophie and myself.'

Except for Linette's incessant song about bacon, the room went quiet as the significance of the words penetrated.

Devlin glanced at Madeleine, who had frozen, looking pale.

'Well,' gulped Devlin. 'I see.'

Poor Bart and Sophie stared at them warily and Sophie looked about to cry.

'Why, it's wonderful news!' Madeleine jumped out of her seat and rushed over to hug Sophie. 'We were taken by surprise by it, were we not, Devlin?'

'Yes, surprised,' he agreed. He followed Madeleine's example, clapping Bart on the back. 'God help our Sophie, marrying this crusty fellow.' They all laughed except Sophie, who rarely expressed that much emotion. She did manage to smile.

Devlin reached into his pocket and pulled out a pouch of coins. He counted out a generous amount. 'Here you are, with extra for a betrothal gift.'

'No, it must be three times what you owe,' Bart protested, pushing the stack of coins away. 'You must save the money, Dev. We mustn't go short again.'

'Nonsense.' Devlin pushed the stack of coins back and sat in his chair. 'Now that I intend to assiduously follow my brother's wishes, he will continue to fund me.'

Linette, attracted by the coins, climbed on Devlin's lap, now singing nonsense words. She peeked inside the pouch. Devlin let her pour the coins on the table.

'See? We are flush in the pockets again.' Devlin gestured to the pile of coins.

'Fush,' Linette said, intently concentrating on stacking the coins as Devlin had done.

Madeleine watched Devlin finger Linette's soft curls, the expression on his face soft and tender. She stared as he gingerly kissed Linette on the top of her head.

'If it is agreeable to you, we should be about the business.' Bart had spoken. Perhaps he had spoken before, but she had not heard and, apparently, neither had Devlin.

'By all means,' said Devlin. He pushed a few more coins to Bart. 'Here. This will pay to fill our cupboards and settle our accounts. Will you see to it?'

Bart laughed and, as tenderly as Devlin behaved with Linette, reached out his hand to Sophie and assisted her from the stool.

'I want to go, too!' Linette cried when she saw Bart and Sophie leaving.

'No, Lady Lin,' Devlin crooned to her, holding her on his lap as she tried to propel herself out of it. 'Stay with me a bit. Would you like a walk in the park while your mother cleans up?'

'I want to ride your horse.' Linette turned to face him, and she played with his neckcloth and gave him her most appealing expression.

'The horses cannot come today,' he said. 'But we might see some in the park.'

Madeleine felt a chill run down her back. She did not wish to believe he might be conspiring with his brother, but the park would be an excellent place to hand over Linette.

She took a deep breath, deciding to trust him. 'You will have a lovely time, Linette.'

Chapter Fourteen

Devlin stood at the entrance of Almack's with Serena on his arm. He had never attended the assembly room, too occupied with Spanish battlefields or, when in town, with pursuits of a baser nature. The room itself was unexpectedly plain, but the pale-coloured dresses of the *ingénues* gave it the appearance of a formal flower garden in full bloom. In his youth he might have relished the prospect of gathering a bouquet, but, on this night, one suitable flower would be sufficient.

Dozens of female eyes fixed upon him, the older ones coldly calculating, probably tallying what they'd heard his fortune to be. Younger eyes might be assessing other attributes as well, but would likewise not be insensible of his monetary worth.

Devlin thought he heard the pounding of cavalry hooves, but his mind played tricks on him. The sound was merely the buzz of so many voices over the music. Perhaps the analogy to an impending battle was more apt than a flower garden. He certainly felt like the target of a frontal assault.

Truth was, he entered this room with as much intent as the flowers before him. He only hoped it was possible to find a biddable female who would welcome marriage to a man whose heart was engaged elsewhere.

Madeleine.

She had offered to play valet for him, but he had undressed her as quickly as she tried to dress him. He could still feel the heat of her body next to his, still feel the raw rush of pleasure as he entered her—

'Devlin?' Serena shook his arm.

Serena had been speaking. He forced himself to attend to her.

'We must greet the Patronesses first of all.' Serena led him into the room, seeming to know in just what direction to go. Had Serena met Ned in these rooms? Perhaps Ned had scanned the flowers with as much detachment as Devlin, since his blossom had been previously selected for him.

Serena led him to where the Patronesses held court. Three in attendance this evening, all looking more ordinary than he had expected. He would not have picked them from the crowd, except perhaps for their vigilant eyes.

'Dear Serena,' one said as they approached. The woman extended her hands to Serena and seemed genuinely glad to see her.

'Maria, how glad I am you are here,' Serena responded in kind. She nodded to the two other ladies who were busy scrutinising Devlin.

He hoped his neckcloth had remained in place and that they would not notice the mended place on his long-tailed coat. He had insisted Madeleine repair the damage she had done, although she begged to have Sophie do it. Devlin wanted to assure Madeleine that her sewing was equal to the task. She had laboured hard to learn the stitches, after all.

Serena urged him a step forward. 'Lady Sefton, Lady Cowper, Mrs Drummond-Burrell, allow me to present to you Lord Devlin Steele, who is Heronvale's youngest brother.'

Devlin bowed to the ladies and managed to push a little charm into his smile. 'It is an honour, ladies.'

'We have not seen you here before, Lord Devlin,' Mrs Drummond-Burrell said, her eyebrow raised suspiciously.

'I have not previously had the pleasure.' Devlin met her gaze and tried to sound sincere.

Serena spoke quickly. 'Devlin—Lord Devlin—was with Wellington. He is recently recovered enough to come to town.'

Serena had drilled him in the proper topics of conversation, which were pitifully few. He hoped oblique references to war wounds were included as acceptable. Not that he wished to speak with these ladies of such matters.

'Indeed. I believe I recall the story,' Lady Cowper said. 'Heronvale fetched you from Brussels. Is that correct?'

'Yes, ma'am, I am indebted to my brother.' Talk of the battle was thus avoided by mention of the rescue.

Lady Sefton took his arm. 'I am certain Lord Devlin did not come here to discuss such unpleasantness. He came to meet our young ladies, is that not so, sir?'

'I am found out.' He smiled.

Mrs Drummond-Burrell tilted her chin in the direction of an exquisite blonde creature surrounded by a group of fawning gentlemen. 'Amanda Reynolds is the current Diamond, I believe. She is not within your touch, however.' The Patroness sniffed. 'Your brother might have tempted her, but not an untitled younger son.'

'You spare me from wasting my time. I am grateful to you.' He bowed.

The Diamond would not have tempted him in any event. The fire within such a lady was as much an illusion as the sparkle of a gem. Devlin preferred the burning passion of a dark-haired woman with fine blue eyes.

But he must not think of Madeleine while here. If he did, he would never find a woman needing marriage and not much else.

'How about Lady Allenton's daughter?' Lady Cowper suggested, glancing pointedly at a plump, rather frightened-looking girl.

'Hmmph!' snorted Mrs Drummond-Burrell. 'She lacks wit,

sense and beauty. Her fortune is impressive, but that is the end of it, and Lord Devlin has no need of her funds.'

'Come, my lord.' Lady Sefton, still holding his arm, pulled him away. 'We shall introduce you to many young ladies before the night is over. I suspect they will be eager to add you to their tally of partners.'

So Devlin met many agreeable young ladies, danced many pleasant dances, and gradually felt more and more depressed. Some of the *ingénues*, particularly the youngest ones, were insecure and full of anxieties, others blatantly forward, as if already composing an engagement announcement. None were Madeleine, however, and all suffered in the comparison. He longed to be at Madeleine's side, even if merely seated in the parlour watching her struggle with her sewing. He longed to bounce Linette on his lap and hear her delighted squeals.

That morning he'd held Linette up next him at the mirror, their heads together. He saw identical shapes of the brow, identical dimples. For his child and her mother he would perform his duty.

He begged leave of the forgettable creature who had partnered him in the last country dance and joined Serena, seated with Lady Sefton among the matrons.

Serena regarded him worriedly.

Lady Sefton smiled. 'You are doing very well, Lord Devlin. I believe you have made an impression on our young ladies.'

'They are quite lovely.'

She laughed. 'Charming, sir! You shall have your pick, I am sure.'

He frowned. 'This is my first evening among society, ma'am. I mean only to enjoy myself.'

Serena avoided his eyes. He supposed she knew he was lying. Or perhaps she continued to disapprove of his decision to marry.

'Would you ladies like some refreshment?' He may as well be useful.

'An excellent idea.' Lady Sefton nodded.

Devlin walked to the room where the refreshments were served. The ladies had requested lemonade.

'Steele! Upon my word, it is you.'

Devlin turned to see who spoke to him. A slim man in an impossibly high collar and tiers of intricate neckcloth grinned at him.

'Duprey.'

The young man smirked. 'Steele, I have not seen you since you were sent down from Oxford, I declare. Been up to no good, I expect.'

Robert Duprey had been a particular stickler at school, always eager to turn in a pupil who deviated from the rules.

'I've been in the army, Duprey.'

'Indeed? Well, I suppose that makes sense. Keeps you out of trouble, eh?' He laughed the same squeaky laugh he'd had in school.

'You have the right of it.' Devlin picked up the two glasses of lemonade.

'I say, have you tried the orgeat? Dreadful stuff.' Duprey took a sip.

'I beg your pardon,' Devlin said, stepping around him.

Duprey followed him into the ballroom. 'I say, who is that creature seated with Lady Sefton? She is perfection.'

'My brother's wife.' Devlin strode away. He served the ladies their lemonade and idly surveyed the room.

Duprey sauntered over to converse with a young lady dressed in a pale yellow gown. Devlin watched her as she spoke to his old schoolmate. She seemed familiar to him, the way she moved, the expression on her face. She had brown hair, facial features of no distinction, a passable figure. There was no reason he should recall an acquaintance with her.

Devlin walked back to Duprey and stood at his side.

'I did not mean to leave you so abruptly, Duprey,' he lied. 'I thought you meant to follow.'

Duprey gave a snorting laugh. 'I say, I would have appreciated a presentation to that exquisite angel; that is, before I knew who she was.'

The young lady attended this conversation composedly, pale blue eyes resting on each speaker.

Devlin favoured her with a smile, and received one in return. 'Perhaps you would present me...?'

Duprey clapped the heel of his hand on his forehead. 'Oh, indeed.' The man waved toward the young lady. 'My sister, Miss Emily Duprey. Or I should say, Miss Duprey. Our other sister finally legshackled some viscount a year or so ago. Piles of blunt. Emily, Lord Devlin Steele.'

'Miss Duprey.' He bowed to her.

'Lord Devlin,' she murmured through downcast lashes.

Miss Duprey was at least in her twentieth year, Devlin guessed. Perhaps if she had seen one or two unsuccessful Seasons, she might welcome an offer such as his with pragmatism.

'Do you enjoy yourself this evening, Miss Duprey?' he asked.

'Oh, yes, indeed,' she replied. 'Almack's is always agreeable, don't you think?'

'I have not had the pleasure of attending before this night.' He smiled at her, sure now he'd not met her before.

Her brother piped up, 'Steele was at Oxford with me, Em. That is, until he was sent down and joined the army.'

Leave it to Duprey to place him in a negative light. The lady's countenance remained complacent, however, so hopefully his less-than-pristine past would not disfavour him in her eyes. Devlin secured the next waltz with Miss Duprey and took his leave of her.

When he presented himself to Miss Duprey for the dance, her mother took far more interest in him than the daughter had, but the dance was pleasant enough. They made predictable conversation. Devlin knew Duprey stood to inherit a barony, not a lofty title. He knew little else about the family. If they had married one daughter well enough, there might not be a need to seek a title for the other.

The rest of the night dragged on. Devlin was surprised to see the Diamond, Miss Reynolds, eyeing him curiously. Perhaps she had not yet heard he was a younger son. Everyone else seemed to know his situation and fortune, accurate to within a pound. Devlin ran into a couple of acquaintances, including one fellow officer he had known slightly when in Spain. He supposed the few officers left alive would be, like he, searching for a wife. There was little else for a former soldier to do.

When Serena had finally indicated that they might leave without disgrace, Devlin was grateful. As they waited for their carriage, Devlin found himself standing next to the Diamond. Serena, acquainted with the aunt who chaperoned Miss Reynolds, made the introductions.

'You did not seek a dance with me, Lord Devlin,' the Diamond said, while her aunt and Serena chatted together.

'I am afraid I was warned that the competition would be too stiff,' he replied.

She laughed and grinned conspiratorially. 'A dance with any gentleman serves to cause worry to those truly in the running.'

Her carriage arrived and he bid her goodnight.

When he and Serena finally were seated in her carriage, Devlin breathed a sigh of relief.

Serena glanced at him warily. She hesitated before speaking. 'I hope the evening was to your liking.'

He gave a sardonic smile. 'It was up to my expectations.'

'You did well,' she faltered. 'You danced many dances.'

'I did indeed.' He crossed his arms over his chest and retreated into his own thoughts of the evening, thoughts he would not dare speak aloud to Serena. How boring the evening had been. And how he hated himself for performing his expected role, when he would have rather been with Madeleine.

Serena glanced at Devlin, sitting silent and sullen next to her in the carriage. She had detested this evening, having agreed to accompany her husband's brother only because her husband wished it. She could not help but think of the beautiful young woman Devlin had brought to their house and how Devlin had gazed at that beauty throughout the evening. Miss England seemed perfectly suitable to Serena. She was polite and well mannered and obviously educated. Surely those things would make her suitable? What did it matter if she had come from trade or something equally as shameful?

Serena wished she could discuss the matter with her husband, but she dared not. He had been in such a temper about his brother, she might aggravate the situation if she interfered. Besides, she never interfered with her husband's affairs. She never even knew what they were.

Ned would not understand if she talked with him of her conviction that Devlin loved this mere girl whom he had kept secret for so long. Ned should make Devlin marry the girl. Surely it would not be too scandalous for the family for a younger son to marry a mistress who had already borne him a child? Why did Ned not consider it Devlin's duty to marry Miss England?

She feared she knew the answer to that question. Ned still wished to adopt the child. Of course that was the reason. He still hoped to convince Miss England to give him her little daughter, because his wife could not bear a child of his own.

Tears welled up in Serena's eyes. Sniffing the tears away, she fussed in her reticule to find her handkerchief.

Devlin turned, looking concerned. 'What is wrong, sister?'

'Nothing,' she mumbled.

'Fustian,' he said. 'Tell me what is upsetting you.'

He put his arm around her and leaned her against his shoulder. The comfort almost opened the floodgates, but Serena refused to give in to the impulse to weep.

'I…' She searched for something to say, something other than the real reason for her tears. 'I…I cannot like this search of yours for a wife. Your heart is engaged elsewhere, I am convinced. It…it seems dishonourable.'

He stiffened. 'I have no other choice. I need to support her and the child. How else may I do that? Your husband controls my money, so I must do as he bids.'

'I still cannot like it,' she murmured.

'I cannot like it either.' He gave her arm a fond squeeze. 'I promise you I will be honourable to whomever I marry, Serena.'

'Oh, Devlin!' she sighed.

The carriage pulled up to the Marquess's town house. Devlin hopped out and turned to assist Serena.

He walked her to her door. 'Thank you, sister, for accompanying me. I could not have endured this evening without you.'

Serena did not know what to say in return. She knew she would attend another such evening if Ned required her to do so, but she felt sick at being a part of something that boded so ill for everyone.

Devlin stepped into the hall with her and gave her a quick peck on the cheek before leaving. As Serena turned to the stairs, she saw Ned staring down at her. Her heart quickened. He had waited for her! She hurried up the stairs, his eyes watching her every step. As she neared the top, he turned and walked into his bedchamber, shutting the door loudly behind him.

When Devlin returned to his apartments, Madeleine was sitting on the stairs, hugging her knees.

'I waited for you,' she said.

He gathered her into his arms with the overwhelming feeling that he had arrived home where he belonged.

She drew him into his room. 'Tell me of Almack's.'

He kicked off his shoes and unbuttoned his coat. She helped him remove it.

'I shall play valet again,' she said. 'But, please, tell me of Almack's. Was it beautiful? Tell me of its decorations.'

He tried to remember enough to answer her questions. 'It was plain. Indeed, I cannot recall that there were any decorations to speak of.'

Madeleine gave him a sceptical look as she untied his neck-cloth. He must be joking with her. She recalled her sisters rhapsodising about the day they would attend Almack's. At the time, she thought it silly, but she'd always taken for granted that her future would include visits to 'the seventh heaven'.

'Do be serious, Devlin. I truly wish to know of it.'

He exercised his neck, free of its confining collar. 'I speak the truth. The assembly rooms were plain, nothing to signify. Seating around the edge. Plenty of space for dancing.'

She sighed, exasperated. 'Very well. Tell me of the dresses. What did the ladies wear? Were the dresses beautiful?'

He sat on the edge of his bed and removed his stockings. 'The dresses were of light colours, mostly. Lots of white.'

'Well, of course.'

She thought about the young ladies in dresses of white or pale pinks, yellows, and blues. Privileged, protected, caring only for the clothes they wore, the parties they were to attend, the prospective husbands they were to meet. Had he met a young lady there this night? Had he been attracted by her beauty and poise? Her unblemished reputation? It did not bear thinking of.

She hung his coat and picked up the scattering of clothes he had left on the floor. As she turned back to him, he was pulling his white linen shirt over his head, leaving his chest bare. She must become accustomed to the thrill of seeing him so, his muscles defined, the hair of his chest an inviting shadow.

She must also become accustomed to the idea that another

woman would claim the privilege of running her hands up that expanse of male beauty. She brushed his jacket. 'Tell me of the music, then. Was it wonderful?'

He stood, barefoot, bare-chested, clad only in his knee breeches. 'The music? The orchestra played dance music. You know, country dances, waltzes and such.' He walked to her, placing his hand on her shoulder.

'Waltzes?' The scandalous dance in which ladies and gentlemen touched each other. Had he touched one of Almack's elegant ladies in a waltz? She began to regret her curiosity of this night. 'I suppose you danced the waltz?'

'Indeed,' he murmured, turning her around. She refused to look at him. 'It is now accepted at Almack's. Have you not had the pleasure of dancing the waltz?'

'My duties at Lord Farley's did not include waltzing.'

He lifted her chin so that she was forced to see his eyes in the candlelight. He placed her hand on his shoulder and took her other hand in his. 'I shall show you the steps.'

He counted out the steps. Back step, side step, together. Forward, side, together. His hand at her back guided her as he performed the steps slowly, gradually increasing the pace. Back, side, together. Forward, side, together.

Soon they were swirling around the room, and Madeleine was swept up in the dance and the pleasure of being in his arms. He hummed the music. Bump, bump, bump. Da, da, da. She laughed at how silly he sounded, and he continued louder, smiling at her.

As they twirled to the music he made, he drew her flush against his chest. With only her thin nightdress between them, she felt as well as heard his resonant voice. Her hand moved to his neck, her fingers into his hair. The music stopped when his mouth found hers and a new tune commenced, a new rhythm that carried them into his bed and relieved them of the remainder of their clothing.

This was a dance she still feared a little, but so much more did she crave it. His hands on her flesh. His tongue dancing with hers. The excitation when he entered her. The transport when her pleasure exploded.

The climax of the dance left her panting.

'That is not precisely as the waltz is done at Almack's,' he said.

She smiled. For the moment, she would pretend she was his exclusive partner in this waltz, and would content herself with that fact. 'It is a lovely dance,' she said.

Chapter Fifteen

As time progressed, Madeleine's days were spent in glorious domesticity. She could almost pretend she, Devlin and Linette were a family. She and Devlin shopped together, purchasing various sundries they'd previously done without, finding treats to bring home to Linette. They took Linette to the park. They sat in quietly in the parlour, Devlin playing with Linette and her wooden horse, Madeleine stitching laboriously. Soon, however, it became necessary for Devlin to make afternoon calls, shortening the illusion. Every evening was taken up with some splendid event. This night it was the Elbingtons' Ball, purported to be the event of the Season. Invitations were highly prized.

Madeleine helped Devlin dress as she'd done each night he left her in search of a woman to marry.

As he tried tying his neckcloth for the third time, he said, 'Maddy, we must talk of the future.'

She could not think of the future. Her mind was too filled with the present, with the idea that another woman would be in his arms tonight, dancing the waltz, perhaps planning a different future with him.

He went on, 'I think the country, don't you? A place for you to have a horse, and Linette a pony…'

'Whatever you decide, Devlin.'

What did it matter, after all, when another woman would spend both days and nights with him?

Madeleine smoothed the lapels of his coat and stood back to survey her handiwork. He looked dazzlingly handsome in his black coat, snowy white breeches and linens. How could any woman resist him? She kissed him goodbye and sent him off, pretending good humour, and returned to sew by candlelight, feeling empty inside.

When Devlin entered Lady Elbington's ball, the noise and crush was as unwelcome as the memories of battle. Indeed, settings like this one, with its noise, bustle, and discreet forms of indiscretion, were now the only places unwanted memories of battle threatened to intrude. Madeleine had chased them away from other parts of his life.

Hearing the faint echo of French cannonade in the rumbling of the voices, Devlin scanned the room. Miss Reynolds gave him a meaningful look from the far corner. He made his way to her side, where two gentlemen half in their cups paid court to her, undoubtedly drawn by her fair hair and skin, and the décolletage of her gauzy lime gown.

Amanda Reynolds and Devlin had developed an understanding of a peculiar sort. Neither had any particular interest in the other, but each found the other to be of use. Miss Reynolds used Devlin when she needed to rid herself of the unwanted attentions of other men, or to make her chosen suitor jealous. Devlin used Miss Reynolds as protection from young ladies who might pin hopes on him. As long at his attention seemed at least partially engaged by the current Diamond, no matchmaking mama fancied her daughter his favourite.

Devlin bowed to her. 'Is this my dance, Miss Reynolds?'

'I do believe so, sir,' she replied. Some poor hapless soul had lost his moment with her. He suspected it was the young buck approaching whose eyes bulged with anger.

As they began the set, she thanked him. 'I do not know when I was in such need of rescue.'

Miss Reynolds delighted in the dance as she appeared to delight in every activity associated with courtship. When the set ended, Devlin caught the eye of the Earl of Greythorne, the gentleman Miss Reynolds hoped to bring up to scratch. Greythorne looked daggers at him.

'My rival has arrived,' he said.

Miss Reynolds grinned. 'Looking deliciously jealous. My thanks to you again.'

Devlin delivered Miss Reynolds to a group of her friends and made his way to Miss Duprey, feeling faintly guilty at the pleased expression on Miss Duprey's face as he approached. It would not be a disservice to her to engage her in a loveless marriage, would it?

He bowed to her. 'Good evening, Miss Duprey.'

She smiled shyly. 'Lord Devlin.'

He chatted with her in the inconsequential ways expected— of her health, her family's health, the weather. He engaged her for the supper dance, which happened to be a waltz. When her next partner came, he withdrew.

Devlin went in search of Serena, who he knew would be seated among the dowagers. Ned had taken to accompanying Serena and Devlin to the various entertainments. Very unusual of him, Devlin gathered from Serena. Ned spent little time in the card room, instead staying within sight of his wife, though dancing rarely with her. Devlin presumed the main purpose of Ned's presence was to keep watch over his younger brother, but it was not well done of Ned to so ignore his wife.

Devlin found Serena and sat beside her.

She cast him a look that barely disguised her concern. 'You dance often with Miss Reynolds.'

'We have become friends of a strange sort,' he replied. 'She relishes all this nonsense and I—' He was about to say that he detested it, but caught himself in time. 'Worry not, sister, there is nothing in it.'

While he tried to decide which of the young ladies present would be safe to dance with, Serena's gaze never left the couples performing the set. A wistful expression came across her face. Curse his brother for neglecting her.

'Are you engaged for the next dance, Serena? I would be honoured, if you are not.' The music had stopped. He stood and extended his hand to her.

'Devlin, you need not waste your time dancing with me,' Serena said.

'Indeed,' came a cold voice behind him, 'you ought to look to the unmarried ladies, not the married ones.' Ned moved beside Serena. The look he gave Devlin was stony at best. 'I will dance with my wife.'

'Ned.' Devlin forced a cheerful tone to his voice. 'What a surprise to see you on this side of the room. I all but forgot you were here.'

His brother glared.

'Serena, I leave you to your husband.' Devlin bowed and walked away.

The Marquess had lately become damnably ill-humoured. Steady Ned had become a man of erratic moods. No telling when he might erupt. Those days when Devlin could pour all his troubles into his brother's willing ear had vanished. Devlin could not even bear to ride to these evening events in Ned's carriage. Accompanying the silent Marquess and Marchioness was too unpleasant by half. What had so changed this brother he idolised, Devlin could not understand.

He collected Miss Duprey for the supper dance. She kept her eyes demurely downcast except when he spoke to her. Her blue eyes were her best feature, Devlin thought. If he were hard pressed to describe her, he could say only that the rest of her was unremarkable. Conversation with her was easy enough, though no different than with the other young ladies he partnered. He listened with half an ear.

'Do you go to Vauxhall Gardens this Wednesday, Lord

Devlin? My mother says we do not, but others have talked of it.'

Vauxhall. Good God, why had he not thought of it before? He could never take Madeleine to Covent Garden or to Almack's, but he could take her to Vauxhall! With the black cloth masks so common at Vauxhall Gardens, they could dance under the lights and watch the illuminations. They could stroll along the hedged paths or seek shelter in one of the grottoes. He quickened his step with happy anticipation.

'Do you go to Vauxhall, then?' she asked again.

He had almost forgotten her presence, even though he held her in the dance. 'I had not planned to go,' he said. But he began planning an excursion now.

He escorted Miss Duprey into the supper room and seated her at a table with some friends of her acquaintance. He offered to fill her plate, to which she pleasantly agreed.

Making his way through the crush around the sideboard, he heard a voice hail him.

'Steele?'

Devlin turned and saw a ghost, a most welcome ghost. He'd last seen Christian Ramsford struck down on the battlefield and had mourned his loss, but this was truly Ramsford, walking toward him.

'Ram,' he rasped, at first grasping the man's hand in greeting, then ignoring all propriety and embracing him in a hearty hug. 'Ram, I thought you dead.'

Ramsford gave an ironic smile, but his eyes glistened as Devlin supposed his own did. 'I thought you were long since put to bed with a shovel, as well. So, I suppose all those bottles of brandy consumed in your memory were for naught.'

'Damn, brandy's never a waste.' Devlin took a good look at his friend, outfitted in a superbly fitting coat of black superfine. Though the penniless son of a country vicar, Ramsford's size and presence always had commanded attention.

'What the devil are you doing here?' Devlin asked. A London ball was the last place he expected to find Christian Ramsford.

'Both my uncle and my cousin had the misfortune to drop dead.' Ramsford's voice was almost mournful. 'My father inherited.'

'Good God, Ram. You are heir to an earldom.' Devlin grinned at him.

His friend shrugged. 'I am escorting one of my sisters, and am also directed to consider the succession in my family line.'

'Come, I must select some food.' Devlin grabbed Ramsford's arm and pulled him into the throng around the food. Ram took a glass of champagne off a tray, downed it, and took another.

'You will sit at my table. I insist.'

Ramsford shrugged again, but followed him to the table where Miss Duprey sat. Devlin introduced him to the young people who had joined her, noticing the curious glances from the ladies present. Devlin was suddenly impatient to be rid of all of them for the sole company of his old friend.

Finally he was able to deliver Miss Duprey back to the ballroom. He drew Ramsford aside again. They stood near the open windows where the night breeze cooled the room and spoke of the war.

Amanda Reynolds, temporarily detached from Greythorne's grasp, boldly approached. She entwined her arm in Devlin's. 'You have all but deserted me this evening, sir.'

Devlin knew he was being used again. Miss Reynolds's true concern was the presence of a new gentleman, whose admiration she had not yet procured.

'Doing it up too brown, my lady,' Devlin said.

He introduced Amanda to Ram and realised the once-penniless vicar's son had the greater chance with her. He left them conversing in a strained manner until a red-faced Greythorne came to collect her. Before she was too many steps away, she turned, giving Ramsford a backward glance.

Devlin collected Miss Duprey for his second dance. Knowing that two dances was the limit propriety would allow, he then felt free to make his escape. After saying his goodbyes to the hostess and Serena, and ignoring his brother, he left the ball with Ramsford.

The two men found a comfortable tavern near St James's and spent several hours there toasting comrades they would never see again. The tavern, smelling of hops, gin and male sweat, was nothing like ones he and Ram frequented in Spain, but the camaraderie was identical. Devlin had missed it acutely.

When the night was well advanced, they finally emerged into the chill night. Devlin embraced his friend. The drink had turned him maudlin, but he was too foxed to feel embarrassed. He stumbled his way home, his baritone voice singing one of the raucous ditties still echoing from the tavern.

Near his residence, a man stepped in front of him. 'Good evening, Steele. I see you've had an entertaining evening.'

Devlin squinted, bringing the figure into focus under the lamplight. Farley.

'Bugger off.' Devlin shoved him aside, almost losing his balance. He was directly across the street from his apartments. It penetrated Devlin's foggy mind that Farley must know where he lived, that he was lurking in this neighbourhood for that very reason.

'Bugger off,' he said again, staggering as he started off across the street.

A whim had sent Lord Farley to spy on Steele this cool, mist-covered night, a whim and the frustration of an empty bed. The gaming hell's full coffers were not satisfaction enough.

Farley had known for weeks where Steele had taken Madeleine to live, had made it his business to know. Indeed, he knew all about Steele, his falling-out with his brother, his need for money, his search for a wife. The time was ripe to get Madeleine back.

Lord Farley gave one final glance toward the retreating figure of Devlin Steele and disappeared in the growing mist.

Chapter Sixteen

Madeleine was startled awake by a slamming door and pounding feet on the stairs. She'd dozed off while wrapped in a blanket on the windowseat of Devlin's room, where she worriedly waited for him. He'd never been so late before. He burst in the room, swaying as he swung around, looking for her.

She shot up in alarm, dropping the blanket. 'What is it, Devlin? What has happened?'

He clutched at her, pushing her nightdress half off her shoulder. His breath smelled foul with drink.

'Maddy.' His voice rose in urgency, but his words slurred. 'Promise me never to go outside unaccompanied.'

'I do not, unless for a little walk with Linette.' She pulled away from him. She had never seen him this way.

'No more. Promise me!' He shook her by the shoulders.

Why treat her in this manner? He was like a stranger. 'What has happened?'

He let go of her and rubbed his forehead. 'Nothing has happened. Nothing at all. But you will obey me in this. You will do as I say.'

Madeleine folded her arms across her chest, massaging sore shoulders. 'You are foxed.'

He glared at her. 'I am not foxed.' He took a step toward her, touching the wall for balance. 'Merely a bit disguised.'

She edged away from him. 'I have no wish to engage in a conversation with you when you are foxed.'

'Oh, stubble it, Maddy, and get into bed.'

She straightened. 'I will not.'

He held his hand against the wall and looked as if he would slip to the floor at any moment. 'I said get into bed. I cannot stand up much longer.'

Having enough of his behaviour, she marched past him, avoiding his attempt to grab at her. 'I will sleep in my own bed this night.' Reminding herself in time that slamming the door might wake Linette, she closed it quietly behind her.

Once in her own room, she leaned against the post of her bed, squeezing her eyes shut. She must remind herself that men disappoint. It had been foolish to believe Devlin an exception. She crawled into her lonely bed, its linens cool against her skin. His body would not warm her this night.

Devlin woke in his clothes, half sprawled across the bed, a whole arsenal of French cannon pounding in his head. Rain darkened the sky and he had no idea of the time of day. He sat up, and the room started to spin. As he waited for it to come to a stop, he tried to stop his thoughts from spinning, as well. What the devil had happened last night?

He remembered Ram. He remembered the two of them drinking toast after toast to dead comrades. He remembered shouting at Madeleine, God help him. He could not remember how he got home.

Devlin gingerly put his feet on the floor and took careful steps over to the wash basin. He splashed water on his face and rinsed out the foul taste in his mouth. He poured the pitcher of water over his pounding head. Still dripping, he glanced about the room.

He could not recall telling Madeleine about meeting Ram. He'd shouted at her, though. Why?

Devlin fumbled through his trunk for a worn pair of trousers and an old shirt. He flopped into a chair and tried to pull on his clothing. His head spun around like a child's toy top.

He sat bolt upright. Good God! He had got drunk and shouted at Madeleine. What else had he done?

As he took careful steps into the kitchen, he resolved to set about correcting his wrongs. Still struggling to recall what wrongs he needed to correct, he warmed himself in front of the fire. The kettle was hot and he brewed himself some tea, wondering where the others were.

Where Madeleine was.

Bart entered the room and shot Devlin a disapproving look.

Devlin waved his hand. 'I know. I know. I've been a wastrel. A miscreant. A scapegrace.'

Bart pursed his lips. 'Well, you've upset the lass.'

Devlin gaped at Bart. 'I did something to upset Sophie?'

'Not Sophie,' Bart huffed. 'Miss Madeleine.'

Devlin groaned. 'You do not know what I did to upset her, do you? I confess I remember little of it.'

Bart cut a piece of bread and handed it to Devlin, who accepted it warily, taking a cautious nibble. 'The lass did not tell me the whole, but I collect you were drunk as an emperor.'

Devlin chewed a piece of crust. 'Indeed.'

Bart opened his mouth. Devlin stopped him. 'Before you jump down my throat, I was with Ram.'

'Captain Ramsford?' Bart's expression changed to surprise. 'He is alive?'

'Alive and very well. I thought him dead, too. I saw him fall...that day.' He lifted his mug of tea and his hand shook.

'I'll be damned.'

'We left the ball together and found a friendly tavern.' He paused, taking a sip of tea, and closing his eyes. 'There were many toasts to be made.'

'By God, I'll drink to the fellow myself.' Bart opened a

cabinet and removed a bottle. He poured a generous supply in a glass for himself and a dollop in Devlin's cup.

'To Captain Ramsford.' Bart raised his glass.

Devlin clinked his cup against Bart's glass.

Right at that moment, Madeleine walked into the room. She stared directly at the bottle on the table and then to the two men. Bart quickly drained the contents of his glass and hastily exited. Silently, Madeleine walked over to the kettle.

'There is tea brewed in the pot,' Devlin told her.

Without a word, Madeleine put a half-teaspoon of sugar and a mere drop of cream into her cup and poured the tea.

As she turned to leave, Devlin put a hand on her arm. 'Stay a moment, Maddy.'

She sat, her face expressionless, her posture rigid.

Devlin's stomach roiled and he took a bite of the bread hoping to quiet it. He gave up the idea of telling her about Ram. It would sound like excuse-making. He needed some explanation, however, but what to say when the events were obscure to him? Worse, he had this awful feeling of foreboding.

'I remember little of last night, except that I behaved badly toward you.' He lifted her chin with his finger.

She swatted it away.

'I apologise, Maddy. I am sorry.'

Madeleine tried to avoid his intent expression. It conveyed a sincerity she could not quite believe. 'Apology comes easy when you do not know what it is for.'

He took her hand and stroked it, holding it in his grip when she would have pulled it away. 'I apologise for being drunk and for shouting at you. That much I do remember.'

She wished he would not touch her. His green eyes reflected the fire in the stove, his hair was tousled, and he had not yet donned his waistcoat and coat.

'Maddy,' he murmured, his voice low. His arm drew around her, pulling her close. 'Maddy.' The cotton of his shirt was cool against her skin, but a furnace seemed to burn inside her. His lips hovered over her ear, his warm breath tickling. 'What injuries did I inflict on you, my love? I wish to make amends.'

How was she supposed to tell him of his ridiculous dictate to be chaperoned, or his abominable order to get in bed, when his lips sent shivers directly to…to that part of her body that craved him? A true lady would not run her hands under his shirt. A true lady would not kiss him back. A true lady would not position herself upon his lap, straddling him, wanting him.

'Deddy!' Linette burst into the room.

Madeleine pushed away, but Devlin would not let her escape. Linette flung herself at Devlin and scrambled into what scant space was left on his lap.

'Deddy!' she shouted directly in his ear.

He let go of Madeleine and grabbed his head.

Madeleine chuckled. 'Linette, do not scream so. Deddy has the headache.'

'Poor Deddy,' Linette crooned, only a fraction lower. 'I will kiss it and make it aaallll better.'

Linette pulled down Devlin's head, squeezed it between her chubby little hands, and gave him a big smack of a kiss right on his crown.

'Dam— Dash it all.'

As he lifted his head and Linette beamed at her apothecary skills, Madeleine laughed.

He managed a wan smile. 'I think I shall be right and tight now, if I may only finish my tea.'

Linette stood on his lap to reach the mug. Madeleine tried not to laugh at his pained expression. Linette handed Devlin the mug. 'You slept all day,' she scolded, settling in his lap.

'I have no idea of the time.' He glanced at Madeleine.

'Near three o'clock,' she said.

'Da— Dash it. I have an engagement.'

Madeleine's smile faded. A peculiar feeling settled in her stomach. 'Do you need any assistance dressing?' Her words sounded stiff, even to her.

He gave her a pained expression. 'I can manage, I think.'

'I...I don't mind helping.'

'I want to help!' Linette jumped up and down in his lap.

'Linette!' He grabbed the child. 'Stop it!'

She stopped. Fat tears gathered in her wide blue eyes. Her lower lip trembled. Devlin, his head still pounding like a hammer to an anvil, felt like a cad.

He wiped a trickle of a tear from her cheek. 'Don't cry, Lady Lin. Jumping on me hurt me a little, you see.'

She sniffled.

He shot a look of appeal to Madeleine, who simply stared at him.

'No more crying now,' he said to Linette in a soft voice. He brushed the little girl's hair with his fingers.

Madeleine spun around and ran out of the room.

A few minutes later, Devlin hurried out of the house, barely pausing to close the door behind him. Soon after, Bart and Sophie took Linette to purchase beefsteak pies and sweetbreads for supper. Madeleine was left with nothing but her thoughts.

She went to the kitchen and filled a bucket from the pump. On her knees she attacked the floor, rubbing the hard bar of lye soap on the brush and scrubbing the wood, rinsing it with wet rags. She'd watched Bart do this job and it seemed not too difficult, but the lye soap stung and reddened her hands. She dipped them in the cool water. She considered what delicate white hands the lady Devlin called upon would have, and scrubbed harder.

She could barely help thinking about Devlin's afternoon calls. What clothes did the ladies wear? Were they all as elegant as the Marchioness? Did they smile prettily at him?

Had Devlin selected a lady to marry? He had not said so, but she sensed it was true. He had become quieter, no longer describing the entertainments he attended or the people he encountered.

What did *she* look like, this woman he must have selected? Was she beautiful? Intelligent? Accomplished?

Madeleine pressed the scrub brush down more firmly, the scraping sound drowning out her thoughts. Unbearable thoughts. She attacked the floor as if scrubbing dirt that had accumulated over eons. The apron covering her dress became damp from where she knelt, but at least she was being of some use. The pungent odour of the soap, the smell of the wet wood, the rhythm of scrubbing back and forth, even the sting of the harsh soap, distracted and somehow soothed.

Perhaps this was how people endured lives of drudgery. In any event, she vastly preferred numbing herself with hard labour than willing herself numb from the labour she had once been compelled to endure. Until Devlin rescued her and showed her joy.

Madeleine threw the scrub brush in the pail, splashing water on the floor. She would not think of Devlin. She would think of nothing at all.

A knock sounded at the door, firm and officious. Callers were rare at the house. In fact, the Marquess had been the only one. Madeleine hastily wiped her hands on her apron and rose. Cautiously, she peered from the parlour window and saw familiar matched bays harnessed to the elegant carriage bearing the Heronvale crest. He had come for Linette, after all.

Madeleine quickly stepped back from the window, her hand flying to her mouth and her heart pounding. Perhaps if she stood very still, he would think no one at home and would leave.

The knocker pounded again. She heard a voice. 'There seems to be no one at home, my lady.'

Through the slit in the curtains, Madeleine saw the Marchioness lean out of the carriage.

'I am sure someone is at home, Simms. I saw movement at the window. I shall knock myself.'

The footman descended the steps from the house and as-

sisted the Marchioness out of the carriage. Beautifully dressed
in a deep green walking dress, spencer and plumed hat, she
seemed to float up to the door.

More knocking. 'Miss England, are you there? Please open
the door.'

The Marchioness's behaviour was most improper. Ladies
of rank did not knock on doors, nor did they visit this part of
town. Only extreme foolishness or some urgent situation
would explain it.

Blood drained from Madeleine's face. Devlin!

She ran to the door and flung it open, throat tight with
anxiety. The Marchioness's hand was poised to knock again
and the delicate blonde gasped with surprise. Madeleine could
not speak.

'May…may I come in?' The lady's trembling smile did
nothing to allay Madeleine's fears.

She stepped aside for the lady to enter. The Marchioness
turned to the footman. 'Thank you, Simms. You may wait
with the carriage.'

The footman bowed and, with one eyebrow arched, gave
Madeleine an appraising look before retreating.

Madeleine closed the door and faced her visitor. 'Please tell
me…has something happened? Is Devlin…?' She could not
make herself coherent.

The Marchioness blinked her eyes in confusion. 'Devlin? I
have not seen him.'

Madeleine's muscles, all taut for disastrous news, relaxed
measurably. 'You have not come to tell me Devlin is hurt?'

The Marchioness blushed. 'No. Indeed not.' She cast down
her eyes. 'The matter I have come upon is personal.'

Madeleine nearly laughed in relief. Devlin was not dead
or hurt, or married. She pressed her fingers to her temples,
only then realising her hair hung in damp clumps around her
face. She tried to smooth the tangled mess.

The Marchioness cleared her throat. 'May I speak to you
for a moment?' She glanced toward the parlour.

Madeleine peered at her. 'I will not give up Linette. Devlin promised to make that clear to you.'

The lady blushed again. 'This is not about...I am so sorry... My husband meant no harm to you, I assure you.'

Madeleine regarded her with scepticism. 'He wished to take my child.'

The Marchioness's eyes pleaded. 'He did not realise. I do pray you will forgive him.'

'Forgive him?' Madeleine said, her voice rising. 'I doubt my forgiveness would be worth a farthing to him.'

The lady straightened and gave Madeleine a direct gaze. 'You sorely misjudge my husband, Miss England. He is the best of men. His interest in your child, misguided as it was, was motivated solely by a desire to please me.' Her voice changed to one of conviction and authority. 'May we retire to the parlour, please?'

Madeleine nodded coolly, though somewhat abashed at her lapse in manners. She led the Marchioness into the small parlour, shabby looking compared to the one in Grosvenor Square.

'Some tea, my lady?' she asked with inbred hospitality.

'That is kind of you,' the Marchioness replied, a slight tremble to her words.

As Madeleine rushed to the kitchen, she glanced at herself in the hallway mirror. She was a fright, her apron wet and dirty where she had knelt. Her hair had escaped from its braid and was a tangle of wayward dark curls.

She set the kettle on the fire in the kitchen and pulled off her apron. The blue cotton day dress she wore would have been presentable had it not been soaked with water. Madeleine measured out the tea and poured the water into the pot. She attempted to rebraid her hair, wishing she had pins to bind it into some sort of submission. She found a few lemon biscuits to add to the fare and hurriedly assembled the tray.

She entered the parlour and placed the tray on the table next to the Marchioness. As Madeleine poured the tea, she noticed the lady twisting her fine lime kid gloves in her smooth, delicate, ivory hands. Madeleine handed her the cup and hid her own beet-red hands in the folds of her skirt.

'How may I be of service to you, ma'am?' Madeleine asked, determined to display good breeding, though not feeling gracious inside. Indeed, this interview was too puzzling by half.

The Marchioness's teacup rattled in its saucer. 'I do wish you would call me Serena.'

'I would not presume, madam.'

The Marchioness looked so disappointed, Madeleine thought the lady might cry. She felt a sudden sympathy.

'Perhaps you ought to tell why you have come,' she said in a soft, inviting tone.

The Marchioness burst into tears. 'I have nowhere else to turn. I do not know what to do.' She rummaged in her reticule and pulled out a white linen handkerchief, edged in elegant lace. She turned away and dabbed at her face.

Madeleine wrinkled her forehead in concern. 'Are you in trouble of some kind?'

The Marchioness shook her head, fair tendrils shaking.

'Is it your husband? Has he hurt you in some way?' Madeleine would not put it past that man to be cold and cruel to his wife, not after his treatment of Devlin and, above all, his eagerness to steal a child.

The Marchioness's head shot up. 'My husband is the best of men. There is no more honourable a man on this earth. He is nothing but good to me, always.' Her face crumbled again. 'It is I who am at fault. I am a poor wife. I cannot please him in the most basic of ways.' She dissolved into tears again.

Madeleine went to her and, crouching next to her chair, took her hand. 'Now, you mustn't cry. Whatever it is, I am sure Devlin can help put it to rights. He will be home shortly.'

The lady's eyes flashed pain. 'No, not Devlin. You.'

'I?'

'There is no one else I can ask. You are the only one I know who can help me.'

Madeleine stared at her in confusion. 'It is not my position to help a lady. I am the lowest of creatures, I assure you. What could I possibly do to help you?'

The Marchioness looked directly into Madeleine's eyes. 'You must teach me how to seduce my husband.'

Chapter Seventeen

Madeleine gaped in disbelief.

The Marchioness twisted her handkerchief. Her words came out in a rush. 'You see, I have been such a failure as a wife. I...I do not know how to give a man pleasure *that way* and my husband...he is very dear to me, you see. He is patient and makes no demands at all, but he cannot bear to bed me.'

Madeleine returned to her chair, collapsing into its cushion.

Tears poured down the Marchioness's cheeks. 'He knows I pine for children, and that is why he sought to adopt your daughter. For me! To make me happy. A wretch such as myself who cannot please him!'

Madeleine took a fortifying sip of tea.

The Marchioness sniffled, even that managing to sound ladylike. 'I thought perhaps if I had lessons in lovemaking, I could learn how to please him. I would be a willing pupil. So, you see, I thought of you.'

Madeleine's breath quickened. The Marchioness knew of her past? Perhaps the Marquess had discovered her identity. Had Devlin told him? Her cheeks burned in mortification. Surely neither of them would have spoken of it to this lady.

'Me? I know naught of love between a man and his wife.' Madeleine's voice was tight.

The Marchioness twisted her hands nervously. 'Not *marital* love, exactly. The other kind.'

Madeleine pretended calm as she took another sip of tea.

The lady continued. 'You see, it is clear Devlin is besotted with you. It fairly took my breath away, the manner in which he looked upon you that awful night. You are not married, so the attachment must be of another kind.' Her voice turned low and tentative. 'At least that is what I thought.'

Devlin besotted with her?

The Marchioness continued, 'Please help me, Miss England...Madeleine. Where else might I turn? I have not been exposed... That is, I have led so sheltered a life. I am not acquainted with anyone else who might...'

Madeleine understood. Only an improper female could speak of such matters. Ladies of the *ton* would not sip tea while chatting about the most effective way to arouse a man. Madeleine's stomach clenched with the memory of how she had learned such lessons. Farley had taken her step by step through what she must do to bring a man to pleasure. Over and over. Again and again. She had learned where to touch, what to say. Such lessons should never soil the ears of so delicate a lady.

She glanced at the Marchioness, who regarded her with a hopeful, pleading expression. Madeleine was unconvinced that the fault of the lovemaking rested upon this creature's shoulders. The Marquess showed no warmth.

She bit her lip. The Marquess had been kind and gentle to Linette, she remembered. Perhaps there was a bit of his brother in him.

She sighed. 'Very well, my lady. I shall try to help you.'

The lady's smile was beatific. 'Please call me Serena.'

Madeleine laughed in defeat. 'Serena, then.' If she were about to provide sexual lessons to a Marchioness, she might as well be thoroughly improper and use the lady's given name. 'Shall we go above stairs? I do not think I can discuss such matters in the parlour.'

Serena sprang to her feet.

Madeleine brought her into the bedroom she shared with Linette. Serena glanced around the room, her eyes resting on the child's bed. 'Is this where you and Devlin…?'

'My goodness, no!' Madeleine replied. 'This is the room I share with Linette…sometimes.' She added, 'Do you wish to see Devlin's room?'

'Yes.' Serena nodded firmly.

Madeleine groaned inwardly. How much more improper could they be? She opened the connecting door and they walked through.

Devlin's room looked as if a whirlwind had been trapped inside its walls. Madeleine had forgotten she had not set foot in his room since stalking out the previous night. She had not straightened the linens, nor picked up his clothes.

Serena's eyes grew wide with wonder. Her gaze fixated on the tangle of sheets and blankets on the bed.

'Let us return to the other room,' Madeleine said firmly, ushering her back through the door.

Serena spoke excitedly. 'When I was young, my bosom bows and I would sit upon my bed for a comfortable coze. Shall we do the same?' The fine lady planted herself cross-legged upon the bed. She pulled off her hat and spencer, placing them on the side table. Madeleine had no choice but to join her.

Madeleine faced Serena's bright, eager countenance. Serena looked as youthful as she must have been with those bosom bows.

Where to begin?

'Have you and the Marquess ever had…um…have you bedded?'

Serena leaned forward with enthusiasm. 'Oh, yes, indeed, but I fear I did something wrong, because it was so very *painful* the first time, and somewhat so every other time. My husband obliged by being very quick about it, so as to not distress me overmuch.'

So the Marchioness had not experienced the pleasure of lovemaking. Madeleine felt sorry for her. But was a lady supposed to experience the kind of frank pleasure she knew with Devlin?

Serena stammered. 'I…I am not sure I can explain all that happened. I was so nervous, you see.'

'That is of no consequence,' Madeleine said hurriedly. She had no desire to hear the details of the Marquess and Marchioness in bed. 'I must think a moment where to begin.'

She glanced at Serena, feeling the wiser, though the lady was at least ten years older. Madeleine had vastly more experience, but what did she truly know of love between a husband and wife? Farley had not taught her about that kind of love.

She closed her eyes and thought of Devlin. He had shown her all she would ever know of love. She set her chin firmly and began. 'I think you will find that lovemaking is very easy. Composed of easy parts.'

After all, it took a mere glance from Devlin to set Madeleine's senses aflame.

'First,' she said, 'you must look at your husband. Make sure he knows you are doing so. No glancing away, until you are certain he has felt your eyes upon him.'

'I shall look at my husband,' Serena repeated.

What else made the blood thunder through Madeleine's veins? When Devlin touched her.

'Next, you must find reasons to touch him,' she said in an authoritative tone. 'Take imaginary fluff off his clothing. Brush his hand with yours. Arrange his hair with your fingers. Just touch him in ordinary ways.'

Serena's eyes glittered excitedly. 'What does that do?'

What it did for Madeleine. 'His body will come alive to you.'

Serena nodded. 'What else?'

'Well, you must contrive to get in bed with him.' Perhaps that was too obvious.

Serena's expression turned bleak. 'How can I do that?'

Goodness, Madeleine had forgotten that Devlin had resisted her initial attempts at seduction. Her cheeks grew hot as she recalled how she'd thrown herself at him. What had finally induced him to accept her?

His nightmare of Waterloo. 'You might pretend to have a bad dream. Would he come to you if you called out?'

Serena frowned. 'I doubt he would hear me.'

'Then you must go to his room and wake him. Seek his comfort. He would wish to comfort you, would he not?'

'Perhaps.' She sounded uncertain.

'Of course he would!' At least Madeleine hoped so. She had not been able resist Devlin's need for comfort. 'You must insist on not being alone. You must contrive to stay in his bed.'

Her pupil nodded resolutely. 'Then what?'

Then let nature dictate the next course, unless the Marquess and Marchioness had somehow thwarted nature. This was becoming absurd. 'You must cling to him.'

Tears formed in Serena's eyes. 'Will he allow me to?'

Madeleine took a deep breath. The Marchioness was truly an innocent. What man would refuse such a creature? Had any man ever refused to touch The Mysterious Miss M? Serena was so much more beautiful. 'You must ask him to hold you, then. He will not refuse, believe me.'

'What then?'

What happens after should need no lesson, if they both allowed what comes naturally to man and woman.

Madeleine's pupil needed very explicit instructions. 'If you feel the time is right, you remove your clothes, remove his clothes, and make love to him.'

'How?' She gave an anguished cry.

There was a limit to how much she would discuss. 'Serena, merely touch him all over. Anywhere. Kiss him. It will suffice, believe me.'

'What if it does not?' Serena's lip trembled.

'Then, what have you lost? You will have tried, after all. Would you wish to go on with the rest of your life, thinking you might have had happiness if you had only seized the chance?'

Unlike Madeleine, Serena had every reason to expect happiness, but Madeleine pushed that thought away.

Serena set her jaw firmly and sat up ramrod straight. The lady had made her decision. Madeleine smiled inwardly. Finally she felt useful.

Devlin had endured his promised calls to Miss Duprey and Miss Reynolds, mainly because he had hit upon the idea of bringing Ram with him. He still felt like weeping with gratitude to have found his friend left alive.

Ram's presence this day prevented Devlin from feeling too much obligation toward Miss Duprey, and, since Ram and Amanda Reynolds had taken such a dislike to each other, the sparks flying between the two of them diverted Devlin from his sour stomach and still-aching head.

He begged off Ram's invitation to pass more time in the tavern and made for home. As he neared his apartments, he tried to recall what had disturbed him so the previous night. Some ominous presence he could not grab hold of. He glanced toward his building. His brother's carriage was pulled up to the front.

Devlin broke into a run. What was Ned doing here? Why would his brother visit? To take Linette?

'What goes on here?' he snarled to the coachman.

The man looked puzzled. 'I've walked the horses, m'lord.'

Devlin jumped on to the side of the carriage and peered inside, ready to confront his brother.

The carriage was empty. 'Where are they?' he demanded.

The footman pointed to the house.

Devlin bounded into the house and found the parlour empty. The kitchen floor was dotted with puddles, a bucket and scrub brush lying in the middle of the room. Voices sounded above him.

Giggles?

He tore up the stairs. 'Ned! Ned! Where are you? By God, if I find you…'

He flung open the door to Linette's room.

Two female heads popped up in surprise.

'What the devil…?'

Madeleine and Serena sat on the bed, looking like two little girls caught in mischief.

'Hello, Devlin,' said Serena, who broke into giggles.

He scowled. 'Where the devil is Ned?'

'Ned?' Serena gave him a puzzled look. 'At White's, I should think.'

'Then where the devil is Linette?' Women. They made no sense.

'Linette went with Bart and Sophie to purchase some meat pies for supper. I suspect they may have also made a stop at the confectioners,' Madeleine said, barely concealing mirth.

Devlin put his hand up for her to stop talking. He rubbed his brow. 'Then Ned did not take Linette?'

'No, indeed!' a shocked Serena said. 'How absurd.'

'How could you think such a thing?' Madeleine scolded.

Serena bussed Madeleine's cheek. 'I think perhaps I should take my leave.'

Madeleine looked regretful. She reached for Serena's hat and helped Serena place it becomingly on her head. Then she assisted her into her spencer. The two smiled at each other.

'Would you mind telling me what the devil is going on?' Devlin said.

'Oh, Serena is leaving.' Madeleine smiled.

'I surmised that.' He touched his forehead. 'Why the devil is she here?'

Madeleine gave him an impatient glance. 'Devlin, I do wish you would not swear.'

'Damnation, tell me why my sister-in-law is visiting my…is visiting here.'

Serena swept over to him and gave his arm an affectionate squeeze. 'A mere afternoon call.'

He gave her a sceptical look. The two women walked down the stairs, arm in arm, chatting companionably. Madeleine rushed ahead to the parlour to gather Serena's gloves and reticule. Serena gave her a big hug, and Devlin thought he heard Madeleine whisper, 'Good luck.'

Why the devil was Maddy wishing Serena good luck?

Madeleine stood at the open door as the footman assisted Serena into the carriage. Serena waved out the window. Madeleine watched for several minutes after Serena had gone out of sight.

'She's left, Maddy.'

'I know,' Madeleine said in a dreamy tone. 'I was placing her in memory.'

The Marquess sipped his sherry and gazed absently out the window as he waited for his wife to appear for dinner. His heart was sick with grief, but he promised he would reveal nothing. He had seen a glimpse of the Heronvale carriage on St James's Street, near Devlin's residence. He had casually checked with Jem to see if Devlin had the use of it, but, as he feared, it had been Serena.

He gulped the remainder of his sherry. His wife having an affair with his brother? How much more painful could it be? Damn Devlin! Pretending to court one young lady while setting up housekeeping with another while dallying with his brother's wife. Ned squeezed the crystal wineglass, shattering it in his hand as Serena entered the room.

'Oh, my! What happened?' She ran over to him, behaving as if she cared that he bled.

'It is a trifle,' he said, wrapping his finger with his handkerchief. He twisted away, refusing to be duped by her solicitude.

She pulled the bell, and Barclay appeared. 'Some bandages, Barclay, if you please. And I'm afraid there is broken glass.'

'Immediately, my lady.'

Barclay returned almost at once with a basin of clean water and the bandages.

'Sit down, Ned,' Serena commanded, 'so I may tend to you.'

He opened his mouth to protest, but she took his arm and pushed him gently into a chair and knelt in front of him. Perhaps if he endured her ministrations he could dispense with them as soon as possible.

She held his hand over the basin and carefully removed his handkerchief. 'You have a piece of glass piercing your finger.' She placed her delicate finger and thumb around the piece of glass and pulled it out, dipping his finger into the soothing warm water. Patting his finger dry, she unrolled the bandage and wrapped it around the wound.

Ned could not bear another moment of this. In a voice tight with restrained emotion, he asked, 'Where were you before this?'

She glanced at him anxiously, biting her lip. He steeled himself for her lie.

'Ned, please do not be angry. I called upon Miss England.'

'What?'

'I know you will think it dreadfully improper, but I have worried about the girl since that night she ran out.' Though she was finished wrapping his finger, she held on to his hand, stroking it with torturous gentleness.

He pulled his hand away. 'Was my brother also there?'

'He arrived as I was leaving.' She stood up, but, before she moved away from him, did an unexpected thing. She stroked his cheek.

'Shall we go in to dinner so that the glass may be cleaned up?' She extended her hand to him, so he had to grasp it as he rose out of the chair. Then she took his arm and leaned against him as they walked to the dining room.

Dinner was an excruciatingly confusing affair. He halfway believed her story about visiting Devlin's mistress. It was the sort of kindness Serena might undertake, but he sensed she was not telling all. Throughout dinner, he felt her gaze upon him. Whenever he looked up, she gave him a smile, not at all like an unfaithful wife—or at least how he imagined an unfaithful wife would act. In addition, she looked extraordinarily beautiful. She wore a silk dress of the palest pink. A matching ribbon threaded through the loose curls of her shining hair. There was high colour in her cheeks and sparkle in her blue eyes.

'Where do you go this evening, Serena?'

She sighed. 'I have decided to stay home. I am sick to death of society.'

He raised a sceptical eyebrow. 'What of Devlin?'

She gave him a puzzled look. 'Devlin? Oh, can he not manage on his own now? He seems to get about well.'

Ned fixed his attention on his buttered lobster. When she spoke like this, he could almost believe her. After all, Devlin had his young lightskirt…and that beautiful child. He had no need for Serena.

What gnawed at Ned the most was that Serena ought to prefer his younger brother, with his easy, ne'er-do-well ways. Devlin could charm with a mere smile. Ned had always marvelled at that ability because he so thoroughly lacked it. What did he know of charm? Serena had married him because it was what her father wished. It had been a splendid match on both sides, true, but Ned had loved everything about her from first sight. It mattered not that his father had dictated the marriage.

He glanced up. Serena sat with her fork poised in her delicate hand, her eyes on him. After a long moment, she cast them down with a flutter of her long lashes. Ned grew warm.

'Do you retire early, then?' Ned asked, though it did not help his sudden flare of heat to remind himself of how Serena looked amidst white sheets.

Angelic.

'I am not tired,' she replied. 'Merely tired of the noise and crowds and gossip. Do you go out tonight, Ned?' She looked at him again, her gaze hopeful.

But for what? Did she hope for him to be gone? Or to stay? By damn, he'd not give her the satisfaction of wishing him away.

'I prefer a quiet evening. You know that, Serena.'

She tilted her head, pursing her perfect rosebud of a mouth. 'You have put yourself out in society very much, these past weeks.'

And how could he not? To avoid the parties and balls meant leaving Serena to Devlin.

Ned's jaw muscles clenched. 'To keep an eye on my brother.'

He took a long sip of wine. Her brow creased, looking disappointed.

She excused herself shortly thereafter, to leave him to his port. As she walked by him, her hand slid across the back of his chair, her fingertips lightly touching his back. The sensation remained long after she departed.

He went straight to his room after that, carrying a brandy decanter with him and freeing himself from his neckcloth as soon as he crossed the threshold. His valet appeared to assist him out of his coat and waistcoat. After his man hung up the clothing, Ned dismissed him.

He kicked off his shoes and sat in the worn leather chair that had been in this room for as long as he could remember. Stretching his legs, he poured himself a generous supply of brandy, but his hand hurt like the devil when he picked up the glass. No comfort in brandy if it brought pain. After draining the contents, he set down the glass and replaced the decanter's glass stopper. He hoped the brandy would help him sleep.

The drink fulfilled its promise, and dreams drifted though

his slumber, disturbing dreams of Serena and Devlin and losing them both.

A soft voice called his name. 'Ned? Ned?'

He opened one eye and shot out of the chair. Serena stood in front of him, her pale hair and thin white nightdress glowing in the faint light from a branch of candles behind her.

'What has happened?' he cried, sure that only something dire would bring her into his room of her own accord.

Her hand swept through her long silken tresses. 'It was awful, Ned.'

'What?' He could not help it. He reached for her.

She seemed to crumble in his arms. 'The dream.' She shuddered. 'I could not find you anywhere. You were gone.'

Returning to the chair, he settled her on his lap. She cried softly against his shoulder.

'Shh, my love,' he murmured. 'I am here now.' He stroked her hair, inhaling the rose scent that always lingered there. She felt soft and warm, and his loins ached with a need he could scarce bear not filling. She'd best leave soon or he could not vouch for his control.

Her breathing finally relaxed. Not knowing if he wished her to stay or to go, Ned asked, 'Are you ready to go back to bed now, love?'

She grasped his shirt tightly. 'No, please. May I sleep with you? I cannot bear to be alone.'

When he placed her in his bed and stripped out of his clothes, he could have sworn that she smiled.

Chapter Eighteen

'Dearly beloved, we are gathered here…'

The sonorous voice of the rector echoed through the small church. Tears streamed down Madeleine's cheeks.

Sophie looked beautiful as she never had appeared to Madeleine before. She supposed beauty had led to Farley's interest in Sophie, but by the time Madeleine got to know her, fear had obscured the girl's looks. This day, standing next to her stalwart protector, Sophie looked radiant.

The dress Sophie had fashioned for herself was a vision of pale pink that swirled like a cloud whenever she moved. The colour put a bloom in her pale cheeks. Madeleine had woven a crown of tiny pink roses, the same colour as the dress, for Sophie to wear in her shining gold hair. Sophie gazed upon her loving groom with all the wonder and innocence of a virgin.

The clergyman droned, '…signifying unto us the mystical union that is betwixt Christ and his church…'

Madeleine was grateful beyond all measure that her friend had found the love of the good, solid Bart. She also envied Sophie painfully.

The humble furnishings of the church suited the parishioners—shopkeepers, merchants and other working people, useful people. It was not dissimilar to the church in her home parish where she used to receive angry glares from her governess for her fidgeting. As a child, she'd never been able to sit still for Sunday services. Now, what she would give for the peace of that country church. Perhaps if she had attended to her vicar's sermons, she might have avoided her sinful life.

Sophie coughed, bringing such a look of loving concern to Bart's face that Madeleine nearly started weeping again.

'Wilt thou have this woman to thy wedded wife, to live together after God's ordinance in the holy estate of matrimony? Wilt thou love her, comfort her, honour and keep her…'

Madeleine glanced at Devlin. Linette's tiny hand nestled in Devlin's strong one as they stood in front of the altar. He had never looked so handsome. He wore a simple morning coat of tobacco brown. Except for the superior cut, his clothes could not be distinguished from the style worn by Bart and other men walking about their business in this neighbourhood. He'd chosen attire that did not outshine the bride and groom.

Madeleine sighed. Truth was, Devlin looked exactly as she'd so often fantasised him, an ordinary man with whom she might share a cottage and a simple life. She shook her head. It was nonsense to hope. Soon she would never see him again.

Linette pulled away from Devlin's grasp and lifted both hands in the air. Automatically, Devlin reached down and picked her up. She leaned her head against his shoulder.

Madeleine's throat tightened. How would losing Devlin affect Linette? He had become so much a part of her world.

'…keep thee only to her, so long as you both shall live?'

Bart responded in a strong, firm voice. 'I will.'

Madeleine imagined Devlin standing before an altar making these same vows. It would be a grander church, of course, St George's, perhaps. Would his bride, like Sophie, radiate innocence and suppressed passion? Would Devlin look upon her with the same astonished joy as that written all over Bart's face?

It did not bear thinking of.

Devlin turned toward Madeleine. His eyes, which he quickly averted, were filled with pain.

'I now pronounce you man and wife,' the rector concluded, raising his voice as if there were a church full of people to hear. 'You may kiss the bride.'

Sophie blinked rapidly and Bart's face turned beet red. He bent toward the tiny woman, his movement tentative, but he raised Sophie's chin with a gentle finger and placed his lips lightly on hers. They held the kiss for a long time until Madeleine thought she might break down in sobs from the pure beauty of the moment.

Bart and Sophie put their marks in the register, and the small party left the church to walk to a nearby inn. Devlin had arranged a private parlour for a proper wedding breakfast for the five of them. The room was comfortable, a place where Sophie and Bart could relax. Breakfast consisted of all manner of fare: chocolate, sliced ham, boiled eggs, pastries, sweetmeats and dishes of berries and cream. Devlin proved an excellent host, keeping up cheerful banter, so that Madeleine was able to laugh when she otherwise might have dissolved into tears. Even Sophie smiled, though Devlin's gentle teasing made her blush.

Devlin had secured a room for the night for the couple, stocked with wine and other delicacies. He had offered them a wedding trip, but Bart refused. Neither had family to visit, Bart explained, and unfamiliar places would only unsettle Sophie.

Madeleine hugged her little friend tightly when they said their goodbyes. Though it was for a mere night, the marriage meant that she and Sophie would never have quite the same relationship as before. Sophie clung to her for a moment, whispering in Madeleine's ear, 'Oh, thank you, Maddy. I am so very happy.'

Evening shadows darkened the bedroom while Devlin sat with Linette, trying to encourage her to sleep. Her eyes were red and puffy with fatigue from the excitement of the day, but stubbornly she refused to keep them shut.

After leaving Bart and Sophie to their wedded bliss, Devlin had been loath to return home. He had insisted upon taking Madeleine and Linette to the nearby shops where he showered trinkets on a reluctant Madeleine and an eager Linette.

Linette's bed was now littered with a family of handsome horseflesh. A mare, stallion and filly, finely painted with acute accuracy and beauty, were nestled next to the child, but were not helping sleep. Linette checked and rechecked to see if they were tucked in properly. Devlin made up stories about them, setting their antics in the rolling acres of Heronvale, where they galloped and frolicked and got into mischief.

Linette's eyes widened and twinkled, but did not close.

'I believe you need nice, dull nursery stories.'

Devlin glanced over to see Madeleine in the doorway. His heart leapt into his throat. No more than a silhouette in the dim light, the curved lines of her body made his pulse quicken.

'I can remember none of them. We need to purchase a book, I suppose,' he said, trying to ignore the alluring scent of lavender that always surrounded her.

'Perhaps if you sang to her.'

He gave her a soft laugh. 'If I sang to her, she might never sleep again.'

'Fustian. You have a fine voice.'

He reached out his hand. 'Come. You sing to her.'

Madeleine walked over to the bed, and he nestled her in front of him, wrapping his arms around her and resting his chin on her shoulder.

'My sweetling,' she said, fussing with Linette's blanket, 'you must try to sleep now. It is very late.'

Linette gave her a mutinous look.

'What if we sing to you together?' Devlin asked.

Linette nodded, eyes stubbornly open.

In a quiet baritone, he began, 'Hush a bye. Don't you cry. Daddy's gone for a soldier…' Madeleine joined in with her sweet clear voice, 'When you wake, you shall see all the pretty little horses…'

Neither of them could remember more of the song, so they repeated the lines over and over until Linette's eyes finally grew heavy. Devlin admired her will. The child clung to her happy day.

It had been a happy day indeed for Bart and Sophie, but for Devlin, one of excruciating agony. At the church, the vow Bart spoke to Sophie was the same one he would soon speak to a woman he did not love. He would never feel the unrestrained joy that shone on Bart and Sophie's faces when they were pronounced man and wife. By that time he would have packed Madeleine and Linette off to some comfortable cottage, never to see them again.

'…Daddy has gone for a soldier…' Madeleine sang. As Devlin accompanied her, the words echoed in his mind, *Daddy has gone…has gone…has gone.*

Linette's eyes remained closed, surrendering to the inevitable, as he would ultimately do.

Madeleine rose from the bed, a finger to her lips. He followed her silently out the door, which she closed soundlessly.

'Finally.' She sighed. 'I thought she would never sleep.'

Devlin could not speak, his emotions too raw. The faint pounding of French drums touched his ears.

Madeleine smiled at him. How did she remain so calm when life was a shambles? 'You must be late dressing for the evening. Shall I assist you?'

He stared blankly. 'I am not going out.'

Her shoulders relaxed slightly. Perhaps she was not so calm after all.

'I would not leave you alone, Maddy.'

As soon as he'd said it, the irony of those words struck him like the Frenchman's lance.

He stroked her hair away from her face and leaned down

to touch his lips to hers. Her arms wound around his neck and he lifted her, kissing her as if she were the air he breathed.

How could he ever let her go?

In the days ahead, he vowed, he would savour each moment with her. He would provide her with as many pleasures as he could contrive. Dancing at Vauxhall. Riding in Hyde Park. Searching nearby shops for whatever she fancied.

This night he would love her with every muscle in his body, every sinew, every nerve. He would give all of himself, and glory in her response. He would show her that, although they must part, his love would endure throughout eternity.

Devlin swung Madeleine into his arms and, like a groom might carry his bride over the threshold, he carried her into his bedchamber.

The next evening, the air was chilly as the boatman's oars splashed rhythmically into the Thames. With shaking fingers, Madeleine adjusted the black mask covering her face. Wearing a mask again reminded her of her nights with Farley, although this soft cloth rested almost like a caress against her skin. With a shiver, she wrapped her paisley shawl more tightly around her shoulders. When they reached the dock and Devlin assisted her out of the boat, the night air felt warmer.

She took Devlin's arm as they walked to the arched entrance of Vauxhall Gardens. He grinned at her, his matching mask making him resemble a devilish bandit. In his trousers and coat, he might have been any young man about town. He'd promised her anonymity, more important to her than a night of music and dancing, or a chance to again wear the golden evening dress he had purchased for her.

People from all walks of life crowded the entrance, many masked like she. Shop girls, she imagined, and clerks, maids and footmen, all mingling freely in their finery, differences of class obscured by the darkness. Was it the chance to pretend or the chance to hide that led others to conceal their identities? For Madeleine, the need to hide provided the chance to pretend. She vowed to pretend that life existed only within these intriguing walls, at least for the space of this one night.

Devlin paid the six-shilling fee, and they stepped through the entrance.

Madeleine gasped. She had stepped into the heavens. Glittering lights shone everywhere like stars come to dwell on earth. Not stars, really, but Chinese lanterns hung everywhere in the elm trees flanking the Grand Walk. The faint sound of music grew louder with each step they took.

'What shall we do first, my love?' asked Devlin, holding her tightly against his side. 'There is much to see.'

'I hardly know.' She glanced around her as they came to the Grand Cross Walk.

'Let us walk the paths, then, 'til you fancy to stop.'

Devlin took her for a stroll down the South Walk with its arches and painted ruins. He kept a wary eye on the young bloods waiting to pull an unsuspecting female into the darker byways. Plenty of men ogled her, and he was glad the glittering surroundings caused her not to notice.

The music was near as they wandered through the Grove, strains of Haydn contributing to the magic that was Vauxhall. As they walked past the supper boxes, Devlin noticed several familiar faces. This had been deemed the fashionable night for the *ton*, he supposed, but who decided one night over another was a mystery to him. Emily Duprey had told him she would not be in attendance. He was pleased. He wished to forget her existence for this one night and pretend there was no one but Madeleine.

Wearing the mask gave him a freedom he would not otherwise have enjoyed. With the mask, he could stroll through Vauxhall, brushing elbows with earls and dukes, Madeleine proudly on his arm, not hidden in the apartments near St James's. He was merely a man escorting his woman, not a gentleman with his mistress. In anonymity, he and Madeleine were like all the other strolling couples.

He smiled at Madeleine's delight, as they passed each new

sight on the South Walk. She swore the painted ruins looked so real, she could walk into them. He wished they could walk into them and never return.

But the South Walk ended, returning them to the Grove. 'Time for us to dance, my love.'

He led her toward musicians playing in a balcony near the supper boxes. The conductor started a waltz just as they arrived, as if he were signalling their appearance. Devlin took Madeleine in his arms and, smiling down at her joyous countenance, whirled her to the strains of the music.

A short distance away in a supper box nearest the dancing, the Marchioness of Heronvale tugged at her Marquess's arm.

'Ned, did you see? I believe that is Devlin and Madeleine.'

He circled his arm around her waist. 'Madeleine, is it? Informal, are you not?' He nuzzled her neck, more interested in the scent of her hair and the softness of her skin than in two people dancing.

'Do behave, Ned,' she scolded, making no effort to move away. 'Look over there. It is Devlin, I am sure.'

He glanced where she had indicated. 'Wife, they are masked.'

'I am sure it is they.' She pulled him out of the box. 'Come, dance with me. We will get closer to them, and you will see. She wears the same dress as she wore to dinner.'

He needed no coaxing to hold her in his arms. These past nights together had been filled with a passion he had not dreamed existed for him. He knew not what had caused the transformation, nor did he care. Happiness was too tame a word for what he felt.

In his gratitude, he would do anything for her. Anything. Even dutifully dancing her near the couple who gazed at no one but each other.

Serena stood on tiptoe and whispered in his ear, 'See, it is they.'

Ned took the opportunity to hold her closer. He agreed it could be Devlin and his Miss England. He recognised the look in the man's eyes. It reflected what sang in his own heart. A pinprick of guilt pierced his happiness, for if that were his youngest brother, Ned's dictates forced the loss of that love. Now Ned understood how that would feel.

'Forget them, Serena,' He murmured gruffly. He clasped her against him in a manner that would get them banned from Almack's forever and would help him not think about the decisions he had forced on his brother.

Serena laughed, a sound more beautiful than the music. With a wicked gleam in her eye, she rubbed her hips against a part of him that now ravenously craved her.

Ned forgot about his brother and turned his thoughts to private recesses of the Gardens where two lovers might retreat. He swept Serena to the edge of the dancing area and led her by the hand to the narrow pathway of the Dark Walk.

Devlin barely heard when the music ended, barely registered the other dancers moving off the floor. Dancing with Madeleine had been magical. Stopping had been like coming out of a spell. She shook her head, as if sharing the same feeling.

He glanced around him. He was not two paces from Amanda Reynolds. Momentarily fearing she would recognise him, Devlin shifted away from her sight. He quickly realised it did not matter. Miss Reynolds would not trouble to notice someone dressed as gentry.

Madeleine uttered a weak cry and pulled at Devlin's arm, as if ready to bolt. She was also looking at Miss Reynolds and he had a moment's anxiety that Madeleine knew her, as well.

'What is it, Maddy?' he asked as she pulled at him.

'Oh, please, let us leave,' she cried, fear etched on her face. 'It is Greythorne.'

Devlin put his arm around her protectively and rushed her away from the dancing area. Finding a quiet spot near a fountain, he sat her on a bench. She trembled under his arm.

'What is it, Maddy? What frightened you.'

She gulped in air. 'Greythorne. I saw Greythorne.'

'You know him?'

She nodded, rocking back and forth.

A sick feeling came over him. 'From Farley's?'

She nodded again. 'Farley banned him from me.'

A man as depraved as Farley banned another from bedding her? 'Why?'

She shook her head, moving away from him.

He drew her closer, blood draining from his face. 'Tell me, Maddy.'

'No. I cannot.'

Devlin thought about Amanda. 'I need to know, Maddy. You must tell me.'

She looked at him worriedly. 'You will not confront him?'

His worry increased. 'Is it so bad?'

She nodded.

'Good God.' He rubbed his forehead. 'Very well, you have my word I will not confront him.'

She twisted her hands in her lap. 'I cannot speak this out loud.'

She knelt on the bench and whispered into his ear, in painful detail, the violence Greythorne had inflicted upon her to fulfil his perverted desires. He had read of such practices, having perused forbidden copies of de Sade's *Justine*. He had witnessed such cruelty during the war, but to have it inflicted upon Madeleine? Rage coursed through him. He clenched his fists, regretting giving his word. Greythorne would not live otherwise.

As if reading his mind, she warned, 'You promised, Devlin.'

He relaxed his hands and caressed her cheek with his finger. Folding her against his chest, he rocked her to and fro as he might have done to soothe Linette.

'Greythorne will never hurt you again,' he murmured. And the man would not hurt Amanda either. Devlin resolved to warn her before tomorrow's end.

'I know.' She cuddled against him. 'It was merely remembering.'

Well he knew about that. 'Let us not let this spoil our evening. Come. We will avoid Greythorne and get refreshments. Our enjoyment need not end.'

He rose from the bench and tugged her to her feet. She came into his arms and he kissed her tenderly. She clung to him for a moment before taking his arm and strolling back to the revelry.

'I want to dance with you again,' Madeleine said, pulling him back to the place from where she had so recently fled.

They danced each waltz and strolled along the paths, enjoying each sight. They sat at one of the Garden's restaurants and ate paper-thin slices of ham, and the tiniest chickens Madeleine had ever seen, washing them down with arrack. When the bells rang, they watched Madame Saqui walk the tightrope.

When it was time for the fireworks, Madeleine hurried Devlin to the best vantage point and fairly jumped up and down. The display began, exceeding all her expectations. Rockets exploded in the air. Sparkles rained down as if all the stars in the sky suddenly fell. Catherine wheels hissed, shedding shards of lights as they spun. Words appeared as still more star showers brightened the sky. The air smelled of sulphur, and the acrid smoke blurred the scene, but still the fireworks boomed and burst in the air.

Devlin's hand dropped from Madeleine's arm. She turned to look at him, to share the excitement. His hands covered his ears. His eyes were clamped shut, a look of anguish on his face.

'Devlin, what is wrong?' She grabbed him as he started to sink to the ground.

He regained his footing with effort, but his whole body trembled. 'Have…to…leave.' The words barely escaped his lips.

She pulled him through the crowd, hurrying toward the

gate. He allowed her to guide him, barely looking up, lost in a nightmare world she could only imagine.

'We are through the gate, Devlin,' she said as if speaking to a blind man. 'Let us go to the boats.'

When they were safely on the water and the sounds muffled by the cool air and the lapping of the oars, he relaxed a fraction. They pulled off their masks and he finally looked at her as if really seeing her.

'Devlin, please tell me. Are you ill?' She still held his arm tightly.

He gave her a wan smile. 'I am afraid the war came back to me.'

She stroked his cheek.

'The sound of the fireworks. It was like the cannon. And the smell…I…I thought I was there again.'

She hugged him fiercely. 'I am so sorry. I did not think. We stayed too long.'

He put his arm around her and she rested her head on his shoulder. 'You could not have known what I did not know myself, but it is all right now, my love.'

He held her close against the chill of the river air. 'I am sorry to have ruined our evening.'

She took his hand in hers. 'It shall always be a magic memory for me.'

As they neared the shore, Madeleine felt a shiver that had nothing to do with the night air. It was a premonition.

Her time with him was nearing its end.

Chapter Nineteen

The next day Devlin called upon Miss Amanda Reynolds as early as propriety would allow. He had borrowed Ned's curricle and meant to induce her to ride with him, the only way he could think to speak with her alone.

'A delicious idea,' she exclaimed. 'Greythorne usually appears at this time and he shall be told I am gadding about with you.' She clapped her hands merrily. 'Give me a moment to don suitable clothing.'

She left the parlour in a rush, obviously not noticing the serious look on his face.

Hyde Park was nearly empty this early hour. Amanda prattled on about Greythorne, the poor refreshments at Vauxhall, and the ball being held that evening. She enquired politely after his friend Ramsford, but in a way that quickly went to a change of subject.

Devlin scarcely heard her.

He drew the horses to a halt. 'Let us walk a little.' Handing the ribbons to Ned's groom, he lifted Amanda from the vehicle.

He seated her on a bench set a little away from the path.

'I must talk with you, Amanda.' They had become friends enough for given names, at least in private.

'So serious, Devlin,' she said with mock solemnity. 'Not some contretemps with the our dull little Miss Duprey, I trust?'

'No.' He took her hand. 'I am afraid it is a topic that is quite improper, but I must pursue it with you.'

An anxious twitch appeared at the corner of her mouth, but she continued to smile. 'Improper? La, you intrigue me, sir.'

Devlin took a deep breath and dove into the tale of Greythorne's predilections.

Her smile quickly fled. She blushed and turned pale by turns. She stared at him with wide eyes or glanced away in embarrassment. His own words sickened him and he could not still images of Greythorne inflicting these debaucheries on Madeleine.

Amanda Reynolds, cosseted darling of the *ton*, could not have imagined half of what he told her. He regretted having to impart these sordid vagaries of intimacy to her and tried to describe the whole to her without graphic explicitness. At the same time, the matter needed to be understood. Amanda must realise the kind of man she intended to marry.

When he finished, she shook her head. 'Such things are not possible! Why would you tell me this?'

He took her hand. 'Believe me, I did not wish to relate these matters to you, but when the knowledge of this came my way, I had to warn you.'

'How did you hear of this?' she stammered.

Devlin rubbed his brow. 'I cannot tell you. Suffice to say that I know of it from one who was his victim.'

She raised her brows.

'I will not say who it might be, so do not ask.'

She rose to her feet. 'I want to go home.'

'Of course.' He offered her his arm. She shrank from it.

They walked silently back to the curricle. He lifted her into the seat and climbed in himself, taking the ribbons while the groom hopped up on back.

When he pulled up to her town house, he said, 'I am truly sorry, Amanda. I had no wish to hurt you.'

She tried to smile at him, but her eyes were pinched with anxiety. 'I suppose I should thank you.'

He lifted her down to the pavement. 'You do believe my tale, don't you?'

'Oh, yes, I believe you.' She sighed. 'Why should you risk your reputation otherwise? I could ruin you for talking of such things to me.'

Devlin shrugged. 'I confess, I did not consider that.'

She did smile, then.

Devlin regarded her anxiously. 'Has he offered for you?'

She shook her head. 'Not yet.'

'Refuse him.' It was simply said.

Her smile fled. 'I will.'

Devlin watched her enter the town house. A horseman rode up beside him.

'Rather early for the Hyde Park set.'

It was Ram. Devlin still felt his heart swell at the sight of the friend he'd thought he lost.

He ignored Ram's comment. 'Good to see you, Ram. Calling upon the Diamond?'

Ramsford gave a snort. 'Don't be absurd. She would hardly find my presence creditable.'

Devlin tossed him a sceptical look. 'If you are not engaged, follow me to my brother's stable so I can rid myself of the curricle.' He had promised to call on Miss Duprey and would value Ram's company.

'I am not engaged. This gentleman's life is totally devoid of purposeful activity.'

They proceeded at a comfortable pace, Devlin feeling the company of his friend an effective antidote to dashing the dreams of the season's Diamond.

The visit with Miss Duprey was pleasant, but without a moment of interest. There was not one thing about her to dislike. Nothing to anger or irritate. Nothing to arouse any form of passion. For that he was grateful. He wanted passion from no woman except Madeleine.

Drums rumbled in his ears as he thought of giving up nights of loving her, days spent in her company. He almost felt as if the darkness would descend upon him, as it had at Waterloo, and he would again be alone with his pain with no one to see his suffering. No one would notice his life ebbing into oblivion.

He glanced at Ram seated across the room, conversing with a young lady also calling upon Miss Duprey. Perhaps some day he would tell his friend about Madeleine and Linette. Then at least one person would know that a piece of Devlin Steele lived and flourished somewhere in England.

'You are quiet today, my lord.' Miss Duprey's voice broke through the drum rolls. 'Are you unwell?'

Her discernment of his mood and her concern were to her credit. She might be bland, but at least she was not insensible.

'I apologise, Miss Duprey. I was merely woolgathering.'

She poured a cup of tea and handed it to him. 'If you are in need of a friendly ear, I am available.'

He gave her a wan smile. 'It is nothing, I assure you.' The drums grew louder. All the thoughts that swam through his head were none he could confide to her.

She cocked her head, a gesture that inexplicably appealed to him. It puzzled him how he'd singled her out for his damnable plan, but then a gesture, such as this, a fleeting look, a trill of her laughter, caught his notice and surprised him each time.

A quarter of an hour later, he and Ramsford departed the lady's parlour and walked to his brother's stable where Ram had left his mount.

'I should call upon the Marchioness, Ram. Are you game to keep me company?'

'It cannot be more of a deadly bore than the last place,' Ramsford said in a dry voice.

When they followed Barclay to the front parlour, the sounds of male and female laughter met their ears. Serena had other callers, no doubt. Perhaps she had given up on his brother and accepted the attentions of one of the many men who sought her.

As they stepped through the doorway, however, the only people present were the Marquess and Marchioness, standing quite close to each other, faces flushed.

Ned strode up, hand extended. 'Dev, good to see you.'

Devlin took his brother's hand, as surprised by the warm handshake as the friendly greeting. He introduced Ram, and presented him to Serena.

'I have seen our new Lord Ramsford many times. How lovely to meet you. You are most welcome as a friend of Devlin's.'

Ned sent Barclay to arrange refreshment and begged leave to speak to Devlin alone.

They entered the library, and Devlin could not help but remember the heat of temper that flared when he last set foot in the room.

'Forgive me for leaving your friend, but I wished to speak with you. Serena and I leave tomorrow for Heronvale. I...I have some business there and she accompanies me.' Ned's face flushed red.

Why should his brother bother to explain this? And why show embarrassment?

Ned gestured to one of the leather chairs in the room and Devlin sat. He poured them each a small glass of sherry.

'There is nothing amiss, I hope?' Devlin took the glass.

'No...no, nothing amiss. All is well.' Ned looked away, but Devlin thought he saw a grin on his brother's face.

'I doubt we will return before the end of the Season,' Ned continued, seating himself in the chair adjacent to Devlin's. 'I thought I should check your...your progress, so to speak.'

Ned's tone and demeanour might be convivial, but he remained thoroughly in control of Devlin's future.

'I have made no commitments as yet.' Devlin tried to sound matter-of-fact.

'The Season will be over in a matter of weeks.' Ned's voice turned tense.

Devlin released a fatalistic breath. 'I have made a selection.'

'And who is the lady?'

'Miss Emily Duprey.' It was as though a cage door closed upon him. Speaking of this out loud to his brother made it all too real. Too final.

'Indeed?' Ned sounded surprised. 'I had thought your interest lay with Miss Reynolds.'

Devlin met his brother's eye. 'My *interest* lies elsewhere.'

Ned had the grace to look faintly ashamed.

Devlin took another sip of the sherry. 'Miss Reynolds and I have an odd friendship. We harbour no other form of attachment.'

Ned fiddled with the stem of his glass. 'I know little of the Dupreys. Malvern, is that the property? A barony?'

'Yes.' Perfectly acceptable, thought Devlin. His brother ought to approve.

'Well...' Ned paused. A softness came into his voice. 'Have you settled Miss England and the child?'

Push the sword in deeper, brother, thought Devlin. 'Not as yet.'

Ned rose and walked to his desk and busied himself writing. He came back to Devlin and handed him a paper.

'This will allow you to draw money in my absence. You will need extra funds to procure a proper place for your...your charges. She must be well situated. Perhaps in Chelsea.'

Devlin accepted the draft and responded in a cool voice, 'I thought the country to be a better choice.'

Ned sat again and spoke as if they were settling some piece of property. 'Much better for them to be among an assortment of the middle classes. You do not wish for there to be questions about them. A ''widow'' and child will not draw attention in Chelsea.'

'No attention at all,' said Devlin mechanically, wishing to blurt out that Madeleine needed the countryside so she could ride. More so, he wished to tell his brother that sending away Madeleine and Linette was tantamount to destroying his own soul.

Devlin glanced at the bank draft. His eyes widened. Ned had written an uncommonly generous amount.

'We do not wish them to suffer,' Ned said softly.

Devlin eschewed a hack and slowly walked home. A persistent drizzle fell, turning the day uncommonly cold. The weather suited his mood.

When he opened the door to his apartments, Linette squealed, 'Deddy!' and bounded into his arms. His eyes moistened as he hugged her to him.

Madeleine appeared from the kitchen, wiping her hands on that abominable apron she wore.

'She has been asking for you all this day. I am nearly mad with it.' She smiled in amusement.

He drew her into the hug. Clasping them both to him, he thought he would be the one to go mad without them. When he loosened his grasp, Madeleine stared into his eyes. With a gentle finger, she wiped moisture from the corner of his eye.

'Come, let me take your hat and coat,' she said. 'You are damp and chilled.'

He put Linette down, but she continued to cling to his legs. 'Play horses with me.' She tugged at his trousers.

He patted the child's shiny curls. 'In a moment, Lady Lin.' Madeleine helped him out of his coat. 'Maddy, I would like to speak with you. Not this moment. When you are able.'

She smiled at him, but the emotion in her eyes was solemn. 'I am in the midst of learning how to cook dinner. Sophie and Bart are teaching me to make boiled beef and oat pudding. Does that not sound delicious?'

'Indeed,' he said, kissing her lightly on the cheek and allowing Linette to pull him into the parlour where her toy horses awaited.

There was not time enough to speak alone to Madeleine until well into the evening after Linette finally lapsed into slumber. Madeleine came into his bedchamber to set out his clothing.

'She is becoming more difficult to get to sleep.' Madeleine raised his evening coat, examining it carefully.

'We need to purchase a book of fairy stories,' he said.

'Indeed,' she agreed. 'Why, I can hardly remember when I last read a book. There is much I ought to read for myself. My mind is in sad need of improving.'

His spirits rose, but only a bit. It was something he could do for her. 'We must go to a bookshop. You may select whatever you wish for yourself and Linette.'

She blushed. 'Please do not countenance my hasty words. I do not expect you to—'

He raised a hand to silence her. 'We will go there tomorrow. I think if we go early you should feel comfortable.'

She was always more concerned about being seen with him than he was with her. For his sake, he supposed, although no one would look upon him with disfavour for being in the company of a beautiful unescorted female. They would merely assume he had an arrangement with her.

'I have brushed your evening clothes,' Madeleine said.

He was expected at the Catsworths' ball this evening, as were Miss Duprey, her brother and her ever-present mother. Amanda, Greythorne, and, thankfully, Ram also planned to attend. Devlin was especially concerned about Amanda Reynolds having to encounter Greythorne.

Devlin stripped down to his small clothes. 'Thank you, Maddy.' He fingered the cloth of his jacket. 'Well done.'

It was painfully ironic that Madeleine acted as his valet when he dressed for these evening entertainments.

She turned to get his clean shirt and he grabbed her arm. 'Sit with me a minute.'

Her eyes lingered on his bare chest, but she dutifully sat next to him on the bed. He should have planned for a neutral setting. The bed brought too many ideas to his head.

He leaned against the pillows and settled her in front of him, his arms around her, her soft hair tickling his chest.

'We must talk of where you will live,' he said.

She stiffened.

'There is little time left,' he continued.

'I told you that it is of no consequence to me where you place us.' Her voice seemed determinedly devoid of emotion.

It was detestable that she must be sent away where he would never be able to check on her, to make sure she was safe. He would never know how she fared. How his daughter fared.

He buried his face in her hair. 'Forgive me, Madeleine.' His body shook. 'I have made a mull of all of it and I cannot make repairs. Forgive me. I never meant to hurt you, to bring you to this end…'

She turned around, coming on to her knees in front of him. She took his face in both her hands. 'Oh, no, you mustn't say so!' She pressed his cheeks firmly. 'You saved us, Devlin. *Saved* us. What would my life be like—Linette's life—if you had not rescued us? Even Sophie. Would she have had any chance for the happiness she now possesses? You did this for us.'

She brushed his hair with her fingers and gazed tenderly at him. 'I shall be grateful to you my whole life. I shall never forget you. Never stop loving you.' Her hands flew to her mouth at these last words.

'Maddy,' Devlin managed, his arms going around her. To hear her say she loved him was unbearable, yet at the same time his heart soared with happiness. Madeleine loved him. She was not merely repaying him with her body. She loved him and, by God, he loved her in return. 'Maddy.'

He could not help himself, needing to show her his love. He rained her with kisses, freed her from her clothes and what few were left of his own. He poured himself into her, desperate to make the moment last, knowing it would be fleeting.

By the time he walked into the Catsworths' ball, almost too late to be fashionable, he moved in a haze of sexual satiation. His soul remained with Madeleine, but his body walked dreamlike through its paces. She loved him, and nothing else seemed the least important.

'Stee-eelle,' slurred a nasally voice. A tottering Robert Duprey grabbed his arm. 'M'sister's awaiting you. Bad form to neglect the chit. Ought to declare y'rself. Common knowledge, y'know.'

Devlin shrugged him off. 'You are presuming, sir. And you are drunk.'

Devlin might next have sought out Miss Duprey, but her brother's insinuations, correct as they might be, angered him. He went in search of Amanda instead. It was never difficult to find her, since she shone more brightly than the other marriage-mart hopefuls. He spied her across the room. Greythorne was speaking animatedly to her, looking very cross. Devlin took a step toward her, but Ram appeared at her side. Ram clamped his fingers into Greythorne's arm and, a moment later, led Amanda into a waltz.

Devlin's throat tightened. He was turning maudlin at seeing his friend assume the role of protector over the fair Miss Reynolds. He glanced around the room and spied Miss Duprey and her mother. She did not see him.

Stepping back, Devlin turned on his heel and fled the ballroom, seeking the chill air of the evening…and home.

Farley hid in the shadows outside the Catsworth town house. Steele would be there. It was *the* event of the evening, after all. The ball would last into the wee hours, but he could stand the wait. He had decided to shadow Steele this night. If the opportunity presented itself, he'd plunge a knife in

Steele's back. With Steele out of the way, Madeleine would have no choice but to return to him.

Carriages continued to arrive and a bustling of people crowded the pavement and the entrance. Farley hardly noticed the man walking in the other direction. It was not until the man disappeared around the corner that he realised the figure had resembled Steele.

Impossible. The ball had hardly started.

Farley would wait. Steele was bound to leave at his usual time and Farley then would be ready.

Chapter Twenty

'Oh, my!' Madeleine cried as she entered Lackington's bookshop on Finsbury Square. She had not imagined so many books to exist in the world.

'Devlin, this is impossible. I will not know how to look.'

He patted the hand holding his arm. 'We shall ask for assistance.'

They walked up to a large circular desk with four clerks behind. Two were idle at this early hour.

'May we assist, sir?' one asked.

Devlin asked the grey-coated clerk to escort them to books suitable for young children. They made a few selections, Aesop's Fables, one book both could recall from childhood, among them. Devlin then requested they be shown the equestrian section. He had in mind that what Linette would enjoy most of all would be a book with engravings of horses.

Unfortunately, such books also captivated Madeleine, and he, of course, could never be uninterested in such a subject. They pored over volumes containing a wealth of information on breeding, riding, equestrian care. They examined fine engravings of handsome horseflesh, arguing energetically over which volume would be most pleasing to Linette.

* * *

When their selections were made and they readied for their departure, Devlin glanced at the large store clock. It read half past one.

'We have been here almost three hours,' he told Madeleine as they stepped out the door.

She grabbed his arm and squeezed it in pleasure. 'I was not aware. Time passed so swiftly.'

The streets were bustling and Devlin looked about, realising the fashionable shoppers were out in abundant numbers, people he'd hoped to avoid, but only because they would distress Madeleine.

Her hand trembled as it clutched his arm. They stepped onto the pavement. Two ladies, one young, one middle-aged, approached.

Emily Duprey and her mother, Lady Duprey.

It was impossible to avoid them. Damn his carelessness. The most efficacious solution would be to pretend he did not see them. They, in turn, would ignore the beautiful creature on his arm, relegating her to a part of a gentleman's life that bore no speaking of.

Miss Duprey glanced up, a shocked look on her face. Devlin felt Madeleine hesitate.

Deuce. He had hoped to spare Madeleine this moment. Walking by would convey that Madeleine was his mistress. Miss Duprey was no naïve miss. At her age she was bound to be realistic about the dealings of men. She could weather the sight of him with a prime article on his arm, as could her mother. But could he bear Madeleine's humiliation?

He could not.

When they were abreast of the two women, he smiled and gave them a small bow. 'Lady Duprey, Miss Duprey, good afternoon.'

The two ladies gaped. Lady Duprey appeared as if she would pop a blood vessel.

Devlin remained undaunted. 'May I make known to you Miss Madeleine England? She has accompanied me to this

excellent bookshop.' He stepped aside to present Madeleine,
who grasped his arm so tightly it hurt. 'Miss England, Lady
Duprey and her daughter, Miss Duprey.'

Madeleine gave a stiff curtsy. 'How do you do,' she said,
her voice barely audible.

Lady Duprey hissed, muttering under her breath, 'This is
the outside of enough.' She pulled at her daughter.

Miss Duprey paused and gave a shaky nod of her head. As
her mother hurried her off, she turned and took one last brief
glance at Madeleine, the shock still plain on her face.

After they disappeared through the doorway of the bookshop, Madeleine went limp beside him. He dropped the
wrapped package of books as he caught her, easing her to sit
on some nearby steps.

'Maddy,' he exclaimed, alarmed. Retrieving the books, he
sat next to her. 'I am so sorry. Shall I get a hack?'

'Give me a moment, if you please.' She hugged her knees
and rocked, hiding her face from him.

Passers-by began to take notice.

'I shall secure a hack.' Devlin hurried to the street and
waved a hand to an approaching hackney coach. He almost
carried Madeleine to the vehicle and bundled her inside.

'I am recovered now,' she said in a weak voice, her hand
covering her eyes.

'Damn.' He rubbed her arms bracingly. 'There was no call
for them to look at you such. They could not know…'

'It is of no consequence.' She continued to shield her eyes,
and he feared she was crying.

'I am sorry for that, Maddy. You have probably deduced
who they are.' He expelled a tense breath. 'Believe me, I
would not for the world wished you to encounter the lady
I…I mean, the one I…'

'Oh, no.' Madeleine felt her moan emerge from the depths
of her heart. It was worse than she imagined. Much, much
worse.

Devlin continued, 'Damn them. Their treatment was rag-
mannered in the extreme. You appear perfectly respectable.

You could have been my cousin or Ram's sister, for God's sake. They had no right to treat you so.'

She lowered her hand and gazed out the window of the hack. 'They had every right, Devlin.' She took a breath and faced him, looking directly into his eyes. 'They are my mother and sister. They thought themselves rid of me after I shamed them so.'

He stared at her, speechless.

The calm of fatalism descended upon her. 'Let us not go home just yet. Ask the driver to drop us in the park. I once promised to tell the whole of my story. You shall hear it now.'

He rapped for the coachman to stop.

They found a bench in the park. Devlin protested that she would be chilled, but Madeleine assured him the brisk air served her well. They sat in silence.

'It is unusually chilly for June.' He drummed his fingers on his knee.

She smiled at him, capturing his hand and squeezing it. Nearby, a bird flapped its wings, aiming for the sky. She fully expected any regard he had for her to also take flight.

'I grew up in Wiltshire,' she began, 'though I suppose your acquaintance with Emily has told you that. I was the youngest. There was my brother, my oldest sister Jessame, Emily, and me. I believe my mother was tired of children by the time of my birth. She bothered little with me. Our father had no interest in any of us, I do not think. In any event, I was a difficult child. Wilful. I never heeded governesses, or tutors or anyone. I was sent down from the few schools I attended. All I ever wished to do was ride my horse.'

He placed his hand over hers. 'You could be speaking of my childhood, you know. Except my father took an intense interest in every niggling aspect of my life.'

'But your life has been worthwhile. Mine has…' She cleared her throat, and took a deep breath. 'I was fifteen when Farley came to visit. He had some business with my father, I know not what, but my older sisters were allowed to take meals with him, while I was confined to the nursery. I cared not for stuffy dinners, but my sisters teased me about it ceaselessly. When Lord Farley saw me out riding one morning, I was ripe to have some revenge upon them.' She glanced at him, blinking rapidly. 'But I have told you this part.'

His gaze searched her face. She'd once spoken lightly of Farley's seduction. 'I suspect there was more to it than the trifling occurrence you made it out to be.'

'I suppose.' She crossed her arms over her chest. 'It was a fine jest on my sisters, you know. The man they spoke of incessantly was paying me attention. Imagine. *Me*. He spoke pretty words to me.' She hugged herself tightly. 'I had no idea the impression I made in my brother's old clothes. The shirt had become tight around my chest, and I could barely lace up the pants. I thought nothing of it. I simply loved to ride like a boy. In those days I'd wished I was a boy, for boys could do all sorts of exciting things, like race and be soldiers and such. I hated to sit still for sewing or pianoforte or French lessons.'

He regarded her, tenderness filling him. He wished he might have ridden over the countryside with that young girl.

She continued. 'Lord Farley told me later that my clothes would have aroused any man. I should have known that, but I never paid attention when the governess talked of such things.' She bit her lip. 'When Lord Farley kissed me, my only thought was that I had achieved something my sisters endlessly dreamed about. I could not wait to tell them.'

She stood up and paced. 'Lord Farley suggested we retire to the hunting box nearby. His kisses were not unpleasant, and I was eager to try anything, so I did.' She stared at him. 'He showed me more than kisses. I do not know how it progressed as it did, but I made no effort to stop him. My body responded to him, Devlin.' She stopped to see how her words affected him.

She sunk back next to him on the bench. 'I vowed never again to allow myself such feelings.' She stared straight ahead of her, as if the bushes and trees held her fascination. 'And I never did, until that night with you.'

He put his arm around her, laying her head on his shoulder.

It took several seconds for her to continue. 'He told me to come to his room that night. I did, of course. It was so exciting, you see. At the worst possible time…my father opened the door.'

Madeleine pulled away from him and buried her face in her hands. 'I knew I was doing wrong. I knew it was sinful. I deserved for my parents to send me away. It was only fitting.'

'The deuce it was,' he muttered. 'At your age, they ought to have had Farley drawn and quartered.'

'Oh, no. I enticed him, you see. Both he and my father said so. It was not his fault. A man cannot be expected to control those…those urges.' The expression on her face was resolute. She believed this nonsense.

Devlin grabbed her shoulders and made her look at him. Though his grip was firm, his voice was soft. 'Maddy, a gentleman must control such urges. Did I not do so when you first came to stay? It was not easy, believe me.'

She blinked and knit her brows together. 'But I seduced you, too. When…when I wanted to make love to you, you could not resist.'

He could not help but smile. 'Goose, you did not seduce me. There was no need to resist when we both were willing.'

She shook her head. 'You do not understand.'

'I understand Farley took advantage of an innocent girl.'

She shrugged. 'I suppose it makes no difference. When the deed was done, my fate was ordained.'

He stood and extended his hand to her. 'Come, let us walk.'

She rose and took his arm.

He kept her close beside him. After a while he said, 'I still cannot believe your parents allowed you to be carried off by Farley. Surely they must have known who he was.'

'Indeed, they did. My mother told me she always knew I

was a shameful girl. She said I deserved to be with such a man. I was so foolish, I thought he would take me to Gretna Green. Only when we reached London did I realise what my mother meant.'

Devlin felt sick with rage. What kind of parent would send an innocent young daughter into the clutches of a man like Farley? It was unconscionable.

'In any event,' she went on, her voice curiously devoid of the hot emotions firing off in him, 'it was not long after that Lord Farley showed me my obituary in *The Times*.'

'Your obituary?'

'My parents fabricated my death. Farley told me there was a grave marked by a stone with my name upon it.'

'Damn them all.'

Devlin tried to convey some semblance of calm, but inside rage burned. Damn them all. They had taken a fresh, headstrong, spirited girl, robbed her of her life, and sent her into hell.

And he had left her there, all alone, when she had been only fifteen. He should have sent her to Serena or one of his sisters. Their kind hearts would have understood how to help her. Instead he had walked away, content to consign the pleasure of her company to fond memory.

Without speaking more of the matter, they walked through the park to their apartments. Madeleine busied herself with housework, while Devlin, still feeling the burden of abandoning Madeleine, turned the pages of the book for Linette, showing her the pictures of horses. His mind simmered. He did not make his afternoon call to Miss Duprey as had been expected. He did not attend Mrs Drummond-Burrell's musical evening that was touted the event of the season. Instead, he took a long walk in the drizzle and chill.

When he returned, Madeleine was in her own bed. He came to her side and her eyes fluttered open. In the light of the candle he carried, her eyes looked red and puffy. He blew out the candle, picked her up, and carried her to his bed.

His room was plunged in darkness. Wordlessly, they made love. The darkness and silence heightened the sense of melancholy in their lovemaking. Devlin felt rather than saw her and heard nothing but her breathing and the sounds of their bodies coming together. It was as if she had half-disappeared already and he was desperately clinging to what was left of her. When both were sated, he held her against him, his fingers combing her hair off her face, wet with tears. He still could not speak, but simply tightly held on to her until sleep finally came to him.

When morning came, Madeleine carefully manoeuvred herself out of the bed so as not to disturb Devlin. She found her nightdress in a heap on the floor and, as she donned it, gazed at the sleeping man. His handsome face was relaxed and peaceful, as it had not been since that fateful meeting with her mother and sister. At this moment he looked so much like Linette no one would doubt his paternity. She no longer doubted it, but accepted it as another of the painful paradoxes of her life. Like loving him and, therefore, having to lose him.

The foreboding sense that their idyllic interlude would soon speed to its end had lingered with her since the bookshop, and, thus, this day seemed grave indeed.

The feeling did not leave her when she busied herself preparing Linette's breakfast, accompanied by the child's irrepressible chatter. It was unusual for her to rise before Bart and Sophie, but perhaps the newly married couple were beginning their day in a happier mood than she.

Madeleine cooked coddled eggs and toast. When first Devlin brought them here, she could do nothing so useful; now she had learned so many skills. She could cook simple meals, scrub a floor, dust furniture and do simple sewing. She knew how to shop and how to bargain with shopkeepers. There was no doubting it. She was prepared to leave.

Bart came into the room, his face pinched with worry.

'What is it, Bart?'

'Sophie is feeling very poorly.' His voice was stressed.

'Shall I go to her?' Madeleine wiped her hands.

Bart nodded, giving her an agonised look.

Bart's room was spare but as orderly as Devlin's was disordered. Sophie lay on the bed, each breath coming with effort. Her face was nearly as pale as the linens she lay upon and dark circles showed under her eyes. She woke as Madeleine came to her side and gave a wan smile.

'We shall get the doctor for you, I think,' Madeleine said.

'Oh, no,' rasped Sophie, her voice thin and weak. 'There is no need. I shall be all right directly.'

'Indeed, you shall.' Madeleine patted her reassuringly. 'I will bring you some tea. Would you like that?'

Her waiflike friend nodded and wearily closed her eyes.

Madeleine returned to Bart in haste. 'Fetch the doctor. I cannot like the way she breathes.'

Bart immediately grabbed his coat and hat, hanging on a hook by the back door. 'I thought so, as well. I will get the man right now.' He let the door slam behind him as he rushed out.

Not long after, Devlin came into the kitchen.

'Deddy!' Linette squealed, scattering her wooden horses with a clatter as she bounded into his arms.

Her heart lurching as it always did at such tender scenes, Madeleine asked, 'May I prepare you some food, Devlin?'

He gave Linette a hug and a kiss and set her back on the floor. She happily returned to the corner where her horses lay. 'No, I must be off…a…a piece of business that must not be delayed.'

Madeleine faced him. She'd been about to tell him of Sophie, but changed her mind. No need to add to the stress evident in his countenance.

'Very well,' she said, trying to keep her voice even.

His mouth was set in a firm determined line. He held her gaze for a moment before he turned on his heel and left.

Madeleine squeezed her eyes shut and took long steadying breaths. Linette banged her horses on the wooden floor, saying, 'Gallump. Gallump,' as they galloped around her. Before Madeleine allowed herself further thoughts of Devlin, she hurried to check on Sophie.

His first piece of business complete, Devlin proceeded to Mayfair, knowing the hour was early for calls, but he had no wish to postpone this meeting. Best to dispense with it.

The Duprey butler ushered him into the parlour. Devlin paced the room where he'd spent several exceedingly boring afternoons.

The door opened and Emily Duprey crept in, glancing furtively behind her.

'Lord Devlin.' She cast him an anxious glance and shut the door.

'Miss Duprey, forgive the early hour. I wished to speak with your father.'

'As I understand. But if I could have a moment…' She regarded him with a worried expression.

He had no idea how to act with her. Since learning she was Madeleine's sister, dealing with her seemed an impossibility.

Suddenly he realised what had attracted him to her. The tilt of her head, the gesture of her hand, the shape of her brow and chin were Madeleine's. It was his attachment to Madeleine that led him to this woman, who at present was wringing her hands and regarding him anxiously.

He had wronged Emily Duprey. Led her to expect from him an offer now repugnant to him. According to her brother, the family considered it a settled matter, and it was for this sole reason he had returned to this house.

'Miss Duprey, I must beg your forgiveness, but after yesterday, you must realise that any further—'

'Never mind that, sir.' She cast him a pleading glance. ''My sister—'

Before she could continue, the butler arrived to escort him to Lord Duprey's study. He bowed to Miss Duprey, who wore a stricken expression on her face.

Lord Duprey, sitting behind a large desk, rose when Devlin entered the room. Lean and sallow-skinned, with a shock of white hair framing an aristocratic face, he approached Devlin. As he came close, Devlin recognised eyes of the same shade of blue as Madeleine's, except in this man bloodshot red surrounded the blue, and his lids were half closed in an expression of dissipation.

'Lord Devlin,' the man said formally, 'please sit down.' He gestured to a chair next to a table, where he poured them both generous glasses of sherry. Duprey, not waiting for his guest, took a long sip of the nut-brown liquid.

Devlin remained standing. 'I am very conscious of the early hour and have no wish to detain you beyond a moment.'

Duprey peered at him through the slits in his eyes. 'On the contrary. I am pleased that you have come. We have business to transact.'

'We have no business to transact. I came to make that clear to you.'

The older man walked back behind the desk and sat, taking another sip of his drink. 'You have singled out my daughter for your attentions in a way no one could dispute. It is time for you to honour this declaration you have implied so strongly.'

Devlin blanched. Surely this man had heard of the events of the previous day. 'I dispute your words, sir. I have shown no partiality, as anyone on the town knows. I have no intentions toward your daughter Emily, and I wish to make that clear.'

Lord Duprey's eyebrows lifted in a mocking expression. 'And I wish to make clear to you that you will honour your obligations to my daughter. You have been sniffing around her all Season, like some mongrel around a bitch. You will come up to scratch, or else.'

Devlin bristled under the crude threat, but he was determined not to lose his temper. He sent Duprey an equally mocking, but menacing look. 'Of which daughter do you speak?'

Duprey drained the contents of his glass and poured himself another from a decanter on the desk. 'So the chit told you, eh?' He laughed, a dry mirthless sound. 'Well, you will marry Emily Duprey and make this family an honourable connection to Heronvale's fortune. I care not a whit how much you bed that little whore.'

Devlin dove across the desk, grabbing Duprey by the knot in his neckcloth and scattering the desk's contents to the floor. The man's cheeks turned red as he sputtered for breath.

'You dare speak of her that way again and I will kill you.' Devlin released him and Duprey fell back into his chair.

When Duprey regained his breath, he smiled sardonically. 'I wonder what story she concocted for you, Steele. Probably some nonsense. I tell you, my luck was with me when she could not keep her skirts down for Farley—or, should I say, she could not keep her breeches up? Let me tell you, she was quite a sight in those clothes. Wished she wasn't my daughter once or twice.'

Devlin clenched his fists. Duprey again laughed, the racking sound repellent. 'Yes, indeed, her lustiness quite settled my debts. Got rid of the expense of another useless daughter, as well.'

'Do you mean you gave her to Farley in payment of gaming debts?'

Duprey drained another glass of sherry. 'Glad of it. Kept me from ruin.'

'Damn you, Duprey,' Devlin said through clenched teeth.

The smile remained frozen on the older man's face. 'Well, damn *you*, Steele, because you are going to marry Emily or suffer the scandal. Your brother dislikes scandal, I'll wager.'

'The scandal is on your head, Duprey. No one will receive any member of your family after I tell them what you did to Madeleine.'

'If they would believe you. My youngest daughter died, you see. There is a grave to prove it.'

'An empty grave.'

'Oh, it is not empty. I purchased a suitable corpse as soon as it became available.'

Bile rose in Devlin's throat.

Duprey raised the ante. 'So you would only expose the chit to much sordid attention.'

Devlin gaped at the malevolent man seated so casually. Surely he was bluffing, a gamester playing the cards the only way possible when the deal was a poor one.

This wager, however, involved not cards, but the reputations of the people Devlin held most dear. What effect on them if he played the game poorly?

Devlin spun on his heel and left the suffocating atmosphere of the Duprey town house. Inhaling fresh air into his lungs. Devlin hurried to call upon his brother, only to discover he and Serena had left early for Heronvale. He begged paper and pen from Barclay and then rushed to his brother's stable.

Jem was inside.

'Jem, thank God you are here. I need your help,' Devlin said, not bothering with a greeting. 'Is there a mount to carry me to Heronvale?'

'Yes, my lord,' Jem responded. 'His lordship took the carriage with m'lady. How may I serve you?'

'Have someone get the horse ready immediately and you deliver this letter to my apartments.'

The doctor gestured for Madeleine and Bart to follow him out of the room where Sophie coughed softly as she lay abed.

The doctor spoke in hushed tones. 'She has a touch of consumption.'

Bart wrung his hands. 'Is there some palliative? A poultice?'

'I am afraid there is little I can do. Country air would be as good as any tonic I could concoct. Alas, this city…' The doctor shook his head. 'It is bad for the lungs.'

Bart gave Madeleine an agonised glance.

'Then she shall go to the country,' Madeleine said. 'Bart, you could take her, could you not?'

'It might be the very thing,' the doctor said.

Bart knitted his eyebrows. 'Perhaps I could take her to Heronvale. They would take us in. The Marquess said he was in my debt. I should ask Dev.'

Madeleine grabbed his arm. 'You must not wait, surely. He might be gone all day.'

'But what of you, Miss Maddy? I should not leave you.'

She smiled. 'You must. It is the only thing to do. I have become quite useful, you know. I am well able to care for things here. Do not give us a thought.'

Bart needed no more coaxing. As soon as the doctor took his leave, the worried new husband was off to hire a posting chaise for his ill wife. Madeleine set to the task of packing Sophie's belongings, refusing to listen to her friend's protests.

'Do not be nonsensical, Sophie,' Madeleine scolded. 'Devlin and I can manage very well.'

Sophie curled up on her cot, making herself even smaller. 'I cannot like being separated from you.'

Madeleine came to her side and put her arms around her. 'Please do not fret. Bart will care for you very well. He loves you, you know.'

Sophie's face took on a dreamy look. She nodded her head and lodged no further complaint.

Within two hours, Madeleine and Linette watched the chaise drive away, driven by four sturdy but otherwise unremarkable mis-matched horses. Linette, as always, was in raptures about the beasts, but whimpered to see the coach drive away. She hugged her mother's neck. Madeleine thought she might nap for a bit and took her upstairs.

She had no sooner put Linette down upon her small bed when she heard the knocker. Thinking perhaps Bart and Sophie had forgotten something, she rushed down the stairs and flung open the door.

Her sister Emily stood before her.

Chapter Twenty-One

Emily let out a gasp, her gloved hand flying up to cover her mouth. 'I had thought…I thought this Lord Devlin's residence.'

Madeleine eyed Emily warily. 'It is, but he is not here presently.' What could have induced her sister to come here? Surely their mother would not allow such an improper visit.

Emily twisted the cords of her reticule, looking even more discomposed. 'Oh, dear.' She glanced back at the street where a carriage drove out of sight. 'The hack has left.'

'Then you'd best come in.' Madeleine stepped aside, holding the door ajar so Emily could pass into the hallway. She continued to look anxious and confused.

Madeleine's heart beat with excitement. She had not spoken to a member of her family for almost four years.

Emily turned to her. 'I did not know you would be here. That is, I did not realise…' She gave a deep sigh. 'I do not understand any of this!'

Madeleine remembered her sister Emily, two years older, as far more knowledgeable and worldly than she. At this moment, however, she felt herself to be the wiser one. Among the jumble of feelings swirling around inside her was a strong desire to throw her arms around Emily in a sisterly embrace.

'Come into the parlour.' Madeleine led the way and closed the door behind them.

Emily spun around to her. 'Oh, Madeleine! I had no notion...' Tears welled in her eyes. 'I thought you were dead.'

Had news of Madeleine's fall from respectability been kept from Emily? Madeleine always assumed her sisters knew all about it and welcomed the ruse of her demise as her parents must have.

Emily continued, 'How came you to be with L...Lord Devlin? Oh, I do not understand any of it! And Mama would tell me nothing, and Papa said I was a fool and had better keep my mouth shut.'

'You did not know?' Madeleine still could not believe it. She took a tentative step toward her sister, who quickly closed the distance and gave her the embrace Madeleine had longed for.

'Madeleine, Madeleine.' Emily choked back sobs. 'I have felt so guilty. Jessame and I had teased you so, and then you disappeared. You were not found for ages. Papa said no one could see the...the body, because it had been outside so long... Although it could not have been, because you are here, so it must have all been a hoax.'

Madeleine patted her back. 'Now, do not cry, Emily. There is no need. Indeed, I am so sorry to have given you such a shock. Come, sit down and I will get us some tea.'

She persuaded Emily to sit on the settee until she brought the tea and, when they were seated together, gave her sister a somewhat amended version of the events that brought them both to the present moment. Among the details Madeleine neglected to mention were a precise description of the duties required of her by Farley, the exact nature of her relationship with Devlin, and, of course, the existence of Linette.

'So, you see, Lord Devlin has been so kind as to assist me, and when he comes into his fortune he will lend me the money to set up a...a dress shop.'

Perhaps this rose-colored version would help to preserve

Devlin's opportunity to marry Emily, if that were still his intent. To think he might become a part of the family Madeleine had lost, however, was very difficult to contemplate.

She changed the subject. 'Emily, why have you come here? You really should not have. This is a single gentleman's residence.'

'I know I should not have come, but I could not let Papa—' She grabbed Madeleine's arm. 'Papa means to force Lord Devlin to marry me. He threatens to send a notice to the *Gazette* that Lord Devlin has offered for me, but it is all untrue.'

'It is untrue?'

'Indeed.' Emily sighed heavily. 'I must stop him.'

Madeleine stared at her sister, fumbling at her words. 'But I thought…I thought Devlin did wish to marry you.'

'No, I do not think so.' Emily's brow furrowed. 'He courted the Season's Diamond as much as he did me, and I think she may have refused Greythorne for him…'

Madeleine's eyebrows lifted. Devlin courted a Diamond of the *ton*?

Emily continued. 'At least that is what they say. I am persuaded Lord Devlin never intended to marry me, no matter how much our brother Robert boasted of it all over town. Indeed, I tried to explain to Papa, but he would not listen.'

But Devlin said Emily had been his choice. Had that been untrue? Did he say that to cover up his wish to marry a Diamond?

'Why do you think Devlin would not marry you?'

Emily gave a little laugh. 'Oh, Madeleine, look at me. I am no beauty. There is nothing to distinguish me from other ladies. Certainly nothing to compete with the pick of the Season.'

Her sister looked well enough, Madeleine thought. Indeed, Emily's face seemed comfortably dear. Madeleine had not realised how much she'd missed this sister she'd thought never cared a fig for her.

A door slammed and halting footsteps sounded on the stairs. 'Mama! Mama!'

Madeleine froze. Emily stared at her, eyebrows raised.

Linette ran in, coming to a stop when she noticed the strange lady seated next to her mother. Her thumb went into her mouth.

Resigned, Madeleine said. 'It is all right, Linette. Come give a curtsy to Miss Duprey.'

Linette, still sucking on her thumb, wobbled on one leg as she tried to accomplish her mother's request.

'Your child?' Emily asked, her eyes wide.

Madeleine nodded.

'Lord Farley's?' she asked.

Madeleine shook her head.

Emily stared at the little girl who climbed into her mother's lap and laid her head against her mother's breast, rubbing her eyes.

Emily's gaze met Madeleine's and held there for several moments. 'She is Lord Devlin's.'

Madeleine nodded. She did not expect Emily to understand how wonderful it was for her to have Linette, to believe that Devlin was indeed Linette's father and that a part of him would always be with her in Linette.

Emily walked to the window. 'Why should Lord Devlin pretend to be courting me or any other lady while living here with you and…and this child? What game has he been playing?'

A game to win money, money enough to support her and their daughter, a coil Madeleine had forced upon him.

She could not tell her sister this. The best she could do was preserve Devlin's chances to marry whomever he wished.

'I am not fit to be his wife, Emily. Not after Lord Farley. I assure you, I was no more than a momentary indiscretion on Devlin's part, but he would not abandon us.'

Emily rubbed her brow. 'It is of no consequence, I suppose. Tell Lord Devlin he may resist Father's trickery. I will not place any damage to my reputation at Lord Devlin's door. He has no obligation to me, and so I will say to anyone. I'll threaten to expose what Father has done to you. That will stop him.'

It would also expose her family to terrible scandal. 'I do not wish for our family to be hurt—'

'Father, hurt? He would never take such a chance. Leave it to me.' Emily briskly retrieved her reticule from the side table and headed toward the door. 'I must leave.'

'No, not so soon,' cried Madeleine, jumping to her feet with Linette still in her arms. Please, allow her a little bit of family for a few minutes more.

Emily turned back to her, the pinched expression on her face softening. Gently she touched Madeleine's cheek. 'I was always so jealous of you, Madeleine, more reason for me to feel guilt when I thought you dead.'

'Jealous of me?'

'You are quite a dazzling beauty.' Emily smiled at her with a wistful expression. 'That year before you disappeared, you had grown so pretty, you cast Jessame and me into the shade. We were green with envy.' She gave a little sigh and kissed Madeleine's cheek. 'I am glad you are alive. Please thank Lord Devlin for being so kind to me. I have had the loveliest time this Season.'

Madeleine could think of nothing to say to this. Emily strode purposefully toward the door, pausing on the threshold. 'Madeleine?'

Madeleine rushed to her side. 'Yes?'

She gave a little laugh. 'I do not have the least notion how to get back home. Do you know where I can find a hack?'

Madeleine gave a tentative smile. 'Wait a moment. Linette and I will walk with you. There will be a hack near the shops.'

As they walked toward the shops, Madeleine begged for news about Jessame and Robert, thirstily drinking in each small tidbit of information Emily provided. Neither spoke of their parents. As they walked, a stylish phaeton came into view, the gentleman holding the ribbons doing an admirable job controlling a pair of spirited chestnuts.

'Oh, my goodness,' said Emily. 'It is Amanda Reynolds.'

The young lady seated next to the phaeton's driver was the loveliest creature Madeleine had ever seen, fair, delicate, with blonde curls peeping out of a modish bonnet. Her stylish fawn-coloured dress, topped by a matching spencer, adorned a perfect figure.

'Who is she?' she asked.

The two sisters paused to watch these passers-by.

'The Diamond I told you about,' Emily said. 'And I believe that is Devlin's friend with her. She does not like him above half. How shocking for them to be riding together with no more than a tiger for chaperon. What could it mean?'

Madeleine only half attended to these words. Her eyes were fixed on the Diamond, who looked beautiful even seated in silence next to the gentleman. Devlin's friend, another unknown piece of Devlin's life on the town.

Her knowledge of him was confined to their apartments and the few places he could take her. She could not have known he'd attracted this exquisite lady.

As the phaeton rolled past, the Diamond turned around and caught Madeleine's gaze.

Emily quickly covered her face with the brim of her bonnet. 'I must not let her see me.'

A hack pulled up at the end of the street, and Madeleine and Emily rushed over to it. After a swift hug, Madeleine bundled her sister into the vehicle and waved her goodbye, watching until the hack drove completely out of sight.

Lord Farley paced the pavement across the street from Devlin Steele's apartments, waiting. It had become his practice to spend some part of each day or night in this neighbourhood. He often caught a glimpse of Madeleine, but she was always accompanied by Steele, that brutish-looking man of his, or that insipid little maid.

He could hardly believe his good fortune when she bid goodbye to the female who walked out of the house with her. She was alone at last. The child did not matter. Farley crossed the street, timing it so that he placed himself between her and her door. She was as absorbed as ever in the child and did not attend to his approach.

He stepped directly in her path. She looked up and gave a strangled cry.

He smiled at her, his most winning smile, the one he'd used to attract her in the first place. 'Madeleine, my dear, it is my pleasure to see you.'

Her eyes darted to both sides and she protectively grasped her daughter's hand. 'Let me by, if you please.'

'I wish to speak to you.' He placed his hand on her shoulder. She wrenched away.

She picked up the child and tried to walk past him. 'I have no wish to speak to you.'

He blocked her way, putting his arm tightly around her waist so that she could not easily squirm away. She struggled nevertheless. He held her more tightly against his side. With his mouth tantalisingly close to her ear, he said, 'I want you back, Madeleine.' He did not resist the opportunity, but let his tongue lap the delicate skin of her earlobe.

The sharp heel of her walking boot pounded into his foot. Pain shot through him and he dropped his hold on her. She hurried away, but not quickly enough.

He caught her arm and held it vise-like, his lips again near her ear. 'You will return to me, Madeleine, or one dark night that pretty soldier of yours will find a knife in his back.'

'No!' She struggled. The child began to cry.

Farley wrapped his fingers with Linette's curls. 'I wonder how easy it would be to snatch this child? The chimney sweeps would pay a pretty price for her, I own. Or perhaps a gentleman might fancy some sport with her?'

'Do not touch her!' shrieked Madeleine.

'I repeat, Madeleine. Return to me or I will carry out my

threats. You will never know when I am about. I will get them, both of them, you may be sure.'

A man walked up to them with a swift step.

'Sir! Sir! Help me!'

The man faced Farley. 'Let the lady go.'

'This is not your affair,' Farley protested. 'It is only a trifling bit of spirit from my fancy piece here. Nothing to trouble you.'

'No, do not heed him,' Madeleine pleaded.

The man grabbed Farley by the back of his collar, pulling so forcefully, his breath was cut off.

'Unhand her,' the man growled.

Farley, gasping futilely for air, knew when the cards dealt could not be played. He acquiesced.

'Be gone.'

Farley brushed off his coat. Before he turned to leave, he bowed to Madeleine. 'Remember what I said, my dear. I will carry out my plans.'

Farley strolled off, taking care not to look nonplussed.

Madeleine clutched at Linette, whose little arms were tight around her neck and whose head was buried into her shoulder. 'I cannot thank you enough, sir. We are truly in your debt.'

The man bowed. 'Glad to be of service. May I escort you to your destination?'

Madeleine recognised the gentleman as the man who, moments before, had driven by with the Diamond. Devlin's friend.

'Thank you, but I am near my residence...' Madeleine glanced toward her door, just a few houses away.

The Diamond stood at the top of the steps at her door, watching her with interest. Madeleine could not avoid her, too afraid to go somewhere else until they drove off.

She allowed Devlin's friend to walk her to her door as Miss Reynolds watched. Madeleine halted. 'We are here. Thank you, sir.'

'Here?' he asked. 'These are Devlin Steele's apartments.'

As Miss Reynolds stood decorously, Madeleine said in a feeble voice, 'I…I am in his employ.'

'Indeed?' A smile, somewhat cynical, flashed across his face. Miss Reynolds looked shocked.

'Well,' said the gentleman agreeably. 'Let me make our introductions.' He gestured to the ethereal creature at his elbow. 'This is Miss Reynolds, and I am Captain Ramsford, a friend of Lord Devlin's.'

'Mama, I want Deddy!' whimpered Linette.

Ramsford's eyebrows shot up, and Miss Reynold's mouth fell open.

Blushing, Madeleine hurried to the door. 'I will see if Lord Devlin is at home.'

She rushed inside with Linette, caring not if they thought it rude to be kept waiting on the doorstep like tradesmen. Linette curled up on the stairs, still looking frightened. Madeleine called for Devlin, but there was no answer.

Before she stepped back outside she heard Lord Ramsford and Miss Reynolds through the crack in the door.

'Oh, my goodness,' Miss Reynolds cried.

'Compose yourself. You will see Devlin by and by.' He added in a mocking tone, 'In the meantime, you may depend on me.'

Noting Miss Reynolds used Devlin's given name, Madeleine stepped back outside. 'Lord Devlin is not at home.'

Ramsford peered at her quizzically. 'A pity.' He turned to Miss Reynolds. 'We have come on a fool's errand, as I predicted. Now, perhaps you will allow me to convey you home.'

Miss Reynolds gave him a scathing glance. Her forehead wrinkled, and she spoke to Madeleine. 'Who was that man who accosted you?'

Madeleine blinked. 'No one you should know, my lady.'

'Are you all right, Miss…?' Miss Reynolds lifted her eyebrows, obviously wanting Madeleine to reveal her name.

Madeleine lowered her eyes. 'I shall require no further assistance.' She ignored the other request. 'If you will forgive me, I must see to my daughter.'

Without a glance back, Madeleine rushed through the doorway, bolted the door, and went directly to Linette. 'Come, darling,' she said soothingly. 'The bad man will not scare us again.'

The afternoon crept by, spent soothing Linette, entertaining her and attempting to still her own agitation from the afternoon events. Madeleine longed for Devlin to return home. She had decided to warn him only about her father's trickery and Farley's threat. If he did not wish her to know of the Diamond, she would pretend ignorance. In any event, her future would be unchanged.

As time wore on, Madeleine grew more uneasy. When she peeked out the front windows, there always seemed to be some man loitering near the lamppost across the street. Not Farley, but familiar figures. His lackeys. He was having her watched.

Each minute Devlin did not return caused her increased agitation. She pictured him bleeding in some alleyway, a knife thrust into his back. And if that image were not disturbing enough, she envisioned him in the arms of the beautiful Diamond.

She jumped at a sharp knock on the door. With a pounding heart, she peered out the window. It was not Farley, nor one of his men, but a footman dressed in Heronvale livery. She opened the door. The footman handed her a note and left.

The note was addressed to her. With trembling fingers, she broke the seal and read: *My dearest Maddy. I am called away on urgent business. Everything will be settled upon my return. I will be gone only one night and will be home for dinner tomorrow. Explain to Bart. Kiss Linette for me. Yours, etc., D.S.*

She folded the paper again, her heart pounding in her chest. What urgent business was this? Did it involve the Diamond, perhaps? Well, at least Farley could not make good his threat. Devlin would not be killed in some alleyway this night.

Madeleine sat down again with her sewing, trying to calm herself. Linette played close by at her feet. Through the crack in the curtains, she watched two men conversing. They scrutinised the house. How long before they determined she and Linette were alone?

She pricked her finger with the needle and put her finger to her mouth to stop the bleeding.

She'd be damned if she would sit here and wait for Farley to come after her. Even if Farley captured her, he would still make good on his threats to Devlin and Linette. She knew Farley too well. Nothing would save the two people she loved as long as that man breathed life.

Madeleine's pricked finger remained poised in the air. Was that something she could do? She set her sewing on the side table and absorbed herself in thought. She could sneak back to Farley's establishment and wait for him. Surprise would be on her side. She could wait until he slept. Then she could kill him.

Almost without effort, the plan formed itself in her head. First, she would take Linette to the Marquess and Marchioness. They wanted to adopt her and would be very pleased to have her. Linette would receive every advantage under their care, and, if things went wrong, Farley would not dare to touch a child under the Marquess's protection.

But would Devlin be safe? The only way to be sure was to kill Farley. Devlin could then marry Miss Reynolds with no impediment. And have a happy life.

If she were caught, she would be hanged. If she escaped, she must disappear forever. If she failed…well, she must not fail.

Rushing over to the desk, she composed a farewell letter to Devlin. She had to write it several times before sealing the final effort. The bleakness of the task made her hand tremble.

How to tell him to forget her? How to tell him how much she loved him? How to explain this was the only thing to be done?

At dusk, Madeleine, donned yet another costume. With her newly acquired sewing skills, she altered some old clothes of Devlin's, stitching the trousers so that they fit her slim hips and came over her walking boots. She found an old cap of Bart's to cover her hair, and a caped coat. Shortened and its cuffs removed, the coat was large enough to hide Linette beneath and Devlin's sabre behind. Farley's lackeys would be watching the back door as well as the front, but the house shared an area with other residences, so a boy walking out the back would not arouse suspicion. She took the risk of leaving candles burning in the house to look as if they were at home.

She enlisted Linette's cooperation by promising her a visit to the Marquess, who would let her see his horses. She also promised that Linette would see Devlin soon, and that she would have a supreme adventure, but first she must be quiet and still, so the bad man would not discover them.

Linette played her role beautifully, as did Madeleine. A boy in a big coat sauntered down the street to no one's notice.

It was dark when Madeleine reached the Marquess's town house. She had no idea how to discover the servants' entrance, so she strode up to the front door. The huge brass knocker was removed. There was nothing to do but rap on the door with her knuckles.

The Heronvale butler opened the door and looked disapprovingly at her.

'Be gone, ruffian,' he ordered through a crack in the door.

'Please, sir, wait. It is Miss England. Do you remember me? I must see the Marquess. It will only take a moment.'

The elderly man's eyes grew huge as he gaped at her. 'The Marquess and Marchioness are not at home.'

The strap that she had devised to hold Linette dug into her

neck, but she dared not reveal the child's presence. 'May I wait for them, please?'

The man regarded her with a concerned look. 'His lordship and ladyship intend to spend an indefinite time at Heronvale.'

Heronvale?

Madeleine walked down the long steps to the street. This spoiled her plans to be rid of Farley and herself before Devlin returned. She must travel to Heronvale first.

She found her way to the Marquess's stable, where once she had come with Devlin for an early morning ride. She crept inside when the stable boy was not looking. It was not difficult to find a secluded corner in which to hide, nor to convince Linette to be very quiet so they could sleep next to the horses.

When the first rays of light shone through the stable windows, Madeleine rose and searched for the saddles. She was tightening the cinch when the stable door opened and the head groom walked in.

'See here!' he shouted, rushing over to her and grabbing her around the waist.

'Mama! Mama!' Linette shouted as she flung her arms around Madeleine's legs.

'What the devil…?' the groom exclaimed.

Madeleine recognised him as the man who had been with Devlin the night she had run away from the Marquess's town house.

'The Marchioness gave me permission. Do you recall me, sir? I am Lord Devlin's…friend.'

'Does he know you are here?' the man asked.

'No, Lord Devlin is away. That is why I must go to the Marquess. Lord Devlin told me I should.' Madeleine struggled for an explanation that would win his cooperation.

'Mama?' Linette gripped the cloth of Madeleine's trousers.

The groom straightened. 'Who is this?'

'My daughter.'

He regarded her, a thoughtful expression on his face. 'Why are you dressed like that?'

Madeleine thought wildly. 'I feared riding all that distance to Heronvale. It would not be safe as a woman. Please, let me borrow the horse. I promise to return it.'

He rubbed his chin. 'I do not think his lordship would like it if I let you ride off to Heronvale.'

'But you must!'

Already she was terribly delayed. It would have been so much better to have Linette safe and the deed accomplished by now. She needed to do this before Devlin returned. Before he stopped her.

The groom put his hands on his hips. 'I'll take you in the curricle. It will be faster and I think Lord Devlin would charge me to keep you safe.'

Madeleine thought she might kiss the man, so grateful was she. 'Thank you, sir.'

Farley fumed as his carriage sped along. The chit had hood-winked him. It was late before his men realised that she had been alone in the house and, by the time he had given the order to break in, she and her child were gone.

It took more time to discover that Steele had hotfooted it to his brother's estate. Farley wagered that, somehow, Madeleine was headed there, as well. Farley and his men would reach the outskirts of Heronvale at dawn. He would send his men ahead to discover if she'd arrived there. If not, he would lie in wait for her.

She would not foil him again.

Chapter Twenty-Two

Devlin woke in his old room at Heronvale. For a moment he thought he was an invalid again and the past months merely one of his fevered dreams. A disquieting sense of unease lingered. It had nothing to do with the heated words he and his brother had exchanged. No, something more elusive.

He had confessed the whole to his brother, which had gone rather better than he could have expected, but they did not agree on the solution. Ned was in accord with Devlin about the impropriety of marriage to Emily Duprey, but did not agree that Devlin must marry Madeleine.

Ned's reasoning was sound, Devlin supposed. Ned had argued that Madeleine and the child deserved a peaceful life after all they had endured. As the wife of a Steele, she would be scrutinised. Would not some eager gossipmonger expose her past?

Who in society would trouble themselves with his business if he reactivated his commission in the army? Devlin had countered. Ned nearly turned apoplectic at that suggestion.

Devlin sat up in bed, stretching his limbs and trying to let the new day give perspective on the past one. In any event, Ned could not stop him from rejoining the army. Ned had, after all, given him the bank draft for Madeleine. It provided enough money to repurchase his commission. But how the deuce was he to silence Duprey?

At least Ned cared not a fig for the dust that would be kicked up if Duprey made good his threat, though Ned did not relish becoming the latest *on-dit* for the *ton*. Serena might suffer from it, he had said. Devlin had been surprised by the softness in his brother's expression when he spoke Serena's name. Come to think of it, Ned and Serena seemed unusually at ease with each other.

Devlin shrugged. Whatever the reason, he was glad of it.

He dressed quickly and headed for the stables. A hard ride would clear his mind and rid him of this sense of foreboding.

As he set the horse into a trot, he thought of Madeleine. What a race they could have if she were to ride the estate with him. They could explore all his childhood haunts, the special places he treasured from those simpler days.

The fields stretched ahead of him, some thick with crops, some fallow. He knew every inch of this land. Urging his horse into a gallop, he sped over them, jumping hedges, clearing fences, and letting the exhilaration replace all other thought.

Farley settled himself in the windowseat of the village's posting house. The ale was tolerable and the breakfast generous. More important, any traveller to Heronvale would by necessity pass directly in front of the window. His horse was kept ready, and he could depend on his own eyes if his lackeys failed to warn him if she came into view.

He regarded the innkeeper's daughter with an appraising eye. She was comely enough, but too common for his tastes. He wondered how many men had their first tumble with a tavern wench. It would make a fetching costume for Madeleine to wear. He could just see the simple dress dipping low, revealing her full breasts as she bent to pour a drink. Farley took a deep swig of his ale. He'd be damned if he'd share her this time.

This time she would be all his, to do with as he wished.

*   *   *

Devlin's ride was ill fated, a bad omen to be sure. After his horse threw a shoe, he led her home on foot, taking up precious time he needed to conclude matters with his brother. The sun was high in the sky when he delivered the horse to the head groom.

'What's amiss, m'lord?' the old retainer asked, having spied him walking with the horse.

'Threw a shoe,' Devlin replied, handing over the reins.

As the man examined the hoof, Devlin made the mistake of mentioning Jem to him. This launched the proud father into a long discourse about his son and how the Marquess was right to value Jem so highly, him being very much like his father. Devlin attended to the conversation with disguised impatience. He had not eaten a bite that day and had much to do before he could return to Madeleine.

'And I was saying to your man yesterday, how I wish the young'uns could live here in the country where the air is not carrying some disease or another, but Jem would not hear of it, nor that wife of his…'

'Saying to my man?'

'Yes, m'lord. Mr Bart. And what a poor little thing that new wife of his is, so sick and all, but she'll be well enough staying with Nurse. Nurse still knows just what should be done, though I'd wager she is five and seventy, if she is a day.'

Devlin grabbed the groom's arm. 'They are here?'

The old man gave him a puzzled look. 'They arrived soon after you.'

Not waiting a moment for the groom. Devlin threw a saddle on one of the other mounts and raced for Nurse's cottage.

She was in her front yard, leaning on her stick, a basket over her arm. She dropped the basket and threw a hand across her chest when he thundered toward her.

'Goodness! Master Devlin, I declare. 'Tis so good to see you. I'm about to make a nice posset for that dear little one.'

'Where are they?' He swung his leg over to dismount before the horse had quite stopped.

'I have the dear girl all right and tight, Master Devlin, never you fear, but you must take a care you don't break your neck. I've told you many a time—'

He ran inside with her limping behind him.

Devlin found Bart seated by the bedside where a pale Sophie lay. Bart's face was pinched with worry.

'My God, what happened?'

Bart glanced up in surprise. 'Dev!'

Nurse poked Devlin on the shoulder with her bony finger. 'You'll not go racketing in this house, m'lord, and waking the girl. She needs her rest. If you want to be talking, get into the other room and keep your voices down.'

Devlin did as he was told, Bart rising to go with him. They went into the main room in the cottage.

'Is Madeleine with you?' Devlin asked anxiously.

'No, but she thought… What are you doing here?'

'Never mind that now. What of Sophie?'

Bart rubbed his face and flopped into a chair. 'She could hardly breathe. The doctor said the only hope was country air. Dev, I would not have come had I known you would be absent.'

'Now, no fussing,' said Nurse, walking in. 'I told you she'd be right and tight. Sleeping like a baby, she is.' She limped over to the fire and busied herself with the posset.

Devlin placed his hand on Bart's shoulder. 'You were right to bring Sophie here. I promise you Nurse will know just what to do for her. I trust Madeleine and Linette have done very well, so do not worry on that side. I had sent word to her that I would be away, but to be prudent I will return to London immediately.'

'We should not have left her,' Bart said.

'Nonsense,' countered Devlin. 'It was my error, leaving as I did with only a note. I must not tarry.'

As he galloped back to the house, that sense of dread returned. Madeleine was alone and she knew no one who could help her if anything went amiss. He must reach her without delay. Devlin ordered a fresh mount, and hurried to inform his brother.

Madeleine pretended to be calm as she sat beside the chattering Linette, who was in transports over riding behind two horses and spying so many more along the way. Jem patiently answered Linette's endless questions about the beasts, at the same time asking no questions of Madeleine. She was grateful to him for that.

They passed through a small village. 'Not long now,' he said.

Not long before she would hug Linette for the last time; kiss her little cheek for the last time. Madeleine might have managed it well enough if she could have handed Linette over to the Marquess in London, before she'd had all these hours to contemplate never seeing her little girl again. With each mile her soul ebbed away, bit by painful bit.

After this wrenching deed was accomplished, the rest of it would seem easy. She would travel back to London, to the gaming hell where she would find Farley. She feared killing him, but only because she might be wicked enough to enjoy it. It should be a comfort to know that Devlin would have the life he deserved, with a beautiful wife who could be a credit to him instead of a mistress who placed his life in danger.

It was no comfort, however. Losing him would hurt as much as losing Linette.

Horses' hooves pounded behind them, and Jem steered the curricle to the side to give the riders room to pass. One rider came aside the curricle's team and grabbed the harness while others surrounded the vehicle, their horses whinnying and breathing hard.

'Get her!' someone shouted.

Madeleine immediately clutched Linette, holding the child tight while men grabbed at them both. The curricle came to an abrupt stop, Jem was on his feet, snapping at the men with his whip. Madeleine crouched on the seat, the shouts of the men harsh in her ears and the smell of horse sweat filling her nostrils. Jem's whip snapped and cracked above her head. A shot rang out, and Jem tumbled from the curricle.

Madeleine forced herself not to think of him. She tucked Linette beneath her feet and unsheathed Devlin's sabre, slashing it at her attackers as Devlin had demonstrated. She drove them back again. Through the din she could hear Jem moaning.

'Damn you, I said get the chit.' That was Farley's voice. He had come for her and to make good his threat toward Linette.

'Mama,' Linette cried, cowering at her feet.

'Cowards!' shouted Farley. 'Seize her now.'

The sabre sliced at the arm of one of the attackers. He fell back, cursing, blood spurting from his arm. Madeleine swung at another, but another man climbed on the curricle and grabbed her from behind. He squeezed her wrist until the sword clattered to the ground. Madeleine struggled against him. Farley rode near and plucked Linette from the vehicle.

'No!' Madeleine screamed.

She clawed at her captor's eyes and kicked him in the groin with all her might. With a cry of pain, he pushed her away. She lost her footing and fell hard on to the ground, the breath knocked out of her. With her cheek flat against the ground, she saw Jem writhing in pain, white-faced, blood staining his shoulder. The horses' stamping hooves sounded perilously close, the animals as panicked as she. The dirt they kicked up rained down on her. The horses bolted, sending Farley's man sprawling off the back in the wake of the curricle clattering down the road.

'Mama! Mama!' Linette's screams rose above the din.

Madeleine forced herself to rise. She groped for the sabre.

Farley dismounted, holding Linette as if she were a parcel of old rags. His men, one mounted, one not, circled around their comrades. The two on the ground were helped to their feet.

Ignoring that she was outnumbered, Madeleine took advantage of the distraction. She strode toward Farley, sabre in hand.

'Release my child.'

Farley laughed, the evil sound stilling Linette's cries. Gazing smugly at Madeleine, he held Linette in front of him, protecting his chest with her little body. 'Still wish to thrust your sword into me, my dear?'

'Let her go.' Her demand was useless, she knew. Two of his lackeys closed in on her again. She turned, slashing the sabre at them. Out of the corner of her eye a third man aimed a pistol at her.

'Do not damage her!' Farley ordered. 'Surround her. There are four of you and one of her.'

The men did as they were told. Madeleine spun around, turning to each of them as they jeered at her.

'Drop the sword, my dear,' Farley said, his voice sickly smooth. 'You and your child are mine now.'

Madeleine closed her eyes. Her heart despaired.

She heard a galloping horse and cries of surprise from Farley's men. Her eyes flew open, and she saw the horseman.

Devlin.

He had no weapon save savage cries and murder in his eyes. He charged straight toward the men surrounding Madeleine, grabbing one of them as the man attempted to run. Devlin lifted him by the collar of his coat and tossed him down again. Madeleine raised the sabre, and Devlin grabbed it out of her hand. He became someone she had not imagined before, a demon on horseback, who easily scattered Farley's men. One reached a horse, mounted and beat a hasty retreat. The others ran for the woods.

With only a glance toward Madeleine, Devlin dismounted and approached Farley, sabre menacing. 'Unhand the child, Farley.'

Farley took a step back. Before Devlin could reach him, Farley drew a silver-bladed knife from his belt and held it against Linette's tiny throat. Its blade flashed in the afternoon sun.

'I would drop the sword if I were you, Steele.' Farley's upper lip curled.

Devlin lowered his sword very slightly.

'I mean it,' growled Farley. He pressed the blade against the child's neck, drawing a trickle of blood. She shrieked.

'No,' pleaded Madeleine.

Devlin watched the blood drip over Farley's fingers to stain the front of Linette's dress. The child, her face chalky white, was rigid, terror bulging her eyes. His vision blurred, and, distinctly as if it were happening to him again, he felt each stab of the French cuirassier.

He shook his head clear, ignoring his old demons and the panic that accompanied them. 'Let the child go, Farley.' Devlin's voice was steady.

'I'll give you the brat.' Farley sneered. 'But I keep the mother.'

'No deals,' said Devlin, advancing.

'She's mine.' Farley's voice went up a pitch and he placed the point of the knife below Linette's chin. 'You stole her from me and now I want her back.'

Devlin halted. There was no way to disarm Farley or strike him before he cut deep into Linette's throat.

Panic rose again and again he pushed it away. Battle was much like a game, he reminded himself, a series of points and counterpoints. As in the card came they'd played not more than three months ago, Devlin must wait until Farley made a mistake.

'I did not steal her.' Devlin kept his voice deceptively calm. 'You offered her, remember? You lost at your own game.'

'Your play was dishonest!' Farley waved the knife.

'It was not, as you well know. You gambled and lost,' he continued reasonably.

'Now you lose!' Farley gave a mirthless laugh. He swung the knife dramatically back to Linette's throat. Devlin's grip hardened on the hilt of the sword.

Suddenly, Farley's gaze left Devlin's face and focused behind him, his jaw dropping open. Devlin turned.

Madeleine had mounted one of the horses. The agitated beast bucked and twisted and kicked. It huffed and blew, its eyes wild. Devlin fell back, away from its kicks. Farley gaped, eyes frozen on the out-of-control animal.

How was Madeleine able to remain in the saddle? Devlin had visions of her falling off and being trampled to death by the horse's hooves. Somehow she hung on. The horse leapt and vaulted ever closer to Farley, who gave a terrified cry. He dropped Linette to the ground, and covered his face against the lethal hooves of the approaching horse.

Devlin grabbed Linette, covering her with his body. Let the hooves kick at him. He would use his body to protect his child.

'Drop the knife, Farley.' Madeleine shouted from the rearing horse. Devlin glanced up.

The horse came under perfect control, advancing slowly toward Farley. White-faced, Farley sank to his knees.

Devlin stood, holding Linette, who had her small arms tightly wrapped around his neck.

'Is she all right?' Madeleine asked, her voice trembling as she backed up the horse.

'I think so,' Devlin replied. He gave her a half-grin. 'Excellent horsemanship.'

She shrugged.

With an enraged cry, Farley charged toward Devlin and Linette, his knife raised.

Madeleine kicked at the horse. The animal shot forward, rearing and whinnying. Its hooves came down on Farley, knocking him to the ground. Madeleine pulled the animal away and forced it back under control. Farley moaned and rolled over. The knife protruded from his chest. Blood soaked his clothing and pooled next to his now-still body.

Chapter Twenty-Three

Madeleine stared out the window. The setting sun cast a reddish glow over the impressive Heronvale park and the rolling countryside. A fire crackled in the ornate marble fireplace at the end of the room, but the cup of tea on the table beside her grew cold. She tucked her feet underneath her on the settee and tried to banish the image of Farley's death from her mind.

The door opened.

'There you are.' Devlin walked into the room.

She looked up at him for a moment and back to the window.

He sat beside her and put his hand gently under her chin, turning her face to him. 'Are you all right?'

Concern shone in his eyes. She could not bear it. She nodded.

He smiled at her, drinking her in with his gaze. 'I see Serena found a dress for you.'

'She has been kind.'

The Marchioness had taken Madeleine and Linette under her wing as soon as they reached Heronvale. They were cosseted and pampered, cleaned up, and dressed in clothes that were hurriedly found in attic trunks.

He put his arm around her and tucked her next to him. She rested her head on his shoulder. It was enticingly comfortable.

'Where is Linette?' he asked.

'I believe the Marquess and Marchioness took her to the stables.'

'Ah, that should please her.' He kissed the top of her head. 'Did you visit Sophie?'

'Yes.'

Sophie had burst into tears when she'd seen her. Madeleine held her and rocked her as if she had been Linette.

'Did you…settle things?' Madeleine asked.

There had been much commotion when they arrived at Heronvale. Devlin had carried the injured Jem on his horse. They had left Farley's body where it lay.

He snuggled her closer to him. 'All is set right, Maddy. Ned spoke to the magistrate, and no further enquiry will be required.'

She closed her eyes. 'I thought I would enjoy killing him.'

He stroked her hair. 'Death is not something to enjoy, but you did not kill him, my love. His own treachery did that.'

He should not call her his love, she thought. Did he now feel even more obligated to her? He should not.

She turned her gaze to the scene from the window. 'Heronvale is very beautiful,' she said.

'I am pleased you like it.'

His arm felt so strong around her and his body warmed hers. She wished she could remain in his warmth and strength forever, but it was time to settle the matters between them, as well.

'Perhaps Linette would be happy here.'

'Linette?'

Madeleine pulled away from him. He regarded her with a puzzled expression.

'I have decided that I should…should agree for Linette to be adopted by the Marquess.'

Devlin's brows lifted. 'Are you mad?'

'It would be best for her, do you not think?' She forced herself to speak casually.

'No, I do not think.' He scowled. 'Perhaps you had better tell me where this addled-brained idea came from.'

She rose from the settee and folded her arms across her chest. 'Well, they can offer her so much more than I. I am persuaded her life would have more advantages.' She walked toward the window. 'She would still see you from time to time, as well.'

He stood as well, matching her tone, but with an edge of sarcasm. 'And where will you be while Linette has this idyll?'

'Oh, I shall do well, I think. You needn't concern yourself.'

He gripped her by the shoulders. 'Tell me what this is about.'

She avoided his eyes. 'My sister Emily visited me—'

He interrupted her. 'And she said I was to marry her. Well, I am not.'

Madeleine tried to pull away from his grasp, but he would not release her. She tried to boldly meet his eye. 'She told me you did not court her, but another lady. The Diamond of the *ton*.'

He blinked in surprise. 'Amanda Reynolds? Not exactly so.'

'I met Miss Reynolds, Devlin,' Madeleine said, her voice soft. 'She would make you a lovely wife.'

'You met Amanda Reynolds as well?' His hand flew up in surprise. 'I was only absent a few hours.'

She continued earnestly. 'She is beautiful, Devlin. The catch of the Season, Emily said. And I thought she had such kind eyes…'

'Damn her eyes!' he barked. 'What do her eyes matter to me?' He grabbed her shoulders again. 'I am not going to marry Amanda Reynolds.'

She pulled back.

'Do you know why I came here, Maddy?' He spoke softly. She shook her head.

'It was to inform my brother that I would marry you.'

Her gaze shot up.

'You, Maddy. Not your sister. Not Amanda Reynolds. You. It is you I love.'

She stared at him, her eyes wide and wary.

He gazed at her with tenderness. 'I came to inform my brother that I would marry you. I did not ask his approval. I checked with my old regiment. If I rejoin the cavalry, I may be able to support you and Linette, if you can bear following the drum. Others have done it, Maddy. Perhaps we can, too.'

'Follow the drum,' she repeated.

'We may be sent to Canada, at best, although it might be Africa or India or some other ungodly place, but we would be together.'

'You cannot mean to rejoin the army. Not after Waterloo.'

He set his jaw firmly. 'I can master Waterloo.'

She reached up and stroked his cheek with the back of her soft hand. 'But what of your inheritance? Your estate?'

'What good is money to me, my love, if you and Linette are not with me?'

'Oh, Devlin,' she whispered, 'have we not always known we could not be together?'

'We must be together, Maddy.'

Laughter sounded in the hallway. Ned and Serena walked in the room, Ned carrying Linette on his shoulders. He leaned over and flipped her over, causing a squeal of delight.

'Mama!' Linette ran over to Madeleine and jumped into her arms. 'I saw a pony and Markiss let me ride her!'

'That is wonderful, sweetling.' Madeleine hugged her daughter for a moment before the child squirmed out of her arms, reaching for Devlin. He squatted down to her level, giving her his total attention, though she told him exactly what she'd told her mother.

Madeleine stared at them, trying to memorise the moment. It was so beautiful, it hurt.

The Marquess regarded her, his expression of concern much like his brother's. 'How do you go on, Miss England?'

She shot him a suspicious glance. 'I suspect you know that is not my name.'

He smiled at her. 'Madeleine, then, if I may?'

His wife took his arm, approval shining in her eyes.

'As you wish, my lord,' Madeleine murmured.

Devlin stood, facing his brother. 'I have asked Madeleine to marry me, Ned.'

'How lovely,' exclaimed Serena.

The Marquess, however, knit his brows.

'I have not accepted, my lord,' Madeleine was quick to add.

'Oh, dear,' said Serena.

Devlin put his arm around Madeleine.

The Marquess pursed his lips. 'It is not a wise course.'

'Oh, nonsense!' Serena broke in. 'It is plain as a pikestaff they are in love with each other.'

'Darling,' Ned said, his voice softening as he turned to his wife, 'there is more to marriage than love.'

'A contract? A business matter? A merging of two fortunes?' Devlin spoke with heat. 'That may have suited you, Ned, but not me. I am a younger son. I will not even reside in England. What can it signify who I marry?'

Ned's cheek twitched. 'This plan of yours to rejoin the army is unconscionable.'

'If it is the only way I may be with Maddy, it is worth it,' Devlin said.

'You will be with no one if you lie dead on some battlefield,' his brother shot back.

Devlin's teeth clenched. 'I love Maddy and I will do anything to stay with her. Loving her is the only thing that matters.'

'You have to stay alive, don't you?'

'Oh, please stop.' Madeleine cried. 'Stop arguing on my account.'

'Oh, pish. Of course love matters,' exclaimed Serena, her

eyes flashing at her husband. 'If you love Devlin, Ned, you ought to simply give him his estate and have done with it.' She placed her hands on her hips. 'More to marriage than love... Nonsense. Ned, you told me you loved me from our first meeting, as I have loved you. It has made all the difference.' She spun around to Madeleine. 'Tell me, Madeleine. Do you love Devlin?'

Madeleine gazed at Devlin. 'I love Devlin more than life itself, but he deserves a better wife than I can be.'

Devlin gave her a returning look of adoration.

Serena smiled at them. She turned to her husband. 'See?'

Ned shook his head. 'What I see is trouble ahead for them.'

'Did you know that Madeleine taught me how to love you, Ned?' Serena persisted. 'I went to Devlin's apartments and begged her to teach me what to do.'

Ned's jaw dropped.

'So, you can place our happiness at her door.' She placed her hand on her stomach. 'We would not have this baby if not for Madeleine.'

Both Madeleine and Devlin gaped in surprise.

A slow smile lit Ned's countenance. He moved toward his wife and took her in his arms, lifting her, and twirling her around. While Madeleine and Devlin watched in astonishment, Ned placed his lips on Serena's and held them there, deepening the kiss until it was clear they had forgotten there were witnesses in the room.

'Mama,' Linette piped up, 'Markiss kiss.'

Serena and Ned broke apart, red-faced.

'Um,' Ned mumbled. 'If you will pardon us...'

As Serena's laughter trilled, Ned took her arm, but paused, turning back to Devlin. 'We'll settle the estate papers and the bank draft later.' He escorted his wife out of the room.

Devlin stared at the door. He turned to Madeleine, amazement on his face. 'You are responsible for that?'

Madeleine felt her face grow hot. 'I told her only what you have taught me about love.'

He walked over to her and gently lifted her chin with his finger. 'I have not yet begun to teach you about love. Marry me. Come live with me at Edgeworth. We shall breed a stable of horses.'

'I cannot.' Her voiced cracked. 'My past.'

His arms encircled her. 'No one will know of your past. Your family will be ruined if they speak of it, and Farley is no longer a threat. No one else knows of you.'

'People will wonder.'

'Then we will give them a fiction to believe.' He held her close against him, her head resting on his chest. 'Perhaps you could become the daughter of a merchant or some such. We could say we secretly married years ago when I was on leave from Spain. Linette would be legitimate, then. How would that suit you?'

She relaxed against the steadiness of his heartbeat. 'Oh, I suppose. It is merely another mask, is it not? But not a shameful one.'

'I will give you the life you deserve.' Devlin took a deep breath and squeezed her tighter. Lifting her face to his, he placed his lips tenderly against hers.

'Deddy kiss!' Linette squealed, running over to them.

Laughing, Devlin and Madeleine lifted her up between them and kissed again.

Epilogue

The two magnificent horses raced over the countryside, neck and neck, clearing every fence and hedge. Their hooves beat the earth like thunder, until at the stone marker on the rise, their riders drew them to a halt.

'I won,' Devlin said. 'Arrived before you this time.'

'Oh, no, indeed,' said his wife. Her apparel gave her the appearance of a slim lad, but the cascade of mahogany-coloured hair down her back belied that impression. 'I won.'

From this high vantage point, Devlin surveyed the fields of his estate, thick and fragrant with hops. He gave silent thanks to his brother. For the first time in Ned's life, he had acted in a way their father would have disapproved. He had given Devlin Edgeworth, and his fortune, as well.

In the centre of this picturesque scene was the house, not as grand as nearby Heronvale, but more precious to Devlin because he shared it with his wife. In the distance Devlin watched their daughter, mounted on a white pony, jumping the low bars set up by Jem, as their best breeding mares grazed nearby. Unseen but also busy at work were his steward, Bart, who managed to recall every niggling task necessary to run the estate, and Sophie who, under much protest, had created Madeleine's unusual riding outfit.

'It is beautiful here,' sighed Madeleine. 'I never hoped for so much happiness.'

He grinned at her. 'Do not be so happy. I won this race, you know.'

She pursed her lips. 'Only because I have been a little tired of late.'

'Tired?' He gazed at her, worry furrowing his brow. 'Maddy, are you unwell? Perhaps you should not be riding today.'

'Not unwell precisely,' she said, turning her steed to make a more sedate way down the hill.

He rode beside her.

She sighed. 'I could not resist one more run. I shall not be free to do so again for some time.'

'What the deuce are you talking about?'

She grinned at him, a mischievous twinkle in her eye. 'I am due to give Linette a brother or sister next summer.'

He pulled his horse to a halt. 'What?'

Madeleine rode back to him. 'I am increasing, husband.'

'Good God! And you are racketing all over the countryside, hell for leather? I ought to throttle you!'

'Not throttle,' she said, coming along beside him, the two horses head-to-tail to each other. The sultry look on her face heated his loins. She smiled and leaned toward him. 'Kiss.'

Devlin Steele did as his wife bid him.

* * * * *

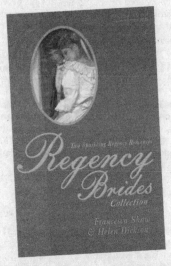

2 FREE

books and a surprise gift!

We would like to take this opportunity to thank you for reading this Mills & Boon® book by offering you the chance to take TWO more specially selected titles from the Historical Romance™ series absolutely FREE! We're also making this offer to introduce you to the benefits of the Reader Service™—

- ★ FREE home delivery
- ★ FREE gifts and competitions
- ★ FREE monthly Newsletter
- ★ Exclusive Reader Service offers
- ★ Books available before they're in the shops

Accepting these FREE books and gift places you under no obligation to buy, you may cancel at any time, even after receiving your free shipment. Simply complete your details below and return the entire page to the address below. *You don't even need a stamp!*

YES! Please send me 2 free Historical Romance books and a surprise gift. I understand that unless you hear from me, I will receive 4 superb new titles every month for just £3.59 each, postage and packing free. I am under no obligation to purchase any books and may cancel my subscription at any time. The free books and gift will be mine to keep in any case.

H4ZED

Ms/Mrs/Miss/Mr ....Initials...........................
BLOCK CAPITALS PLEASE
Surname ....
Address ....
....
....Postcode ....

Send this whole page to:
UK: FREEPOST CN81, Croydon, CR9 3WZ
EIRE: PO Box 4546, Kilcock, County Kildare (stamp required)